GONE WITH THE VINDALOO

Vikram Nair is a post-graduate in History from Delhi University. He has been self-employed for most of his life and is, in fact, a serial entrepreneur of sorts because not many people agreed to employ him. Presently, he is the promoter and CEO of a chain of Indian restaurants, Khaaja Chowk, which goes by the byline 'Full Full Indian'. Vikram and his wife, Shefali (the woman of his dreams, for the most part), are thrilled grandparents of Amaan, aged two. This is Vikram's first novel.

GONE WITH THE VINDALOO

Vikram Nair

hachette
INDIA

First published in 2014 by Hachette India
(Registered name: Hachette Book Publishing India Pvt Ltd)
An Hachette UK company
www.hachetteindia.com

SRD

ISBN 978-93-5009-589-8

Hachette Book Publishing India Pvt. Ltd
4th & 5th Floors, Corporate Centre, Plot No. 94,
Sector 44, Gurgaon 122001, India

Typeset in Granjon Lt Std 11/14.4
By Eleven Arts, New Delhi

Printed and bound in India by
Manipal Technologies Limited, Manipal

MIX
Paper from responsible sources
FSC™ C104740

To my grandson, Amaan

BOOK I

Dream Sequence

DINNER had been simple vegetarian fare, the once-a-week-every-Tuesday convention in the Mahadev household. Simple baingan ka bharta – aubergines, plump and purple, roasted over the fire and skinned, the smoky flesh sautéed lightly with onions and tomatoes – and urad ki daal, fluffy and moist, equal portions of the lentil and water pressure-cooked till soft and tempered with ginger, onions and tomatoes. For the greens there was palak paneer – a purée of dark green spinach flavoured with cumin, or jeera, and saunf, anise, and flecked with the brilliant gold-white of cottage cheese. All of it served with crisp, flaky parantha sprinkled generously with the roasted tartness of carom seeds, or ajwain. Surprisingly, the children, devoted carnivores, loved the meal and complimented Pakwaan, the passionate cook, blessed with flair and able assistant to his father, Param.

Pakwaan bathed as soon as he had finished cleaning the kitchen, scrubbing off the sticky humidity from his skin, luxuriating in the freedom that comes from wearing only a lungi at the end of the day. He felt the cool breeze blow past his legs as he scratched his balls, pinched, squeezed and stretched his foreskin. Then he slept and dreamt magnificently.

Full orchestra! *Kha-chaang! Kha-chaang!* Clashing of glittering cymbals – their metallic thinness echoing into space. Thousands of violins tucked under chins, faces rapt, eyes closed, heads and bodies vigorously swaying, engrossed in making melodious music. Highways, caressed by white billowy clouds, floated across a clear blue sky. Sensuous nymphs in sheer Banarsi brocades wafted by, flashing their breasts and deliciously flared hips. Pakwaan felt a flutter of excitement, the beginning of a glorious erection.

A tall and massive man dressed in a shimmering robe, flowing and fabulous, now filled his dream. A Rajasthani saafa, six yards of beautiful bandhani fabric, was tied around his head, the fabric stretched, flat and broad on one side and, on the other, lovingly coiled like sensuous snakes.

'I am the God of Magic and in my hand I hold a pen, a most important discovery, for it will improve both the memory and the wisdom of people who will use it,' said the shiny figure in a loud and important voice.

The figure shrank suddenly, receding, allowing space for a familiar character.

Enter Kalaam, Pakwaan's grandfather, wearing a dhoti, his torso draped in a crisp, clean gumchha.

'O God of Magic, Paragon of Inventors, Father of Writing, you are mistaken,' he said gravely, shaking his head, looking sorry for the showy giant of a man. 'You have attributed to this pen quite the opposite of its real function. Those who acquire it will cease to exercise their memory and become forgetful; they will rely on external signs instead of using their internal resources. What you have discovered is a receipt for recollection, not for memory. And, as for wisdom, your pupils will have the reputation for it without the reality. They will receive an overload of information without proper instruction and will be thought of as knowledgeable when they are, for the most part, quite ignorant. And because they will be filled with the conceit of wisdom, instead of *real* wisdom they will be a burden to society.'

On hearing this, the shiny giant was *lum-late* – passed out, horizontal – stunned, the pen still in his hand. The nymphs floated back into Pakwaan's dream, clapping, celebrating his grandfather's words. But in a flash the giant was up, his eyes full of venom, his mouth twisted into a vicious sneer. 'You bloody dhoti-gumchhawalla, what do you know?'

Then came a storm of great ferocity. A terrible tornado that brought whooshing whirlpools of wind, ripping the giant's saafa from his head, the robe from his body, sucking his body out of the dream. A moment of pitch-black emptiness was replaced by the gushing waters of the seven seas sloshing inside a massive cauldron, a ship stuffed with spices sailing effortlessly across the waves.

'Land ahoy!' a sailor yelled and a gust of wind carried chillies red and green, cloves and cardamoms, onions, cinnamon and cumin, coriander seeds and turmeric, garlic and ginger and black pepper, and meat, fat, juicy and pink from the legs of a young pig – ingredients for the salivating spiciness and tart hotness of delicious Vindaloo. People poured out of their homes, women with flowers in their hair, men with their musical instruments, excited, chattering children in tow. Pakwaan saw himself in the dream, leading the way.

The marination began. Pyramids of chillies, cardamom, cloves, peppercorns, whole cumin and coriander were ground in toddy vinegar under Pakwaan's enthusiastic supervision, and kept aside. The marinade was then worked into the mounds of juicy pink pork. Pakwaan showed the crowd the way, his fingers kneading in the paste so that each piece was soaked completely in spicy tartness. Onions were fried till golden, tossed with turmeric, garlic and ginger, and the marinated meat, red and full of hot promise, was thrown into the cauldron and left to simmer till the meat was cooked.

'VINDALOO!' The crowds happily announced and the tasting began. Taste buds exploded in congratulatory applause, curry dribbled down the chins of the greedy, and the etiquette-wallas pat-patted their napkins on their lips. At this point, from the ocean, a woman emerged, her top clinging to her sinewy, shining white body. She ran towards the cauldron and dipped her hand into the Vindaloo, sensuously licking the curry from her fingers, astonished by its taste. Her eyes sought out Pakwaan, who was standing at the front of the crowd, and she embraced him, caressing his body greedily. Pakwaan experienced full-full arousal, his huge straining erection anticipating joys of entry. *Kha-chaang! Kha-chaang!* The cymbals clashed amidst the thrusting and thrashing of their bodies, and in the end there was a volcanic, splotchy release. He felt a warm, sticky wetness and woke, startled by his dream.

Hey Bhagwaan! What a dream, he thought, as he changed into a fresh lungi and walked out of his room, looking up at the sky. He could sense the beginnings of a coastal monsoon. Raising his arms skyward, he thanked God for blessing him with an instinctive, primal passion for cooking and a natural flair for proportion, taste and texture.

Since Pakwaan could remember, his father's kitchen was a magical place. Mouth-watering smells surrounded him, and the sight of curries on a simmer, gently bubbling, enthralled. His father chopping onions, holding one end firmly with the tips of his fingers, exposing just enough so that very thin slices could be cut. *Schlick, schlick, schlick,* the knife moving in a blur, and in an instant it was done. Spices being roasted, cumin seeds popping on hot tawas, paneer and mushroom being diced, fresh meats marinated in yogurt and spices, the marination worked in with the hands. Ah! For him it was an indescribably sensuous feeling. And the transformation

– the food changing colour and texture over heat – the gobi just the right golden-yellow, the chicken and mutton the desired rich dark brown. All this achieved without written recipes, without a reminder from wound-up clocks that time was up. Just smell, feel and texture to determine the doneness of a particular dish.

'Beta,' his father used to tell him, 'from Mother Earth sprang herbs, from herbs came food, from food seed and from seed man. Man thus consists of the essence of food – from food are all creatures produced and by food do they grow. And placed in the centre of all this is the cook, solely responsible for the taste of food. Ah, food! Made well, it can be the start of contented conversations; badly made, it can lead to disgruntled hunger. Appreciative *wah-wah*s after meals are heady for the cook but bad meals leave diners with silent hostilities. Yes, cooking can be as cruel as it can be enchanting. Spices have to be tempered and balanced so that taste buds enjoy the right kind of titillation, the kind that pleasantly fires the edges of the tongue and spreads a delicious warmth over the scalp and ears.'

His father's repertoire was vast. Dosas and marchwangans, idlis and tamatar gosht, dhokla and machher jhol, biryanis and pulaos, and sarson ka saag and Kerala chemmeen. Pakwaan was a passionate learner, absorbing, sponge-like, his father's experience. Impressed by his son's passion, Param too poured out his knowledge, and by the end of Pakwaan's eighteenth year, exquisite badam pasandas came off his chulhas, crisp paranthas spun off his tawas and flaky lachchedaar rotis rolled off his belan. Confident of Pakwaan's capabilities, Param gently supervised, calming the boy's restless excitement, reminding him about the hazards of over-enthusiasm. When the food was ready, Pakwaan always asked his father for his opinion. The ritual remained his most nervous moment – a shishya asking for the guru's approval.

'Shabash, beta,' Param would say, and hug him. The compliment always thrilled Pakwaan.

It was the day of the marchwangan korma, the first time his father had allowed him to make a dish from start to finish. Pakwaan was thrilled at the privilege, at his father's admission that he had finally come of age. Whole, wrinkled red chillies lay soaking in warm water, moments away from being ground into a rich red paste. The spices were laid out on a plate – little heaps of saunf and saunth, the sweet-sour chutney made from dried ginger and tamarind, a sprinkling of green cardamom and cloves, a pinch of cinnamon and a bowl of perfectly set yogurt. In another ceramic bowl, blood-red food colouring dissolved in two tablespoons of water waited for its moment. He would never forget the flawless white of the yogurt, the blood-red food colour, the greenish-brown saunf and saunth, the brownish-rust of the well-used cooking utensils, and his father telling him, 'The essence of the korma is dalchini, fragrant cinnamon. Put in just a bit too much' – his thumb and forefinger pressed lightly together for emphasis – 'and mouths will *burn*.'

Such precision, so vast a repertoire and his father's quotes from old religious texts suggested great and ancient cooking repasts. While Pakwaan tap-tapped two spoonfuls of desi ghee into the kadhai and watched it slide down the sides, gently melting across the bottom of the kadhai like golden honey, his mind sped off, conjuring images of much ancientness. He imagined his ancestors being rewarded with rare and expensive gifts by a Mughal badshah, as an expression of appreciation for a marchwangan korma stupendously made.

The ghee, like his imagination, was hot now. It was time to plop in the yogurt. Cool yogurt hitting hot ghee – a delicious hissing sound at the moment of impact. Pakwaan's imagination, already in full flow, catapulted him further backward to visions of more ancient ancestors who had served as heads of kitchens supervising delicacies for maharajas, rajas and an assortment of powerful nobles who waited gratefully for the food cooked by their magical hands.

Thoughts of such a glorious past convinced him that he could do no wrong. He moved the ladle vigorously, and with reckless flourish threw in that extra bit of cinnamon and red chillies. As he removed the korma from the fire, he asked, 'Baba, how old is the cooking tradition in our family?'

'Beta, you are just the third generation. Your grandfather was the first for whom cooking was a profession. We are, traditionally, Kathuas.'

Three short sentences, and Pakwaan's flights of culinary fancy into ancient times simply crash-landed. Kathua – slang, generally derogatory, for the circumcised members of 'a certain minority community', as the newspapers would describe. He covered his face with his hands, and moved dejectedly to the far end of the kitchen. He was lucky that the button fly was the common closure in those days, so he had no problem in sliding his thumb and forefinger between the buttons and reassuringly pulling at his fleshy protrusion.

Pakwaan did not have a problem being Muslim. He had heard much from his father about their culinary skills. In fact, marchwangan korma was from their traditions. Besides, there were seekh kebabs and kakori kebabs, tamatar goshts, ishtoos, biryanis with their regional variations, roomali rotis, khameeris and bakarkhanis – the list was endless. But he knew, too, of the rumblings within the nation. The khaki-pant movement was marching ahead. Mosques had not been demolished yet and the movement was still to be jaundiced into starker saffron, but Pakwaan had the foresight – and, indeed, the foreskin – to see the dangers that loomed ahead.

'M' for Muslim – the letter M, the thirteenth letter in a language made of only twenty-six letters, right in the centre of the near-universal language of the powerful, the language of thought, history and commerce. There, right in the middle, hounded by twenty-five others – what temptation it provided to twist myths into reality and reality into myths. What power it possessed to disguise, what power to mystify. Imagine histories read and written from right to left instead of left to right – handle-ghumanewallas, historians, scholars and students, zindabad, zindabad!

He looked at his father, astonished by the irony (and the humour) of the moment. He was a Kathua with foreskin intact, but with his fabulously imagined culinary heredity drastically circumcised! He began to laugh – a slow, rumbling laugh that soon became a loud hysterical cackle. Param, father of his only son, knew instinctively the reason for this sudden expression of his disappointment. Damn itihaas, he fleetingly thought. But dinner had to be served and explanations could wait. Yet, the more Param tried to calm his son, the more hysterical the boy became, till his father had no option – he swung his arm, and *phattack*! And even before four crimson fingers could leave their mark on Pakwaan's cheek, there was absolute silence. In the midst of all the commotion, the ritual of son asking father to taste was forgotten. The marchwangan korma left the kitchen dangerously spicy and a touch raw.

The Happy and Not So Small Mahadev Parivar

'FULL plate in the centre, quarter plate to the left, full plate in the centre, quarter plate to the left,' Pakwaan muttered to himself as he went about laying the dinner table. It was the first time his father had smacked him. He rushed through his task, placing knives, forks and spoons, and quickly placed the mats for the serving vessels for the marchwangan, daal, rice and vegetables. There was a hint of desperation as he went about setting the table, imagining his own embarrassment if the family, especially the children, saw the four red fingers on his cheek.

Mahadev, translated literally as Great God, was the head of the household. He was born at a time when the land and the minds of the subcontinent were being fertilized and cultivated under the colonial yoke, and the Indian Civil Services, or simply the ICS, was one of the most important torchbearers of the fertilization flame.

The civil servants were extraordinary. Vilayat-educated, suited-booted, living in big bungalows with orderlies, khidmatgars, hookabardars, bawarchis and syces, they were, despite their colour, almost as important as the rulers themselves. Their powers fascinated him. And so from village primaries to suburban secondaries and on to urban universities, Mahadev made his determined way to join this educated elite who exercised such enormous clout. In 1949, two years after the country was partitioned, he found that a slice of history had been thrust upon him! He was a member of the desi elite, the Indian Administrative Services, or simply (and quite powerfully) the IAS. His was the second batch, almost at the head of the vanguard of fulfilment, his young shoulders carrying a noble and heavy burden.

There were only a few bureaucrats of his vintage in Bhubaneswar, the movers and shakers who could shape the destiny of the masses. As he sat in his room, the Burra Sahib with his chhota peg, Mahadev reminisced about his day. He had lost count of the number of obsequious people who had flattered him to curry favours that he could easily grant. As he sipped his second chhota, his being was filled with the warm glow of self-importance. He looked forward to dinner.

The rest of the family was getting dressed for dinner, too. Freshening up before meals was the convention laid down by Mahadev for his household. He loved the idea of a warm, loving home and mementoes of his two favourite homilies were displayed in all the houses he had stayed in. The first, 'A house is made of bricks and stones, but a home is made of love alone' in white lettering on four black metal strips encircled by small copper leaves, found its place at the entrance to the house, and the second, 'The family that together eats and prays, together forever always stays', occupied a prominent place in the dining room.

His wife, Jhelum, beautiful, milk-white fair, was the youngest of six brothers and sisters. With the passage of time, coastal colour had crept into her cheeks and facial freckles stayed as reminders of childbirth. While the Great God sipped his chhota, she sat facing the mirror in her bedroom, patting powder on her face to restore the freshness that might have been lost between Mahadev arriving from work and dinner being served.

With her freshness patted back on, Jhelum made her way to the kitchen to check the dinner bandobast. It was a formality. Param hated supervision; in fact, he discouraged any interference in his kitchen. But he made an exception for Jhelum because she had added an angrez dimension to his formidable skills. She had introduced him to the refined and dainty art of baking. For her it had been an added qualification for matrimony and a coming closer to memsahibdom; for him it was a unique addition to his culinary talents. The varieties of cakes, scones, buns, puffs, sweets and spongy soufflés that could be baked were a revelation for Param, and with his natural feel for taste and texture his skills had soon matched those of his tutor.

Tuesday was baking day in Jhelum's household, and every Tuesday, Dadu, the gentle old ex-Chief Secretary of the state (and retired ICS) ambled his way to the house to sample the day's fresh baking. Post retirement, Dadu lived in Bhubaneswar and had developed a great fondness for Jhelum – the fondness of an old father for his youngest child. And there was Uncle Chuk, also a senior IAS officer and still in service, his rotund, balding, thinning hair brilliantly Brylcreemed and his bushy moustache peppered by age. He would announce his arrival by hauntingly whistling 'Que Sera, Sera' as he walked across the polished red cement floor of the veranda. 'Jhaay-lum,' he would call, stretching her name affectionately. 'My coffee and your baking.'

And so, the Great God was doubly blessed. He was a Burra Sahib and also the undisputed head of a household that was recognized for its kitchen. The taste of power and the power of taste! What a heady combination!

Mahadev was the eldest son in a family of five. His selection in the IAS had been a great source of pride for his family. In fact, with Mahadev's selection, their cup overflowed with joy, for only a few months before Mahadev's entry into the elite bureaucracy his younger brother had been selected for the Indian Railways. Their family's status in the small town they lived in assumed gigantic proportions. Imagine, two sons, both 'prestigiously posted' – like two rare invaluable stamps. They were matrimonial medals waiting to be worn. Missives and messengers were sent to mothers and matchmakers for suitable spouses. Jhelum was identified as a suitable life-partner for the Railways man and Mahadev, being older, was deputed to conduct the once-over, the dekho, for pyari Jhelum. Jhelum's family loved the idea of a life partnership with the Railways. 'Imagine,' they said, 'free railway passes for our Jhelum to come home whenever she wishes.' But kismet, ah kismet, was about to switch the tracks to take her on a different journey. Mahadev arrived at Jhelum's house and was received warmly by the family. While Jhelum made tea and sandwiches in the kitchen, they indulged in polite chit-chat, and Jhelum's eldest brother quickly realized that Mahadev's placement was more prestigious than the prospective groom's. The demure damsel entered with a tea tray, followed by a servant carrying the sandwiches covered with a doily with colourful beads sewn on its edges. Jhelum, head bowed in shyness, placed the tea tray on the table and as the servant did likewise with the plate of sandwiches, Jhelum removed the doily, Mahadev looked up at her and kismet intruded. Struck by her beauty, he decided to marry her. The odds were stacked in Mahadev's favour – he was older and his posting more prestigious. Both families readily agreed, and immediately after Mahadev's short and concentrated training in the art of running an independent nation barely two years old was complete, the Great God and Jhelum were wed.

Tek Ram was the eldest of their children. Govinda, their second child, was three years younger – the correct gap between siblings for the mother to remain healthy. Gauri was the youngest. Only eleven months ('Legs, Number 11,' as the compere would announce at tambola sessions) separated Govinda from Gauri. Gauri was a mother's wish for a daughter finally fulfilled, an accident of passion born at a time when a two-child family was about to become the national norm.

'We are the first country in the world to have a family planning programme,' Mahadev would proudly remind his family as he ticked off his own achievements as well as those of the IAS for a newly independent India in all sorts of throes. Family planning was national priority – sizes of families had to be rationalized, awareness of birth-control methods had to be spread, condoms had to be worn, and passion, in general, kept in check. The fresh, young batch of administrative gladiators moved with firm resolve to ensure success in these endeavours and Mahadev himself was involved in policy at the highest levels. He was Collector of Sundergarh at the time and determined that his collectorate should be the finest example of population control.

The Centre had decided that the best way to spread the message would be via giant billboards displayed across the state. The message would have to be short, have a ring of divinity and, if possible, rhyme. And so the slogan was coined:

'Great Mother Orissa beckons us all
To keep our families happy and small.
So come, let us all check the population wave,
Chief minister, health minister and Mahadev.'

Below this bouncy ditty was the drawing of a family showing a father holding his daughter and a mother with her son, and below it the message, 'A small family is a happy family. Ek ya do, bas!', followed by 'Use Nirodh (Made by the Govt of India)'. It was another matter that Nirodh, which meant to stop, control, block, had been a popular enough boy's name till the campaign began, but after the name became synonymous with 'condom' in India, all the boys named Nirodh became Niraad, the Nirudhs became Anirudhs and the name dropped off the lexicon of good Hindu names for boys.

Mahadev's campaign was ready, the billboards mounted across roads and busy intersections, the posters typeset, the copy read and corrected, all set to go to the press. The use of Mahadev was not an attempt at self-glorification on his part (though it was, no doubt, an added benefit). It rhymed with 'wave' and called on the blessings of Shiva, the most popular god of the Hindu triumvirate, giving the message a ring of divinity. Mother Orissa beckoning, the chief minister and health minister sanctioning, Great God willing, the campaign was success guaranteed!

But kismet, an unpredictable, never-to-be-taken-for-granted force, willed it otherwise.

With Govinda's delivery a few months away, Jhelum had left with Tek Ram for her maikaa. It was customary for the sisters to go home to roost and this time she had company as her older sister, also pregnant, was there as well. They spent more time at their maikaa than usual and by the time Jhelum arrived in Sundergarh, the Collector, her husband, in the prime of his youth, had missed her intensely and she him.

The sun had set and a cool coastal breeze blew, lush with passion. Their bodies touched, skin on skin. Feeling-fooling, kissing-shissing, feeling-fondling followed. The condoms be hanged, control be damned, and Mother Orissa looked the other way. Jhelum was into her third month when the doctor confirmed she was pregnant and advised against abortion. Mahadev was stunned, embarrassed – the passionate pillar of population control, now guilty of having one child over the about-to-be prescribed norm.

The Centre was informed, and the chief minister and health minister did not miss the irony. A guilty Mahadev suggested the last two lines of the slogan be expunged from the ditty, but they insisted it was too late. 'Mahadev' implied cosmic connotations necessary to control the overactive libidos of the superstitious masses. And if babudom wills it, babudom gets it – jahan Michael hai wahan cycle hai. So the ditty remained as is, but the slogan was changed – from 'Ek ya do, bas!' to 'Do ya teen, bas!' The drawing of the family remained the same – two kids were still the ideal, but if push came to passionate shove, a third was permitted. Everything was perfect – the baby grew in Jhelum's womb, having allowed masses of families an extra child.

Today Gauri was restless. Bhubaneswar, with its open spaces, cool sea breeze from the coast, its bright crimson sunsets against inky blue skies, games of musical chairs and pass the parcel at birthday parties at the club, was losing its charm. Gauri, constantly battling with her parents to study away from home, longed for the challenge of more invigorating environments. Today, she was determined to 'put up' – as they did with long pending files in the kingdom of bureaucracy – her case at dinner.

Govinda, too, could not wait for dinner to begin – and end. He was plotting a never-allowed shikar that night with his friends. They had secretly taken shikar-organizing to a high and exciting art. Whenever their bloodlust beckoned, or they missed the excitement of entering the forests at night, they would stroll to each other's gates and whistle, lips slightly parted, teeth almost clenched, mimicking the call of a partridge – *si-si, si-si, si-si*. Three pairs of whistled *si-si*s would come in short, sharp, morse-like bursts announcing their shikari intentions. Today, the signal had come only minutes before dinner and they were at the gate of his house, seemingly nonchalant, discussing the logistics of a secret hunt in hushed bottom-of-the-larynx voices.

The planning had to be meticulous, for the consequences of discovery would be deadly.

The painful memory of the time he had been found out was still fresh in Govinda's mind. Mahadev and Jhelum had been out for dinner and had told the children they would be back late. Govinda saw his chance and seized it. As soon as they left, the partridge-call signal was made and the shikaris gathered around. His friend's father's car was available; Gauri the restless, caught up in the excitement, had insisted that she be taken along. So off they went, guns, spotlights and all.

But the parents got back much earlier than expected. Tek Ram was the only one at home, burning pre-midnight oil, ostensibly studying. But what should have been a reassuring scene for any parent, their eldest hunched over books, studying for his future, became charged with a tense and ominous rage when Mahadev realized that his younger son and his precious little Gauri were nowhere to be found.

'Where are they?' he bellowed, his angry face close to Tikky's. In a state of panic, Tikky jumped up in fear and said he had no idea. It was a mistake. While Mahadev paced about angrily, time crawled dangerously slowly. After a while, sick of pacing, he walked up to the gate and waited. They finally arrived, Govinda sauntering in with Gauri in tow. Mahadev's seething anger bubbled over and he slapped Gauri – a sharp, stinging whack.

Brotherly feelings for the protection of his sister – behen ki raksha feelings – welled up aggressively in Govinda.

'How dare you slap my sister?' he asked threateningly.

Mahadev turned around to find his youngest son crouching like a boxer, chivalrously defying paternal authority. Mahadev's eyebrows shot up in surprise and then a blind rage overcame him. His eyes narrowed to dangerous slits, his lower jaw thrust out, he blurted, 'You bloody ba-ba-ba-ba . . .' He almost completed the blasphemous word, but despite the anger that raged inside him, he managed, being a father, not to utter it. The sentence changed mid-flow and after three or four angrily blustered, sheep-like 'ba-ba's he finally shouted, 'You bloody ba-ba-ba-baas-DUNKEE! I'll slap *you* instead.' He lunged at Govinda, landing a painful blow on his head. Govinda turned and ran, the Great God in hot pursuit.

The memory of this event was the cause of much hilarity and admiration among the children. Both Tek Ram and Gauri remembered Govinda's gutsiness with mixed laughter-awe – the sibling pugilist defying a dangerously frothing father, the enraged bull-father bellowing ba-bas after a fleeing son, finally blurting out 'dunkee' instead of 'donkey'. 'The communal roits were a terrible chapter in the nation's history,' Govinda would mimic his father, the 'o' in 'riot' coming before the 'i', with Gauri adding, as if on cue, 'Look at the Mahatma, fearless as a loin, defying the might of the British Empire wearing only a loin cloth,' amidst much laughter.

But enough about pronunciations. Dinner for Govinda would be deliciously deadpan. The marchwangan would be inviting, but the excitement that his post-dinner plans promised would have to be effectively masked – nobody should get a whiff of the hunt!

Tek Ram was also ready for dinner. Back home for vacation from boarding school, where food was mass-produced for hungry boys, where watery daal was served with mushy vegetables and breakfasts consisted of congealed, cement-hard fried eggs with mouldy toast, where Tek Ram ate to live and sustained himself on countless home-food memories. Warm, crisp toast, generously dolloped with malai and marmalade; fried egg on toast so perfectly done that the yokes spread evenly across the white, the gratifying crunch of toast and sublime taste of yellow-white in perfect harmony; crisp, flaky paranthas, their brittleness crackling at first bite, his mouth exploding with the flavours of jeera and ajwain.

At home, Tek Ram lived to eat. And eat he did, with an appetite that bordered on gluttony, and today his appetite was edged by a particularly satisfying evening of cricket.

Four for 20, after 10 overs. Tek Ram had diddled the opposition with his left-arm spin. Those deceptive donkey drops that started, temptingly, as half-volleys waiting to be smashed to the fence but dipping just before the good-length spot, with the batsman stranded outside the crease, committed to playing the drive. He could either drop his wrists and smother the spin, or complete his drive hoping to loft the ball over the fielders' heads. In either case he ran the risk of being caught or stumped. Tek Ram had outwitted four batsmen in this fashion – two were caught and two stumped. With the compliments from his teammates marvelling at his guile still ringing in his ears, dinner would be doubly delicious.

And so the parivar of five gathered at the table looking forward to an excellent meal, but Pakwaan's overconfident flourishes were about to serve up a disaster.

It was Mahadev who served himself first, and his first swallowed bite made his eyes bulge in watery shock. The curry burnt his insides as it made its treacherous way down. With one hand he grabbed a napkin to wipe away spice-induced tears and with the other he gulped a glass of water, hoping to quell the fires that raged inside him. His thoughts rushed to his early morning ablutions. By then his piles would have painfully reacted and the grape-like bunch at the end of his rectum would be angrily inflamed. No amount of water could calm their red hotness and the next day would be spent on a burning arse – the hot seat, in a manner of speaking – acknowledging the fawning minions who pampered his ego to curry (how he hated the word now) favours for themselves.

Jhelum, all set to take the metaphoric bow at the end of the meal, straightened up in shocked disbelief, while the children, mouths wide open, vigorously hand-fanned their mouths and inhaled-exhaled mouthfuls of air to get some relief. Yet, despite the scalding the family had experienced, they merely voiced murmurs of disbelief. They seldom openly expressed their displeasure at food produced in their kitchen. It could drive Param into a sad, vengeful mood for days and the food they would then be served would be pedestrian, to say the least. Only Jhelum would gently criticize him later, and Param would offer sincere apologies.

Pakwaan, his normal colour restored to his face, had set about the task of cleaning up. In the kitchen, there was an unspoken routine between father and the son. The halka kaam, or light work – cleaning up of surfaces where chopping was done, wiping off spillovers around the chulha – was Param's responsibility. The bhaari kaam – the washing of plates, scouring of degchis, cleaning of crockery and cutlery, and swabbing of the kitchen – was Pakwaan's. Param's after-dinner chores finished earlier than Pakwaan's. He always helped Pakwaan with unfinished work, but today he left the kitchen and stepped out into the courtyard. He paced up and down furiously, thinking of what to say to his son. This nonsense of imagined antiquities had to be sensitively handled.

He slapped his forehead with an open palm. Curse bloody history, he thought to himself again. His view was simple. The country was a giant degchi in which the ingredients of myths, legends and bits of reality either simmered gently or were transformed over high fires to suit the tastes of the handle-ghumanewallas. Only, the handle-ghumanewallas changed. Ah! The handle-ghumanewallas, or ladle-stirrers. But ladle-stirring had a gentler connotation. The image that came to mind was that of a cook gently stirring a pot. But handle-ghumana was more vigorous. Imagine a car that has stalled, and no amount of pushing or shoving could coax even the slightest splutter from its lifeless engine. A rod is pulled out and connected to the crankshaft; the other end is gripped with both hands and rotated with great force, one's entire body weight behind the effort. *That* is handle-ghumana. Param viewed events through cooking metaphors and his objectivity was astonishing. After all, concoctions were the order of the day.

Param felt sorry for having slapped his son but he knew it was necessary. He could hear Pakwaan in the kitchen, vigorously scrubbing stubborn stains from plates and degchis and banging them down aggressively, an obvious display of a hurt child's temper tantrum to get a parent's attention. The sounds irritated Param, but in a while the winding down of kitchen sounds began. He could hear his son swabbing the kitchen floor – the swish-swash sounds of the pochha, the squish of a damp cloth being squeezed and the trickle of water into a bucket immediately afterwards.

It was the pochha, a thick absorbent cloth made from yarns spun from waste cotton that reminded Param of his origins, the start of a story that held the promise of delightful adventure. His father had spun yarn, 'kathna' in the lingua franca. His caste was determined by his profession – 'Kathua' the moniker for their caste. 'Kat' as in cut, 'hua' as in happened. Kathua, also slang for the circumcised. As he sat on his haunches, chin cupped in large hands, he chuckled at the irony. Here I am, a Kathua with foreskin intact, a spinner of yarns by caste but not a storyteller, a Hindu whose father spun yarn with the Julahas, or Muslim weavers, and now a second-generation cook by glorious, timely accident!

'Pakwaan, beta,' he said affectionately,

'Ghumao the handle and make some tea,
Some for you and some for me,
Father and son shall sit and chat,
Of tradition, of history, of this and that.'

Param spoke in a bouncy sing-song voice and Pakwaan loped across the courtyard, two glasses of piping hot tea in hand. Param sipped, a long, noisy, slurping sip, and felt the hot, sweet liquid caress his throat.

'Aah!' he sighed with pleasure. Memories of his father sprung to his mind with a fragrant freshness. A huge, vicarious nostalgia gripped him, and he began his tale.

The Spinner of Yarns

'OUR story begins in the city of Banaras – Varanasi, Benares, Kashi, the starting point of all stories in India – more than seventy-five years ago. Banaras – the epitome of great holiness, where the majestic and mysterious Ganga flows, carrying in her watery belly unfathomable secrets of an ancient civilization. On its banks sat many mystic sadhus and assorted holy men in various stages of nangapan and ardhnangapan, of abstinence and indulgence, of dhyan and gyan – all looking to Ganga Mata, the Mother Ganga, for classic, timeless inspiration. Banaras was an ancient memory fixed in time, where everything, it seemed, began and ended.'

Param congratulated himself on this opening touch. He had spoken in a low, faraway sort of voice that arose from the depth of his belly, like a classic yogic chant in a soothing baritone. He knew it had pleasantly washed over Pakwaan.

'But,' said Param, pausing for a long, slurping sip of his tea, 'these images of Banaras that I have just described are borrowed from the eyes of Chatur Chuttar, who found all this mysticism, all this religion-shiligion, so strange and new that this is what he chose to see.'

'Chatur Chuttar?' Pakwaan asked with a grin. 'What sort of a name is that?'

Param smiled wickedly at the memory. 'Later, Beta. I will tell you all about how the man got his name, but before that let me tell you about Banaras. The city was much, much more than an assortment of holy men. It was a city of great activity, famous for its musicians and poets, its food, and the intricate and beautiful brocade sari that needed such skill in spinning and weaving.

'Brocade,' he said longingly, stretching the last syllable, his eyes half-closed, 'was woven in Alaipura, where we lived. It was a district of Banaras and the centre of this most enchanting fabric. Ancient legend has it that powerful kings and nobles insisted on the Banarsi brocade for their ranis' wardrobes. Even when the great Mughal, Prince Saleem, met his Anarkali, he was as smitten by her beauty as he was by the brilliance of her Banarsi lehanga.

'Kin khwaab . . .' he lingered over this word, 'beautiful little dreams. That is what my father wove on the silk with rich gold and silver threads. Weavers and spinners were considered just that – mere weavers and spinners, simple "kaarigars",' he sneered at the word and waved his hands dismissively. 'But those like my father, who spun and wove fabric of such intricate beauty, were artists or "kalakaars". And, my son,' Param said, his eyes widening with admiration, 'brocadery was truly an art.

'Imagine a large room where every square-inch of floor space was covered with looms, yarns stretched across their warp, and from the top, as if from the heavens, flowed streams of yarn of different hues, which narrowed as they passed through the small space made by two wooden bars over each warp. A massive, magical mingling of chaotic colour – of brilliant blues and bright yellows, shimmering greens and subtle saffrons, blood-reds and crimsons, oranges and gorgeous golds! But this colourful, crowded arrangement of threads would seem chaotic only to the eyes of the novice for this random riot of colour was a large and exact version of a small, fixed plan, the naksha – a design or a map.

The naksha was a paper sketch of the design of the fabric, but it was the nakshaband, or the rendering of the sketch into threads, that required immense skill. It was from the nakshaband that the number of threads for every colour and every motif were calculated so that the design could be woven. And what designs we created! Flowers and peacocks, birds and animals, hunting scenes, simple bootis and complicated pallus! Imagine arranging thousands of threads in the correct sequence so that a hunting scene with caparisoned elephants, horse-riders, deer and wild boar could be woven with them! It required great skill, and the kalakaari of nakshabandi represented a great tradition, of learning-from-young and instincts of touch and feel. The nakshabandis of Banaras were so well known for their artistry that their nakshas were sent to brocade weavers in faraway places like Surat and Chanderi.

'And if nakshabandi was magical, the process of its transformation into fabric and the weaving of patterns that followed were equally enchanting. The master weaver, often the nakshabandi himself, like your grandfather's dearest friend, Mateen, would sit at the base of the loom. Opposite him, at eye-level, behind the cascading yarn that came from above to be attached to the warp, sat his chela – your grandfather, Kalaam – waiting for instructions from the guru. The stage was set for the predetermined, intricate yarn dances to begin in slow motion – its beauty a result of perfect harmony and understanding between guru and chela. The correct number of yarns had to be lifted in the right order so that weft shuttles could pass between the opening and closing of warp shafts – *khataak*, *khataak*, *khataak*!' Param's hands powerfully sliced the air, mimicking the classic weavers' motion on a hand loom. 'And slice by slice, yarn by yarn, the motif would emboss itself on the fabric as if it had a life of its own.'

Pakwaan was amazed at the tenderness, power and pride with which his father recounted these memories.

'There was a joy of life in the very soil of Banaras, and being Banarsi was unique,' Param continued. 'They were free-spirited, the Banarsis, not enslaved by work nor dominated by services or salaries. Theirs was a close-knit biradari, a brotherhood where privacy was public preserve. But it was not an intrusive, needling, or smug curiosity about others' problems. Dukh–sukh were genuinely shared, and life, like Ganga Mata, went placidly by. In this biradari there were three who were like this,' said Param, clasping his hands tightly to indicate the closeness of the bond, 'your grandfather, Kalaam the Kathua, Mateen the master weaver and nakshabandi, and Arth Purabiya, the storyteller without an equal.

'Arth Purabiya was the badshah of kahanis.' Param's voice was heavy with awe and admiration. 'A conjurer of delightful images and *the* master of the spoken word. He was gifted and skilful with its use – like a great painter blessed with an instinctive feel for colour and strokes. And the way he told his tales, and the tales he told! At the slightest hint of a story getting hold of Arth, entire mohallas would gather to hear him – such was his power.'

'Uncanny,' Pakwaan muttered, remembering his dream, and his father looked up at him, surprised. There was a moment of silence, his father waiting for Pakwaan to speak. 'No, carry on, Baba,' Pakwaan said.

'It had been a satisfying day at the karkhana. Mateen had, after much trial and error, finally perfected the naksha of a unique but particularly complicated brocade and the first yardage that had been woven matched the naksha exactly. As always, there was more work to be done, but a complicated task done to perfection called for celebration. And so off went the two friends, your grandfather the Kathua and his good friend Mateen, savouring the flavours of their beloved Banaras with its narrow galis, its brightly decorated shops, its sounds of busybodies asking for their right of way, buyers bargaining with shopkeepers for better prices and friends greeting each other warmly. The smell of peanuts being roasted on tawas; hot, strong, milky tea; aloo tikkis and samosas being fried; the sweet-sourness of saunth being splashed on the yogurt over chaat, the spicy mintiness of jeera-paani with gol gappas, a jhalak – a quick glimpse – of the masti of Banarsipan.

'They reached their favourite paan shop in Alaipura and placed their order: "Oye, Guru, let's have two magnificent maghais – soft betel nut, cardamom and perfumed tobacco. Splash on the katha daringly but use the chuna sparingly." As they chewed their paan, swishing its taste around in their mouths, enjoying the flavours of cardamom, the aroma of scented tobacco, the tart-sweet taste of chuna-katha, they ambled without a care in the world along the banks of the Ganga, where they met, by joyful accident, their friend, Arth Purabiya, enjoying the pleasures of a head massage.

'"Aah!" he groaned, when he saw his friends approaching. "This maalish lightens the load of time. The masti of maalish is more blissful than the heavens. My spirit feels it is bubbling like water on a slow-rolling boil, relaxed and mischievous. You have done your kathna, Kathua; now it is time for me to spin my yarn," he said.

'Mateen and my father laughed, admiring his wit. Mateen was the circumcised one, the Kathua, your grandfather was the Kathua-by-caste, and Arth the spinner of yarns! No offence taken, no offence meant, it was just another celebration of bhai-bandi and easy camaraderie. Their hands cupped around their mouths and their heads thrown back, Mateen and Kalaam announced in happy voices, "Suno! Suno! Listen you all, citizens of Banaras, the great Arth Purabiya is ready to tell a story."

'When people heard the announcement, they left whatever they were doing and gathered to hear Arth's tale. Some were happy to have dropped the daily drudgery of work to enjoy the outdoors and an entertaining story, and some felt their happiness smudged with the guilt of not completing their everyday tasks. Arth dipped himself in the river and dried himself vigorously. Dressed in a fresh dhoti, a crisp, dry gumchha across his shoulders, he began the story of the sly and cunning tiger

"'Once upon a time . . .' spoke Arth in a voice loaded with ancientness, "there was a forest so dense that even the Sun God had to strain through the blackness to show his power, like the belly of a deep-deep well. Thick-thick, tall-tall trees stretched towards the sky . . ." He stretched his arms as high as they could go. "And fireflies winked like little diamonds in the midday sun. The forest teemed with life. There were birds – big ones and small ones, colourful and dull ones – barasingha and spotted deer, hogs and blue bulls, rabbits and jackals, musk deer and peacocks, and the hero of our story – an old, sly, cunning and ferocious tiger. But age and injury had slowed him down, and hunting for food had become a problem. So he turned to the village at the edge of the forest where there was easy game. At first, his shikar was cows and goats. But as the burden of age grew heavy and his strength and speed sagged, he had to satisfy his hunger with prey that was the slowest and easiest to kill," he paused, looking up at his audience. "MAN."

"'When the villagers found their cows and goats missing they were worried, but when the tiger killed a little child – baap re baap – there was gadar in the village. Drums were beaten," Arth thrust his hips at the crowd and mimicked the beating of drums with his hands. "Announcements were printed and messages passed from mouth to mouth, offering generous rewards to any shikari who would kill the dangerous beast.

"'The villagers were in luck – the news reached the famous and legendary Galeecha Shikari. Galeecha was brave and cunning and carried many guns. He was tall and fair, his shoulders were broader than the broadest, and his aim was absolutely deadly.

Galeecha was not his real name, but it had stuck because he always carried a carpet that he spread on the machaan while he lay in wait. The carpet was made in Persia and was soft to the touch, and depicted the scene of a tiger hunt. Imagine the guts of this man! Hunting an animal as dangerous as the tiger and having a tiger hunting scene under his bum! This show of guts was admirable and it gave the great Galeecha an aura of fearlessness. But . . ." Arth's eyes became big-big, round-round in frank admiration. "What the tiger lacked in youthful vigour, he more than made up for in sheer cunning." Arth put his hands on his bent knees and thrust his head at his audience, his face sly and conspiratorial. "This tiger could throw his roar like a ventriloquist, always confusing the enemy about his location – and this the great Galeecha did not know.

"'The plans were made. The machaan was placed in a tree with a generous, leafy canopy so that Galeecha would be hidden from view, and a goat tied up as bait. At dusk, Galeecha took his gun, his carpet, a thermos full of tea, and sat and waited. He carried only two bullets – so sure was he of success. As darkness descended, black and heavy, the poor goat shivered with fear and the great Galeecha sat with the hunting scene padding his bum, imagining the appreciation and applause that awaited him after he had made his kill.

"'The jungle was filled with an eerie silence and Galeecha's senses were finely stretched. In the distance, he heard the sound of a twig snapping. It came from the right of the goat. The tiger realized that he might have given himself away. So he purred like a cat and threw his mew to the left of the goat. Galeecha swung the barrel of his gun, took careful aim and *thain, thain! bang, bang!* two bullets crashed into the undergrowth, and clods of earth and broken branches flew around. During all this confusion the tiger rushed at the goat, killing it with a vicious blow. While it sat down to enjoy the juicy meat, Galeecha waited. In a little while, a satisfied burp slipped from the tiger's mouth and then he threw his roar, wild and ferocious, straight at Galeecha's face! Galeecha jumped up, petrified, his sphincter almost giving way, but he managed to save himself the embarrassment of explaining a smelly stain on the hunting scene.

"''COME DOWN!' roared the tiger, and Galeecha, hypnotized by fear, climbed down as if in a trance.

"''TURN AROUND!' the tiger bellowed," Arth said as he turned his back to the audience.

'"Then the tiger roared again, 'PATLOON UTAARO – TAKE OFF YOUR PANTS!'" Arth thrust his arse at the crowd and mimicked the pulling down of trousers. "And then," said Arth, a smile of victory on his face, 'usne uski gaand maar di – the tiger took the shikari's arse. Or, as the angrez would say, he buggered the hunter."

'Shocked, coquettish, hand-covering-mouth laughter tittered through the women's section; loud, lewd, wicked laughter echoed amongst the men. Arth raised his hand, hushing the crowd.

'"But you have to salute Galeecha's bravery – he did not run away, and the fires of revenge raged in his heart. He admitted to the disappointed villagers that this tiger was more cunning than he had thought but, ultimately, it was just good kismet that had saved the animal. In a voice full of passion and courage he promised the villagers he would drag the body of the dead tiger to the village the very next day. The villagers were relieved. Another machaan was set up, with fresh bait. This time Galeecha took a more powerful gun with many bullets and, for the first time, he did not carry his favourite carpet. The memory of the hunting scene was now inside his bum, not under it.

'"But the second time was just like the first. Many bullets were fired and more damage done to the flora and fauna. Galeecha was again called down, told to strip and buggered by the sly animal. Despite the two-time buggery, Galeecha's courage did not fail him. His honour was at stake, and he had to wipe out, *obliterate*, the humiliation of the anal assaults. The third time, he took his most powerful gun, whose bullets were as big as cannon balls, and lay in wait. This time, too, the tiger appeared and tricked him. Once more, Galeecha fired into emptiness and big-big, tall-tall trees were uprooted as if there had been an earthquake, but when the dust, smoke and confusion settled, the tiger roared for Galeecha and, for the third time in a row, buggered him. This time the tiger could not help himself and after he finished he asked the great Galeecha, his voice heavy with victorious sarcasm, 'TELL ME, GREAT HUNTER. TU YAHAN SHIKAR KHELNE AATA HAI YA GAAND MARWANE. ARRE, DO YOU COME HERE TO ENJOY THE PLEASURES OF SHIKAR OR DO YOU COME HERE TO GET BUGGERED?'

'The men slapped their thighs, thumped each other's backs, roared and guffawed, tears streaming down many faces. The women also laughed, but theirs was an embarrassed tinkle, as if they were admitting that they too enjoyed the humour in such crudity. Arth waited for the laughter to subside and then asked, "Tell me, you people, what is the message in this story?"

'Silence. Everyone was deep in thought and then a voice broke in. "It's just a joke, this story. It has no message."

'"I have to agree that this is a story full of jest but . . ." Arth's voice dropped, becoming low and heavy with wisdom, "it says a lot about storytelling. This is the tiger's tale, glorifying his cunning in stripping the hunter – a pathetic, idiotic figure with only a hat-trick of buggery behind him – of his pride and bravery. If the hunter told this story it would be different – the hunter would glorify his hunting and the tiger would be weak and cowardly. You see, this is the problem with a story – where the truth lies, nobody knows. It all depends on who narrates it. In war and in peace, the victorious vigorously tell their tales and the vanquished lose their voices and are stripped of their virtues."

'An appreciative murmur passed through the crowd and a few clapped softly, amazed by what Arth had just said. Sounds of, "One more, one more," came from the crowd but Arth had had enough.

'"Bas, yaar, bas! Enough! Friends, enough!" he said. "There will be another time. Till then, khuda hafiz, may God be with you." The crowd went its way and Mateen, your grandfather and Arth went off to celebrate his success and their friendship.'

The effects of the tea had worn off and Param felt the need for sleep, but one look at his son and he knew he had told his story well. There was a longing in Pakwaan's eyes, as if he missed the aura of an era gone by.

'But, Baba, how did we become cooks?'

'Patience, Beta, patience,' Param said teasingly. 'I promise to tell you the next instalment tomorrow.'

Matters of State

JHELUM and Mahadev sat on the veranda on white wicker chairs, gifts from the inmates of Sundergarh Jail given to Mahadev in honour of his visit to the prison as Collector.

'Namaste, Ji,' said Param as he presented the tea-service. 'Namaste, Param,' said Jhelum. Mahadev nodded his head in stiff acknowledgement, his bum, still burning from his morning's ablutions after the marchwangan, resting gingerly on the wicker. He preferred to keep the help at arms-length. 'Always appear distant and stern with the subordinates. It keeps them in their place, prevents them from getting too familiar,' the angrez had taught him during his training.

Param left, and Jhelum waited for the tea to brew to perfection. Then she poured a cup for Mahadev. 'Aah,' he said in appreciation, and Jhelum smiled with relief.

He finished the first cup and asked for another. It was time to wake the children and educate them on the benefits of morning exercise. He turned up the volume of the music system and put on the Mahatma's favourite bhajan, 'Aum Jai Jagdish Hare'. The loud sound of temple bells rung with great devotion, and the chorus of the devout singing boomed through the house, shattering its peaceful stillness. The children leapt out of their beds muttering protests, and made their groggy way to the veranda.

Mahadev always enjoyed this joke. 'Wake up! Wake up!' he gleefully announced. 'Early to bed and early to rise makes a man healthy, wealthy and wise. Exercise! Exercise! You have to exercise. It is a good habit. It energizes the body, keeps you in top gear for the day. And you know about habits – they make good servants but bad masters,' he jumped up from his made-in-prison chair and enthusiastically began his routine.

Standing straight, with his legs together, arms by his sides, he bent his knees and threw his arms forward, bent his knees, threw his arms forward – seven, eight, ten times. Arms on his hips, he kicked his legs forward and sideways, forwards and sideways, always grimacing, neck muscles taut and stretched as if a giant effort was involved. His exercise routine was punctuated by burps and farts – soft and smelly ones, loud and long ones, wet and dangerous ones – and he explained to his children yet another benefit of regular, early morning exercise: 'It rids the body of all the foul air that it collects the day before.'

Mahadev's departure for work was a ceremony conducted with clockwork precision, celebrating his importance in the household. While he was bathing, his office clothes, immaculately pressed, were laid on his bed. Fresh socks were draped over highly polished shoes. Jhelum would bathe and dress before Mahadev, and inform Param in the kitchen that breakfast would have to be served shortly. En route, she would check if the children were dressed. Just as Mahadev was tying his shoelaces the gongs could be heard, so that by the time he got to the table breakfast would be ready and he would not have to wait.

Breakfast was announced at 8 a.m. sharp by three officious gongs from a brass bell that hung on a thick ebony frame intricately carved by Chinese craftsmen – a part of Jhelum's dowry that had been brought all the way from Delhi. The family, bathed and ready, trooped in for breakfast. Fluffy omelettes, crisp golden-brown on the outside, light and airy inside, stuffed with tomatoes and onion, sprinkled with finely cut green chillies were served with two types of sauces. The common Kissan tomato sauce in a bottle that, more often than not, had to be turned upside down, banged with an open palm to finally have it splotching red all over the plate in squirty bursts, and the second one home-made, tomatoes blistered on a red hot tawa, blended with dried red-hot chillies soaked in warm water with garlic and sugar – chilli-hot with a touch of sweetness. The family favourite.

Mahadev cut his toast in half. 'A sign of elegant English manners,' he said. 'It ensures small dainty bites and avoids ugly mouth-open chomps.' Silence at the table as the family crunched on their toasts and cut fluffy omelettes with their knives and forks, washing it all down with sweet, creamy cold coffee.

'Breakfast like a king, lunch like a prince and dinner like a pauper is the key to a healthy life,' Mahadev energetically announced as he proceeded to demolish his breakfast.

While the meal was in progress, his tiffin or mid-day snacks were being made. He always came home for lunch. Coffee or tea in a shining thermos wrapped in a spotless white damask serviette and biscuits in a small and elegant silver bowl were packed in a wicker hamper, the spaces around them padded with cotton wool to avoid clattering noises as the car moved along – very much like the English chief engineer's hamper during Mahadev's first posting in a remote district in the state. As he left the table to rinse his mouth the hamper was given to Jhelum, who stood in the porch where the car waited. Jhelum handed over the hamper to the driver, while Mahadev's briefcase and a huge red box marked 'Files Urgent' in bold black letters were picked up by a peon and deposited carefully in the front seat of the car.

Mahadev would then arrive, walking across the polished veranda in his highly polished shoes making *thuk-thuk* noises. Another peon, bent and obsequious, followed him to the car and opened the passenger door, overtaking him just before he got there. The children called him 'Fartcatcher' because he always followed behind. 'Namaste, Mai-Baap,' the peon wished him in a voice dripping with exaggerated servility as Mahadev settled into the back seat. Jhelum, waiting at the top of the stairs, waved goodbye. As on every morning, Mahadev was too preoccupied, his mind grappling with the matters of state that lay ahead. The car drove down the circular driveway and sped through the open gate, Fartcatcher running up to close it, and, finally, the house heaved a sigh of relief. Govinda rushed to where Jhelum stood, his chest bulging, his stance totally macho. Thumping his chest like Tarzan, he burst into song:

'I've eaten breakfast sharp at eight
It's time now to celebrate
Let the family flag be unfurled
And we shall rule the bloody world.
Exercise! Exercise! You've got to exercise.'

He mimicked Mahadev's movements – shaking his hips, waving his arms and burping loudly. He could burp to order and make all sorts of farting noises with his mouth, and Tek Ram and Gauri took particular pleasure in egging him on.

In a week, Tek Ram would be leaving for Mayo. His parents had been thrilled when he had got admission after competing in a common entrance exam the year before. Much like the IAS, Mahadev thought fondly, imagining his eldest son as the second in a line of powerful bureaucrats who would carry his name. He considered Tek Ram to be his lucky charm. A few days after he was born, his father was scaled up, from Deputy Secretary to Under Secretary – better pay, more responsibility and, if it were possible, more importance.

While he sat in his gleaming white Ambassador, its white-walled tyres with jet black treads, standard issue, like a uniform for bureaucrats of his vintage 'posted' in the capital of the state, his mind wandered off into the past. A rare occurrence, since his time from home to office was always spent looking through files that lay in the red box.

'My firstborn son, my beta,' Mahadev remembered his mother cooing gratefully as she pinched his cheeks with great affection. He smiled fondly at the memory. Her first two children were girls – the pregnancies were smooth and both were born A-1 specimens of health with all parts intact, but how his mother had wished for a son! Daughters and sons made for a better mix. Sons allowed parents a fling at immortality, the chance to carry forward the family name, the advantages of acquiring dowry notwithstanding.

It had been that time of the year when the pickles soaked in the winter sun. Long, blood-red carrots along with cauliflowers, turnips and small white onions, fresh mustard seeds, large, fiery red chillies slit and cleaned and stuffed with masala, and gul-gul, those large bright yellow lemons almost the size of oranges – all left to pickle in their own juices. Fresh winter produce preserved in large ceramic jars. Tasty little bites with meals, the spicy-sweet, chilli-hot memories of the crispness of winter as spring gave way to summer.

The summer of 1924 – 23 April, to be precise.

George V, 'Panjam' to the natives – the only English monarch to be proclaimed King Emperor live and exclusive in Delhi – was again on a podium, this time in London, declaring the British Empire Exhibition open at Wembley. It was a grand event designed to show the hundreds of people assembled there the 'vivid model of the art, architecture and industry of all the nations that came under the English flag.' Home-turf tamasha showcasing the glory of the Empire while the subject nations fell over each other to get Mother Britannia's attention. Yet, in the end it was the Indian pavilion modelled on Mughal architecture that proved to be the most popular – kudos and standing ovations to their Jewel in the Crown. The exhibition had more than twenty-five million visitors who went back home in awe of the grand spectacle, grateful to have been ruled by the fairest and most just of all empires.

At that very moment, thousands of miles away in Amritsar – morning in Wembley, afternoon in Amritsar – Devi, Mahadev's mother, had woken up and felt the change in her body. She knew, instinctively, that she was pregnant. The timing was loaded with noble destiny – the inauguration of the Empire at one end of the world and the beginning of a life in India, the jewel in the British crown. Kismet lent its shoulder to a native, born and bred to push – dum laga ke, hai-shaa – the burden of improving the lot of hapless natives.

Devi carried the child for a little more than the duration of the exhibition of Empire, full nine months and more, to absorb, Abhimanyu-like, the glories of English rule. When the exhibition was finally declared closed, she could feel the baby kick and move. Palm readers and pandits, soothsayers and women who could tell the child's sex just by looking at the shape of her swollen belly (carrying low – daughter; carrying high – son), were sure it was going to be a baby boy. 'Hai!' Devi said, smiling wistfully, and wished them pure ghee and sugar in their mouths.

For a change, the soothsayers and pandits were right. 'It's a boy! It's a boy!' everyone said gratefully when the child arrived. Mahadev was precious, the harbinger of a hat-trick of sons. Devi would have two more, making the family a three-two combo, dowry cashflow positive and a fling at immortality guaranteed.

Before the Employee Stock Option Plan (now a taxable perk and only an A away from Aesop, the fablewalla) made chauffeurs millionaires, the English had mastered the art of outsourcing. The day-to-day functions, the dreary tasks of keeping records 'up-to-date', of seeing that the enterprise spent more time following policy than being enterprising, the everyday maintenance of the massive machinery of babudom, was, quite simply, outsourced to natives trained in the art of attending to petty detail. The IAS sat on top of this heap, making sure that enlightened governance filtered down to a nation desperate to recover the glory of a lost golden age.

Orissa was Mahadev's choice of cadre. Rich with tribals, men wearing only loin cloths, women in sarees without blouses, their breasts bouncing gaily as they walked or danced, closest to the state of nature – so much for him to do. The batch of would-be administrative gladiators were trained at Metcalfe House, a huge mansion across acres of landscaped lawns and English-style hedges and gardens by the banks of the Yamuna. Once his training began, Mahadev could spend little time with his lovely Jhelum, but he made up for the loss of physical contact with love letters to her that were occasionally Napoleonic (naturally) in content.

Darlingest,

As I sit by my window and muse over the mist that lies yonder, over the Yamuna, I am filled with thoughts of you. My soul aches with sorrow. But there is solace. When profound feelings overwhelm me, I draw from your lips and from your heart a love that consumes me with fire.

But until I see you, meri jaan, a thousand kisses. Give me none in return – for they will set my blood ablaze.

Yours eternally,

M.

He would look at her photograph as he folded the letter. Framed in sterling silver, it was in black-and-white, her face in profile, a touched-up glow of greyish sepia around her head, her soft eyes looking wistfully into the distance. It was signed 'Kinsey Bros' with a flourish on the bottom right corner. Photography and framing by Kinsey Brothers of Connaught Place, the most well-known portrait photographers in the country – a must for upper-class brides and bridegrooms when they sent their portraits for suitable matches. Expensive, but worth it. He shook his head as he imagined her face – even the brothers Kinsey could not do her beauty complete justice. To the letter, he added, *P.S. I realize now how false an image of you your photograph gives.* Jhelum read the letters and blushed happily. She looked at his photograph (also by Kinsey Bros) and held it to her heart.

They had entered their third year as husband and wife when Jhelum realized she was pregnant. It was around the end of April, the month when Mahadev had been conceived. Like him, Tek Ram was born at the end of the year, their birthdays a few days apart. Surely, it could not be mere coincidence – kismet, Mahadev was sure, had willed that his eldest would follow in his footsteps. The early fifties may not have been the grandest of times for the country, no spectacle of Empire to celebrate, but his son was witness to the grandeur of a royalty noveaux. Mahadev was District Magistrate, Sundergarh district, when Tek Ram was all of four, old enough, Mahadev was certain, to keep the memories of the awesome prestige of the IAS tucked away permanently in some significant corner of his mind. District Magistrate, DM for short, was a giant leap in stature in the kingdom of bureaucracy. All aspects of district life – revenue and administration, social welfare and forestry, health and family planning, roads and transport, towns and villages – came 'under' him.

The house allotted to the DM was huge, complete with orchards, stables and rabbit pens, and guards roamed the large premises twenty-four hours a day. A few steps away from the main house was the DM's home-office, with a large hall at the entrance where a 'durbar' was held every Wednesday morning (budh hai shudh, or Wednesday is good) and common folk would assemble and, with great humility, apprise the Magistrate Sahib of their problems. The best trumpeter from the armed constabulary, Hila Bhaiyya, as Tek Ram called him – Hila, short for the full name Hilarious given to the tribal when he was converted to the fold of Lord Jesus – would play the 'Reveille' when the tri-colour was hoisted at sunrise and the 'Retreat' when it was brought down at sunset. Sometimes, Raja Sahib of Gangpur – fat, bulbous-eyed, gin-soaked during the day and pickled in whisky by night – would arrive before sunset and watch the tri-colour being brought down to Hilarious's 'Retreat'. He would put his arm around Mahadev's shoulder and in a voice loaded with nostalgia tell Mahadev how it reminded him of the good old days – a compliment from an old raja to a new king.

Ah, the IAS, Mahadev thought, chuffed by the memory, imagining his firstborn as a bureaucrat. But Tek Ram's academic performance at Mayo niggled dangerously at the back of Mahadev's mind. Tek Ram oscillated between ranking in the middle and at the bottom of the class, and whenever Mahadev stressed the importance of coming first, as he had done through school and college, saying it was 'a step in the right direction to ensure great careers', Jhelum would deflect his concern and spring to Tek Ram's defence. 'Just wait and watch,' she would say enthusiastically. 'He will make you proud.'

Mahadev was never convinced, though he hoped for the best, and Jhelum's motherly protection of their eldest son irritated him. 'Marriage is the union of two bodies but one soul,' was another of his favourite clichés, and his wife's siding with his son did not quite live up to his belief. Mahadev snapped out of his reverie as the car halted briefly at the gates to the Secretariat.

'Namaskar, Sahib,' the guard said to Mahadev, bowing obsequiously before he opened the gates to his office. Mahadev waved dismissively in acknowledgement. Two peons were awaiting his arrival. They rushed to open the doors, one taking the wicker hamper with his lunch, the other grabbing the box of files and running to his room to make sure the files arrived before he did. A glass of water was placed on the table and the table lamp switched on. He left the room as soon as Mahadev entered, and flicked a switch outside. A red light glowed on top of the door indicating that the Sahib was in his room and was not to be disturbed.

'Ah, the IAS,' Mahadev murmured again and plunged into the files, making notations that would affect the destiny of his people. Never have so many owed so much to so few, he thought as he remembered Sir Winston. The civil services was such a great career – he would chat with his son, alone, he decided, and share with the boy his dynastic dream.

Vindaloo and the Hired Historian

VINDALOO – pronounced 'vin-dah-loo', the 'ah' either a gasp of surprised pleasure at the discovery of a new flavour that has revived a jaded palate with delicious, spicy hotness, or the stifled gasp of an insular palate that can never experience joy at tasting fieriness. Vin-dah-loo – probably the oldest memory of Indian cuisine in Vilayat, almost as ancient as curry, that standardized mix of different spices roasted, ground into powder and bottled, dissolved in hot water like a stock to cook anything in, meat, chicken, fish or vegetables, a convenient cuisine, an immediate indulgence for palates desperate for cosmopolitania, or for those who miss the flavours of the exotic Orient. Vin-dah-loo – pickled or curried. Vin-dah-loo – strangely, always pronounced by the Vilayatis as 'vind-uh-loo', the original 'ah' sounding like a constipated 'uh', a full-throated gasp expressing unpleasant shock, as if surprised pleasure is bad manners, a show of too much emotion.

'Baba, can you teach me how to cook Vindaloo?' Pakwaan blurted out.

Param looked up at his son, taken aback by the strange and sudden request.

'If my memory serves me correctly, Beta, we have never talked about Goan cuisine during our conversations. So where did you hear of this dish – in your dreams?'

Pakwaan nodded, blushing at the sensual memories of the Vindaloo and his firangi pari.

'Wah, beta, wah! If you dream about food then cooking has to be a genuine passion,' said Param with so much pride and happiness that it thrilled Pakwaan. 'Well, listen then. A great Vindaloo should never be made on the same day the meat is marinated. It must be left overnight so that each piece of meat soaks up all the flavours of the marinade. The next day it should be cooked on a slow and gentle fire till the meat is done. And ah! The reward of patience! Each bite is a celebration of the juicy spiciness, unlike in hurried marinations where only the surface absorbs the flavours. Meats that have been marinated for a short time and cooked are first-bite delights, but as you chew the blandness of the insides dominate as they have barely been touched by the masalas – the initial promise of delicious spiciness disappointingly diluted in the end.'

Param salivated as he spoke, memories of Vindaloo spreading in his mouth. 'The spices for a Vindaloo are traditionally ground in vinegar that is made from coconut toddy. Making the toddy is an art. Fresh toddy is fermented for a day or two and then poured into an earthen pot. A piece of earthen clay tile, the ones used for roofs, is heated till it glows fiery and passionate and is thrown into the toddy pot. The mouth of the pot is sealed with a cloth soaked in a mixture of red mud and water, and allowed to stay for days. The elements of the earth and nature mingling in harmony produce vinegar of such a subtle tartness that Vindaloos made in this are blessed with a balanced, well-rounded flavour. But before we start, let me ask Jhelum Memsahib if we can serve Vindaloo for lunch tomorrow.' He left the kitchen to ask

Jhelum's permission and came back a few moments later with good news.

'Before we start, I should tell you that traditionally Vindaloo is made with pork – the pig and the red chillies introduced by the Portuguese. But since good pork is not available in these parts, I shall make Vindaloo with mutton. And while I organize the spices, you can chop some onions, garlic and ginger, and pour out half a cup of synthetic vinegar. I know the tartness will be sharp, but what to do – toddy vinegar is uniquely Goan.'

The lesson was about to begin! Pakwaan delightedly chopped the onions, garlic and ginger, and within minutes three little mounds were neatly arranged on the chopping board.

'Put the tawa on the fire, Beta. We will roast the spices before grinding them. And now for the meat,' he said as he carried on cutting the mutton into bite-sized pieces, taking care to leave some fat around the edges. 'Cooking the meat in its own fat guarantees succulence.'

The tawa was hot now and Pakwaan roasted the spices, each spice separately. Cumin and mustard seeds jumped about delightedly on the hot tawa and the kitchen filled with their aromas. The chillies released their pungency and tickled the nasal passages – both father and son sneezed in delicious joy. The roasted spices were then ground with ginger, garlic, vinegar, and a dash of sugar to compensate for the sharpness of artificiality. The marinade was ready.

Lunch was made – soup and sandwiches for the Sahib and Memsahib, thick and rich meat curry with rice for the children. Sharp at a quarter past one, Mahadev's car honked its arrival. Fartcatcher ran to open the gate, bowing low as it passed him on its way to the porch. Jhelum was there to receive Mahadev and the peon opened the door to grab his briefcase and the wicker hamper, to be refilled for the afternoon snack.

Lunch for Mahadev was short and nutritious. He finished quickly and retired to his bedroom for a ten-minute nap, a second wind of energy so that he could deal with official matters more efficiently. 'After lunch rest a while, after dinner walk a mile' – another piece of pithy advice from his training days in the National Academy of Administration that he enthusiastically followed. At 2 p.m., refreshed and ready, he left – another brusque preoccupied-by-matters-of-state departure – and the household retired for the afternoon. Param and Pakwaan cleaned the kitchen, and the marinade for the Vindaloo was put away in the refrigerator.

'We will marinate the meat after dinner,' Param told his son. 'Remember, we have to work the marinade slowly and with feeling into the meat so that the flavour is guaranteed. Come now, you have a story to listen to.' He left the kitchen and ambled into the courtyard, and waited for his son. Pakwaan joined him moments later, and Param started where he had left off.

'Cunningham Sahib was an important man – as important as our own Mahadev Sahib. People sirred him and salaamed him and bowed before him with exaggerated izzat, because in his position he could grant favours, or hurt and harm. Cunning-ham,' Param broke the word into two syllables. "Cunning" in Hindi is "chatur", and "ham" is the thin slice of meat cut from the rump, or the "chuttar" of the pig,' he said, patting his backside. 'Join the two and you have Chatur Chuttar. It was Arth Purabiya, that skilled sculptor of words that gave him his name. It had a tongue-twisting lilt to it and was loaded with playful mischief. "There goes Chatur Chuttar," people would wickedly whisper, and those within earshot would titter with delight. And cunning he was, for he would often disguise himself like us, by staining his white-white skin with the rich brown juice of walnut and dye his hair to match the colour of ours, wear desi garments – dhoti and gumchha, kurta and pyjama – and mingle with the locals to get a feel of their ways and customs.

'It must have been a dull day for Cunningham Sahib. Salaams full of servility, respectful bowing and general grovelling are novelties that please the ego, but when overdone they begin to irritate. The tedium of office and the burden of responsibility had taken its toll on that fateful day. Desperate for diversion, it was time for Chatur Chuttar's favourite sport – the game of the girgit, the creature that skilfully blends itself into his surroundings and, unseen, observes the goings-on before it strikes. He left his office and coloured his skin with walnut juice and disguised himself as a sadhu, wearing only a dhoti and a sacred thread on a naked torso, and smearing parts of his body with holy ash. He walked down the banks of the Ganga where he came upon the gathering listening to Arth Purabiya's story about the tiger and Galeecha, and was amazed by the hold Arth had on his audience. He watched them listening to him as if in a trance, mesmerized by the power that Arth Purabiya wielded. And Chatur Chuttar was not chatur for nothing!' Param smiled at the turn of phrase, happy that Pakwaan was also amused. 'Cunningham Sahib stroked his chin, fiddled pensively with his sacred thread, thankful that he had left his office the way he had. He found what he was looking for, to shoot and bugger the truth with bullets! He decided there and then that Arth would be the medium for his message.

'Meanwhile, the friends were celebrating life's simple pleasures once the crowds had departed. Mateen and my father marvelling at Arth's ability to take a tale of buggery and give it such import, Arth accepting their compliments, enjoying their camaraderie and his hot chai and crisp samosa when . . .' Param paused.

'"Suno!" a voice said loudly above the murmur and chatter of those around. A half-naked fakir looked at them, pointing at Arth, wagging his finger with great authority.

'"Who are you?" asked Arth.

'"I am Cunningham Sahib," Chatur Chuttar said importantly, and the friends laughed.

'"Abbey, sala. Who are you trying to fool? If you are Cunningham Sahib then I am Kaiser-i-Hind," Arth said, acting coquettish and effeminate, puffing up his cheeks, cupping his palms below his chest, mimicking big, saggy breasts, and looking as solemn and dowdy as his mood would allow.

'A vengeful rage surged through Chatur Chuttar. What bloody cheek? The subject race mocking the supreme monarch . . . But he controlled himself. "Look at my eyes, look at my eyes," he hissed angrily, pointing with his fingers so that they could see the blueness. He dipped his gumchha in water and rubbed his forearm vigorously, revealing pale, milky whiteness, stark against a deep rich brown.

'Shocked, desperately afraid of the consequences, the three men folded their hands, bowed their heads and said, "Forgive us, Mai-Baap, forgive us, for we have done wrong. Your shoe and our heads," and they beat their bowed heads with their hands.

'"Suno Arth," said Chatur Chuttar with authority, "meet me at my office at nine o'clock sharp tomorrow morning." Then he got up and left.

'Arth arrived at the sahib's office half an hour early, nervous and afraid. His imitation of Queen Victoria had landed him in trouble, he was sure. On the dot of nine, a peon announced Arth's arrival, and permission was granted for him to be allowed to enter the sahib's room. He bowed with folded his hands.

'Chatur Chuttar smiled. "Namaskar," he said condescendingly. "Sit down."

'"Namaskar, Mai-Baap," Arth Purabiya said as he prepared to sit on the floor.

Chatur Chuttar quickly rose from his seat and motioned Arth Purabiya to sit on the chair opposite his.

'"Listen my man," the sahib's voice boomed importantly. "You tell your stories well and the hold you have on your audience is remarkable. But a God-given gift such as yours is being wasted in the narrowness of mohallas and petty boundaries of small biradaris. You must broaden your vision and, like great artists, create images that are permanent and of immense importance."

'Arth was amazed at his good fortune. Fear flew out of him and he sighed with relief. Chatur Chuttar was praising him, buttering him up!

'"I have great plans for you; plans that will give you the satisfaction of putting your God-given talent to good use. But to do this you will have to cho-though your mohalla, learn our language, and acquaint yourself with the superior knowledge, strength, steadfastness and courage of our race."

'There was a wicked look on Arth's face and his body shook with laughter. It was the sahib's turn to be surprised. "Why do you laugh?" he said, puzzled.

'"It's the way you say 'cho-though'. What you want to say is chho-do," he spoke slowly, elongating amd emphasizing the syllables. "The 'chh' pronounced as in 'chhota peg' – what you Burra Sahibs need after a long day; the 'odo' pronounced as in when you wrap a shawl, with a gentle hint of an 'r' sound – 'ooh-rdo' not 'oh-though'. When you say 'cho-though' you mean leave, but the way you say it, Sahib, gives it a wicked, naughty flavour. Do you know what you actually mean when you say the word like that?"

'Cunningham Sahib shook his head.

'"It means . . ." Arth broke into a smile, his face and eyes lighting up with badmashi. He put his elbows on the table and made a small hole with the thumb and forefinger of his right hand, and with the index finger of his left, all erect and stiff, he pushed it in and out, in and out, in and out of the hole – the action of the joyous joining of the ling with the yoni.

'Chatur Chuttar was shocked. He remembered the number of times he had raved and ranted at his incompetent peons to leave him alone. "Mujhe akela cho-though, mujhe akela cho-though!" he had yelled at them. They must have left the room in fear, wondering what was wrong with the sahib. Thank God, they weren't like the tiger in Arth's story,' Param said, and father and son guffawed loud and long.

'The humour hit Chatur Chuttar as well,' Param continued at length. 'He roared with laughter. A puzzled peon peered into the room, shocked at the sight of his Burra Sahib and the storyteller laughing hysterically.

'"Leave us alone," the sahib shouted in Hindustani, in between fits of laughter, pronouncing the word perfectly, enjoying the startled look on the peon's face. Then he turned to Arth. "Thank you for saving me much embarrassment, by God. But now, you will learn our language, dot your i's and cross your t's. So off with you, my boy," he gestured dismissively. "Pack your bags, pick up your belongings and forget your past. Your education starts tomorrow."

'Arth's ears were filled with instructions, his brain licked for the correctness of the Angrezi nuance, and with his gift for language and his instinct for words Arth became fluent with the Angrezi bhasha and comfortable with their manners.'

Param's voice was filled with sadness. 'And so Arth, the loveable kahanibaaz and dearest friend, changed completely. He changed his name – can you imagine? From Arth Purabiya, he became Arth Dubashi. Dubashi – a person who spoke in do, or two, bhashas – a cunning linguist whose stories could have double meanings. On his trips to the mohallas and biradaris, all suited and booted now, he threw his newly learnt Angrezi at his friends with great bombast. And he began to speak in the sahib's tongue. '"Suno," he would say as if it was a command, and when he referred to himself he would do so in the plural, like he was nobility. The mohallawallas whispered in awe, impressed that one of their own seemed so important.

Back in the sahib's office, Chatur Chuttar thundered, '"We must have a proper history."

"Yes! Yes! I wholeheartedly agree," said Arth. "We need itihaas, Sahib, we desperately need it."

'So, like two skilful handle-ghumanewallas, they stirred the minds of the people with the masalas of myth, garnishing them with bits of reality to create hulchul in people's minds. And how Arth's stories changed! No more mauj, no more masti, no questions from the crowd, no laughter. Only serious stories delivered from lecterns and pulpits to the janta who were in awe of their power. Arth Purabiya allowed himself to become like a performing monkey who danced to the tune of the dumroo that Chatur Chuttar played. And the story was always the same, like ghisa-pita, worn-out plots of Hindi films. The Hindus were the perennial victims, the Mussalmans were the villains who had inflicted all the suffering, with the English in the wings, like reluctant heroes who now had the extra burden of uplifting the nation and restoring to the Hindus their lost golden age.

'Let me read out one of his stories for you,' Param said, unfolding a piece of paper, yellow and brittle with age, handed down to him by his father.

> Those who believe that the English are nothing but looters and plunderers do not want real progress. This fair and just jaati of English deserve nothing but the highest praise. They came here as traders but after they saw the penalty which our great country was paying for its caste division and political weakness, their fair conscience was awakened and they made it their duty to uplift us from our pathetic state and make us rediscover our Golden Age.

> We were a civilized country 4000 years ago, but today we are as lifeless as a dead body that is awaiting cremation on the banks of the Ganga. For the last 700 years, the history of our country has been one solid blank for we have been ruled by the Mussalmans. They are by nature fanatics, commanded by their Prophet to bring the non-believers into their fold by the power of the sword. If they die in battle while converting the kaffir they are promised paradise, where they will enjoy the company of virgin, doe-eyed nymphs and, thus aroused by eternal pleasure, they looted and plundered this country and crushed underfoot our glorious and ancient culture.
>
> It is our good fortune to have people like Cunningham Sahib in our midst, for they have nothing but the benefit of you people in their minds and hearts. It is therefore our God-given duty to help people like him help us restore the glory of our ancient land.

Param sighed, shaking his head as if shrugging off a terrible memory. He folded the piece of paper and put it away in his pocket, and carried on.

'The Hindus thumped their chests, remembering their glorious, ancient heritage, the Mussalmans were now viewed with suspicion for the damage they seemed to have caused and, as if this was not enough, Chatur Chuttar and his chamcha Arth Dubashi believed that the people of the country had to be cut, sliced, categorized and labelled like daal, roti, spices and snacks in a kirana shop, so that everyone knew their place and the country could be effectively administered. Like some sort of bhagwan, Chatur Chuttar, with a stroke of his pen, allocated qualities and characteristics to large chunks of people, stripping them of their insaniyat. He dismissed the Brahmins as scheming and full of intrigue, and thrust upon Gujjars the in-born qualities of criminality and thievery. Julahas like Mateen were seen as bigoted and troublesome; Pathans as fierce and fond of battle; and the Gurkhas – the angrez always had a soft spot for Gurkhas, for they often fought the sahibs' battles – were bold and manly, independent and self-reliant, and admired the sahibs for their superior knowledge, strength and courage.

'Hey Bhagwaan!' Param slapped his forehead with his open palm and shook his head. 'God knows what else he noted,' he said sadly.

'The country became like a giant cauldron where Hindus scurried around nibbling at the roots of their newfound glory, imagining a brilliant golden age. Rajputs, Sikhs and Marathas rediscovered the war-like valour they had possessed when they had fought the Mughal invaders. They sang songs and told stories of the bravery of their men and courage of their women, and their heroes and heroines became larger than life. "We are the descendants of Raja Agrasen, the brave and noble, who even got the better of Indra, the King of Gods," the Agarwals thundered. "We are Ahirs," exclaimed the milkmen, "direct descendants of Lord Krishna – and we wear the sacred thread, wrapping it around our right ear twice just before pissing, exactly like the Brahmins do."' Param paced up and down full-o-full with excitement, waving his hands like a conjurer before an expectant audience waiting for a magnificent jadu mantar. 'The Mussalmans, too, pumped up their chests, changed their names to announce their purity. Singhs became Khans, barbers and butchers became Sheikhs – and Mateen . . . Mateen claimed that the first man on earth, Adam in the Garden of Eden, was the founder of his craft.

'"Suno, suno!" he would explain. "When Eve, the first woman on earth made Adam realize his nakedness, he taught the art of weaving to his sons, who are our original ancestors." He called himself Momin Ansari – Momin for the faithful and a man of honour, and Ansari from Ansaar, our ancient Arab ancestor who practised the art of weaving."

'The handle was turned and turned,' said Param, holding an imaginary ladle with both hands and making vigorous stirring motions. 'After this there was gadar, a hullabaloo of humungous proportions. The Brahmins bambooed the Chamaars and Ahirs for thinking of upper-casteness, and the sharif or respectable Mussalmans bambooed the barbers, butchers and weavers for dreaming of respectability as they were always low and labouring people in their eyes. There was too much hulchul, absolute and TOE-TULL KAY-OSS.'

Param fell silent.

'In all this hungama, Papaji, my father, watched his warm, familiar world crumbling before his eyes. Mateen, in a fit of imagined purity, decided only Ansaris could weave and so he stopped my father from weaving the simplest designs. The karkhana, so familiar till yesterday, had now become a place where my father was reminded of his otherness.'

Param closed his eyes, his face a mask of sadness. His breath deep and deliberate, willing himself to be calmer. He carried on in a low and heavy voice.

'It was early in the morning on the last day of Muharram. Arth had insisted that the three friends meet at there favourite chai shop, the same place where Chatur Chuttar had first met them. Your grandfather had agreed only to fulfil the formality of a once-warm friendship.

'"I tell you, Mateen, you have stopped me from weaving and this has caused me much pain and brought sorrow to my heart," Papaji said.

'"But you are neither a Momin nor an Ansari, and only they have the right to weave as they have been weavers since the time of Adam. Ask Arth, he will tell you all about it."

'Papaji looked at Arth and said in a voice full of sarcasm, "What do *you* think great storyteller?"

'Arth was irritated by Papaji's tone, so obvious was its irony. "An ordered society is the only way the benefits of an enlightened governance can filter down to the most lowly. It is the right tonic, I would say, to rejuvenate an ailing society," Arth Purabiya, now Arth Dubashi finished off, completely self-important and pompous.

'Papaji had had enough. "Bas!" he shouted. "Bas!" He pressed his ears tightly with his palms, trying to shut out Arth's pretension. "Sliced and ***behenchod*** demarcated, effectively ***bloody*** administered, rejuvenating tonic for an ailing society . . . Bloody hell! I've had enough! Enough of your bombastic bakwaas." Papaji's body shivered with an uncontrollable rage, his eyes filled with angry tears. "You have herded people into pens like cattle, chaapoing, branding them with characteristics, assigning them qualities, fixing their statuses and creating a society that is coloured by prejudice. You have moulded a past that will inflict such deep wounds that it will fester for centuries. You have taught the Hindu to dislike the Mussalman, whom he now considers the enemy of his religion and the destroyer of his ancient heritage. The Mussalman falsely believes he was once a member of the ruling race, and is hurt and angry that his status has been relegated. But most of all your stories have destroyed the warmth and easy friendship, the bhai-bandi among the three of us. I curse you Arth Purabiya, Arth Dubashi, or whatever you now call yourself, for the rubbish that you have dumped in people's minds – I hope you rot in hell!" With that he thumped his fist on the table with such force that the glasses jumped up in shock, and Mateen and Arth stared at him in astonishment.

'"A dramatic and, may I add shocking, display of emotion, dear Kalaam. Most unexpected from a person of your temperament," said Arth condescendingly. "But you must admit that what you accuse us of moulding was shaped from the earth of this land, from its very fabric – and I speak figuratively, of course. Perhaps, in the process of categorization and tabulation, the Kathuas have not been adequately represented and you feel slighted that you and your brethren have been robbed of status and importance – but I could look into the matter."

'"Baap re baap! What profit in shouting and screaming? Ancestrally associated with Adam," Papaji said, pointing to Mateen, "and the pompous distributor of identities." He pointed to Arth. "Wah, bhai, wah! I thank my stars, for I am in such exalted company. It seems to me, great kahanibaaz, that you have forgotten the power of the story. Think about your delightful tale of buggery. A tale told by the victor glorifying his victory, the vanquished hunter remaining a pathetic figure with only buggery behind him, and the moral – that the victor will tell his story and the vanquished will lose their voice. Today you have sold your God-given gift of storytelling to the victor and the results will be bloody and disastrous. And coming to your talk of earth from this land and its very fabric-shabrick, come with me, *come with me, I say*." His voice rose as he grabbed Mateen and Arth by their hands, and with great strength dragged them to the karkhana.

'"Observe this room – observe it carefully. To the novice it seems a riot of chaotic colour, but to the nakshabandi it is a prearranged plan and, if well-executed, the result is a fabric of stunning beauty because he understands his craft that has been handed down through generations. That is what we need – enlightened nakshabandis and storytellers, not people like you and Chatur Chuttar, who speak from positions of power and whose minds have preconceived notions about people of whom they have no real knowledge and pump into us strange and weird identities with so much force that ultimately we believe that it is the truth."

'In a low and dangerous voice he asked Mateen, "Where is the naksha for Chanderi? I will deliver it myself and enjoy the escape, welcome the relief from this suffocating mahaul." He grabbed the naksha from Mateen and walked out on to the street, shaking his head in disgust,' said Param shaking his own head to emphasize the point.

Chhutkara, Release

'THE celebration of Muharram had begun and the atmosphere was charged with a fevered energy, celebrating sorrow. Crowds milled around lamenting the sacrifice of their martyrs in loud, wailing voices, working themselves into a frenzy, beating their chests and tearing their hair, some fainting in an ecstasy of sorrow. Papaji pushed his way through the crowds, the naksha clutched safely in his hands, willing himself to banish the memories of Arth Purabiya and Mateen from his mind. He stopped for a minute to pull out a beedi from the bundle of his paanch-sau-ek or 501, his favourite brand. The bundle was wrapped in a pink paper cone, its mouth sealed with a green band which had at its centre a photograph of a man – mushtand, mustachioed and macho, smoking, satisfaction splashed across his face. He lit his beedi, took a huge, primal suck and felt a welcome nicotine rush. He looked up and exhaled.

'As he travelled westwards to Chanderi, the sky darkened dangerously, lit briefly by lightning, and there came a storm of terrible proportions. In the middle of this storm, Papaji came upon a river in full spate. Its waters gushed and gurgled, smashing into rocks, throwing huge sheets of water into the sky. The wind howled through the trees and big-big, tall-tall whirlpools of dust and leaves as tall as the Qutab Minar spiralled upwards into the air.

'But then there occurred the coincidence of coincidences! A miracle of fate, kismet ka jadu! Papaji came across a group of English Burra Sahibs on a camping tour. You know, Beta, in those days, these burra log travelled with lots of bandobast – coolies to carry their luggage, khidmatgars to wait at camp tables, dhobis to wash their clothes, bawarchis to cook and clean, hookabardars to set up their hookahs for the after-meal smoke, even bhishtis or water bearers, who would sprinkle water around their tents so that the earth would be cooler and make hot summer evenings more bearable. But the storm had scared away the servants – they had bolted in fright. Their bandobast lay ruined, and the Sahibs were wet and very hungry.

'"Can you cook?" they asked desperately when they spotted my father.

'"Yes," he said, "a little."

'Papaji realized he was a bit hungry himself and rummaged through their provisions. There was chicken, ghee, tomatoes, chillies, onions, garlic, salt and ginger. While the storm raged, he chopped the onions, scraped the skin off the ginger, peeled and sliced the garlic. He was fortunate that their servants had carried a mortar and pestle. He used it to pound the garlic, ginger and green chillies into a coarse, stringy paste. He motioned to the sahibs to stand around the stoves so that he could light it easily, wiped a degchi clean and put it on the fire. Then he tapped spoonfuls of ghee into the degchi and watched as it melted. He threw in the onions and stirred, and watched, fascinated, at the change in colour and texture – the fresh raw slices changing, turning transluscent at first and then gradually shrinking as they became golden and then brown. The smells changed, too, from strong and pungent when the onions were chopped to a gentler aroma when transluscent and, finally, the stronger, more metallic smell when they turned dark brown. With an instinctive sense of timing, he stirred in the mixture of chillies, garlic and ginger, scraping the mortar clean. He threw in the pieces of chicken, amazed at how quickly the pink flesh changed to a consistent light brown and then to a rich brownish-red. He marvelled at the sensual, soft, yielding quality of the tomatoes, their firm consistency on the surface resisting the knife for a moment, then allowing it to cut through their squishy softness. He eased the chopped tomatoes into the degchi, covered it with a lid, and put the rice to boil on a separate stove.

'The sahibs sat around the stove, with their chhota and burra pegs, waiting for the meal. Every now and then Kalaam would lift the lid to check. Spicy aromas, fragrant and full of promise, would tease his nostrils and he would salivate at the thought of the meal that lay ahead. The sahibs offered him a drink. Papaji refused at first and then allowed himself the pleasure because the sahibs were so insistent.

'"Chicken curry and rice," he announced happily when it was done, and the sahibs queued up for their helpings. Papaji served out generous portions. Conversation stopped as the sahibs began to eat and Kalaam was amazed to see how their hands ripped apart flesh, how they chewed the bones, sucked out the juices, making grateful *soo-soo* noises, curry dribbling down their chins. They rubbed their stomachs lovingly after they finished, and burped, content and sated.

'"Excellent meal, jolly good, old chap," they said in their crisp Angrezi, watching him eat after they finished.

'Whether it was the drinks or the quality of your grandfather's cooking, one cannot really say, but the sahibs linked their arms and kicked up their legs and began to sing an English song sung at farewells and moments of appreciation:

'"For he is jolly good fellow,
For he is a jolly good fellow,
That nobody can deny,
That nobody can deny."

'Their stomachs full, they were mast and swaying, and added their own words as they went along.

'"And the bugger's a jolly good cook, too,
The bugger's a jolly good cook, too,
And so say all of us, and so say all of us."

'And they carried on clapping and dancing.

'"Why don't you come and cook for me?" one of them asked Papaji.

'My father's eyes were lidded, his brain fuzzy with too-quickly-drunk pegs of angrez daru. He felt a sense of bravado at the success of his meal, so he said with a studied nonchalance, "Let me think about it," and retired for the night.

'He woke early. The sahibs were still asleep. He sat on a flat rock, deep in thought. The chicken curry had been delicious and the appreciation that followed heady. He looked up, his palms pointing skyward, and gently, lovingly, kissed his hands, thanking kismet for blessing them with skill. And the ceremony of cooking, what an experience that had been – ingredients all around him and he alone responsible for their proportions, his talent for timing and tempering determining deliciousness or disaster, his mind focused on the end result, completely insulated from bad memories.

'Shoot this history-shistory with bullets, he thought, blow to smithereens all this striving for a magnificent heredity, this glorifying-purifying business. Appreciation or abuse after meals would never be coloured by prejudice – the intensity of praise a reflection of the quality of the meal. It was that simple! He would make his own world where ability would determine his self-worth and every meal would carry his kalaam, his signature. He picked up the naksha and with a magnificent sweep of his hand flung it into the river. It sliced through the air and landed in the water with a plop, and floated away.

'Palmer Sahib, who had requested Papaji to be his cook, lived in Kanpur. Papaji accepted the job in his household and learnt to cook with an obsession that bordered on madness. He dug out ancient recipes, kept only cooks for company, and began to master the art. His kitchen became famous for its flavours and the goodness of the food it produced, and Palmer Sahib's house – like Jhelum Memsahib's, if I say so myself' – said Param, theatrically allowing himself the compliment – 'became famous for its cuisine. The Burra Sahibs longed for invitations from him and took back with them delicious memories.

'My father taught me everything I know, Beta,' said Param to his son, his voice shaky with emotion, 'and that is how a family of Kathuas became a family of cooks.'

The Butler's Revenge

flatulent
adjective
suffering from or marked by an accumulation of gas in the alimentary canal

AMONG those who are flatulent, the quantity and frequency of gas passage can reach astounding proportions. One careful study noted a patient with daily flatus frequency as high as seventy passages in a four-hour period. This symptom can cause great psycho-social distress and usually has three salient characteristics. The first is the Cushion Creeper or Slider, when folks full of social graces and manicured habits desperately feel the urge to pass wind in small gatherings, but have to do so silently so that they can escape detection. This is the 'pssst' type, which creeps up the upholstery and has devastating effects. The second is the Butler's Revenge, or the 'pooh' type. The farter here is caught unawares and cannot plan a Cushion Creeper as the urge to pass wind is greater, but he has the presence of mind to cough loudly and uncontrollably for the time taken to release the air. This is to make sure that those gathered around him do not hear him go 'pooh' though they will be compelled to hold their noses at the smell that follows. The third is the Twenty-One Gun Salute, the 'bhadurr-bhadurr' type, generally passed in privacy or in the presence of people more intimate with the farter, like wives and old friends. This is sort of Shakespearean, 'full of sound and fury, signifying nothing'.

It had been a much busier day at the office than Mahadev had anticipated. He had meetings in various ministries, and by the time he entered his office it was time for lunch. His packed snacks and the red box with urgent files lay untouched. He asked his secretary to dial home. It was Jhelum who answered.

'Mai kya, darling,' he said. 'What are we having for lunch?'

It was rare that Mahadev ever called home while at work but he was feeling hungrier than usual today. The fiery effect of the marchwangan had been pleasantly quelled. It was a forgotten memory, and the idea of a light soup and sandwich meal was very meager, to say the least. 'Lunch like a prince' could be given a miss; good, desi khana was what he craved.

'Rice, Vindaloo and crispy, fried okra,' said Jhelum.

One of my favourites, Mahadev thought, salivating. 'I'll be there within an hour,' he said and cut the line as soon as he finished the sentence.

Overnight marination had coloured the pinkish-red mutton pieces into a delicious reddish-brown, and just before the dish was done, Param told Pakwaan to cook some tamarind paste with garlic, chilli flakes and a pinch of sugar to 'round off' the tartness of the synthetic vinegar. The steamed basmati lay ready, beautifully khilaa-hua, each plump white grain of rice separate, not little lumps of gooey white balls.

Mahadev had a beer with his meal. Jhelum stuck to her soup and sandwiches, but the rest of the family ate hungrily. The children enjoyed the crackling sounds when they broke the crispy okra;

Mahadev ate with a fork but picked the okra delicately with his fingers. A burp, soft and silent, escaped from parted lips, and a delicious laziness overcame him. Fartcatcher was instructed to call the office and say that the Sahib would be resting at home. Eat, drink and be merry, for tomorrow we die, so Khayyamesque, was his last thought before he slept.

'Ah, Vindaloo! Guaranteed to satisfy, guaranteed to slow down busy, important people, and allow them time to savour the simple pleasures of life. Vindaloo, loaded with the memories of a delicious, wicked revenge that turned sour in the end,' said Param, luxuriating in the pleasure of having made a perfect dish. Hurry, Beta,' he called, 'let me tell you the story of the toofani badla, a revenge that expelled the insufferable air of pompous self-importance and an ode to my father's extraordinary cooking skills.' He laughed at the thought of what his son would hear this afternoon.

Pakwaan rushed through his chores and sat opposite his father, his son's enthusiasm allowing Param the occasional flourish and addition of mirch-masala as he went along.

'Palmer Sahib was your grandfather's first employer, the fourth generation of a family that had made India their home. His great-grandfather was a General, a big man in the employ of the Company Bahadur, and had married a beautiful begum of noble ancestry. He loved the country, had none of the pompous phook that filled the likes of Chatur Chuttar, and in many ways was more approachable than our own Mahadev Sahib. He was firm but fair, generous with praise, yet never hesitating to criticize if it was deserved. Palmer Sahib was a much respected, important man in

Kanpur. The angrez asked him for advice because he understood the country better than most. And what a bungalow he lived in! It was set as if in the middle of a forest, with fruit orchards to the left and right, huge servants' quarters at the back, with rabbit pens and stables, and uniformed guards at the entrance who checked all visitors before they entered. "Phrend or phoe?" they would ask when they waited at the gate and no 'phoes' ever came.

'And what to say of the Memsahib? She was the gentlest of farishtas, patience personified, never losing her temper at my father as he passionately stumbled along. With his natural flair he learnt quickly, never repeating the same mistake. He picked up from the Memsahib the proper doneness of roasts, the right flavour of mint in the mint sauce, the correct fluffiness of the omelette, the right milk–flour ratio for the béchamel, and the right glaze and rich brown colour of the sugar for the caramel custard, that standard pudding of old khansamaas sprinkled across circuit houses throughout the country.

'Soon, Papaji's kitchen became famous for its food, but it was the Vindaloo that had its most passionate admirers. Touring dignitaries, commissioners and governors, collectors and surveyors, senior police officials and generals in the army – burra-burra log would request that Palmer Sahib have them over as guests and serve Vindaloo for dinner, and there was always applause at the end of the meal. They envied the Palmers the quality of their kitchen. Accompanying memsahibs hinted at better pay if Papaji decided to head their kitchens, but Papaji was very clear. "Loyalty is a virtue," he always said, for he knew he could not have asked for better employers.

'The Cawnpore Club's kitchen was run by a Gomes Sahib, who had taught Papaji how to cook Vindaloo. Gomes Sahib made a decent Vindaloo himself, but it never quite achieved the natural roundness of flavour because toddy vinegar was unheard of in these northern parts. The local vinegar was too tart and the end result, even though delicious, would always be a bit sour and lacking in fullness. But your grandfather, blessed with his God-given intuition for taste, suggested the infusion of tamarind, sugar, chillies and garlic in the tart local vinegar, and the result was astounding! It was so close to the original Goan version that even Gomes Sahib had to admit that he could not tell the difference. He took my father under his wing and, like a fond guru to his favourite chela, introduced him to the beauty of fiery coastal curries, the nuances of cooking with vinegar and coconut and, of course, the intricacies of the Vindaloo.

'It was Sunday morning. The Sahib and Memsahib, back from the club after their tennis game, had showered, changed, and were waiting in the large lawn in front of their bungalow for breakfast to be served. The guard at the gate approached Palmer Sahib and handed him an envelope – strange for a Sunday morning, for Palmer Sahib was always particular that on holidays no official work would be entertained. 'By Hand' it said on the top, and below it was printed 'Personal, Mr Palmer'.

Dear Mr Palmer,

We have been travelling the length of the land, convincing the subject race about the benefits of the English civilization. Fortunately, I have an able assistant in Arth Dubashi. He is a remarkable storyteller with a fascinating feel for the spoken word. I have trained him well (if I may say so myself) in the nuances of our language and he has proved to be a quick learner. In the process I have learnt Hindoostani and manage to be easily understood, especially when I am giving orders. It is quite a job to convince the natives that our presence in India is for their benefit, and our natural inclination towards fairness and justice will lift them from their present pathetic state into an era where they will rediscover the benefits of a golden age. The entire process of categorizing and compartmentalizing this country involves such painstaking effort that sometimes I feel that the burden of improvement that has been thrust upon us leads to a sagging of spirits, but then the ultimate goal, the vast improvement of the masses, nourishes my soul and enables me to work with renewed zeal and energy.

During our travails we were joined by a devout and most motivated missionary – Peter Hiscock. He is from the Church of England and has shunned the comforts of home to spread the word of our good Lord Jesus Christ. It's an odd name that he has and it is the object of great mischief among the locals, but it is fortunate that he travels with us.

Spending an evening with the likes of Arth can be very trying. After all that I have done for him, he is constantly bowing and scraping. I am sure you know the feeling. With one of our own, we can at least spend the evenings as equals when the day's work is done.

We will be in your town the day after tomorrow. I have heard that your kitchen is famous for its quality. The food on the tour had been most unappetizing. The local zamindars, in an effort to impress, cook English food and the results are disastrous – the sauces are watery, the roasts raw and the caramel custards are an unholy gooey mess! Of course, it is heartening that important natives adopt our ways. These are indications of the successes we have achieved with our dogged efforts. But I yearn for a good Indian curry. Would it be too much of a bother to partake of your hospitality? The thought of a rice and Vindaloo meal made by this cook of yours makes me salivate.

I do hope it is not much of an inconvenience. If it is, do let the bearer know. I look forward to seeing you.

Yours truly,

James Cunningham

'Palmer Sahib handed the letter to his wife, shaking his head in disgust. "I am afraid, darling, we have rather boring company for dinner at home, and much as I'd love to duck it, protocol demands otherwise," he said.

'His wife read the letter and grimaced. Then she walked to the kitchen to discuss the menu.

'"Kalaam," she told Papaji, "we have some guests for dinner and your Vindaloo seems to have become quite the rage. James Cunningham, who will dine with us this evening, has especially asked for it. His companions, Arth Dubashi and the Reverend Peter Hiscock, will be with him. Cunningham is no stranger to India and Arth Dubashi should be able to handle the spices, but the Reverend might find it difficult. So make a nice English roast, too, just in case." She left the kitchen to join her husband for breakfast.'

'This was Papaji's chance for revenge!' Param was excited now, and his voice grew louder as his speech quickened. 'Heeng, asafoetida, was the choice of weapon – his trusty hathiyaar. A paste of hingu made with goats' urine cures the evil effects of the grahas and insanity; mixed with karela it controls diabetes; consumed with raisin it soothes the heart; fried in ghee and added to the latex of the banyan tree and then eaten with a banana it gives you a fine erection,' said Param to his blushing son. 'The Persians call it the food of the gods, the firangi, devil's dung – for it does have a smell. It is a major ingredient in digestive mixtures for it effectively expels wind from the digestive tract. Heeng also has a distinct flavour, a pungency that is easily tasted. But my father, with little flourishes of this and that, masked its flavour and made a Vindaloo which would guarantee turbulence. Abdul the bearer was told to serve the first portions to the guests.

'The guests arrived, all suited-booted, their waists slashed in the centre by shiny cummerbunds. Ah! The cummerbund, the cholera belt as they called it, was the most essential accessory. For a long time, it was advised by angrez doctors, old India hands, English armymen and police officers that it was essential to wear a flannel or woolen cummerbund at all times around the waist, even while sleeping, for it prevented chills and heat-strokes and was solid protection against loose motions. There was a ditty coined for it, which went,

Make sure that the cummerbund snugly fits,
For it is a sure way to avoid the shits.

And then, of course, there was Arth's version, before he became an official historian:

Jab tak angrezon ke kamar pe bandhi hai patti,
Tab tak saalon ko nahin lagegi tattee.'

Pakwaan could not help laughing aloud.

'The evening had begun! The drinks were poured and handed to all.

"Cheers!" said Palmer Memsahib and the gentlemen lifted their glasses in salute.

'"To the glory of the Empire!" said Cunningham Sahib.

'"Let the word of the Lord spread," said Reverend Hiscock.

'"To life," said Palmer Sahib, a tinge of mockery in his voice, his wife squeezing his arm affectionately but firmly as a warning.

'The evening progressed amidst chitter-chatter, the clinking sounds of ice being put into glasses, the murmur of conversations in soft voices while the table was laid for dinner and Abdul began the service.

The Reverend Hiscock said grace, and everyone around the table folded their hands and bowed their heads as he spoke, "For what we are about to receive, may the lord be truly thanked," and then he continued, completely out of character, "I have a definite and delicious little hunch – that this dinner will be better than that terrible lunch." The table tittered and Palmer Sahib looked up at the padre with affectionate admiration.

First, the roast leg of lamb was served. Thin delicate pieces of lamb, the centre a pink-brownish red, the edges a rich, crisp dark brown drizzled with mint sauce, surrounded by potatoes, onions, beans and thinly sliced carrots sautéed just right for that crisp but tender taste. While this was placed on the food warmer, the second waiter arrived with the boiled rice – magnificent long-grained basmati, each grain soft and fluffy. The rice was served, guests first, hosts later. Then came the Vindaloo. In his prolonged fit of vengeful anger, Kalaam had dumped into it disastrous doses of the devil's dung, the lethal heeng. And here his instructions had to be followed to the dot. The red bowl was for the guests and the white for the hosts. "This has more spices," he told Abdul. "My Sahib and Memsahib enjoy the desi taste."

'Chatur Chattar was the first to be served. Memories of the insipid meals on tour, the reputation of the Vindaloo made in the kitchen of Palmer Memsahib's house, made his eyes bigger than his stomach. His was such a giant helping that the padre had no option but to have a small one. And our friend Arth, that saala, had become more English than the angrez. He refused the rice and the Vindaloo, and helped himself to the roast. He was familiar with the use of fork and knife – a deft jab of the fork to hold the meat and neat sawing motions for bite-sized pieces with the knife. At home with English ways, sitting with the sahibs at the same table," Papaji had admitted much later, a twinge of jealousy in his voice.

'"Fantastic," Chatur Chuttar said as he ate and Mrs Palmer acknowledged the compliment. Then he was ready for seconds. The padre found it tasty but too spicy to handle the second time around. He settled for roast. It was mid-way through the seconds that Chatur Chuttar and Hiscock felt the gur-gur-gur inside. Their stomachs had bloated up and they could feel their bowels twisting and churning, their cummerbunds stretched tight. Cunningham lifted a cheek, one chuttar, so to speak, and with great control broke wind ever so delicately. Pssst, the air escaped. But relief was momentary, for he was filled with wind. He leaned forward to pick up the salad, making more space for air to escape, and coughed to avoid detection, but by the time he sat down with his piece of cucumber he could feel his insides going ulta-pulta, upside-down.

'He flung back his chair, clutching his sides. 'The men's room?' he asked Palmer Sahib and ran, pulling his shirt, unbuttoning his trouser and removing the cummerbund to get some relief. He ran down the corridor, flung open the toilet door, shut it with a bang and plonked himself on the pot with a grateful thud – a pathetic figure, with his trousers, underwear and cummerbund bunched in an untidy heap around his ankles – and he farted and farted and farted. Cushion Creepers and Butler's Revenge punctuated by Twenty-One Gun Salutes!

The padre felt the rumblings, too, and gingerly lifted a cheek to let out the offensive air. But the build-up inside him was considerable and, like a good Christian, he lifted the other cheek and let some more air slide by. With great muscular control over his sphincter, he asked in a constipated tone for the second men's room and ran, his black cassock flapping all over, to relieve himself of the unholy flatulence. The smell pervaded the room, and the three left at the table crinkled their noses and vigorously fanned the air, forehead furrowed, completely puzzled at the disappearance of the two guests.

'The padre arrived after a while, relief writ large on his face, and apologized for the commotion. They picked at their meal, worried about Cunningham. Arth had finished his helping, but his Sahib had still not arrived. Worried, he excused himself from the table and went to check. He knocked softly on the door, and there was no reply. He banged harder and in complete panic shouted, "Sahib! Sahib! Theek to ho? Are you okay?" He pressed his ear to the door and heard his mentor moaning painfully, "Mujhe akela cho-though! Mujhe akela cho-though," mispronouncing the word yet again to mean "Fuck me alone! Fuck me alone!"

'His revenge was complete, and there was your grandfather –' Param stood up, arms stretched skyward, shaking his shoulders up and down and doing the bhangra to celebrate a Kathua's badla on the mighty Chatur Chuttar in one full heeng-Vindaloo shot. 'Papaji's head rolled from side to side as if in an ecstatic trance, swaying rhythmically to a victorious beat, smiling all the while.'

Pakwaan smiled as he imagined his grandfather in full flow, wicked grin on his face, and began to laugh a deep belly laughter till the tears flowed.

But Param's voice had changed now as he said, 'Fully mast in his dance of revenge, Papaji did not notice Palmer Memsahib enter the kitchen. There she was, Palmer Memsahib, graciousness and warmth personified, her happiness sucked out of her, her sad, crumpled face fighting back tears of shame.

'"I can't believe you would do something so shameful," she told my father, blinking back her tears.

'Papaji's prayaschit, his atonement, would begin right away. He would comfort the affected immediately and carry the healing concoction to the table himself, even though Arth would recognize him. He mixed two teaspoons of carom seeds, the blessed ajwain, with dried ginger and ground it to a fine paste. Then, he mixed in a little black salt, dissolved it in warm water. The end result was the best remedy for flatulence. He carried his concoction to the dining room.

'"You?!" said Arth, recognizing him immediately, and turned to Palmer Sahib. "I am sure, Sahib, that *he* is responsible for this terrible disaster. A good friend of mine, Sahib, he used to be a long time ago . . . But he is the typical disgruntled native, completely against our mission of improvement. He is a small-minded badmash, a trouble-maker, and nothing else."

'There was Papaji, silent, his head bowed, and Palmer Sahib knew that Arth was speaking the truth. My father left the glasses on the table, turned around and retreated to the kitchen. The concoction lay untouched and the guests excused themselves and left, Cunningham using Arth's shoulders for support, the cummerbund slung across his own shoulder.

'Papaji left the kitchen immediately, went to his quarters, packed his belongings and sat down to write a letter to Palmer Sahib and Memsahib.

Dear Sahib and Memsahib,

I am not a born badmash but badmashi, momentarily, got the better of me. Without thinking, I have indulged in meaningless badla and now our guests have left disgruntled and will talk badly of our gracious home. They will accuse you of not instilling fear and respect in your domestic staff and they will be believed. But I know that they are wrong. You are in the true sense my mai-baap, my mother and father, for you have treated me with warmth and love, have taught me and encouraged me and given me the opportunity to discover my true calling.

But the memories of the past have festered angrily inside me. Cunningham Sahib and Arth Purabiya (this was his original name) destroyed the comfort, the intimacy, of our small biradari, of bhai-bandi, the simple warmth of fellowship. But what I have done is unforgivable. Instead of embarrassing them with kindness and generosity, I have misused my God-given gift to seek pleasure in momentary, petty revenge.

I have forgotten mehmaan-nawazi – that noble and gracious concept that believes that every visitor must be treated like God. I do not ask for, nor do I deserve forgiveness. For if you forgive me I will feel shame. I must atone for this zalil harkat, this dastardly act. I plan to wander, Sahib, and think deeply. I need to get rid of the burdens of my past.

Kalaam

'Papaji was up long before sunrise. He left the letter on the dining table and his wandering began,' said Param, concluding the instalment for the day.

The Meekers

ACROSS the seven seas, America prospered, and prospered magnificently. It was the land of plenty, the janta well fed and clothed; a genial giant slowly awakening to the consciousness of its power. And so, from the Midwest, the food bowl of the United States, from the University of Missouri, Amercians arrived in the capital of Orissa to set up centres of agricultural learning, and Bhubaneswar had a slice of American life served upon it. They were guests of the government and were sanctioned large bungalows set amongst lawns and fruit trees for residence. The way they lived was poshness personified, their homes little islands of luxury in provincial Bhubaneswar. Westinghouse air conditioners hummed gently all day to maintain the desired coolness. Wall-to-wall carpeting covered the floors – thick, tufted machine-made rugs in shades of tan, lilac, grey and other neutral colours were laid over thick sponges, so that the feet sank into their softness. The dining tables were covered with white hand-crocheted lace tablecloths, and candelabras stood in the centre holding elegant, tapered candles. The homes smelt of a mixture of fresh pine cleanser, freshly baked bread and freshly brewed coffee. The station wagons were solid and sturdy, and the Chevrolet Impalas long, sleek, aeroplane-like cars that glided over roads, with seats upholstered in luxurious, padded material and shockers that made going over the deepest potholes a pleasant, bouncy experience. Fiats and Ambassadors looked like shabby, second-hand rattletraps when compared to these superior imported machines.

Cliffard Richard Meeker and Josephine Meeker were, much to their delight, 'Uncle' and 'Aunty' to Mahadev's children. They found it charming, the prefixes of Aunty and Uncle before their names. So much warmer and more personal than 'Jo' and 'Cliff', as they would have been called in their country, irrespective of the age of the person who addressed them.

Cliffard Richard Meeker, tall, balding, with a paunch sitting comfortably over his waist, was a big, jovial American who was light as air on his feet. Aunty Jo was slender and tall, with straight salt-and-pepper hair untouched by hair dye, brilliant blue eyes blessed with an easy, twinkling laughter and that rare gift – the ability to make everyone feel at ease. And with them came the splash of Americana – the Kool-Aids before the Rasna, the introduction to spaghetti and meatballs, lasagna, pizzas, burgers and fried chicken and, right there, at the top of the list, the pull-tab-to-open Coca-Cola can – *tsssh!* – the gulp with head flung back and the delicious taste of cool, fizzy Coca-Cola caressing throats made dry by the Indian summer. Jannat! Paradise! Globalization sprinkled on a lucky few before it became such an important word in the Angrezi bhasha.

Summer afternoons could be hot and humid in Bhubaneswar, and the children would look forward to air-conditioned comfort in the Meeker home. They loved playing with Jo Meeker, Pick-up-Sticks their favourite game. Afternoons were spent in friendly banter, the players accusing each other of cheating. If Aunty Jo won, hugs and kisses from the children were her prize and she would announce in a laughing ha-ha voice,

'Eenie, meenie, miny mo,
Just keep on loving Aunty Jo,

When she cries don't let her go,
Eenie, meenie, miny mo!'

She would hug the children and kiss them. If the children won, it was a meal of their choice at the Meeker home.

The game was on, a best-of-five match, and the three children were running Aunty Jo close (two-all, one to go), keen to win the match and have their favourite meal. Fried chicken and mashed potatoes, with delicious American corn, boiled and dipped in a sweet, rich butter.

'It's two-all and the Pick-up-Sticks series is down to the wire,' Jo announced, mimicking the voice of an excited radio announcer. 'The children have fought back to level the series.' She rubbed the sticks vigorously between her palms and deliberately threw them from a height. The sticks bounced and lay scattered all over. Easy pickings, and Tikky cleaned up effortlessly.

'A fried chicken, mashed-potato-and-corn dinner,' the three children trilled expectantly.

'The bet will be settled immediately and we will all have dinner together tonight,' Jo said. She called Jhelum, inviting them over.

Mahadev and Jhelum arrived in the evening. Scotch had been laid out for Mahadev, ginger ale and bourbon for Uncle Cliff, red wine for the ladies, and Coca-Cola for the kids, served in the red wine goblets to make them feel all grown-up. They toasted the children's victory, and dinner was served. The children gorged on the food, watched by indulgent adults marvelling at the appetite of the young, and then it was time for dessert – a spectacular chocolate cake with sinfully creamy icing, a thick vein of chocolate fudge sandwiched between the moist, spongy layers of cake. A large, triangular chunk oozing with richness, topped with a scoop of vanilla ice cream, was served to each of them.

Sated, the table sighing with pleasure, Jhelum wondered loudly how Jo got her cakes so consistently moist and soft. Jo and Cliff smiled at each other because they knew the secret, and Jo clinked her glass with her husband's and raised a toast, 'To the magician, Betty Crocker,' while the rest of the table looked on expectantly, waiting for explanations.

'Time for my exit,' Cliff said, knowing how much his wife loved telling this story, and Mahadev and Cliff left the table and sat in the veranda, sipping their drinks.

'I'll let you in on the secret,' she told Jhelum, leaving the table and coming back with a box of Betty Crocker Cake Mix in her hand. 'Make everyday home-made', the message on the box read, with Betty Crocker's name signed off in a friendly scrawl and an image of a wedge of the cake that matched the pieces that lay on the table. The box was accompanied by a set of simple instructions that made baking so simple, it was extraordinary! Precisely measured quantities of sugar and shortening, milk, baking soda, eggs and melted chocolate folded and beaten into the mix till smooth, and you were 'ready for a cake that was a chocolate powerhouse', the message proudly proclaimed.

Jhelum longed for Betty Crocker cake mixes, imagining the relief from the uncertainties of inconsistent risings and of assured applause after the instructions were precisely followed. 'What a genius this Betty Crocker is,' Jhelum sighed, 'she makes baking so simple.'

'Baking was just the starter. Betty became the liberator of women from drudgery in the kitchen, touching everything from mixes for salads and pastas, cornbreads and mashed potatoes, brownies and desserts. She was and remains America's first lady of food. She is as loved as the President of the United States and all this in a span of . . .' Jo paused for a metaphorical glimpse at history, 'only forty years.

'It was a few years after the First World War, when our soldiers, christened doughboys, if you please, had tilted the scales in favour of the Allies, when from a mill in Minneapolis came the special Gold Medal Flour. It guaranteed consistent risings but it seemed only for those skilled in the art of baking who were thrilled with their fresh and spongy breads, their sweet and soft cup-cakes, and their brittle and crisp breadsticks. But there were also the not-so-skilled who were keen to become proficient who wrote to the company for tips to help them. It was an opportunity for the company to come closer to the customer, and what better way to build bonds than to reply personally to their letters? Betty was a good first name – it had an efficient, friendly ring to it – and Crocker, so close to Crockett,' Jo Meeker winged along, 'resonated with the pioneering age. And so "Betty Crocker" was coined. Women employees were asked to sign off as Betty Crocker. The most distinctive signature was chosen by a panel of judges and it remains the same till this day. Letters were written, signed off and sent to housewives struggling to improve their baking skills.'

'You mean . . .' Jhelum said incredulously, her eyes wide with wonder.

But before she could finish Jo cut in, smiling,

'Patience, Jhelum, patience. This is only the tip of the iceberg. Betty was an instant success. Three years later she had her own cooking show on radio, the nation's first, and more than a dozen actresses across radio stations in America gave voice to Betty Crocker teaching millions of Americans the basics of baking, of whipping and whisking cake mixes. This became a national broadcast and ran for twenty-four years, just a little less than the ages of these three children put together. From a voice, they gave her a face. Artists studied women's faces, blended the best features in each and crafted a face that was pretty, friendly and concerned. Her face gave her life. A living legend is what she became, and a few years later she had her own TV show. Curvaceous actresses were hired to play her character, and when the big red Betty Crocker Cookbook, complete with pictures, was published, its sales were more than that of the Holy Bible! Her popularity was huge, an acknowledgement of the skills of spin doctors. Many people even swore that they had seen her in flesh and blood.'

'Hey Ram! What a story!' Jhelum said, hitting her forehead with an open palm.

The men entered the dining room as soon as she had finished and unexpectedly announced, 'It's been decided – we are going to Puri for the weekend.'

Khare Masale ki Shaadi
(The Marriage of Standing Spices)

IT was to be an early morning start – 6 a.m. (sharp). They would catch the sea before high tide. The sea could be treacherous at midday, with high, choppy waves that could hurt you if you did not jump or duck in time and strong undercurrents that could suck you in, sweep you off your feet. Jhelum would make the sandwiches – masala omelette between plain white bread moistened with butter and mayonnaise – and Jo would bring the coffee and brownies, another of Betty's sweet magical gifts, for on-the-way drinks and nibbles. There would be little traffic on the road and they would hit the beach by 8 a.m. The waves would be gentle swells, the kind you could float with, feeling their contours. They would frolic for a bit during high tide – it would be a change to enjoy being thrown around after a period of relative calm. The adults would sip their beers, the children their root beer or Coca-Cola. Then they would bathe and change, and lunch at the Bengal Nagpur Railway Hotel, or BNR as it was called. Mr Murthy, the manager and general major-domo there, had been informed of their arrival and that the fixed course meal would have to include spring chicken, golden-fried prawns and bhetki baked in white sauce, and served with sautéed vegetables. The seafood would be fresh, the catch of the day. The prawns, large and luscious, dipped in a beer batter, dusted in rice flour and fried, served with a sweet-and-sour chilli sauce for the dip. The baked bhetki would follow. To round off the meal, there would be shareefa ice cream. Shareefa, sitaphal or custard apple, its delicious flesh, sweet and grainy, removed from the seeds, mixed into vanilla-flavoured milk, churned by hand and frozen. The children's favourite. Lulled by the cool sea breeze, the adults would lounge around and fall asleep in the planter's chairs in the large polished red-floored verandas that overlooked the sea. The children would either be indoors playing ping-pong, or watching hotel guests play an afternoon game of billiards, or playing hide-and-seek or catch in the large lawn, allowing the adults their afternoon siesta.

Param and Pakwaan woke up early and served the Sahib and Memsahib their tea exactly an hour before departure. The children were allowed their extra sleep – 5.30 a.m. was their designated wake-up time – but they shot out of bed when nudged by Ayah. They loved the sea. Fartcatcher came in fifteen minutes before their departure, collected the luggage from various rooms and kept them on the porch. When the Meekers arrived, Fartcatcher ran to the gate to open it, salaamed them in obsequious welcome and ran back to load the luggage in the station wagon. And they were off, Fartcatcher running behind to shut the gate.

The house was empty! Chores would be done as and when they pleased, for Param had begun to enjoy the story sessions. He felt he had a flair for kahanibaazi, like Arth Purabiya, and was sure that Ayah and Fartcatcher would be willing listeners. He now had an audience of three.

'Chalo, Beta,' he clapped his hands authoritatively, like the Burra Sahibs doing the 'Quoi Hai?'. For now he was the head of the house. 'Let's have cheeni ka parantha and chai,' he said, gesturing expansively to include Ayah and Fartcatcher.

Ayah winced, Param's display of arrogance grating her nerves. He was always bossy, throwing his weight around over all and sundry – even the junior bureaucrats who came to visit the Sahib. Ayah and Param's khit-pit was legendary; the tug of war, the bickering over household turf rights was a problem that constantly simmered, sometimes exploding into shouting matches, pushes and shoves. Only Jhelum could deal with it, steel fist in velvet glove. For the moment, Ayah swallowed her anger. Her sweet tooth was her weakness, and cheeni ka parantha was one of her favourites.

Pakwaan put the water to boil and prepared the parantha. Leftover chapatti dough kneaded just a bit to let the air in, sprinkled with sugar, rolled into thin chapattis, fried in a film of desi ghee on a tawa – crisp, flaky and sweet.

They sipped their chai, and as Ayah bit into her parantha, a brittle sweetness filled her mouth. 'Wah,' she said, 'you have taught your son well. I tell you, Param, we have our problems, but I praise your cooking so often and to so many that one day I will get blisters on my tongue.'

Param melted at the warmth of the compliment. 'Thank you, gracious Memsahib,' he said, bowing theatrically and then, completely against character, hugged her warmly. 'Now to the story,' he said, and began.

'Cooking had been my father's nirvana, his chhutkara, his escape from the handle-ghumanewallas. Cooking had been his cure. Like a conjurer, he had cooked up a storm that had given him the pleasure of exacting his revenge in a sense, but it had been so-so and' – he struggled for the word – 'bematlab, without meaning, absolutely pointless. Papaji left Banaras in blind, raging, righteous anger, but he left Palmer Sahib's gracious home with a deep sense of shame and regret.

'Hard physical labour, kathin parishram, he decided, would be his release – dull repetitive actions that required strength and would numb the mind. And so he took up work in a masala factory, one large room of pukka construction that overlooked a large courtyard covered by a shamiana that barely kept the elements at bay. Rows of workers stood in front of large cast-iron mortars and pounded roasted spices with long, heavy wooden poles encased at one end by a cast-iron cap. From morning till night he stood there, as if in a trance, his arms and shoulders moving vigorously, oblivious to heat or cold, sweat or exhaustion, aches or pains. The rhythmic pounding, the brittle crunching noise of the spices being crushed, the *dhuk-dhuk, dhuk-dhuk* noise of pestle hitting mortar was therapeutic, as if he were pounding out the shame that he felt.'

Param paused for his sip of chai and a bite of parantha. 'Delicious,' he said. 'Very well made, Beta – crisp, flaky and yet soft to the bite. The shishya definitely shows more promise than the guru, as it should always be.'

Pakwaan preened and Ayah nodded her head in agreement, looking at Pakwaan with maternal pride.

'He pounded the masalas like a man possessed,' Param continued. 'He would forget his meals and at the end of the day he would be drained of all energy, his mind a dull, unthinking hole. He lost weight, his eyes had black rings around them, his skin was dull and lifeless, his palms cut and bleeding, his body sore from constant standing, but he carried on, glad in a perverse sort of way that he was punishing himself.' Param paused, shaking his head.

'Terrible times were written in his fate. But God in his wisdom does everything for the good and with my father he did not make an exception. Papaji met Vidhaata,' he said. 'My dear mother, fair and freckled, short and pug-nosed, with the warmest eyes and the most comforting smile, a heart of the purest gold and with the calmest and most affectionate temperament.'

There was a lilt in his voice now, a sing-song, naughty quality, and he smiled as he went along. 'My mother may not have been as good a cook as Papaji but she knew the medicinal values of spices. Her little kitchen was like a vaid's dukaan. Nuskas and potions for indigestion and headaches, sore throats and wheezing, flatulence and constipation and other minor niggles lay around in little pudiyaas in kitchen cabinets. Mothers in her biradari came to her carrying their babies on their hips, asking for cures for colds and coughs, stomach aches and gripes and other children's ailments. Young couples in love asked her for special concoctions of mouth fresheners so that their breath remained sweet and fresh when they hugged and kissed. It was rumoured that she had the secret ingredients of the palangtod paan, the after-meal digestive laced with aphrodisiacs of such potency that men swore by it's strength as it allowed them to carry on through the night till the bed gave way.'

Ayah laughed coquettishly. Fartcatcher drooled.

'It was a hot and humid day and Papaji vengefully pounded away, not stopping for a break, not drinking water. Suddenly he felt the world spin frantically and in the next instant fainted in a crumpled heap. The other workers shouted in panic and rushed to his aid. They sprinkled water on his face, vigorously fanning him with their gumchhas. Vidhaata, delivering the day's supply of heeng and haldi, rushed to his aid. One look at him and she ran home to get the nuskaas for revival. For the headache, she prepared her nuskaa of pepper, dried ginger, camphor and heeng ground into a paste with rosewater and applied it on his forehead. She drenched a cloth pad with the hot water and heeng concoction and fomented his abdominal region. She ground a secret herb with haldi, neem leaves and lime juice and applied the paste to his wounds. Relief was immediate, and Papaji's fatigue ebbed away. His pain now bearable, he got up in a state of delirium. She put a palm on his chest and pushed him down so that he lay again on the floor. Years later, he remembered being surprised by her strength.

'"Don't be so foolish," said Vidhaata affectionately applying the balm on his forehead and dabbing his stomach with the hot compress. Her voice was soothing. He felt his body relax and he slept – a deep, deep sleep, completely untroubled, completely dreamless. He woke up many hours later. The workers had left, but Vidhaata was still at his side.

'"Have this," she said, giving him a bowl of steamed rice mixed with a powder of fenugreek seeds, mustard, heeng and turmeric that had been fried in best-quality desi ghee. It will do your stomach good and give you the energy that you need. After you have eaten, bathe, and use this paste to soap your body and your face. It is a special concoction – harre channa ka atta, besan and haldi mixed with my magic touch. It will bring a glow on this dull and lifeless body that you punish with such peculiar pleasure."'

Param smiled and continued, 'Papaji ke to dil ke taar bajne lagey, she had plucked his heart strings with the delicacy of her concern. His heart and mind were in a melodious flutter, singing the praises of the lovely Vidhaata. He began to oil and comb his hair, show concern for his appearance. And her magic potions did their work. His skin began to glow, his sense of taste and appetite returned. On his day off, he invited her for tea, and on that day my father made this cheeni ka parantha and masala chai while he waited for his fair and lovely Vidhaata.

'Papaji chose his ingredients with care and passion. Only the best cardamom pods were chosen – plump, green and robust, not cracked, hollow or shrivelled. He smelled the cinnamon sticks and chose only the most aromatic ones. For the paranthas, he chose best-quality wheat at the local chakki and ground it to perfect fineness in front of his eyes. He ground the spices with his mortar and pestle for special occasions – a small elegantly shaped mortar with a silver-tipped pestle – with the greatest care and tenderness. He kneaded the dough with much love in his heart and firmness in his fingers till it was of the right consistency, and divided it into small portions or pedas.

'He bathed using her concoction, lovingly rubbing it into his skin and washing it off with vigour, and looked at himself in the mirror. Her nuskaas had done him a world of good, his body felt strong, his skin had a healthy glow. He combed his hair, making sure that his side parting was knife-edge straight. He tap-tapped his forefinger on his tongue and ran its moistened tip over his eyebrows so that they sat like perfect arches over his eyes. He thought the better of applying surma, it would be too theatrical, but he dabbed some attar, sandalwood essence, behind his ears, on his neck and on his chest. And he waited. There was a knock on the door and he opened it. There was Vidhaata, framed by the open door, the evening sun setting behind her. She wore a sari the colour of saffron, its border a riot of embroidered ambi designs, and on her forehead was a large red bindi. Her hair was tied in a bun bordered with a kajra of raat-ki-rani. Papaji just stared and stared, mouth open, eyes bilkul gol-gol, as if jolted by an electric shock. Unke to hosh udh gaye.

'"May I come in?" she said smiling, quite aware of the impact she had on him.

'"Forgive me, Vidhaata," he said, coming to, giving the chair a quick dusting with his hands. "Sit here. Sit here, while I make you chai."

'He put the water to boil. The small circular pedas he had prepared lay on a tray. Holding the belan lightly in both hands, he rolled the dough into thin, perfect circles, sprinkling roughly pounded sugar and finely ground flour on its surface. He spread desi ghee thinly over a hot tawa and put in the paranthas, constantly turning them till they were done – thin, crispy, flaky, with the right strength of mithaas. When the water for the tea reached a slow, rolling boil, he infused the masala. The freshness of elaichi mixed with the pleasurable tartness of cinnamon filled the room, and by the time his tea was ready the last of the four paranthas was a moment away from done. With Vidhaata looking on keenly, waiting, he placed the two glasses in the centre of a thali and arranged the paranthas around them as artistically as he could. Then he carried them to her.

'Vidhaata picked up her glass, inhaled deeply and closed her eyes, enjoying the khushboo of elaichi, chai and dalchini perfectly mixed. She sipped the tea and took a bite of the parantha, closed her eyes once again and shook her head in ecstasy. "Heaven!" she said. Papaji's entire being filled with gentle warmth, his eyes watery at the intensity of her appreciation, thrilled that a simple meal of chai and cheeni ka parantha could give his Vidhaata such joy.

'"The true essence of mehmaan-nawazi," he used to say, "is when your guest is mast, completely immersed in the hospitality that the host provides."

'Vidhaata had finished the paranthas and was dabbing at the thali, picking up the remnants of crispy sweetness till the thali was picked clean, as if just freshly washed. She licked her fingers, savouring the taste of wheat and caramelized sugar. "Pyaar ki mithaas main kha rahi thi," she used to tell me, remembering that time. "It was as if I was eating the sweetness of love."'

Memories of Vidhaata, his mother, came flooding back, and this time tears rolled down Param's cheeks. Pakwaan sprang to his feet and hugged him. 'Baba,' he said tenderly. Param put an arm around his son's shoulder. 'Don't worry, Beta, these are not tears of sadness but of warm and happy memories.'

Ayah blinked back tears and Fartcatcher coughed loudly into an open fist to fight back emotion.

Param cleared his throat and carried on. '"What a fabulous meal," my mother said. "You are truly gifted, and what baffles me is that you choose to work as a masala pounder who seems to enjoy punishing himself. My instinct tells me that there is something amiss – zaroor daal mein kuchh kala hai. Tell me, Kalaam, am I right?"

'The concern in her voice was touching and the acknowledgement of his skills thrilled him. He knew he had found a way to her heart and, dil phaad ke, he poured out his story. Of his Banarsi biradari and his great friends, Mateen and Arth, of the stories that Arth had spun and the power he had on his audiences, of the beautiful brocade that he and Mateen made and the kalakaari that they used to be known for, of the chance meeting with Chatur Chuttar. Papaji told me how she laughed at the translation and affectionately slapped his face, squeezing his cheeks for this display of lovely wickedness. He told her then about Arth Dubashi, the man who spoke in two tongues and his bombastic bakwaas, and the bitter division it created amongst the friends; of the day of Muharram; the streets milling with crowds commemorating grief and betrayal by inflicting pain upon themselves; and his escape with the naksha from Chanderi of Palmer Sahib's discovery of his culinary talents, the shame he felt when he saw the Memsahib's face after his arrogant display of his skill for a pointless revenge that sullied the reputation of a household known for its table and its hospitality.

'She listened to his story with absolute concentration, not once interrupting him. Not a sound escaped her.

'"Buddhu," she said, putting her hand on his forearm, rubbing it with warm and gentle affection. "You have seen so much of life, experienced the beauty of texture and taste, felt the sadness of an angered separation from the comfort of warm and familiar milieus. Look at me. I am a supplier of the finest quality of heeng and haldi and a mixer of herbs, a provider of nuskaas for all sorts of maladies. I take so much pleasure in the good my potions do in uplifting the spirit and improving health. I do not know my caste and what my character should be, so where I am placed in the hierarchy of importance is of no concern to me. I find happiness in the insaniyat, the humaneness, of what I do and that gives me peace. And look at you, Kalaam," she carried on, "you are blessed with a God-given skill but are so conscious of your past that it has manifested itself in an ugly, pointless revenge. You have allowed your past to weigh you down and overshadow this glorious skill that you naturally possess. Just forget the past, develop your skill, make food that people will applaud for its taste."' Param was in full flow now, waving his hands for effect, thumping his fist on an open palm as he finished his mother's speech.

'Papaji felt peace and was convinced that his lovely Vidhaata was right. He decided that his prayaschit was over and so were his days of being a brahmachari. He would enter grahasti with nobody else but his Vidhaata. There was no need to pluck up courage, no struggle for words, no humming and hawing. Instinct – unembarrassed, unashamed – took over, and he said without a trace of panic, "Vidhaata, will you marry me?" Just like that,' said Param, clicking his fingers.

'It was my mother's turn to be stunned. Her eyes were circles of surprise. She blushed, she stuttered, her heart simply fluttered. She muttered and muttered. "But, but, but," she began to say, but my father, all mischievous and masterful, cut in as she struggled to express her emotions in words. "No ifs and buts, jaan-e-man, jaan-e-jigar, my dear Vidhaata. We are meant for each other and you will say 'yes', and then there shall be a jhat mangni putt vyaah." He laughed, slapping his thigh.

'"Pagal admi, this father of yours," my mother used to say, with such warmth and pleasure, biting the corner of her lip in mock shyness and partly covering her face with her pallu. "Khilaya, pilaya aur shaadi karvaya."

The wedding date had to be set, so the pandit was contacted. Kismet and cosmic combinations were kind to them, for they were truly in love. Shani, the planet capable of spreading the curse of misfortune, was aligned in a manner that was benign and harmless. Rahu and Ketu were so positioned that good fortune and great happiness was there for the asking. Auspicious dates were available in plenty and shraadh was months away. It was decided, then and there, that the engagement would be in two days and the shaadi five days later. One week and sab kuchh finished and their life of grahasti had begun.

Naturally, Papaji supervised the feast for the wedding. It was a celebration of the end of his prayaschit. It could be called the wedding of the standing spices. All the dishes were made with sabut, whole masalas, meat, spinach, peas, arbhi, gwaar-ki-phaali, and some had a sprinkling of heeng to honour his lovely Vidhaata. Whole bay leaf, whole cardamom, fresh and green, just as he would use in his masala chai, whole cinnamon, plump whole black cardamom, whole seeds of coriander, whole grains of jeera, whole red chillies, glistening and spicy, were gently infused into hot desi ghee of the best quality. As they sputtered and changed colour, releasing fabulous flavours, the memories of his pounding of these very same spices simply faded away, like sins that were washed away when the janta dipped themselves in Ganga Mata on the ghats of his beloved Banaras.

The pandit, a good man, realized that intense longing should not be stretched and he kept the ceremony short. As they circled around the fire, bonded by the knot of matrimony, my mother's friends – the gopis, Papaji called them – stole his juttees made of soft white leather with gold zari embroidery and refused to return them. Papaji begged and pleaded in mock seriousness, telling them about the blisters he would get if he walked barefoot, and how he would spend the night in pain. But the gopis just tittered and laughed, and acted coquettish.' Param bit the corner of his lip and fluttered his eyelashes, mimicking the gesture of flirtation.

'My mother smiled at the playful charade and watched her husband as he valiantly bargained for his shoes. It was Rekha who settled it. "Rekha was the top gopi," Papaji used to say. She was one of my mother's dearest friends and quite a cheez.' Param sliced an hour-glass figure in the air with his hands. 'Big eyes and long hair, slim waist and voluptuous, very conscious of her charm and impact. That night, she clapped her hands, silencing the female chitter-chatter. "On one condition, oh husband of Vidhaata," she told Papaji, and smiled mischievously, "will you get your shoes back. If you eat the paan I give you, your shoes will be returned without any money exchanging hands."

'"I agree," said Papaji.

'The paan was tied in the corner of the pallu of her saree. She walked towards Papaji, swaying her hips, smiling with great badmashi. She bent down as if to adjust her silver anklets and allowed her pallu to fall from her shoulder. Then, ever so slowly, bilkul dheeray, she untied the corner of her pallu and – there it was! Vidhaata's most famous concoction, the palangtod paan.

'"Close your eyes and open your mouth, husband of my dearest friend," Rekha said. Papaji enjoyed this game of flirtation, allowing her to plop the paan into his grateful open mouth. He enjoyed the bitter-sweetness of the katha and choona, of the gulukand and the supari, and the rich, metallic taste of the chaandi-ka-wark. His shoes, as promised, lay at his feet and he walked to the room and waited for Vidhaata. He heard the gopis teasing her, embarrassing her, giving her the first-night blushes and, finally, depositing her with my father before they ran away giggling. Then the two were alone.

'Papaji took Vidhaata in his arms and hugged her with such strength that she gasped for air. Initially, their touches were tentative, the exploring embarrassed and the fondling shy and awkward. But the effects of the palangtod paan had kicked in and

Papaji carried on tirelessly. The bed creaked violently till the wee hours of the morning, and Vidhaata had to push him away. Had she overdone the nuskaa, she thought. That was the night I was conceived. "First day, first show," as Papaji used to say, much to my mother's embarrassment. Nine months later I came into this world. And, before I forget, let me tell you. On the morning after their wedding night, my parents discovered a large crack on one of the bed's frames.'

'What a story!' Ayah said, laughing at Param's naughtiness.

'You tell a story so well,' said Fartcatcher, thumping him on the back and chuckling with delight.

Pakwaan looked at his father, shaking his head, his face the colour of beetroot. He was pleased, nonetheless, with these stories of flirtation, seduction and aphrodisiacs. They were spiced up for the benefit of entertaining the audience, but were also a father's acknowledgement that his son had come of age.

The Transformation of Mateen

LUNCH was light. Daal, chawal, subzi. Fartcatcher deftly mixed the dal and rice, rolling it into little round balls in the palm of his right hand, tossing it as a spinner would a cricket ball and plopping it with great accuracy into his open mouth. He gorged on the sour chilli onions, sweating profusely, wiping it away with the sleeve of his shirt every now and then. All of them slept after lunch, and in the evening gathered around Param for the next instalment of his tale.

Param looked up, his forehead creased in thought.

'Where was I?' he asked, feigning absent-mindedness, checking if his audience had paid attention.

'First day, first show,' Ayah said, a smile lighting up her face.

'Ah yes, the night of my shuruaat, my beginnings – the reason for my name, PARAM, meaning first. Look at the sunset' – he pointed westwards and beyond – 'the sun dipping, marking the end to another day. And as darkness descends, night will follow'.

'There, in Kanpur, after the shaadi of the standing masalas, the sun rose as it always does, spreading beams of warm and gentle light that filtered through the windows and on to the bed that had borne the brunt of the passionate effects of the palangtod paan. A single ray of light, dust motes dancing in its beam, fell on my mother's face. She blinked, stirred and stretched, sighing with satisfaction and pleasure. To her right, my father lay on his stomach, his right leg wrapped possessively round her hips, his left arm under her neck keeping her a gentle tug away from a warm embrace.

'My mother always slept on Papaji's left side, and in this too there is a story. Great cooks will always be sensitive – they have to be, for they must be able to discern the effects of high heat and low heat, of timing and tempering, of spicing and garnishing while cooking their food. My father was no exception. The mantras and shlokas that the pandit uttered on the night of my shuruaat were in the purest Sanskrit. They had the resonance of ancientness, the heaviness of wisdom, and sounded ponderously pious, but Papaji, like most of those present, understood little of what was said. Fortunately, there were occasions when the pandit would translate the meaning of his utterances into simple Hindi to allow the janta little peeks into the great ocean of Brahminical wisdom – and one such gem stuck in Papaji's memory permanently, for it had romance, charm and the gesture of love.

'"Remember," the pandit said, "always remember that she is your Lakshmi, your goddess of abundance and wealth, so keep her on your left side, for that is where the heart is and it is from your heart that you should love her. Good fortune will be showered upon you then, and you will be happy forever." Papaji loved this bit of advice for its simplicity and depth, and followed it religiously. Even when he slept alone he always left a little space on the side of his heart, wishing she would be there when he awoke.

'That morning, my father was fast asleep, snoring ever so gently. He deserves this peace, Vidhaata thought, and buried her face in the crook of his neck, muzzling him gently with her nose. "Ummmm," he said and, with a little pull of his left hand he embraced her firmly.

'"Oof-oh, leave me," my mother said in an affectionate flirtatious voice.' Param's hands mimicked the gesture of pushing away from an ardent embrace. 'Papaji released his hug somewhat, her hand lay on his chest and with great gentleness, using the nail of her index finger, she wrote with such an exquisite slowness that he could feel every word etched onto his skin – I LOVE YOU. His eyes welled up with tears of happiness and he smiled, looked up and thanked the almighty for giving him Vidhaata. He could fill up oceans with his love for her, he used to say. He released her from his gentle jhappi and pinched her cheek with great affection, kissing her forehead. "Let me make some chai," he said, just like that.

'"Imagine, a husband making chai for his wife without concern for being called hen-pecked," my mother used to tell me, "and though my friends giggled and teased me that I had trained my man well, I know that they were envious for that is what they would have liked from their husbands. Early mornings are not the best of times, and being served a cup of hot, steaming tea by the one you love while you stretch and laze, energy warmly spreading through your body to make it ready for another day, is paradise."

'They sat, sipping their tea in silence – my father held the glass with his right hand, his left hand gently massaging her neck. My mother cupped the glass close to her face with both hands, enjoying the steam as it formed little droplets on her nose and cheeks. She had a distant, faraway look in her eyes.

'"You seem deep in thought," Papaji said.

'"Yes, I have been thinking – we should go to Lucknow."

'"Why Lucknow, meri jaan?' he asked, puzzled at the sudden suggestion.

'"Lucknow smiles kindly on lovers," my mother explained. "Love and Lucknow go hand in hand. Love blossoms in that city.

Besides, it is the land of tehzeeb, of ada, of gracious manners and cultured politeness, where mehmaan-nawazi is a refined art. It is a place of magnificent monuments, whose colours they say change with the passage of the day. It is the land of dusehri and chausa mangoes, of poets and poetry, a city of many splendours drenched in culture and with a tradition in food so old and vast that, meri jaan, even you will be surprised. Kanpur . . . Kanpur is industrial and commercial, where people scratch out a mundane existence, but Lucknow celebrates life."

'My father was surprised by this passionate description. "It shall be as you say," he complied, "Lucknow is where we will settle. But before we start our life in this other world, tell me, my love, how do you know so much about Lucknow?"

'My mother had finished her chai and bent sideways to place the glass on the floor. She could be chatpata and mischievous – the palangtod paan was proof. She turned to face him and stretched, holding her hands together and stretching her arms as far as they could go above her head.

"There is a man I know who lives in Lucknow," she said playfully, looking for expressions of jealousy on Papaji's face. "Very gracious, charming and polite."

"Trying to make me jealous, are you?" he hugged her and they laughed.

"He calls himself Ansari," she continued, "and he is full of stories about the graciousness of Lucknow. He scoffs at Kanpur and its obsession with industry and commerce. Kanpurias are like small worker ants that hoard and store for a rainy day, allowing life to pass them by, he says. They think only of profit and are crass and crude, a common failing amongst most people for whom money is an important god. By contrast, the true Lucknawi has time for leisure, a taste for life, for the charm of strolling quite aimlessly in Hazratganj. Wealth is important there, too, but nazaakat –

grace, charm, good manners and consideration for others – is valued above all else. The Gomti flows through Lucknow to join Ganga Mata later. The Ganga is the holy river, heavy with ancient secrets. But the Gomti – ah! – the Gomti is like a playful young girl, a dancer, and rarely floods. It is not intrusive, but flows by like a well-behaved friend. People dip themselves in Ganga Mata to wash away their sins, and the Lucknawi walks on the banks of the Gomti, in crisp mulmul kurtas embellished with the most delicate chikan embroidery, inhaling life and enjoying living."'

Param paused.

'Papaji sat there looking at her, stroking his chin thoughtfully, recalling the day of the cheeni ka parantha and chai. She was wearing a saree embroidered with chikan-kari and he looked at her suspiciously. Was it really an old love she was remembering?

'"And pray tell me, my dear, what does this Ansari do?" my father asked, an edgy irritation creeping into his voice.

'Vidhaata looked up at him, her eyes playful and smiling. "My loveable buddhu," she said, caressing his face and ruffling his hair. "I know you are blessed with taste and magic in your fingers but my nuskaas, too, have a reputation. This Lucknawi, Ansari, is the odd-job man – part-time cook, part-time masalchi, part-time delivery boy – who collects my nuskaas for Ameena Khaala. She is a magician with masalas and has the secret family recipe for the galouti and kakori kebab. It is a recipe that is many years old, passed down from generation to generation orally to only one member of the family, ensuring absolute secrecy. But Ameena Khaala has the strangest affliction – a constant burning sensation in her backside. Some believe that the affliction is a curse on those who bottle up their secrets but, whatever the truth, my nuskaa, which is a simple mixture – roasted liquorice, roasted rind of the cherry plum tree and cardamom ground to a fine powder taken twice a day with water and honey – gives her relief, and her days pass without pain and discomfort. Naturally, she is grateful, and whenever Ansari is sent to collect the nuskaa she tells him that I should leave Kanpur and come to the land of nazaakat. And, meri jaan, Lucknow is kind to lovers like you and I."

Suspicion, jealousy – the deadliest enemies of the mind, dimaag ke dushman – left Papaji in a flash. He lifted her in his arms and twirled round and round, Vidhaata screaming in delightful protest, holding on to him, her hands clasped tightly around his neck. And as he twirled her, her bun became undone and her thick jet-black hair swished through the air as he went faster and faster. "Bas! Bas! Put me down, put me down," she screamed. "I feel dizzy and my head is eating circles!" He dropped her on the bed, for a while a little unsteady himself, and then he flopped on top of Vidhaata and began to tickle her, underarms first and moved down, feeling the fleshiness of her breasts, tickling her ribs, her stomach. "Stop it! Stop it!" she screamed, laughing hysterically and he rolled off her, lifting her on top of him and embracing her in a warm, gigantic hug. "Badmaash aadmi," she chided, not meaning a word. She rolled off him and lay on her back, her hands behind her head, deliciously exhausted, her face flushed with happiness.'

'Kya, Baba,' Pakwaan said, chuckling lightly. 'You can be really filmy when you want – my grandfather the great romantic hero, my daadi the touch-me-not heroine enjoying his attention but not always willing to admit it'

'Wah, Beta, wah, it seems your wings have sprouted. Not a squeak from you so far and now you comment on my style!' he scowled, pretending to be angry but secretly he was pleased. Pakwaan had spoken without hesitation, without fear of upsetting him, as he would have to a friend.

'Beedi break,' Param said and passed one to Fartcatcher. They lit up. Param got up and stretched, straightening his back and rolling his head from side to side, easing the tension in his neck and shoulders. He inhaled deeply, sucking in a lungful, and exhaled blowing out smoke rings. He watched them as they floated away.

'Does life always go according to plan? Thank God not, for we would then never experience the pain or the pleasure of the unexpected – it could make life so placid and dull. Coincidence, kismet, fate, or karma – call it what you may – but strange are the ways of Bhagwaan living in the heavens above and with many hands and many, many fingers playing us like puppets with such glee. They say that fate is pre-determined, written on our palms and etched on our foreheads.'

Param was speaking softly, almost to himself, his audience straining to catch the words. Now his voice rose a pitch and he brought on a little lilt, a pleasant latchak to his voice. Latchak – ah, what a word – best used to describe the naughty, seductive swaying of a woman's hips.

'My mother suddenly remembered. "Hey Bhagwaan!" she chided herself, hitting her forehead with an open palm, "this Ansari will arrive any day now for the nuskaa for Ameena Khaala, and the rind of cherry plum is out of stock." She leapt out of bed, bathed, dressed and dashed off to the market. She was lucky – she found it in her favourite shop – the oldest kirana store in Kanpur, owned by Pyaara Seth, whose name did him full justice. He was a loveable old man, pleasant, rotund, with a luxuriant white handlebar moustache that he lovingly tended, basting it lightly with desi ghee so it glistened. My mother was like a daughter to him and he enjoyed teasing her whenever he got the chance.

'"Pyaare ji, have you got the rind of cherry plum?" my mother asked, concerned, hoping it was in stock.

'"Cherry plum, bitiya?" he shook his head.

'Her heart sank, her face a naksha of disappointment.

'"And what will you do for me, Bitiya, if I have it?" he asked playfully. "Give me a nuskaa so that my beautiful moustache stays as luxuriant as it is now," he said, twirling it with both his hands.

'"Pyaare ji, please don't tease me. My customer will arrive from Lucknow any day now."

'He laughed and gave her the rind of the cherry plum, refusing the money she held out as payment. "In exchange for the nuskaa for the ever-luxuriant moustache," he said, pinching her cheeks affectionately. She thanked him and ran back home, his eyes following her as she disappeared, his face a map of fatherly pride.

'When Ansari arrived, the nuskaa was ready. She asked Ansari to wait. She wanted him to meet her husband. When Papaji pushed the door open, Ansari's back was to him as he was talking to my mother. "My husband," Vidhaata said, pointing over Ansari shoulder. Ansari turned to face him, and lightning struck! The man facing Papaji was none other than his dearest friend, the kalakaar of the brocade, master-maker of nakshas, the one and only Mateen!'

Param's audience gasped.

'My father and Mateen stood like statues, stunned by the turn of fate. Papaji was the first to recover. "Abbe Ansari," he said playfully, not a trace of anger or regret in his voice.

'"Saale Kathua," said Mateen, recovering quickly.

'They leapt into each other's arms and, like madmen, thumped their feet on the floor, jumping up and down and going round and round at the same time. The baggage of the past was dumped in an instant, Papaji's prayaschit was complete.'

The tale had taken its toll. A little diversion, Param felt would be an excellent idea.

'Come on, my friends, Beta. Let's go into town and watch a film,' Param said graciously, and all of them looked forward to their outing.

Movie Break

AYAH, dressed up, bindi on forehead, powder on cheeks, wrapped in shimmering sari, hair tied in a bun, was all set. Off they went on two bicycles – Ayah on Param's, sitting in front, her legs dangling daintily like the Queen's when she rode a horse; Pakwaan riding pillion on Fartcatcher's rattletrap, legs astride.

It was one of those B-grade movies, made in little time with little money. *Pyaar ka Badla, Chand Pe Chadhai, Toofani Badla*, or some such title, starring the impossibly strong Dara Singh and his permanent heroine – the blue-eyed, thunder-thighed, 70-mm hipped, Indira Billi, lusted after by the villains, generally thick-set, lecherous and hairy, armed with chains, lathis and hockey sticks. Dara Singh, was her eternal protector and lover, bashing the villains at random, not a scratch on his smooth, muscular body while they lay around almost comatose, writhing in pain.

But the climax, as usual, was dramatic. Indira Billi was held hostage by the villains. Dara fought them on a rooftop, his loyal steed, Chetak, waiting for him on the ground so the hero could gallop off to save her as soon as he was done demolishing the villains. Sure enough, Dara jumped off the roof once the final villian had been vanquished, landing perfectly, legs astride on the saddle. 'Chalo, Chetak,' he said urgently while the poor animal had shit going up his arse!

Pakwaan laughed hysterically. More comedy than heroism, he thought. Obviously, the scene was being played in reverse – it had been shot with the hero first sitting astride the horse and then being pulled up on to the roof. It must have been the poor animal's first cinematic experience. His bowels had moved during the shot and budgets did not allow a retake. The horse's arse was transformed into a vacuum cleaner, sucking in his shit when the hero 'landed' on his back. The other way around would have been more likely. Dara Singh was well-built and heavy and the impact should have parted the animal's sphincter. Even acts of heroism required the right budgets.

They were home around midnight, Ayah tittering about Dara Singh's muscular body. 'Bilkul dhaasu,' she said, feeling her non-existent biceps.

But the scene with the horses's shit being vacuumed back into its arse was their favourite.

'He should have worn the cummerbund, like the angrez do,' Pakwaan told his father and the two of them laughed.

In the morning, Pakwaan rose early and walked into the kitchen to make some tea. He found Ayah up and about. She had already put the water to boil. Param and Fartcatcher joined them soon, and when the tea was ready they sat, the four of them, sipping and dipping their white bread in chai, enjoying its moist, mushy softness.

They thanked Param for a lovely day and it pleased him. They wanted to hear the rest of the story but he reminded them of their duties. Later, Pakwaan followed Ayah about the house, duster in hand, pitching in. They were in Mahadev's bedroom when the phone rang. Pakwaan answered. It was Jhelum. 'We will be back late,' she said, 'but tell your father to have everything ready for kathi rolls, just in case anyone is hungry.'

Kathi rolls, another family favourite. Succulent kebabs wrapped in thin, crisp rotis. It came in various combinations, single egg–double mutton, double egg–single chicken, no egg–only mutton, double egg–double chicken. This was Sheikh Hasan Raza's gift to Calcutta.

Chaprassigiri – carrying heavy files from one office to another, constant salaaming, and bowing with unnatural humility to the supercilious sahibs – had crushed Sheikh Hasan Raza's spirit. He left his job, made the kathi roll, called his eatery Nizam and it became an institution. Everyone flocked to his eatery – important Englishmen, nearly as important desi babus and hungry workers – for a cheap wholesome snack. It was at Nizam's that Jhelum had tasted the kathi roll and over time had slowly perfected this delicious snack. The kathi roll was comfort food, a must-eat among the grown-ups and children alike, and Cliff Meeker's favourite.

Param pulled out a packet of boneless mutton from the freezer and left it to defrost. While he kneaded the dough for the kathi Param thought about his father. Kalaam's life had been adventurous – he had wings on his feet, his friends used to say. His father's spirit of restlessness had passed him by, but he could sense it in his son. 'May his feet have wings and may life allow him to fly,' he silently prayed.

Housework done, his audience arrived and once again he began his tale.

'So there they were, the Kathua and the Ansari, celebrating the joys of reunion. Wah!' Param said, throwing his hands up in the air, looking into the heavens. 'It was an example of jigri-dosti at its peak, the absolute masti of unconditional camaraderie. But what would their Banaras be without Arth, that magnificent storyteller?

'"What a kahanibaaz!" They both said simultaneously and suddenly there was sanatta, an eerie silence, as if somebody had stolen their voices.'

Param paused, and Pakwaan could sense a strange sadness creep into the story.

'The memory of the day his friend had left the karkhana had stayed with Mateen and he began an awkward apology. Papaji felt Mateen's embarrassment and put his arm around his friend's shoulder, insisting that bygones be bygones. But Mateen pushed Papaji away and insisted that he speak his piece – it would cool his soul. My father understood, for he too had felt the terrible heaviness of guilt.

'"Damn itihaas, this history," Mateen said with passion, smashing his fist into an open palm. "So self-conscious and made up, tailored to suit the occasion. Ancestory so seductively arranged that we called ourselves weavers of light, direct descendants of Adam, the original weaver of cloth. We were Momins, the faithful; men of honour, Ansaris. We loaded ourselves with praise, our egos so pumped that we forgot our insaniyat – the simple pleasures, the deepest wisdom of being humane. We were probably the only pair who could spin and weave, and our solid friendship guaranteed cloth had quality and character. But Ansaripan galloped inside my veins like tharak, or horniness, in a stud in his sexual prime. When you offered help and I knew I needed it, I refused it for nothing but a cheap and vicious victory – a pointless announcement of an imagined superiority. Our teamwork and friendship were destroyed in a flash.

'"And as if this loss was not bad enough, kismet became vicious. Our world became a giant bazaar and price became the worshipped god. Value was completely forgotten. This bloody buttonwalla cloth' – he shook his head in disgust – 'look how it was woven. With a mere flick of a switch shuttles travelled at fantastic speeds across the warp to make these fabrics, flat, textureless and without any character. But in the end daam triumphed over kaam, price ruled over value, and operating my loom any further would mean bankruptcy. When we gathered in numbers and agitated for better prices and easier terms, the Chatur Chuttars and Arth Dubashis of the world never forgot to mention that we were Mussalmans, painting us with the colours of bigotry and fanaticism as if they were inborn traits.

'"My loom, the livelihood for many generations, lay rotting, and without it I felt rootless. So I became a champion odd-job man, doing everything from chowkidari, to lifting bales of cloth, to washing clothes and cleaning utensils. I worked my way through this and that till I made my way to Lucknow. There I was hired as a masalchi by Ameena Khaala, sole keeper of the secret mixes of the galouti and the kakori, the lady with the burning bum. Just look at the extraordinariness of kismet and the chuttars." Mateen looked mischievously at Papaji and his newly married bride, "One chuttar divided us and the other united us."

'"Badmash," my mother said, slapping him playfully on his shoulder. "Kismet and chuttars," she continued, with a wicked lilt in her voice, 'may be extraordinary and all that. But if one bum was responsible for the separation of friends, it is my nuskaa that brought them back togteher. But remember, dear husband of mine, you are a cook and your good friend a masalchi. The Kathua and the Ansar once again complement each other and if God wills it they can start working together once again.' The two men bowed low, saluting her wisdom.

'"Bhai, Lucknow was a godsend," Mateen continued, "as if fate had granted me some measure of happiness – an island of peace in a world gone mad, where grace and manners, skills and subtlety are appreciated irrespective of caste or creed, where Urdu, that language of nuance and subtlety, of tehzeeb and gentility, the bhasha of poets and lovers is spoken and appreciated for its beauty. And yet, the Lucknawi is not a darpoke. When push comes to shove and a stand has to be taken for justice, the Lucknawi comes to the fore. You know, in 1857 – the year of the Mutiny – it was Maulvi Ahmadullah Shah who led an army of Lucknawis who defeated Sir Henry Lawrence, the commanding officer of the garrison at Lucknow. But history does not remember the Maulvi. Instead, it honours Sir Henry Lawrence by making schools named after him for children of officers and men of other ranks of the English army. A deliberate omission that I have often wondered about . . . But enough of this funny itihaas.

'"It was in Lucknow that I perfected the art of roasting khara masalas," said Mateen. 'Lucknow respects great cooks, and legends of Lucknawi cuisine are fondly remembered. The kakori and the galouti – did you know their recipes came from the kitchens of a toothless nawab, an ode to the passion of a carnivore despite the lack of chewing equipment, the meat so soft and tender that gums and the tongue could do the job. I could tell when the spices would release their full aromas by the way they changed colour while being ground. You know, I think I have discovered the secret of the proportions of spices, but to make a great galouti or a kakori the cut of the meat has to be right – always from the inner thigh of a young goat," he said, patting his inner thigh like a pehelwaan.

'"And the murgh mussalam zafraani, a dish – no, a project – that blended meat, saffron, milk and flour to perfection! Thirty chicks, fluffy white, were chosen. Desi ghee, milk, flour and the purest Persian saffron were mixed to form a paste of silken consistency. The next day all thirty of them were fed this mixture. On the second day, one chick was killed, dressed and deboned, its meat minced to soft, silky fineness, the meat kneaded into the paste and fed to the twenty-nine living chicks, and the same procedure followed everyday. On the thirtieth day there was one chick left, now fully grown, its flesh soft and rich, its feathers tinted with the colour of saffron. You could smell saffron on the bird, and for a day the cooks just admired the bird. It was killed in the evening and soaked in a marinade of cloves, cinnamon, black cardamom, a touch of freshly made garam masala and milk thickened till it was almost creamy. Its stomach was cut open, filled with egg and sealed. Then it was cooked on a slow fire – chicken, milk and masala merging deliciously with saffron, the world's most expensive spice at the gentlest of simmers. Yes, this was truly an occasion and it was said that the elite of Lucknow would offer prayers to be invited to Wajid Ali Shah's court when the murgh mussallam zafraani would be ready. 'Nush-e-jaan,' the Nawaab used to say to the grateful invitees at the beginning of this meal, 'enjoy this food of life!' Kamaal, I know a Kayasth family in Lucknow who needs a cook and they would be happy to have you. Come to Lucknow, my friend," concluded Mateen simply.

'My father's move was now a foregone conclusion,' Param stopped as he heard the station wagon's horn at the gate and Fartcatcher ran to open it.

'Snacks, anybody?' Jhelum asked as she got out of the car. The kids were ready to eat. Everybody else said they were full.

'It's kathis,' Jhelum said, looking at Cliff with a smile.

'Yeah, twist my arm,' he said. Jo laughed and Cliff pretended to look sheepish. 'A double egg–double chicken for me, Jhelum.'

A little later he was munching on his kathi, enjoying the softness of the egg and the spiciness of the chicken kebab filling, sprinkled with green chillies and coriander. 'You guys are wasting your time,' he said between bites. 'You should come to America and open a chain of kathi-roll restaurants. It will be the next big thing and give McDonald's a good run for its money.' They all laughed.

As Tek Ram watched Uncle Cliff gorging on his kathi roll and Aunty Jo delicately pecking at hers, all he could think of was Betty Crocker and McDonald's. What a place this America must be, he thought, impressed.

Bawarchi-ki-Toli

'IT is story time once again,' Param said, and his audience gathered around and waited for him to begin.

'I, Param,' he said, thumping his chest, 'son of my parents, the great lovers Kalaam and Vidhaata, a first-day-first-show conception, the best advertisement for the nuskaa of the palangtod paan, was born in Lucknow. I soaked in Lucknawi tehzeeb while I was in my mother's womb. Unlike other newborns, who had to be spanked hard on their buttocks to make them yell like banshees, I needed a little putt, a gentle tap, on my chuttars' – he patted his bums in demonstration – 'to get me going. But I did not wail. My mother used to say that my cries were soft and melodious, like the plaintive bleat of a baby goat. Wah!' he said and lowered his head, his right hand making the gesture of an adaab, looking for appreciation from his audience, who looked amused by this theatrical flourish.

'Bahut khoob, Baba, bahut khoob,' Pakwaan responded generously, in the manner of a gracious patron acknowledging a ghazal well sung. Param looked at him with fondness, put an arm around his shoulder and pressed him close.

'Mateen was true to his word. He convinced the Kayasth family that my father was the man for the job and they employed him without a trial to test his skills. The Mathurs lived in a large, old house. Our quarters were at the back, some distance away from the main house, and my mother made her nuskaas without getting in the way. Law was the family profession and the Sahib was a master on all matters relating to property. His attention to detail was legendary. He could go through pages and pages of complex judicial jargon and in a flash analyse nuances that could put his client in a bind. He had the reputation for drafting fair contracts and the angrez, nawabs, businessmen, zamindars and shopkeepers, all sought his advice. And how he loved his meat! Mutton, chicken, partridge, quail had to be cooked on the slowest of fires ensuring that the masalas seeped through the flesh. He ate vegetables only because they were considered healthy and insisted he would enjoy them better if they were cooked with meat.

'In Kanpur, my father was a one-eyed man in the kingdom of the blind, and Vindaloo was his only signature dish. But Lucknow was culinary paradise, a giant cauldron that bubbled with delicious secrets anywhere you looked.

'Mulayam,' said Param suddenly, rubbing his fingers slowly with his thumb as the others frowned in curiosity. 'It is the perfect word to describe it, silky to the touch, wondrous for the eyes and magical for taste buds. Azhaar Mian's nihari, leftover pieces of meat cooked overnight on the slowest of fires, early morning sustenance for the industrious who worked the night shift in factories and were on their way home. Thick, creamy gravy dipped in taftan, that delicious saffron-laced bread, sprinkled with slivers of ginger and fresh, chopped coriander, just enough to rid the body of fatigue when they had worked through the night, allowing the mazdoor his gestures of affection with wives or lovers. And for the sweet-toothed there was malai-ki-gilauri, dried fruits and nuts sweetened with cream and sugar, folded into thin sheets of cream and sculpted to look like a paan. And nimesh – full-cream milk flavoured with saffron and rosewater, left under an open sky on a wintry night, absorbing overnight dew, then whipped before sunrise, folded into clay sakoras to be eaten before the heat of the day set in. A flavoured, bubbly froth that delicately popped in the mouth, filling it with the flavours of sweetened saffron and rosewater. There is no limit to the delicacies of Lucknow,' Param said, closing his eyes to savour the memory.

'While Mateen tinkered with the proportions for the masalas of the kakori and the galouti, my father roamed the streets, befriending cooks, observing their methods and asking them for recipes. But he found that most were possessive of their secrets, holding back a nuance here, a garnish there, omitting the infusion of some spice or the other. But my father was blessed with a memory for flavours and a natural flair for texture and taste and, with a bit of trial and error, he perfected most recipes. Like a child, he would rush to my mother and ask her opinion and when she would roll her eyes and smack her lips with appreciation, he would hug her and she would look at him, her eyes brimming with emotion, silently thanking God that he was following his true calling. She helped in the Mathur household, cleaning and dusting, while her business of nuskaas grew steadily. Ameena Khaala was her biggest spokesperson, always suggesting her nuskaas to anyone who complained of niggling coughs, body pain, fevers and frequent headaches.

'My father's angrezification in Kanpur proved advantageous for the Mathur household. Shashi Sahib, the respected lawyer, and his wife, Minakshi Memsahib, spoke fluent English and had impeccable manners. Their uthna-baithna, chalna-phirna was with the city's elite, and Minakshi Memsahib loved the English's ways – their obsession with neatness and order, their well-maintained lawns, the sculpted symmetry of their hedges, their lace table cloths, their immaculately laid tables. Properly placed plates and quarter plates, knives and forks laid out as courses demanded, butter knife across the side plate, the napkins, crisp and white, pressed and pleated, pushed through napkin rings to resemble the pankhis, or fans, that the angrez memsahibs used. But entertaining English-style with desi help could be nerve-wracking. One had to constantly watch over them to see that nothing went wrong as the evening wore on. But for my father this was bain haath ka khel, merely left-hand play. Mrs Palmer had taught him everything and there was always the Vindaloo – a favourite with the firangi guests.

'Minakshi Memsahib now entertained with confidence, her table immaculately English, her roasts soft and tender, the caramel custard firm yet soft and never runny, the colour of the caramel always a deep rich brownish-red and not a sickly yellow. Mr Peterson, the Collector, loved their company and admired their table, and was often invited for a meal along with other Angrezi officials and a sprinkling of desi lawyers with their wives. Papaji as cook and major-domo was a feather in the Mathurs' cap and Minakshi Memsahib was admired, albeit grudgingly, by the desi wives. The Memsahib was thrilled but the Sahib, Papaji felt, was sort of non-committal. Angrez ka khana was not really his favourite, and the Vindaloo was too sour and tart for his taste. Bread-butter-toast, boiled vegetables, roast-shoast, stew and puddings seemed to stick to his insides. But kismet usually favours the brave, skilful and passionate, and, ironically, it was too much of angrez ka khana that converted the Sahib into an admirer of Papaji's skills.

'The morning motion – moh-shun,' Param said, extending the word lovingly, 'is the day's most important event. No painful oohs and aahs as you sit or squat, only the gentlest of thrusts that would ensure smooth and easy passage. The consistency firm, but a bit foamy, ensuring the formation of a chonch, a little beak on top of the pile, like the swirl atop an ice cream cone. "Ah!" Vakil Sahib would say every morning, towel wrapped around his waist. "Excellent chonch today." He would announce this to anyone willing to listen and pat his stomach gratefully, and Memsahib would look appropriately disgusted.'

'Chhi, chhi, chhi, I don't blame her,' Ayah said while the others ignored her.

'The hot summer was setting in and the safeda announced the beginning of the mango season – large, fleshy mangoes full of sweetness and with just a hint of flavour. Vakil Sahib seemed busier than usual, leaving early in the morning and coming back late in the evenings, and either going out for dinner, or having the Collector, Peterson Sahib, a few other English officers and some of the city's important lawyers over to the house for dinner. All this formal entertaining and English food took its toll on Vakil Sahib. His early morning ablutions became hard and painful, his mood dark and sullen around the house. He would snap at his juniors for the smallest of mistakes, going through the motions of work without focus or desire. Finally, when the family dined alone after many days, Papaji came to his rescue.

'My father knew that pasanda was Vakil Sahib's favourite and that he loved eating it with sheermal – flour kneaded with ghee, milk, eggs and suger, rolled paper-thin, then layered and baked in an iron tandoor, a soft, flaky masterpiece with a hint of sweetness. He could make it himself, but iron tandoors were a rarity in household kitchens. He would order it from Mahmudi, the most famous naanbhai in Lucknow.

'A good badam pasanda involves the right cut of mutton flattened with care, and that day Papaji had got just such meat from Qureishi Mian, who was known for the quality of his products. Papaji ground some onions, a fair amount of garlic, a little ginger, dried kachri soaked in water to act as the tenderizer, and added the final touch – figs, plump and soft from their overnight soaking, poppy seeds and blanched almonds, and left the pasanda to marinate for the whole afternoon. He would serve the pasanda with biwi-ki-daal – the daal made by his wife, Vidhaata. This was essentially moong ki daal – the lentil served to the invalid and those recovering from an illness, bland, like khichri without a tadka. But in my mother's recipe it was transformed. The daal would be boiled with thin slices of ginger, green chillies and turmeric, stirred gently till it was thick – the procedure till now the norm for daal. But her tadka – Kashmiri tikki (a mix of anise and chillies, garlic and heeng) sautéed in desi ghee, topped with fresh tomatoes and stirred till it formed a paste – was mixed into the daal till it dissolved. From pale yellow, the daal would become a rich yellow-red-light brown and the flavour – bhai, what to say – moong daal's blandness transformed into piquant perfection.

'It was summer, and the vegetables available were limited – lauki, tindaa, tori, watery vegetables that Vakil Sahib hated. Papaji had decided to make him saag masala, the recipe from Mohammad Shah Rangila or Mohammad Shah the Colourful, from a long line of cooks known mainly for their mastery of dishes in disguise. Rangila was an expert with vegetable dyes, dyeing his rice a fiery red from boiled root of the madder and green from a double dye of larkspur and indigo, so that an ordinary pulao looked like a plate of rubies and emeralds. But his recipe for saag masala had no surprises. It was a three-hundred-year-old recipe that had been around since the time of Emperor Akbar and was made from spinach and other greens. A mixture of spinach and dill leaves, finely chopped onions, ground ginger, crushed cloves, green cardamom and a sprinkling of salt and pepper was cooked in desi ghee, ideal roughage for bowels seeking desperate evacuation.

'Papaji laid the table, the sheermal was cut in quarters, the pasanda was served in a degchi of hand-beaten brass. Silver thalis with katoris were artistically placed all around the table and, in the centre, a silver bowl – the shape of an urli – was filled with water that had rose petals floating on the surface. My father had gone back to the kitchen to get the daal and saag, when Vakil Sahib arrived at the table. He was thrilled at the repast. He broke the sheermal gratefully and dipped it into the gravy and, folding a piece of pasanda in the bread, plopped it into his mouth. It was delicious, and he thanked god for the taste of familiarity. Papaji arrived with the daal and saag, and Vakil Sahib congratulated him for his choice of street cook for the sheermal and pasanda. My father smiled and said, "Sahib, It was no street cook. I made the pasanda as Minakshi Memsahib told me it was your favourite. And I could make the sheermal, too, if we had an iron tandoor."

'"Wah, bhai, wah!" he congratulated my father. "Kya nazaakat hai tumhare haathon mein – your hands have such nuance and delicacy. We shall have the iron tandoor installed in the shortest possible time." He enjoyed the daal and the saag and, after dinner, husband and wife went for a walk, Vakil Sahib's left hand rubbing his pleasantly satiated stomach, his right hand across the Memsahib's waist, holding her close to him, like the newly-weds do on Mall Road when on honeymoon in Shimla.

'Vakil Sahib's morning was stupendous. The spices had licked clean his sticky insides and his morning movement was poetry in motion – full-bodied and frothy, rhythmic from the beginning to the soul-satisfying end, his insides bilkul saaf, his stomach soft and buttery. "The best chonch I've had since I can remember," he loudly proclaimed, the Memsahib shushing him, embarrassed at the thought that the servants would hear. But he was unstoppable. "Shabash, Kalaam! You are the discovery of the decade," he shouted, making sure Papaji could hear him. He left for office with a bounce in his step and, as a parting shot, gave Papaji the dinner menu – "Daal gosht, shaami kebab, dum aloo and a green of your choice." It was something he had not done in years.

'Cooking for Vakil Sahib's family became a joyful game for Papaji. Sahib and Memsahib would challenge my father to produce one Lucknawi street delight or the other, and he would prove equal to the task. They knew their food and their compliments were genuine – full of joy and warmth. When they ran out of Lucknawi challenges, they pulled out, from their oldest cupboard, a recipe book from the court of Bahadur Shah Zafar. They dusted its pages, yellow with age, and aired it to rid it of its mustiness. It was a family heirloom, an ocean of delectable recipes, and often they would plonk it on the table and flip it open at random – and the recipe on that page would be the dinner for the next day.

'While my father was playing games celebrating his skills, Mateen was getting closer to discovering the right proportions of the masalas for the galouti and kakori. He had perfected their textures, nearly perfected the taste, but the aroma, that hint of floral sweetness at the end, was missing. But his desire was bulund, irada pukka, and one day while my father and Mateen were enjoying their full plate of korma with crisp khameeri rotis at Mahmoudi's he suddenly realized the similarity of flavour – it was kewra, simple kewra, flavoured rose water, that was the missing ingredient. "I've got it! I've got it! Allah be praised, I've got it!" he whispered excitedly and he bolted out of his chair and ran to his house. He sprinkled rosewater on his spice and meat mix for the dishes, and when he shallow-fried them and tasted, he was sure he had discovered the magical mix. He burst into my father's quarters in the afternoon when the household was resting and asked for his opinion. A bite later, my father said, "Truly you are a kalakaar. This calls for a celebration! I will convince my Sahib to have a feast for his friends where we can showcase our skills."

'Vakil Sahib was thrilled at the idea and a party was planned two weeks later.

'The city's rich and famous, the powerful and the respected, attended. Kakoris and galoutis; bakarkhanis and sheermal (the iron tandoor and sigri had been installed in the lawn at the back, near the kitchen); fish koftaas; whole baby lamb, their insides removed and stuffed with basmati and quail, skewered over a pit of gently burning coal; biryani and korma; and saag, saunf-wale aloo and pasanda of green banana for the vegetarians were laid out in silver dishes. The guests were amazed at the variety and taste of the food served to them.

'While the party progressed in the Mathur household, the pages of history had been turning, and the nation simmered with the masalas of madness and discontent. Since the early days of the Company, Calcutta had been the central player in the angrez's drama. There were Bengalis who so loved the British that they tried to be more British than the British themselves. They wore straw hats and carried their umbrellas throughout the year in the manner of a Londoner, even ate their food by cutting their chapattis with knife and fork, daintily dipping them into a daal or curry, their food never touching their fingers. But Calcutta was also the centre of protest – many Bengalis demanded a larger say in the running of the country. Bengal had become a nightmare, the British felt – a well-behaved pet that hissed and growled at its master, who had trained and fed it well. "United they will stand, divided they will fall," the angrez thought and so, in 1905, they sliced Bengal into two – the western part comprising mainly Hindus and the eastern slice mainly Mussalmans. It was a trial run before the major hacking up of the country forty-two years later – not as bloody and disastrous, but painful all the same. There was lecture-baazi and naare-baazi, protesting and sloganeering, marching and rioting and clashing, and all that goes with the general drum-beating of angst. Day by day, the voices became louder till the noise was almost deafening. The Mussalmans became more Muslim; the Hindus more Hindu – fanatical soldiers desperately entrenched in their own identities.

'Peterson Sahib was enjoying his whisky with soda, the delicious taste of kakori and sheermal still lingering in his mouth. He sought out his host, put an arm around his shoulder and led him to a far corner of the lawn, out of earshot of the party in progress.

'"My friend," he told Vakil Sahib. "Please listen to me carefully and follow my advice. The partition has been a disaster and the decision will be reversed. But most important, and this I know from reliable sources, the capital will shift from Calcutta to Delhi and I sincerely advise you to do the same. Lucknow, I know, is full of old-world charm, but it has become obsessed with refinement and has turned effete, almost decadent. The city lives too much in the past; in fact, it clings to it with a desperation that is dangerous. Delhi promises to be more robust, full of opportunities, and we are going to build a city there in proper English style, with wide, tree-lined avenues, parks and gardens. Properties will be bought and sold, and your practice will flourish. I urge you to buy some land, build a house and settle down there. I know of this area named Gamaswala Bagh, a stone's throw from Chandni Chowk, twenty-five acres of elevated land almost on the banks of the Yamuna, completely secure from flooding in the monsoon when the river swells dangerously."

'Collector Peterson was an important man, well-connected with the influential and the powerful. There was no reason to doubt his information, and Vakil Sahib was in luck. His England-returned barrister uncle, completely at ease with English life and etiquette and well liked by important Englishmen and Indians, was looking to move to Delhi as well. Theirs was a joint family looking for larger accommodation. They had their eyes on Sheesh Mahal, a large haveli in Chandni Chowk, but it was not up to scratch. It was too close to Paranthewali Gali – the street that sold only paranthas, crisp and flaky, stuffed with the greatest variety of fillings – potatoes and radish, cauliflower and mixed vegetables, paneer and eggs. The idea of being woken up in the morning to the hiss of paranthas frying on the tawa, loud voices of hungry customers asking the vendors to rush their orders, was middle-class, to say the least. Vakil Sahib's heart was in suburbia, wide, open spaces reminiscent of the English countryside with lawns, hedges and well-appointed gardens. Gamaswala Bagh fitted the bill perfectly. It was a huge piece of land, full of fruit trees, home to the wild boar and the neelgai, scattered with pieces of history – cannons and cannon balls that lay around as testimony to 1857. Vakil Sahib and his uncle bought the land. His uncle built a home quickly and was the first to move; Vakil Sahib constructed slowly, taking his time.

'The party in Lucknow was the talk of the town but it had other pleasant consequences. It fulfilled my mother's fondest wish. As word of the party spread, stories about the succulence of the galouti and the kakori that had been served reached Ameena Khaala's ears. She knew that the family secret she had so zealously guarded was out!

'"Where is Mateen?" she shouted viciously, stalking across the karkhana like an enraged tigress waiting for her prey.

'"What sort of a man are you?" she shrieked when she saw him. "First you eat my salt and then go on to make a hole in my thali? Have you no sense of shame, no sense of loyalty? There is a limit to ungratefulness – may Allah punish you in the worst possible way," she cursed, spittle flying out of her mouth, her eyes bloodshot like a rakshasi, Mateen would tell my father laughing.

'But as the wise say, whatever happens, happens for the best – and so it was with Ameena Khaala. She spent an entire day knowing something was missing but just could not put her finger on it. It was towards the end of the day, while applying my mother's nuskaa for the pain in her joints that it struck her – her arse had been calm the whole day! The weight of the secret that she had carried for so long had been burning her insides. Mateen's discovery was a blessing in disguise, for with it came a sense of welcome relief that banished her bum-burning forever.'

'And Mateen?' Pakwaan asked.

'Mateen was asked to leave, but Papaji got him a job in the Mathur household as a masalchi. Minakshi Memsahib did not need much convincing. My father told her that it was Mateen who had mixed the masalas on the day of the party. And so the Kathua and the Ansari became working partners once again.'

Param smiled. 'Imagine,' he said, 'they no longer worked as Kathua and Ansari but as masalchi and bawarchi, their religion and caste now a thing of the past.'

'The grandest of grand tamashas held in 1911 to announce the patch-up of east and west, and declare the King of Vilayat as the King Emperor of India – a giant circus guaranteed to deflect attention from all the hoo-haa and the noise – was still a few years away. This third and final tamasha, this display of pomp, would be different in an important way. Unlike the earlier two, during which the then English Rani or Raja was declared the Queen Empress or King Emperor of India in absentia by the Viceroy, this time India would have the honour of welcoming the King and Queen live in India to be bestowed the honour. And as the date of the Imperial Durbar drew closer, kismet once again played its delicious hand.'

Param's voice hinted at the possibility of grand futures and huge successes, like a soothsayer giving hope to people always desperate to see silver linings.

'Vakil Sahib's house was ready before the year of the Imperial Durbar. Thick walls and high ceilings keeping the house warm in winter and cool in summer, a fireplace in the living room where the family would sit on typically cold Delhi winter evenings and enjoy the gentle warmth of a log fire. It was a large bungalow surrounded by verandas and gardens, with garages and servants' quarters at the back and a separate room for Vakil Sahib's office-at-home. When he would finally shift from Lucknow to Delhi many years later, its walls would be lined with leatherbound books, their spines neatly printed with his name. An old neem tree, taller than the bungalow, stood at the entrance to his office, and alongside it were goolar, papal, jamun and nimbu trees, generous with fruit. It was the nimbu tree that was really special, with its big, round nimbus, their skin thick and a deep bottle green, easy to squeeze, and succulent with smell and flavour.

'Bhai wah!' Param pressed his thumb and fingers together under his nose and took a deep breath. 'A fresh blast of lemon that stuck in your memory forever. Nimbu panis in summer were memorable and the smell of the fruit lingered strongly in the house. Friends insisted on planting the cuttings in their gardens, but admitted the flavour was never the same – there was a lot to be said about the soil of Purani Dilli and the water of the Jamuna!

'The time had come for George Nọ. Five, George Panjam to the natives, his Queen in tow, to pronounce himself King Emperor of India. Lord Hardinge was the Viceroy then, the ringmaster of this last and final show. The spectacle had to be spectacular. 'The greatest show on earth', just like the Raymond Circus. Visitors from India and all over the world would be arriving in Delhi and the city had to be readied, all dressed and made-up to reflect the awesome power of the angrez sarkar. It was here that Delhi, not Calcutta, would become the centre of imperial power, to finally show the troublesome Bengali his aukaat, his real place, in the scheme of their grand plans. The maharajas and princes of India and native gentlemen, the flowers of Indian nobility who owed their status to the largesse of the angrez sarkar, would be present to offer homage to Panjam and his Queen.

'The Governor General of the United Provinces, Sir John Hewitt, was the head of the Durbar Committee, responsible for the mother of all bandobasts, to choreograph the pageantry and prepare for accommodation for more than two hundred and fifty thousand people who would witness the coronation and watch Panjam win the hearts of the princes and people of India. No expense was spared, and money flowed like water. Land had to be cleared and levelled, and a temporary township built with a special railway line that would transport people from Delhi station to the durbar grounds. More than two hundred separate camps were constructed to accommodate the desi royalty, both major and minor, of which King's Camp was the largest, spread across more than 80 acres, with luxurious tents in spotless white separated by paths and English-style hedges. Work was carried out at a frenetic pace, and as the important day came nearer kismet once again showed its colours.'

Param paused. He rubbed his hands gently, made his eyebrows dance and flashed the broadest smile.

'Pomp and show are heady, but there are some who are more pompous and showy than others. The Raja of Mysore booked the entire Maidens Hotel, the grandest hotel in all of Delhi. He would attend the Durbar with his entire staff of officials and secretaries, diwans and munims, valets and cooks. Suddenly, accommodation was in short supply for the important. Vakil Sahib's family had built their houses close to the site of the Durbar, and the Governor General, good friend of Peterson Sahib and central figure in this grand tamasha, sought Vakil Sahib's help. The use of his house was no problem but protocol demanded evening entertainment, so Papaji and Mateen were sent to organize the kitchen in Delhi a few weeks before the Durbar. Vakil Sahib reminded them that his honour was at stake – the food had to be delicious and the service immaculate so that guests would have no complaints.'

Param looked at Ayah, the beginnings of a smile playing on his lips, 'Like your Dara Singh, Hewitt Sahib was a dhaasu gentleman.' Param sucked in his stomach, thrust out his chest and in full military fashion pushed his shoulders back as far as they could go. 'Tall, his white skin healthily tanned by the tropical sun, he was a born leader of men. His instructions were clear, his voice loaded with authority and he was blessed with boundless energy. "Darjan Sahib" his juniors called him – he had the stamina of a dozen men. But Hewitt Sahib's efficiency was in no small way thanks to his cook, valet, butler and the manager of all his non-official needs – his all-in-one man, as Ramaswamy himself would proudly announce.

'Ramaswamy and my father became the best of friends. He taught my father the art of making soft and fluffy idli, thin, crisp and flaky dosa, sambars that had piquancy and spice blended in the most heavenly of proportions. And his rasams – my God, his rasams. Thin and watery, quick to prepare and easy to digest, spiced with generous doses of maliga – pepper mixed with thani, or water. It was this maliga and thani that the English mixed with chicken, rice, vegetables and leftovers, garnished with lemon and christened mulligatawny. Eaten as a soup, the mulligatawny was an ideal beginning for any meal – the tangy taste of pepper cleansing the palate, freshening the taste buds and allowing diners to savour the foods that followed. When he taught my father, he did so with a generosity that held back nothing. From the subtleties of tempering spices in desi ghee to the colour and texture of rasam powders, delicious blends of coriander seeds, chilli peppers, peppercorns, daal, cumin seeds and curry leaves – each ingredient roasted individually so that they gave off the right aroma. He would hold the pan close to my father's nose and insist that he inhale deeply so that the smell stuck in his memory forever.

'"Hold back nothing for those keen to learn and share your knowledge and make sure that nothing is left to chance. That is one way to achieve immortality," Ramaswamy would say as Mateen and my father looked on, respect and admiration in their eyes.

'"Secrets are such a heavy load to carry," they all agreed, laughing at the good it had finally done Ameena Khaala when Mateen had discovered the secret spice mix for the kakori and galouti.

'"I am a cook by happy accident, Ramaswamy, my friend. I thank God above that He has blessed me with the skill, but there is so much to learn," Papaji told Ramaswamy one day.

'"Ah! A seeker of knowledge blessed with skill and humility – the ideal mix of masala that guarantees greatness!" Ramaswamy said laughing, but meaning every word. "Seek and you shall find," he continued, clicking his fingers. "I am not an all-in-one man for nothing. Your timing is perfect. Delhi, thanks to the Coronation, will have rajas and maharajas falling over each other to prove the excellence of their kitchens and their best cooks will accompany them, and my position as right-hand man of my boss promises me access to closely guarded secrets."

'He thumped his chest and laughed. He was true to his word, and Papaji's canvas exploded! Maharajas and masalchis, wazas and khansamas, cooks and bawarchis warmed to him. Marchwangans and machher-jhol, gushtaaba and daab-chingri, hilsa and chemmeen, appams and ishtews, daal bati churma and besan ke nimbu, palak rishtaa and mirchi ka saalan – they all came his way, a criss-cross of north, south, east, west, embracing the masalas of the whole of India. Mateen made notes on spice proportions, textures and colours, and Papaji tasted it all with intense concentration, observing procedures and storing everything away in his memory.'

Param's voice rose a pitch in his excitement and he waved his arms expansively as he said, 'Newspapermen and gossipmongers, cameramen, filmwallas and thousands with huge appetites for grand spectacles descended on Delhi. The city was ready – Hewitt Sahib had done his job. The past few weeks had been hectic for him, and he looked forward to an evening with close friends.

'"A table for three," he informed Ramaswamy, "and let's keep the menu simple. Obviously the starter will have to be your mulligatawny" – Ramaswamy smiled broadly at this – "I have heard that the lawyer's cook makes an excellent Vindaloo, and let's follow that with a roast leg of lamb – just in case the palate needs soothing from too much spice."'

'The mulligatawny was excellent – murmurs of appreciation went around the table. "Puts lead in your pencil," Papaji heard a voice, which he was sure was Collector Peterson's, say. There was laughter around the table. Then it was time for the next course – Vindaloo, crisp, fried okra and long-grained, fluffy white basmati. Ramaswamy served the food, a moment of silence punctuated by the sounds of cutlery on china followed, when suddenly a voice loaded with nostalgia and longing, joyous and loud, cried out, "Kalaam! It has to be Kalaam, for only he can make such a magnificent Vindaloo! I cannot tell you how I have missed his touch!"

'Much time had passed, but there was no mistaking the voice. The discoverer of his talent, the giver of his first chance, his karta-dharta and his mai-baap, the most gracious of men, without whom there would have been no escape from his stuffy milieu – Palmer Sahib! Papaji shuffled into the dining room, head down, looking at his feet, ashamed at the memory of Kanpur. Palmer Sahib shot out of his chair and hugged him with the greatest of warmth and affection.

'Palmer Sahib turned to address his friends, who looked at him a bit surprised. "This man you see before you," he said, putting his arm around Papaji's shoulder and making him face the Collector and Sir Hewitt, "is a genius with food and has a sense of humour to match." And he began to describe Papaji's revenge in great detail, embellishing his story with doses of exaggeration. The gathered company laughed and laughed, thumping the table. "Serves him right, that pompous arse," they all agreed.

'The bandobast for the Coronation had been first-class, every detail looked at. Imagine . . .' Param said admiringly, 'the sides of the roads were sprinkled with oil and water to hold the dust down, so that it would not irritate royal nostrils and for those days Delhi crawled with royalty. On the morning of the day, the huge arena at Kingsway Camp filled up with thousands of people, accompanied by the *dhum-dhum* of drums, the *tan-tara-tan* of trumpets and bugles, and the *boom-boom* of guns. Officials and troops in dress uniforms, Indian royalty arranged in a rigid hierarchical order, like castes in the census, their closeness to the angrez sarkar decided by the number of gun salutes that the English granted them. Only five – the Paramount Chiefs, as the Crown had christened them – got 21-gun salutes. The rest were graded on a scale of nine to twenty gun salutes. All were dressed in their finery, in turbans of various colours, wearing their most precious jewels that glittered splendidly in the sun.

'King George and Queen Mary wore their coronation robes, jewels that caught and reflected the noonday sun, their fair skins sheltered by golden umbrellas. Welcomed by the thunder of artillery, they walked, accompanied by liveried attendants, to the central royal pavilion where George Panjam was proclaimed the King Emperor of India. And then, like our netas always do, he made promises for more funds for education, for banishing poverty, granted medals for meritorious service and, finally, he took a document from the Viceroy and announced the decision to shift the capital from Calcutta to the only truly imperial city in India – Delhi.'

'It was a moment of uncontrollable enthusiasm – the audience rose as one, and thousands of throats cheered lustily. The flag of England was unfurled from the central flagstaff, accompanied by a band playing "God Save the King . . .", and, as suddenly as the crowds had roared only a few moments ago, they were silent, heads bowed with thousand right hands on a thousand hearts, listening to the band with the deepest respect. Panjam was overcome at the sight and never felt closer to hearts of the princes and peoples of India.

'Film companies fell over each other to record this magnificent spectacle and be the first to show it to the world. But here the English lost out to an American, who finally won the race. While most companies were content to shoot in black-and-white, Charles Urban – American-born travelling salesman of books who fancied moving images – shot it in colour. He came to India with five cameramen and filmed the entire event, and in a span of only thirty days the movie, *With Our King and Queen through India*, was ready to be shown. It was the first colour feature film ever made, creating a sensation wherever it was screened, cinemagoers impressed by the pomp, splendour and grand tamasha of the real event that had been so vividly captured for posterity. Thousands saw it and gasped in awe, impressed by its realism, pomp and glittering splendour when it was shown in London, till then the centre of the world.

'Desi royalty lined up to pay obeisance, bowing in front of the King and Queen – like you, Fartcatcher, when you see our Mahadev Sahib.' Param's audience giggled good-naturedly. 'The instructions were clear and imperious – bow low before the Majesties, head down to waist height, no adaab please since we are not in the Mughal court, and leave the dias walking backward, not showing your back to Panjam and his Queen as a mark of respect. In all of this it was the Gaekwad of Baroda, a Paramount Chief, no less, who created a bit of hulchul. A bit of an angrez himself, he walked to the dias twirling an English-style walking stick, as if strolling in a garden, bowed with a perfunctory bend at the waist, did a quick about-turn and was off! He had shown his *back* to the Majesties, and there was gadar! All was sorted out in the end, however – explanations provided (it was unintentional, no offence meant), apologies tendered and accepted (no offence taken) and the matter was forgotten.

'Chatur Chuttar and Arth Dubashi were there, gloating over the superiority of the angrez. Arth Dubashi, eternal chamcha, marvelled at the organization of the British camps, which were spotless-white and meticulous in their attention to detail. By contrast, the Indian camps were chaotic with the atmosphere and colour of the grand bazaars. People milled around and the smell of cooking, spices and masala filled the air. Arth immediately pointed this out, not losing the opportunity to show Chatur Chuttar the contrast between order and chaos, sure that it was discipline that allowed one race to control the other forever. Chatur Chuttar smiled, thrilled that he had taught his pupil well.

'Papaji heard later that Arth left for Vilayat to study and he made rapid strides, briskly climbing the ladder of importance. He lived a half-half life, six months in England and six months in India, where he bought a large plot of land at the bottom of a pretty, hilly village called Tikli, some miles out of Delhi. He christened his English-style manor "Tiklibottom",' Param said, patting his chuttars, laughing along with the rest of his audience, 'his salute, in a sense, to his long association with his mentor Chatur Chuttar.'

'Papaji and Palmer Sahib met after the Coronation, and the Sahib talked to him as if to a close friend. He was leaving India, he said, but India would never leave him. He had decided that he would look for space in London and open a restaurant that would serve the finest Indian cuisine. "It will take some time but can I depend on you, Kalaam? Can you put together a team of cooks for a kitchen in London that will be famous for its taste and authenticity?" My father agreed. With this, his prayaschit would be complete.

Param was nearing the end of his story and was surprised at how much he had enjoyed telling it. A Kathua, fulfilling the promise of spinning a good yarn after all! But it was getting late and his eyes were drooping with the heaviness of sleep.

'Chai banao, Beta,' he told Pakwaan. 'Paani, doodh rok ke, cheeni, patti, masala thok ke,' he finished off, gesturing grandly. He had asked his son to prepare the tea of wakefulness – generous quanitities of tea leaves, cardamom, ginger and sugar with less milk and water, a thick, sweet, dark-brown brew that would guarantee energy and a second wind for the storyteller and his audience alike.

They smoked their beedis, Fartcatcher and Param, while Ayah helped Pakwaan in the kitchen. A little while later, they sipped their tea, waiting for Param to begin. Param paused for a sip of his tea, enjoying the spicy sweetness that caressed his throat.

'Palmer Sahib left India a few months after the Coronation. More than a decade later, he fought the war for Britain and fortunately survived. The English were proud of their victory but the nation grieved – many young men had lost their lives. A spectacle celebrating the Empire would be the right tonic to revive sagging spirits, they decided, and so the British Empire Exhibiton was held at Wembley in 1924. At the exhibition, Palmer Sahib constructed a grand Indian pavilion modelled on Mughal architecture. It was the most popular destination in the entire mela. Instinctively Palmer Sahib knew that an Indian restaurant in London would be a grand sucess. He found a place on Regent Street and shot off a letter to Papaji to bring a team of cooks and my mother to England.

'It took some time for Papaji to get the cooks together. Most of the cooks he wanted should accompany him had worked too long as heads of their kitchens and were secure in their milieus. The thought of Vilayat filled them with a deep sense of dread but my father's bubbling optimism convinced them to come along and assured them the pleasures of grand success. And thus began the bawarchi-ki-toli. There was Mateen to make the masalas, Abdul Ahad Waza from Kashmir, Santoo-moshai from Burdwan, Ramaswamy, of course, and himself. Recipes were shared, menus for the restaurant discussed, Papaji writing down each recipe, which they put together and bound into a book. They called it *Punj Pyaaron ki Mehanat*, or *The Efforts of the Beloved Five*.'

Param paused, looking into the distance, recalling the day his parents left India, the initial euphoria watered down by the sadness of separation, Vidhaata and Kalaam assuring their son that they would write, promising him that they would be back for good after they had saved enough to allow them to live comfortably in their old age.

'I was around your age, Beta,' he said, looking at Pakwaan, 'and knew enough about the kitchen to ensure that it would function smoothly despite my father's absence. Vakil Sahib and his family were sad to see my parents leave but knew that this was an opportunity not to be missed.

'Palmer Sahib called his restaurant Veeraswamy, and Veeraswamy was a magnificent place. Tiger skins and portraits of maharajas adorned the walls. Chandeliers from maharajas' palaces hung from the ceiling and the furniture was beautifully crafted in solid teak, imported all the way from Burma. At the entrance, either a Sardar or a Gorkha dressed in full military regalia opened the doors for guests, who were served by waiters in colourful Rajasthani saafas. It was an immediate success. The Prince of

Wales was a regular patron and when ships berthed at the London docks, the restaurant was the first stop for the maharajas, the rich and the famous, like a temple stop for the devout.

'The main attraction of the restaurant was the Menu of the Punj Pyaara, or the beloved five. The top of the menu had a photograph of Kalaam in the centre, flanked by Abdul Ahad Waza and Ramaswamy on his left, and Santoo-moshai and Mateen on his right. And below it, written by the finest calligrapher in London, was the menu:

RAMASWAMY's *Mulligatawny Soup*
ABDUL AHAD's *Kashmiri Wazwaan*
SANTOO-MOSHAI's *Machher Jhol and Chaurchori*
MATEEN's *Kakori, Marchwangan Korma and Sheermal*
KALAAM's *Vindaloo with Basmati Rice and Fried Okra*

'They served these specialties only for dinner and customers had to book days in advance to enjoy the delicacies of the Punj Pyaara. The chefs were presented after they finished and the cream of London society rose from their chairs to give them standing ovations.

'My mother's small nuskaa business still carried on, but it was her nuskaa for constipation that sold best. "Angrez ka khana and bowel movements are always at loggerheads," she believed, and Vakil Sahib would have wholeheartedly agreed.' Palmer Sahib, who used it occasionally and realized its benefits, called it Vidhaata BC. Although it gave the nuskaa seriously religious overtones and lent a hint of ancientness, 'BC' simply stood for Bowel Cleanser.

'You know, Veeraswamy still exists, probably the oldest running Indian eatery in England, known for its authenticity and taste – just as Palmer Sahib would have wished it.'

The effects of the tea of wakefulness were wearing off now – Param's yawns were proof. But he had come to the end of his story.

'My father and Mateen taught me everything I know and I learnt quickly. I am an old man and I admit to my weaknesses without any shame or guilt. I had the skill and the technique to master an art, but the intensity of passion has skipped a generation,' he finished off, looking at Pakwaan with pride and affection.

'Thank you, Baba,' Pakwaan said and got up to hug his father.

'May your dreams have wings, my son,' said Param warmly, putting his arm around Pakwaan's shoulder as they walked back to their quarters, Ayah and Fartcatcher following them.

The Vagaries of Kismet

AH! Look at the vagaries of kismet! One father thrilled that his son has discovered his passion and is proud to carry the family tradition forward; the other doubtful of the fruition of the dreams he had for his talismanic firstborn.

Tek Ram's academic results continued to be middling or below average. Jhelum's constant 'Just you wait and watch, he will make you proud one day' year after year was beginning to get on Mahadev's nerves. The dining table, once a storehouse of delicious memories, had become a battlefield, Mahadev not losing an opportunity to give Tek Ram a vicious dressing down in the hope that it would shame him enough to do better. The constant predictable harangue – not working hard enough, wasting time on extra-curriculars, playing too much cricket – was filling Tek Ram with guilt and buggering his appetite.

Tek Ram had reached his final year in school and his summer break was passing more pleasantly than expected. Mahadev was buoyant. His 'posting' to Delhi had finally been confirmed – a just recognition for the proof of his commitment to developing 'backward areas', in bureaucratese. He was thrilled at the opportunity to display his prowess on a larger stage, and Jhelum was happy she would be closer to her maika.

But then the envelope arrived, marked Tek Ram c/o Mahadev, IAS, carrying the dreaded result. Jhelum prayed for improvement as she opened it, but it was not to be.

'He has done badly,' she said as she handed Mahadev the marksheet.

'Anything new?' he asked sarcastically and Jhelum sensed the angry edge in his voice.

'A bloody disgrace,' he hissed. 'Mollycoddle him a bit more, protect him under your petticoats and this is what you will get.'

Jhelum looked away, not taking the bait, and Mahadev itched for her to respond. But she knew better.

'I'll deal with the duffer at breakfast,' he said angrily and walked off in a huff.

'Well begun is half done, as Sir Maurice Gwyer used to say,' Mahadev quoted at the table the next morning, after helping himself hungrily to plump sausages and fried eggs with their sunny sides up, quivering expectantly, waiting to be pierced. As he lathered his warm toasts with generous lashings of butter, he fixed his eldest son with the most contemptuous glare. He plopped the egg on the toast, puncturing the yoke with his fork, and Tikky watched as the golden-yellow spread across the white and dribble down the black-brown edges of the toast. He salivated over the taste of toast and sausage mingling with the yolk and white of the egg, waiting for more pithy philosophical homilies.

'But badly begun is disastrous,' his father added as he chewed, bits and pieces of crumbly toast flying out of his mouth. Tikky looked down at his empty plate, teeth clenched, fists tightened, toughening up for the abuse that would follow.

'IAS, IAS, this duffer wants to join the IAS,' Mahadev looked around the table, making sure that everyone present was aware of Tek Ram's plight. 'But the way this useless fellow is going, he will be nothing but, nothing but . . .' Struggling for the worst possible vocation, he finally blurted out '. . . a puncture repairman in a Daryaganj cycle shop. And let me tell you what *you* should do,' he said, pointing at Jhelum. 'Instead of protecting him under your petticoats, teach him the skill of sandpapering – it will serve him well in his profession as he smoothens the area around the puncture at his cycle shop. Son of an ass,' Mahadev muttered disgustedly.

'I wonder what that says about you,' Tek Ram blurted out with nervous bravado, looking for the suppressed giggle, the admiring look in the eyes of his siblings for this display of gutsiness. It was a big mistake. There was a stunned silence at the table. Pakwaan had just entered the dining room with chilled, frothy cold coffees on a silver tray. Mahadev slowly pushed his chair back, stretched to his full height, leaned across the table and with a full swing of his right hand slapped Tek Ram hard across his face. An embarrased Pakwaan made a quick about-turn and a quicker exit. Tek Ram followed moments later, feeling the redness spreading across his cheek.

Mahadev left the table, followed by Jhelum. The whole house heard their bedroom door slam shut, the sound of the curtains drawn angrily, muffled voices at first that became louder and louder, Mahadev accusing his wife of spoiling Tikky, ingratiating herself with the children, the occasional protest from Jhelum, her voice rising a bit, followed by the sound of her sobbing in the end. The children heard the bedroom door slam shut once again, then the *thuk-thuk* noises of Mahadev's leather-soled shoes against the polished red veranda floors till he got into the car and left for office.

Tek Ram hurried away from the table to his room, flung himself on the bed and buried his face in the pillow shutting out the infernal noise, guilty of causing all this commotion. He felt nausea rising from his belly and rushed to the bathroom and vomited. He felt lighter and had to admit, feeling sheepish, that he was a bit hungry.

Pakwaan seemed to have read his mind the moment Tikky walked into the kitchen. He whipped up an ande-ki-bhurji, scrambled eggs Indian-style, fried golden yellow, garnished with tomatoes, fresh coriander and green chillies. He had squeezed out the meat from the sausage casing and lightly fried the filling in ginger, garlic and red chilli paste. A touch of pure genius, Tek Ram thought as he ate his breakfast with crisp flaky parantha. The meal magnificently transforming his mood.

Over the next few days, Tek Ram avoided the table, preferring to eat with Pakwaan, Mahadev happy to have him out of his sight. Tek Ram was fascinated by Pakwaan's efficiency – the chopping of onions, garlic, ginger and green chillies in a flash while his masalas roasted on the griddle, the expert little nicks and cuts he made on the pieces of meat like a skilled surgeon, removing fat from flesh, always watched over fondly by his father who would gently instruct him and give his son shabashi when it was deserved. Tikky envied Pakwaan his passion and the relationship he shared with his father.

They would talk, sometimes late into the night, Pakwaan telling him how his grandfather discovered his God-given skill that allowed him and the generations that followed their escape from their stuffy milieu of caste and narrow classifications. Tek Ram spoke to him about America, how he believed it was a land of better futures, and Pakwaan shared with Tikky his deepest, most secret desire – to emulate his grandfather and become known in Vilayat.

Pakwaan had been whacked by his father for dreaming up a fabulous past that had quite simply been kat-huaed, circumcised, by fact. Tek Ram had been slapped by his for being a disappointing start to a gloriously imagined future. In a strange way this strong pull of the past and the powerful tug of the future rooted Pakwaan and Tek Ram firmly in the present and closer to each other than ever before.

BOOK II

The Great American Dream

V-I-L-A-Y-A-T, the word stretched wistfully as Pakwaan reminisced about his dream featuring the long-limbed, golden-haired pari – soft, sinewy and seductive – his wet dream now a passionate memory.

Vilayat, the word for 'phoren', pronounced with the 'v' sound for those familiar with the softness of Urdu but as 'bilayat', with a 'b' for the Hindi-speaking and for some reason always pronounced as 'blighty' by the English when they spoke of home. When they fought their battles for the glory of their motherland how they wished for blighty wounds – deep gashes or broken bones, anything that did not kill or maim – so that they could be shifted from the heat of battle and recuperate in Blighty, living to tell the tales of their brief but heroic skirmishes for the expansion of the Empire.

For Pakwaan, vilayat was only England, but there was another Vilayat, 'phoren' no doubt but never Bilayat or Blighty. It was only America.

1776.

Thirteen years before the people of France threw out their kings and queens forever and opted for liberty, equality and fraternity (instead of cake), the Thirteen Colonies of the New World declared their independence from Mother England. (The number thirteen once again and 'unlucky for some', as the man would announce at tambola sessions at the Bhubaneswar Club.) Away from the hullabaloo of the Old World where HISTORY, it seemed, began and ended, America was the New World free from the burden of tradition to discover its own destiny. But in the end they were their mother's children and, like her, were blessed with virtue and superiority so natural for all those of the Anglo-Saxon stock.

They came to the New World and found a world of noble savages unaware of the great benefits of Anglo-Saxon civilization. So they conferred upon themselves the burden of divine morality and willed themselves their victories to possess the land, from the Atlantic to their east to the Pacific Ocean to the west, creating a heaven where life, liberty and the pursuit of happiness were there for all to enjoy. It took bloody battles and a civil war for them to realize their mission. Four score and seven years after they had split from their mother nation, they shouldered another noble ideal to see that a government by the people, of the people and for the people would not perish from the face of this earth. But they had to wait for their moment – the shakers and stirrers, the shapers and moulders of events, were still in the Old World across the pond.

It was an American who had shown the world the power of the moving image in colour for the first time. Two years after Mr Charles Urban's work dazzled the world, the Old World went to war. America watched from the sidelines as England and its allies, and Germany and its supporters, battled in their trenches, each side claiming their petty victories. Finally, when America sent in her doughboys, it tilted the scales and established a victor. Two years after the doughboys had made their mark, the spin doctors concocted their great ode to dough and a fictitious, made-up Betty Crocker, the baker of instant cakes, breads and meals became a cultural icon, capturing the nation's imagination. Blessed with muscle, confident of its concoctions, this New World was destined for greatness.

World War I was supposed to be '*the* war to end all wars' but it did not live up to its promise. Twenty years later, the Old World was at war again. Until now the sun had yet to set on the British Empire but England's virtuous (and broad) shoulders were tiring of being the flag-bearer of fair and just civilizations. America was a younger, more energetic nation, conscious of the flex of its healthy muscle, the doughboys being posthumous proof. History, heroism and kismet swooshed towards this magical land and America muscled its way to the main page from the footnotes of history.

As with most wars, this grand war, too, brought forth its heroes. On the right, if you faced the Atlantic, there was Mother England, led by Churchill. Churchill was half-American, born of the successful joining of loins of a millionaire American heiress in search of a title that would guarantee status and an English lord with a status but doubtful cashflow, much like England herself as she fought the war. For Churchill's parents it was, perhaps, a marriage of convenience, but there were moments sprinkled with intense pre-nuptial romance. Born seven months after their marriage – premature or conceived out of wedlock, we shall never know – young Churchill seemed to be in a hurry to walk with destiny and make his mark on the world, and even destiny had no choice. When war broke out and Germany got the better of the English they clamoured for someone more belligerent to lead them and Churchill was plonked at the helm of affairs. 'We have nothing to offer but blood, toil, tears and sweat,' Winston Churchill thundered from the floor of the House of Commons and promised to fight the enemy on land, at sea, on the beaches, in the air, on the streets, and wherever else space permitted, but *never surrender*.

On the left of the Atlantic, there was Franklin Delano Roosevelt, abbreviated to FDR by a nation in a rush to realize greatness. Lincoln, responsible for the pithiest definition of democracy – government by the people, of the people, for the people – was the sixteenth president of the USA. FDR was the thirty-second; Lincoln multiplied by two. While Churchill made his stirring speeches from the floor of the House of Commons and general public pulpits, FDR sat by the warmth and comfort of the White House fireplace and chatted with his people on the radio every now and then, on economics, diplomacy, banking, employment, freedom and security – stuff that makes great nations. When he saw the mother country taking a beating again, the time was ripe for FDR to have another chat and declare his country Democracy's Arsenal. He urged America to come together and produce guns, ships and bullets to aid England in its noble effort to check fascism and dictatorships, a major threat to the American way of life.

Art buttressed noble intent and imitated politics, while entertainment fuelled patriotism. Within months of FDR declaring his country Democracy's Arsenal, comic-strip artists conjured up Steve Rogers. Born on the fourth of July, a sickly man (like FDR), who suffered the effects of a paralytic stroke for a third of his life, Rogers suddenly transformed himself into Captain America when his country was in danger. His body sculpted to perfection, all sinewy muscles, bulging biceps, the stars and stripes of the American flag clinging like second skin to a body at the peak of human perfection. He was a patriotic superhero biffing and punching his way through illustrated pages to aid America in its virtuous fight against Hitler and his allies. Millions read the comics, bristling with righteousness, and when Japan attacked

Pearl Harbour, this bristling righteousness found righteous release. The GIs, like Captain America, came to the rescue. The balance slowly tilted in favour of the allies and victory was certain when they dropped Fat Man on Nagasaki and Little Boy on Hiroshima. Japan finally surrendered.

Radio announcers announced the happy news and friends told friends who had not heard. When Edith Shain, dressed in her starched white nurse's uniform, heard the news she dashed off delirious with joy to Times Square to celebrate with the rest. And when that horny sailor grabbed her by her waist and kissed her passionately on her lips, Alfred Eisenstaedt, ready with his camera, froze *the* image of the war being over. It seemed the war had been kissed goodbye, the nation's bristling righteousness nobly spent.

Young America was feted by the world as the champions of freedom and democracy and, feeling virile and virtuous, the entire nation, it seemed, rediscovered its libido. Over seventy million offspring exploded across America in the next eighteen years, all set to become teenagers and young adults in the sixties. Their marketers labelled them 'baby boomers', a catchy alliteration for a new generation that had different tastes and held the promise of exciting capacities to consume.

Svetlana Terishkova was part of this extended surge.

The Terishkovas had left Russia before World War I, bound for the New World that delivered the promise of bright and glowing futures, of ranch-like houses with crew-cut lawns, wide-bodied cars that glided along on broad, smooth roads and television channels that promised wholesome family entertainment throughout the day.

Theirs was the immigrant's story – they worked hard, scrimping and saving and educating their only child, Mikhail. The boy, ever conscious of his parents' sacrifice, was the ideal son, obedient and hardworking, and married a girl of their choice – Anna. She was a comely girl, skilful in the kitchen, familiar with the art of sewing and knitting, possessing a way with children that everyone found amazing. The cranky and the mischievous, the bratty and the spoilt, would all coo contentedly when she held them to her ample bosom, their irate mothers looking on in happy disbelief at her maternal talents.

Mikhail and Anna were married in a simple ceremony before World War II. By the time their children, Svetlana and Vladimir, were born, they already had their piece of the American dream – a large house in suburbia, an airy kitchen with all the modern conveniences, two large American-made wide-bodied cars with stylish fins and the mandatory lawn at the back of the house. Here, every weekend, Mikhail would wear his I LOVE AMERICA chef's apron and grill burgers, basting the patties with Anna's home-made stroganoff sauce – a Russian garnish to the Terishkovas' salute to Americana.

Svetlana was a rebellious, restless child, constantly testing Anna's god-given mothering skills. She threw shrieking tantrums, taking longer to pacify than any other child Anna had known. Vladimir dutifully learnt Russian while Svetlana thought it a waste of time. She hated the matryoshka dolls, those rotund matronly figures with their shapeless sarafans, but loved her Barbies. She collected them with a passion, lining them up in neat little rows, marvelling at their long model-like legs that met at pinched-in waists, topped by perfectly proportioned breasts sitting lusciously on slender chests. Whenever Svetlana passed by mirrors, she stopped and tucked in her stomach and willed her breasts to sprout. And when Ken came along with his clean-cut looks, Svet had a Ken for every Barbie, dressing him in tuxedos and her in frilly white wedding gowns. Barbie could be stripped completely naked when she undressed her, but Ken was born with a set of permanent underwear, the area between his legs, the area of the GREAT TABOO, securely fastened and out of bounds for little girls. While Svetlana imagined the pleasures that lay there, dreaming of her very own Ken to sweep her off her feet into a world of sweet, sexy, syrupy romance, the chill of the Cold War allowed America's spin doctors – their own handle-ghumanewallas, their Chatur Chuttars and Arth Purabiyas – to concoct fear to keep the new champions of freedom and democracy alert and ever-ready.

A few years after World War II, the dreaded A-bomb was no longer America's sole preserve. The Cold War was in vogue and Russia, ally only a few years ago, the new bugbear. Red menaces and nuclear explosions were real threats to the nation, and its people had to be protected. Fears were advertised, pamphlets distributed, teachers instructed, nuclear shelters constructed and movies made so that the nation knew what to do just in case Russia dropped the A-bomb on the land of the free and the home of the brave.

'Duck' and 'cover' were the buzzwords, and Bret the Turtle their heroic and entertaining instructor. Bow-tied, bow-legged, with top hat, Bret the Turtle in cartoon animation would be shown walking down a street when a naughty monkey would let off fire-crackers. But Bret the ever-vigilant would smartly fall to the ground, sucking his head into his shell. He was saved, but the monkey blown off by his own devilish prank. 'Duck and cover, duck and cover is what we all must do – You, You and You,' the chorus would sing in a happy, bouncy sort of way, info-taining the janta, hoping that it would go down well with the generation of baby boomers. And to keep them in good nick, sirens would occasionally go off, Svet and her friends ducking under tables or running into the safety of shelters, protecting themselves from a nuclear boom that never came.

But there was always the thrill of danger, and on a lovely spring day kismet laced it with romance. Svet got off the school bus to walk to her house when the sirens went off, wailing their warnings. She ran to the closest nuclear shelter and shut the door behind her. Rob was the only other person there. Love was instant, like the food stacked on the shelves around them, and with the sirens screaming menacingly in the background the two of them looked at each other with desperate longing.

'Hello,' he said, 'my name is Rob and I am so pleased to meet you.'

'My name is Svetlana, but people call me Svet.'

'Well, then I shall call you Svetlana, for I want to be more than just people to you.'

Svet's heart melted into a mushy pool of sentiment. *Robber, your name should have been Robber, for you have stolen my heart*, she thought to herself.

The bunker became the love nest where they romanced, eating instant food out of cans, their love defiant against the wailing warnings of false alarms. Rob, the first thief of Svet's heart, ran his fingers through her soft, fluffy hair, pressing against her body – Svet finally discovering the pleasures in the area of the GREAT TABOO.

The first crush, the benchmark to measure future romances against scales of sweetnesses and intensities, was supposed to be intense, fiery and short. So believed the pundits of romance, but Svet and Rob's romance defied the pundits' usual predictions. It had the promise of longevity, an ease of comfortable togetherness, dreams of doting on a brood of grandchildren bouncing on their rickety knees as they grew old together.

But kismet, oh kismet, had other plans. Solid, secure love stood little chance against an aroused patriotism. Across the seven seas (and a bit beyond), tiny Vietnam seemed to be going the communist way, the dreaded red virus threatening to spread rapidly. The civilized world needed saving once again, or so their leaders said, and American righteousness sought heady encores and standing ovations. So they sent in their soldiers to do heroic battle halfway across the world. It was time for comic entertainment to buttress war efforts and Captain America, assumed dead since the end of World War II, was resurrected as the leader of the Avengers, the most awesome collection of superheroes who fought injustice in every part of the world. These superheroes had their hands full. As Rob and Svet sat together, flipping through the Avenger comics, enjoying their BIFF!s, POW!s and powerful WHAAM!s Rob's patriotic urges would bubble forth, but Svet's feathery fondling quickly doused a rising patriotism. But she had not bargained for the Green Berets, the ultimate seduction for the true patriot.

The Green Berets. *The* elite fighting force, many notches above the G.I. and future inspiration for *Rambo* films with a muscular Stallone grunting his way through calculated mayhem, overcoming impossible odds to emerge victorious in the end (like our very own Dara Singh, but without a thunder-thighed Indira Billi by his side) – the movies always backed by million-dollar budgets, no chance whatsoever of heroes landing on horseback while the animal sucked up his shit. When Staff Sergeant Barry Sadler (returned-alive Vietnam War veteran) composed and sang 'The Ballad of the Green Berets', it sold millions of copies and catapulted to the No. 1 single of the year in 1966. Patriotism surged ahead and the patriots thumped their chests, sure that an encore for American righteousness was around the corner.

Trrrr-rum, trrr-rum, the kettle drums rolled, horns in the background playing softly in rhythm, a marching tune not really sung but recited with a bit of lilt in the Sergeant's baritone voice:

Fighting soldiers from the sky,
Fearless men who jump and die,
Men who mean just what they say,
The brave men of the Green Beret.

Silver wings upon their chest,
These are men, America's best.
One hundred men will test today,
But only three will win the Green Beret.

Trained to live off nature's land,
Trained in combat hand to hand,
Men who fight by night and day,
Courage take from the Green Berets.

Silver wings upon their chest,
These are men, America's best.
One hundred men will test today,
But only three will win the Green Beret.

Back at home a young wife waits,
Her Green Beret has met his fate.
He has died for those oppressed,
Leaving her this last request

Put silver wings on my son's chest
Make him one of America's best
He'll be a man they'll test one day,
Have him win the Green Beraaaaaay.

The ballad had everything – heroism, pathos, patriotism, bravery, good solid ingredients to make men out of boys and heroes out of ordinary men. Rob hummed the song incessantly, singing it at parties at the drop of a hat when asked. Hand on his proudly puffed chest, eyes looking intensely at Svet with special pride when he lamented the death of 'her green beret', he would belt it out like a tragic hero from a Bollywood film. Svet found it too melodramatic, but no amount of cooing and cuddling, fondling and feeling afterwards would shake his patriotic resolve. Like a devout believer who hears mystical voices compelling him to visit sacred sites, Rob felt the pull of the Green Beret.

America's Best Men

ROB was in the army for a year when he was sent off to Vietnam, but never survived to tell the tales of his trysts with heroism. They buried Rob in Arlington with full military honours. Guns fired in the air and trumpets wailed their sorrow for America's fallen hero. White-gloved soldiers smartly folded the Stars and Stripes, briskly rolled it into a neat bundle and handed it over to his parents before they lowered his coffin into the grave. Svet surprised herself by the vehemence with which she threw that traditional handful of mud on the coffin before the shovelling began. She was through with the heroics of patriotism, tired of her country's arrogant, bristling righteousness, and found, in her indignant sorrow, her calling, her bulawa: To protest against the war and whatever else was wrong with America. Sixties' America boiled over with all sorts of angst. It was impossible to be a rebel without a cause.

As the body bags came in from Nam, 'The Ballad of the Green Beret' was knocked off its perch. Female, teenaged baby-boomers cried, laughed, shrieked hysterically when John, Paul, George and Ringo sang out that they did not care too much about money because money couldn't buy them love. Blacks fought for fair treatment, railing against a society that judged people by the colour of their skin. Women protested against being treated as sex objects, burning their bras, objecting to beauty pageants and demanding equal treatment with their men. Lovers found commitment stifling, fucking and fondling anyone with the right vibrations. And lovers of peace wanted a swift end to the violence of war. Hippies and beatniks, poets and artists rebelled against America's mindless pursuit of materialism and America's spiritual emptiness. And, if at the end of the day the dreariness of too many angsts got too heavy, there was always the nirvana pill. LSD, sucked on the tongue or popped in the mouth – tune in, turn on and simply drop out and see your mind colourfully expand into a world of tangerine trees and marmalade skies.

Svet spent some time grieving over Rob. She visited the bunker, the storehouse of so much of their tenderness, and was amazed at its state. The paint on the wall was peeling off and there were signs of seepage everywhere – large damp patches, all proof of fears that had fallen out of favour. She left home and 'shacked up' in the East Village, New York, 'digging' the scene and lending her angry voice to the chorus of 'MAKE LOVE NOT WAR'; 'ONE-TWO-THREE-FOUR, WE DON'T WANT YOUR FUCKING WAR'; 'HEY, HEY, LBJ, HOW MANY KIDS HAVE YOU KILLED TODAY?'

She lay down with street protestors when they had their lie-ins, listened intently when students had their teach-ins, celebrated with the free lovers after their bed-ins, smoked with potheads at their smoke-ins, dropped acid with acid-heads at their trip-ins, sat with much earnestness with the anti-war and civil rights activists at their sit-ins, mourned for the dead at kneel-ins and was there when the entire motley assortment would gather around for their be-ins. Anything she liked, she 'dug', what she disliked was a 'bummer'; anything meaningful was 'heavy'; money was 'bread'; her conversation became sprinkled randomly with 'like' when she spoke.

She 'dug' and 'did' the whole counterculture scene, watching Billy the Kid, the fastest roller of the joint, rolling with panache, elevating it to an art form. The finest hash plopped into a small brass ball etched with many OMs on the outside and tied with a black thread around his neck. 'My peace ball,' he would say, heating the ball over a candle with one hand, twirling the cigarette between thumb and forefinger with the other, emptying out the tobacco with practised ease. The joint would be passed around and greedily inhaled, and nirvana would slowly set in – the world would suddenly be a calmer, beatific place blessed with gentle, joyous rhythms. She tripped with Tripper Dan, Uncle Timothy's zealous child, 'popping' the purest Orange Sunshine, convinced that she saw huge wells of love and trust bubbling up for humanity and the world at large.

But protest, too, had its fashions – and India, *the* land of hashish and *great* holiness, sadhus and spiritualism, yoga and meditation, was the flavour of the decade. Svetlana wore her worry beads, burnt incense, slipped on voluminous voile skirts gathered tightly at the waist with ethnic prints in bright reds and oranges, her cheesecloth peasant blouses smocked with the brightest of threads, her tie-dyed tee-shirts in multi-neon colours, the peace sign resting on her chest, heaving for peace on earth and goodwill to all mankind.

She would rarely visit home, and always regretted her decision when she did. Mikhail and Anna would look at her strangely, shocked at their daughter's new avatar. Vladimir was always held as the example of how a normal life should be led – the standard preachy 'study hard, get a job, raise a family', the nine-to-five way of looking at life. Svet was tired of suburbia's unthinking capacity to conform. Her friends wanted nothing better than to look like Barbie and wish for clean-cut all-American boyfriends who looked like sterile Kens, or boys in tight trousers and leather jackets, their hair slicked back, James Dean wannabes with an aura of cultivated danger around them. Barbie and Ken were the first to feel her disgust. She dumped them in an incinerator, wickedly wishing them their hottest dates. Barbie's latest direction to the victims of her fashions – frilly overcoats, mini-skirts and the black net stockings – were given away to her friends, who squealed with delight. Svet looked upon them with amused condescension, sure that she now sat on a much higher moral plane, and promptly rushed back to the hyper-exhibitionism of bohemia.

But protest wobbled in the glare of publicity, becoming more spectacle than dissent, more designed to be in the news. Anarchists like the Motherfuckers wanted an end to hippie capitalism, getting their fair share of attention because of their name. Radicals like the Weathermen declared war against the State, bombing a building every now and then to announce their presence. The League For Spiritual Discovery left little to the imagination. LSD was cult-like, its believers sure that tripping was THE way to psychedelic nirvana. Peter the Handyman walked around the Village, poncho thrown over his head, five plastic arms sticking out on either side, asking flummoxed pedestrians if he could lend them a helping hand. The Knock-Knock Man meandered, a doorknocker hanging from his neck like a giant pendant, and spoke, if he felt like it, only after someone knocked. There was circus, burlesque, theatre and, to add some sort of balance to this hyper tamasha, the born-again Christians, who stood at street corners warning all and sundry that an angry Jesus was all set to arrive and drive the fornicators and the hallucinators to their fate in hell. The time was ripe for a grand entry of some sort of a spiritual messiah to apply the soothing balm of a warm, fuzzy spirituality to counterculture that was losing its way.

The time was ripe for another FDR. This one was named Firangi Das Ramka, the foreigner soldier of God – to enjoy more than just a moment in the sun. FDR, a Brahmin of protest, had done more than his share of acid trips and protests against the war and, sickened by America's mindless pursuit of materialism and the general noisiness of protest, had gone on the Cat-man-doo trail, meditated with ascetics at the foothills of the Him-aa-layas, swung by Banaras and found himself a goo-rooh.

As with the arrivals of most messiahs (only after they have successfully arrived), there were 'signs' that had heralded the arrival of a spiritual leader. The night before was ominous, the sky displaying a reddish-brown ring outlining a near full moon, signs of terrible storms at sea. Dogs howled mournfully into the night, the wind whooshing through the narrow streets, suggesting tragedies around the corner. Tripper Dan, Billy the Kid and Svet lay huddled, shivering, suffering the effects of a 'bum trip'. But the morning after was dramatically transformed. The sky was a bright azure blue, crisp bright sunshine lighting up the day with the warmth of promises to be fulfilled. Even Tripper, Billy and Svet's heads had cleared. They had woken up eager to face a new day.

FDR drove in that day in a Volkswagen Van, the hottest mobile accessory of sixties' angst. The van had been given a fresh coat of paint and 'AUM SHAANTI' had been stencilled below the windscreen, saffron painted over Peter Max pop art, its plump letters in bright neon colours peeping through. A 'Make love not war' here, a 'Superzap them with love' there, just about readable if you squinted. The doors slid open and framed between them stood FDR, his long, carefully tended hair resting on his shoulders, his rich, flowing beard lit golden by the sun.

He walked to the centre of the park carrying a cushion, a table lacquered in a beautiful shiny red and a photograph of a bearded man lying on a charpoy, his body covered by a coarse blanket and his smiling face propped up on his arm facing the camera. He placed the photograph on the table, lighting an incense stick as a mark of respect. With folded hands and head bowed, he asked for his goo-rooh's blessings. 'Jai ho Maharaj-ji, jai ho,' he intoned with great devotion and sat beside the photograph, eyes closed, in padmasana, the lotus pose. He inhaled slowly from the pit of his stomach, his breath moving upwards, filling his lungs, expanding his chest to the full. He exhaled slowly and when he opened his eyes, people had gathered around. He inhaled once again, held his breath for a moment and while he exhaled he chanted, 'Auum Shaanti,' stretching it till his breath allowed, but buggering up the pronunciation of 'shanti', making it sound like a temporary structure in a slum. He held his palms over his head in the gesture of a blessing and, as if sensing the general despondency around him, began with his goo-rooh's favourite utterance, 'The temple of God is within you, like perfume inside the rose. Drugs and dope are useless, no matter what the dose.' Admiring 'ooh's and fascinated 'aah's were sighed through the crowds, the gathered flock marvelling at his capacity to sense the confusion in their troubled minds. 'My goo-rooh,' he said, pointing to the photograph, breaking up the word into two syllables – 'goo', which meant shit, and 'rooh', spirit. Spiritual mentor linguistically transformed into Shit Spirit.

FDR spoke softly, his speech punctuated by heavy, meaningful, spiritual silences, Svet straining to hear his every word. 'My goo-rooh was a spiritual master for he had forgotten ego, that terrible "I" that comes in the way of a loving awareness. His eyes glinted with mischief and there was laughter when he was around and all those around him felt bliss and peace pouring down on them. I feel connected to him twenty-four/seven.' He paused, looking up at the sky. 'And when I feel moh, that is desire, well up inside of me I remind myself that moh should be less and less till it is whittled down to nothing. Once moh is whittled away, ego disappears and is replaced by a deeper "I" that loves awareness, loves the simple fact of just being. I have a practice in which I say to myself, "I love awareness." To begin, I focus my attention in the middle of my chest, on the heart. I breathe in love and I breathe out love. I watch all the thoughts that create the stuff of my mind and I love everything that I can be aware of. I just love, I just love, I just love,' he wound up with feeling and looked up at the crowd.

'I love you all no matter how rotten you may be, because you are the manifestation of God. In this state I am not FDR, or a yogi, or a holy man. In fact I am not even a man. These are just roles, like costumes hanging in a closet. All I am is loving awareness and this is the most fundamental love of God operating in the human heart. When you accept that kind of love, you can give that love to everything you perceive. Say to yourselves: "I am loving awareness".'

'I am loving awareness,' the crowd murmured.

'Louder and with feeling,' he said.

The crowd responded, much louder this time – the chant whispering through the streets of the East Village, purifying it, Svetalana was sure.

Love welled up amongst strangers, who hugged each other with a warmth reserved for old friends. Some openly wept with loud wracking sobs that could be heard across the park. Tripper Dan, Billy the Kid and Svet collectively and with feeling swore never to do acid or hash ever again. Svet loved everything about FDR – the aura of peace and calm around him, his limitless, unconditional love for the world, his ego-less, moh-less existence, all guarantees for permanent spiritual happiness, the really high moral ground where one could watch, amused, ordinary mortals struggling with day-to-day hassles. She developed a desperate moh for him, but this one moh was fine, she told herself – it had nothing to do with the terrible 'I', the dangerous ego.

After depositing his things in the van, FDR walked in the Village, so sure of his way it was as if he had been there many times before. Svet followed him as he made his way to Wonderpussy, famous for its erotic desserts. She found it strange that a man like

FDR would visit a place such as this. But the owner, Magnolia the Magnificent, was clearly a friend.

'Welcome back, my favourite holy man,' said Magnolia as she hugged FDR. They laughed, looking at each other for signs of change like friends who meet after ages. 'You need to get some flesh on your bones,' Magnolia said, and ordered his favourite – the Pineapple Pussy, a hollowed-out pineapple filled to the top with a mix of frothy whipped cream and strawberry ice cream, garnished with small chunks of the freshest, reddest strawberries.

Svet waited for him to sit. 'Hi, I am Svet,' she said, going up to him, grasping his hand and shaking it gratefully. 'How do I achieve my nirvana?' she blurted out.

FDR laughed, told her to sit with him and asked Magnolia to get a dessert for her.

'Let it flow, let it flow. Work on yourself, trust and obey your kare-maa,' he said with feeling. 'Quieten your mind, soothe it, control it's present restlessness, meditate, practice pranayam, deep breathing and yoga, visit India, that land of great holiness. And you shall find your path.'

Her dessert arrived, the Cantona Banana, a firm ripe banana nestled between two balls of chocolate ice cream, a swirl of whipped cream on the tip of the fruit, leaving nothing to the imagination. It was the closest they came to consummation. The year was '69 and, like the position in the Kamasutra, an exciting one.

Svetlana was fascinated, her moh for FDR heightened, her desire to visit India bulund. Her kare-maa lay in India, she was sure, just like FDR had told her. India was the place where she would shed off her terrible 'I' to discover true egolessness. India was the place where she would become Svetlana the spiritual. India just had to be done.

History and Tradition

WHILE Svet resolved to whittle down her mohs, sure that she would find salvation when she did India someday, Tek Ram's future in the country of his birth seemed bleak, to say the least.

This was his final year in school, the final exams only six months away. His disastrous show of bravado in front of Mahadev after his mid-term results had been painfully embarrassing. On the day he left for Mayo, his father had taken him aside. It began as a quiet, gentle lecture, his father explaining to him the importance of doing well academically – it made admissions to good colleges possible and allowed the application of the right kind of spit and polish, which in turn would equip him to appear successfully for the civil services examination. 'The top job in the country, without any doubt,' Mahadev asserted. 'This is your final term,' he reminded his son, pursing his lips for emphasis, his voice losing its gentle quality, 'your final chance to redeem yourself. There are *no* chances of doing better next time,' he said a bit testily, finishing off with, 'You better show *drastic* improvement,' uttered like a command.

The *chug-hiss, chug-hiss* of the steam engine, the rhythmic clickety-clack of steel wheels over the railway line as the train gathered speed, the wispy steam-clouds that sped by his window, the sudden rush of noise as it sped over a bridge sounding its mournful warning whistle, and Tek Ram alone and despondent

– *the* atmospheric props and ambience ripe and ready for that clichéd FLASHBACK.

He remembered his days as a child, Jhelum teaching him English with brightly coloured alphabet books. 'A for –' she would say in a sing-song voice, pointing to the bright red picture of an apple. 'Sev, apple,' he would say and on it went. 'B for balla/bat, C for billi/cat,' Tek Ram happily translating from the vernacular to English, mother and son laughing as he learnt his 'Twinkle, Twinkle' and 'Jack and Jill'. And then on to his convent school, where the love for the good Lord Jesus was abundant and unwavering, solid among the nuns and the mother superior. But the last one he attended was run by Irish Brothers. Here the nature of the good Lord Jesus changed from the good kindly shepherd he had previously known. DOMINI TIMOR PRIMA SAPENTIA, their motto, meant 'the fear of the Lord is the beginning of all knowledge'. Suddenly the kindly Lord had become a fearsome fellow. English language, grammar, punctuation and pronunciation were taught with enthusiasm, and speaking in Hindi was mostly frowned upon. 'Hindi is the language of the street, of the "chokra boys",' the Anglo-Indian teachers would say.

In the schools Tek Ram studied in in Orissa, the sons of sahibs mingled with sons of businessmen, but outside school contact between business and bureaucracy was discouraged. Wealth was grudgingly admired, but profit was somehow a dirty word. The noble cause of nation-building had been hijacked as the sole preserve of the bureaucracy and money-making was just not considered noble enough. Children of bureaucrats stuck together after school. Sons of Orissa Bureaucrats, or SOBs they were called, Tek Ram remembered. They devoured Enid Blytons – Tek Ram and his friends graduating from Noddy to Famous Five and Secret Seven. Theirs became a world of Julians and Georges, Peters and Janets, Jacks and Barbaras, Daisies and Pips, Fattys and Larrys, Timmys and Busters. Prakash became Praks, Chakraborty was Chuk, Niraad became Noddy, Randhir was Randy, Rakesh was Rocky, Bhagwan became Bugsy, and Tek Ram became Tikky. Holidays, were always hols. Hindi was spoken only to the malis, peons, guards, plumbers, cooks, who were all called 'Bhaiya'; the maids and cleaners, 'Didi'.

Mayo College was different. 'Steeped in history and tradition', the first and 'most Royal amongst the Royal Chief's Colleges' in India, conceived in 1870, thirteen years (the dreaded number, thirteen, again) after the Mutiny or the First War of Independence in 1857, the watershed year when the Company gave way to Sarkar, when from simple traders they burdened themselves with the noble conscience of passing on the benefits of civilization. The native princes were their natural allies, spectators first and later collaborators in quelling the rebellion. The battle of Waterloo was, after all, won on the playing fields of Eton, and an Eton in Rajasthan would be appropriate – Rajasthan crawled with royalty. And so, the then Viceroy of India, Lord Mayo, called a Durbar (what else) to announce his grand idea.

The royal salute was fired, 'God Save the Queen' sung, all those present standing up with right hand devoutly placed on chest waiting for the Viceroy to make his announcement. With passion in his voice and hope in his heart, he exhorted the Rajput princes, minor nobility and heads of thikanas big and tiny to fund this noble endeavour, which sought to educate them *and* their future generations, to protect an enlightened power that wanted nothing else but their progress and well-being. Education was outsourced to create Macaulayan delights that were Indian in blood and colour but English in opinions, morals and intellect.

The assembled princes dug into their coffers with enthusiasm and His Highness Maharaja Mangal Singh of Alwar (HH to the teachers and his nears and dears) was Mayo's first student. He entered the gates on elephant-back with a retinue of two hundred servants and a menagerie of tigers, camels and horses – yet another piece of exotica for sepia-tinted memories of the Raj. Mayo College was nestled between the hills of Taragarh and Madar, an insular, royal haven that would try in its little way to see that the sun never set on the British Empire.

When the British did leave – or had to, who knows – it took royalty by surprise and the blue-blooded protected their Mayo turf. Six years after India's historic tryst with destiny, it took an Englishman to fling open Mayo's royal doors to people other than royalty. Trust the English, Tek Ram thought, to ring in the changes. Jack Gibson, Headmaster, toured the country, convincing parents that the Eton of India was open to all. And Tikky was ready – son of IAS, royalty noveaux, Britannica-ed by Blyton, proud of the English chip on his desi shoulder.

There were many like him at the desi Eton who hardly, if ever, spoke in Hindi and, in fact, considered it a bit beneath them to do so. They cringed if someone called them 'haramzada' or 'behenchod', but it was par for the course if they were called 'bastard' or 'sisterfucker', even though it meant the same thing. Learning Hindi was compulsory, and it was studied only because it had to be. Maithili Sharan Gupt may have been christened the Wordsworth of India, but the fact that he was compared to an English poet to confer stature was proof of the superiority of English. The Hindi 'ispeaking' type (for they always pronounced speak as 'ispeak') on scholarship, bright, intelligent, became a source of pretentious amusement due to their lack of familiarity with English. Architect was 'aarchie-tect', school was 'ischool', they 'vaaked', 'cuffed' and 'did latreen', never walked, coughed or shat. Testicle was 'tutta', hairy was 'jhaantu', penis either 'lauda' or 'ghanta', arse always 'gaand'.

And then, of course, there were the Rajputs. Proud, aware of glorious traditions, always introducing themselves by first mentioning their names, followed by *of* the place they came from, as if somebody else were calling out their name when they made their imagined entry into a grand durbar. They stuck together, reminiscing about those good old days at Mayo when their forbears were the only ones present. They were more than a little piqued that the most royal of Chiefs' Colleges had opened its exclusive doors to commoners.

Yet, there were some who were comfortable in their skins. Dharam Singh the Hindi-type, spoke Hindi as well as he did English. With spiky hair that was oiled till it shone, thick bifocals that made his eyes bulge grotesquely, he was a 'local' as the English-type, like Tikky, would call him, but a legend in senior school, admired for his guts.

Dharam was a great fan of Hindi cinema and broke bounds every time a new movie came to town. *Jewel Thief* was the new release at the time and the trade pundits had predicted it would be a super-hit. '*Jewel Thief* is the most mast picture I have seen in a long time, yaaron,' Dharam said, flitting between two languages. 'I was there first day, last show, dressed in striped pyjamas and a torn white vest with thin canvas shoes and a rough chaddar wrapped around my body. I looked every bit the chowkidar as I made my way to Ajanta Talkies to see my favourite hero sing his songs and romance his women, Vyjayanthimala, doe-eyed and generous-hipped, and Tanuja, all buxom and voluptuous. And Helen, oh-my-god Helen,' he said breathlessly. 'Kitni sexy hai, yaaron. Her figure is so slim and slender as she slithers and shimmies in red stilletoes and black fishnet stockings along a circular bar. She contemptuously dismisses the lecherous and the horny, with eyes only for the hero, Dev Anand, who ignores her – can you imagine – because he is on the lookout for the jewel thief. Mera toh, I tell you, khada ho gaya, my penis straining against my underwear,' he said as parts of the English-speaking crowd winced. 'I will not spoil the mazaa for you, yaaron, by telling you the story, but this movie has everything – suspense, drama, twists, turns, sex, love, and its end is a complete surprise.

Full paisa-vasool guaranteed. While I was leaving the hall I was stopped by our very own Rampoo and Sampoo.'

'WHAT?' Tikky and friends chorused in horror.

'"Are you a Mayo boy?"' Rampoo barked out menacingly. My gaand was fluttering in terror but, yaaron, bravado was my only hope and as they say in my mother tongue, it was aar ya paar, nahin to do laudon ka haar. In Angrezi, I'll bluff my way, what the heck, for if I get caught, two thick penises around my Mayo neck.'

The English-speaking winced once again.

'"Vaat bloody Mayo you two taak, you bloody gaandus can take a vaak," I barked back, amazed at my own rhyme, and then let fly at them the maderchods and behenchods, haramzadas and chutiyas. A crowd had gathered, and one brother pulled the other away telling him that this chokra boy could not be one of their own. I was saved and giddy with relief, but the use of "chokra boy" rankled. They called me that just because I let fly in Hindi. Bloody English,' spat out Dharam, as if accusing the lot of them, disgusted by the hypocrisy of it all.

And Dharam had his revenge. There it stood – the statue of Lord Mayo, founder of this Eton in India, made of polished white Italian marble, glistening in the desert moonlight. He clambered onto the pedestal and smeared honey on the founder's crotch. The beehive grew quickly and within a matter of days Richard Southwell Bourke, Earl of Mayo and Viceroy of India, had a giant beehive jutting out like a pregnant belly from his crotch and creeping, like tentacles, all the way down to his knees.

The amusing apparition stood at the entrance to the school and it was imperative that the sweet tumour was removed quickly. The bees had to be smoked out, and six farashes, their bodies wrapped with thin strips of cloth, small slits cut out for their eyes, worked in tandem, dipping their lit torches in water, shoving them between the statue's legs, smoking the bees out of the giant hive. By sunset, the bees had flown out of the school's grounds, buzzing their way towards Ajanta Talkies. The hive was sawed off the next day and the polishers arrived. It took a week of washing-scraping and polishing-waxing to restore its flawless whiteness. But there was a problem. The Italian marble, softer and more buttery than the Indian variety, had got soot embedded in the veins. Parts of the Lord's crotch and thighs now had the thinnest lines of black running through.

Mayo was lucky. Four generations of male heirs to the thikana of Kadchipur had studied in Mayo and a member of the fifth, Chhota Thakur Ranveer Singh, was finishing his last year in school. Kadchipur was an ancient thikana that owed its existence to the British sarkar and their thakurs were known for their weakness for luxury. Their khujaals, or scratchers, were famous for the hereditary skill passed on from father to son of removing the irritating itch on parts of the body that the thakurs could not, or did not, want to reach.

The khujaals were called in and, with their long, tapered fingers and finely manicured nails, they delicately picked the veins clean of the soot. The house of Kadchipur is doubly blessed, thought the heir apparent. From kissing British arse to picking crotches clean, sycophancy had come full circle. Although it was a small principality and lower down the hierarchy of royal Rajput houses, the house of Kadchipur was lauded for its efforts to prove that the Rajputs were the true inheritors of tradition in the Eton of India.

From the Eton of India to India's Cambridge was logical progression. St. Stephen's the pit stop en route to the IAS, as his father never failed to remind him. St. Stephen's, where boys stayed in residence and not in hostel, ate in the café and not in a canteen, snacked on scrambled eggs on toast and never pakoras and samosas. His academic performance in school had to be stellar for him to be allowed admission into India's Cambridge. As he unpacked his things in his room, Tikky prayed for a return of the academic form that had eluded him so far in Mayo.

The Making of a Spiritual Warrior

MEANWHILE, Svetlana was consumed by India. She was back at home, relieved that her self-indulgent fling with the countercultural sixties was over. Anna welcomed her back, playfully chiding her for her misdemeanours and grateful that her daughter was back, safe and healthy. Vlad joined in the fun of good-natured teasing and Mikhail took his time to thaw, making it a point every now and then to remind her of her irresponsible behaviour and the pain that the family went through wondering about her safety, praying that she had not become one of those 'hippie drifters'. Svetlana looked at him affectionately, never taking up cudgels for counterculture and apologizing without any rancour. Mikhail enjoyed this bonding with his daughter and soon it became a game, her father putting on the pretence of anger, throwing his arms open, expecting a hug and Svetlana always obliging.

The family gathered around the television every evening, catching up on Nam, Svetlana noticing the subtle shift in the nature of the broadcasts. Their soldiers carried the stigma of being baby-killers and executioners of innocent villagers. Once heroic America, protector of freedom and democracy now seemed less heroic. The Vietnamese were being admired, those little men in black pyjamas, mere peasants who took on mighty America. With the passage of time, Vlad and even her parents, staunch believers in the American dream, had begun to believe that the little people were somehow more heroic for fighting an army of occupation.

Svet missed being around her FDR, but had news of him because he was often in the news. Like a wandering Indian sadhu, he travelled across the country applying a spiritual balm, trying to alter the spiritual consciousness of America. He was popular on the lecture circuit, so popular, in fact, that he would endearingly say that the 'RAM' in his name was the acronym for Rent-a-Mouth. His audiences would titter with delight, amazed that he could take his God-given spirituality so lightly. 'Better to do good than to be good', 'Follow your kare-maa and see how far it takes you' – and other little spiritual tidbits that sounded so good, so soothing to the lost and burnt-out souls now sure they could see the light at the end of their black and barren spiritual tunnels.

Svetlana took to yoga and meditation, looking inwards into her soul. Up before sunrise, she washed and bathed, stood facing the sun, pouring water from cupped hands in obeisance to the giver of life. 'Auummm Shaanty,' she chanted, grateful for the beginning of another day. She tried to rid her mind of all thought, training it to be still, not to jump about restlessly. An hour of yoga and deep breathing, and her mind focused, aware of her breath rising from the depths of her stomach, moving up and filling her lungs. She tried her hardest to imagine that she was breathing in love, breathing out love, but could never convince herself. Her nirvana lay in India alone, she was sure.

Nevertheless, yoga and meditation calmed her, allowing her to gently ease into her working day at a convenience store – the humdrum nine-to-five routine with half an hour for lunch and weekends off. She welcomed the rhythm of routine, tired of the do-what-you-like-when-you-like scene at the Village. It gave her a sense of direction as well as an opportunity to save money for her trip to India.

At the store, she had started at the till and soon realized she had a head for numbers and an innate ability to do simple sums mentally and rapidly. It served her well when her till was short on change. When she rang up an $11.25 bill for a customer and he gave her $12, she asked for a quarter and returned a dollar. Her lines moved quickly, regular customers seeking her out instead of joining other lines where the not-so-numerate store personnel asked their supervisors for change, loudly counting the balance while handing it back to the customers to make sure they gave back exact amounts.

It was when she worked in the aisles that she was surprised by her innate, almost reflexive ability to spot trends. The American palate it seemed had become more adventurous, showing a sudden fondness for piquancy, heat and spice. Tabasco in its entire range of hot avatars sold quicker than tomato sauce; the granier, more pungent mustards sold faster than the bland, thick and yellow Coleman's; and in the ready-to-eat foods section, pithily christened Heat-and-Eat, the sales of chilli con carne with its spicy mix of beans, tomatoes and ground beef showed the beginnings of becoming a rage. She noticed, too, the sale of spices – ginger, garlic, chilli peppers, black pepper, white pepper, star anise, sesame paste – increasing. Almost instinctively, she collated these trends into dollar terms, sure that the market for spicy foods was about to explode and she found it strange that India, the flavour of the moment, known for its hot and spicy cuisine, was barely present in supermarket aisles.

The natural ability to spot trends, the hallmark of all great marketers, would have been a source of much pride in anyone else, but Svet's attitude to her gift was ambivalent. In a strange way she felt these qualities were too business-like and that they went against the grain in her quest for spirituality. But the store's management was pleased, her talents were recognized and her salary rapidly upped. She was sure now that she could do India quicker than she had planned.

Kismet ka Jadoo

COINCIDENCE of coincidences! Kismet ka jadoo! On Friday, the fifteenth of August 1969, as the swinging, psychedelic, promiscuous sixties wound down, two major events worth mentioning took place at two ends of the world. There was a third event, which, though minor, would give Tikky another chance to redeem himself.

India, the world's largest democracy, celebrated its twenty-second year as an independent nation. Living freedom fighters were given their annual dusting and dead heroes were remembered for their sacrifices to the nation. Indira Gandhi stood on the ramparts of the Red Fort, just like her father before her, and addressed the nation. She reminded her countrymen of the sacrifices her family had made for India and, like all good leaders, swore to banish poverty from this ancient and glorious land. 'Garibi hatao,' she said with believable passion, and the people went back to their homes happy that the country was in caring hands. It was a one-day affair – a passionate construction of patriotism forgotten by the weekend.

While Indira Gandhi addressed the nation, Mayo College warmed up for friendly battle. India's Eton versus India's Cambridge, a three-day cricket match to celebrate the nation's twenty-second year of independence. Before the match, the senior school assembled in front of Lord Mayo's statue in white trousers, black bandhgalas and starched pink Rajasthani saafas. The national anthem was sung, the boys standing at attention, and as the tri-colour was unfurled, rose petals cascaded down and were carried gently by the breeze. 'Jai Hind,' those assembled shouted in passionate unison, watching a few rose petals settle on Lord Mayo's statue, deep red caressing brilliant, flawless white, before floating down to the ground. The polishers and the Khujaals had done a marvellous job.

The captains of the two teams walked to the green top of the central grounds for the toss. The red-sandstone Bikaner pavilion was packed with Mayo students and staff, all praying for victory. The planets, the stars, fate and kismet in general, were clicking into place to bring Svet and Tikky together. And, for once, kismet smiled on Tikky. The honours were shared at the end of the first day's play, but Tikky was noticed for his ability to spin the cricket ball. It was one of those days when everything – his action, run up, delivery, flight – clicked into place from the first ball he bowled, and his rhythm never deserted him. The inside edges, the nicks, carried easily to fielders, Tikky finishing with 6 for 150. He led the team back to the pavilion when the stumps were drawn, his captain and teammates cheering him in, thumping his back in congratulations. Mayo ran St. Stephen's close, losing the match by a narrow margin, Tikky once again playing his best in the second innings. There was a sports quota, the captain of St. Stephen's told him, a back-up in case his academic performance was below par. The college needed good cricketers, especially from public schools. Ah, insurance, Tikky thought, and heaved a sigh of relief. Cricket, the game of glorious uncertainties, had given him something to be certain of after all.

While the sun set in India after the first day's play, another event (and, in the end, culturally very significant) occurred across the oceans when the sun rose in America heralding the beginning of a new day. More than half a million baby-boomers, Vietnam-returned war veterans, music lovers, peaceniks, beatniks, hippies and free lovers gathered in Woodstock to celebrate the dawning of the 'Age of Aquarius', three days of music, peace, love and a long weekend. It was counterculture's last, massive stand to usher in peace on earth and goodwill to all mankind. Even Svetlana, who had shoved counterculture on the back-burner, could not resist its pull. Woodstock promised to be the be-in of all be-ins and Svet felt the beginnings of nostalgia for counterculture nibbling at her edges. She got to Woodstock early and was awestruck at the sight.

The New York State Thruway was closed, jammed with cars packed with devotees on their way to this mammoth event. Musicians, singers and swamis were being deposited in instalments, the crowds cheering on their icons as they made their way to the gigantic stage to sing about the horrors of war, the loss of freedom, doing your own thing, and all other manifestations of heartfelt angst. The air was thick with hash smoke and whiffs of booze. Acid did its frequent rounds, sucked up on tongues, and bodies lay in wait for pscychedelia to kick in. The whole area was randomly dotted by people hugging, kissing, petting, feeling, fooling, fondling, fucking, as if celebrating desire in the open air. It was a Friday, the day named after the Nordic goddess Friga, the free-sprited goddess of love and fertility. She would have been pleased with such devotion.

Svetlana heard Richie Havens belting out 'Freedom', shaking his head, tapping his feet and saying 'Freedom' on a loop, improvising his way as best as he could, waiting for the rest of the performers to arrive. The New York State Thruway was closed, jammed with cars packed with devotees on their way to this mammoth event. People had begun to park their cars and walk to Woodstock. After a while, the only way to get there was by air and when the helicopter did arrive. The first person she saw stepping out of the copter was an authentic Indian Swami, in flesh and blood!

The Swami, resplendent in a saffron shawl draped across his body, thick, long, wavy, salt-and-pepper hair down to his shoulders, and a brilliant white luxurious beard that came all the way down to his chest. Svetlana ran to him, taking off her rudraksha string from her neck and thrusting it in his hands. He closed his eyes, cupped the beads between his palms and jiggling them as if rolling dice softly muttered his mantra, 'Easeful. Peaceful. Useful.' Then he asked Svet to repeat after him. 'Ease-full. Use-full. Peace-full,' she said closing her eyes, with so much feeling that he put the beads back on her neck like a spiritual medal, placing his hand on her head and blessing her. Svet felt deep spiritual vibrations and India tugged at her heartstrings. She was sure that her bulawa was round the corner.

The Swami sat on an elevated stage, his devotees below him, three rows deep, waiting for their goo-rooh to begin. He lifted his hands to hush the crowd and there was silence. 'Auumm Shaantii,' he intoned, the chant rising from his belly, stretching as far as his breath allowed. 'Aum shaanty,' the crowd, topped up with acid, hash and other intoxicants, loudly reciprocated, as if it were a cheer.

On this date when Indira Gandhi promised to banish poverty, allowing the nation to dream their dreams of prosperous futures, here was Swami Satchitananda showing half a million baby-boomers all the way in America the way to spiritual well-being. India, spiritually shining but materially fucked, America the other way round. Woodstock would catapult the Swami to the top of the spiritual charts, his lithe and lissome devotees doing sewa for him, massaging his tired legs at the end of a hard day, moving up slowly into the area of the GREAT TABOO, releasing him of spiritual and other tensions. Artists, musicians, celebrities, would gush about their transformations from miserable, unhappy, selfish people to loving, positive, selfless humans after they felt the Swami's aura of positive vibrations.

The Swami yummed his Ms, yenned his Ns, yaayed his As and yeed his Es as he went off on all sorts of tangents, pontificating on grand themes of music and the oneness of Yeast and West. His accent was strange, his grammar unique, his English tutti-phutti, broken and confusing, but Svetlana just loved this layered, wrapped-up piece of exotica, and with her necklace blessed a few moments ago wanted nothing else but to enjoy her spiritual ride.

'Woodstock yis Yummerica's first step in the spiritual direction and the right thing to do for the yalready yestablished leaders of the material world. Yeast and West yis one,' Satchitananda proclaimed. 'I believe that the youth yassembled here will show the world the right path.' The audience cheered and clapped till he held up his hands and gestured once again for silence. A holy hush fell over the crowd, allowing him his final flourish. Hands up in the air, like a victorious messiah sure of converting his flock, he reminded them of the awesomeness and power of sound and asked them to chant after him, 'Hari Om, Haro Om, Hari Hari Om, Rama, Rama, Rama, Rama'.

At first the chant was repeated a bit hesitantly by the crowd. But as the chanting went on, the voices in the gathering got surer and louder, the devoted swaying from side to side, and Woodstock resonated with Hari Oms and Ramas from the throats of half a million angst-filled baby-boomers. The Swami looked heavenwards, closed his eyes and probably thanked God for his good fortune. Even Banaras would have blushed at this display of devotion.

But India had not finished with Woodstock. The Swami had played the spiritual Pied Piper, and now it was time to bring in some Indian sound. 'RAHVEE SHANK-ER,' the compere announced ('Shanker' rhyming with 'wanker', the way he pronounced it), and the maestro began. He started slowly, gently plucking his sitar's strings, outlining the melody of the raga, then picked up the tempo, his hands a blur as he plucked and strummed. He would stop after playing a fast, complex melody and look across at Allah Rakha, the virtuoso tabla player, playfully challenging him. Allah Rakha would look back, shake his head in admiration, then match him note for note with his beats, the rapid, dazzling dialogue enthralling the audience. They finished to a standing ovation, and it began to rain, as though even the Gods were pleased and were weeping tears of joy.

As rain continued to pour down on Woodstock, the farm turned into a slushy mud pool. The portable toilets overflowed and garbage lay all across the farm. The stench was awful. But there was no violence. The crowd, toked to the gills with pot and hash, floated above it all. Wet clothes clung to young bodies, outlining breasts and nipples, pert arses, taut young stomachs and broad chests that tapered to sexy, narrow waists. Some, tired of the clinging wetness, threw off their clothes and jumped into the pond on one side of the farm, washing off the mud from their bodies, now clean and pinkish white. The war seemed to have been pushed back into some insignificant corner of collective memory, and Svet felt the beginnings of an inexplicable unease.

Joan Baez was the last to play that day and Svet was lulled to sleep by the hymn-like melody of 'We Shall Overcome'. Yeah right, she thought as she closed her eyes and slept.

By the next day, Woodstock had lost its charm for Svetlana. The wetness had dampened the collective spirit, though the devout still swayed and chanted in some sort of a primitive rain-dance chanting of 'No rain, No rain', flashing peace signs at the sky.

The skies cleared as if by magic, and on a soaking stage under a beaming sun the music began once again. As bodies dried under the sun, Joe MacDonald belted out 'Give me an EFF, YOU, SEE and KAY,' insisting that the crowd join him. 'FUCK,' the crowd roared back with passion, each 'fuck' louder, more passionate than the last. Hormones, pheromones and plain moans zipped through the crowd, horniness reigned in random pockets, couples drying and making out under a summer sun.

Disgusted, Svetlana left Woodstock for home. She missed Janis Joplin, high priestess of rock, whiskied and heroin-ed, trying to perform. She missed a completely stoned Jimi Hendrix playing 'Star Spangled Banner', squeezing out the noises of the battlefield, the whistling of bombs and the wailing of sirens from the strings of his guitar. Thirteen months to the date after he performed at Woodstock, Hendrix died of an overdose and Janis Joplin followed sixteen days later from the same.

Counterculture was in shambles. Svetlana was now convinced more than ever that her nirvana (to rhyme with Savannah) lay only in India.

Dilli Darshan

THE trucks loaded with Mahadev's household effects left Bhubaneswar for Delhi around the middle of October. Pakwaan and Param were to leave a few days later. They would arrive in Delhi before the trucks did and make sure the kitchen was functional before Jhelum and the children arrived. They took the Puri Express for an overnight journey to Howrah. The office peons accompanied the Sahib's cooks, carrying their luggage, announcing their 'coming through' with such authority that the crowds parted easily, allowing them their passage and making sure that they boarded the train without inconvenience. The Station Master had been informed to make sure that both had the lower berths and the Travel Ticket Examiner, TT for short, told that the Sahib's cooks should be well looked after. Param and Pakwaan enjoyed the looks of admiration from their fellow travellers when the TT offered them the free cups of tea and politely enquired whether they were comfortable enough.

The next morning father and son boarded the Kalka Mail, the 1UP/2DN from Howrah to Kalka via Delhi. The Kalka Mail, pride of the Eastern Railways, chugging along the route for a century or thereabouts, had been *the* mode of transport for the angrez when they shifted from the capital, then Calcutta, to escape the heat and dust of summer, to Simla, the queen of the hills. The Kalka Mail had pride of place, arriving on Platform No. 1 at Old Delhi Railway Station. As the train wheezed into Delhi, sidling along the platform, Pakwaan saw the signpost: PURANI DILLI.

P-U-R-A-N-I D-I-L-L-I, rolled off his desi tongue so naturally. It was here that his grandfather had rounded off his vast range of food. It was here that his grandfather made the promise and fulfilled it, paying back his dues to Palmer Sahib and completing his penance to mehmaan-nawazi at Veeraswamy in Vilayat. This was Purani Dilli, splattered with rich culinary histories. Pakwaan shivered with excitement.

'It was fourteen years ago,' Param reminisced. 'Fourteen years, Beta – the time that Ram spent away from Ayodhya in banvaas.'

Param had always known that one day he would be back in Delhi to stay. Delhi had until now been a brief stop to get a connecting train en route to his village in the hills from Orissa for his annual holiday. After his parents had left for Vilayat, he had worked with Vakil Sahib for a long time and remembered the day he received the letter from his parents in Vilayat telling him how much they missed him, how they longed for their homeland and were planning to return for good. But the timing of their departure had proved fatal. It was the beginning of World War II and their ship had been torpedoed. No one had survived that disaster, and the original, handwritten recipe book, *Punj Pyaaron ki Mehnat* had sunk, like the *Rubaiyyat of Omar Khayyam* on the *Titanic*, to the bottom of the sea.

Orphaned in an instant, Param had been bereft – no amount of affection and counselling from Vakil Sahib's family could console him. He wanted solitude and left their services, living by himself in the house in the hills made with the money his parents had sent. He worked only as a replacement when the heads of kitchens in decent households left for their annual holidays, never for more than a month, two at best.

When Jhelum's sister's cook in Delhi went on leave, Param had filled in for a month. Both sisters had arrived from Amritsar, newborns and little Tikky in tow. Jhelum, en route to Orissa and desperate for good help, her experience with ayahs and cooks in Orissa nightmarish to say the least, had asked Param if he would come along. Life, as Vakil Sahib and Minakshi Memsahib had kept reminding him, had to carry on, and he finally felt the time had come to plant his roots. He was competent, looking to settle down with a good family as long as quarters for his wife and six-year-old son could be provided. This was no problem for an IAS officer's household. Once again, kismet, glorious kismet, whooshed around fortuitously and the stars ordained that Jhelum's kitchen would be blessed with great gifts and talents.

Param and Pakwaan passed the India Gate, monument to the Indian soldiers who gave up their lives for the cause of Empire and freedom. The canopy that had sheltered the statue of King George V, responsible for Delhi's capital status, lay bare. There had been talk of a statue of the Mahatma being placed there as replacement, but Nehru's death was more recent, fresher in people's memories. A statue of a tall and erect churidaar-and-sherwani-clad man with a red rose in his buttonhole, it was thought, would be more aesthetic than a slight, bent man with a lathi and dhoti. But there were others who wanted heroes from their own biradaris to be honoured and as a result of the difference of opinions the space remained vacant. What was it with this zaalim itihaas, this dangerous history, that needed constant meddling to announce the arrival of each new power, Param wondered.

When they reached the quarters that were to be their home now, both father and son were shocked at the size of the house – shrivelled when compared to the grandeur of the Bhubaneswar residence. Not an indication of the Sahib's importance, they hoped. A rectangular double-storied box, the monotony of the façade broken by small balconies and slatted windows painted in a bright shade of green, bordered by small balconies with barely enough space for two to sit or stand. Their rooms were above the garage – small airless spaces with narrow slits for windows – overlooking a driveway all of fifty paces long and a tall wrought-iron gate that opened out on a broadish, treeless road. What was it with the Sahib's progress, Param wondered, the more he climbed the ladder of importance, the smaller his houses seemed to become.

As they trudged up the flight of stairs, bent under the weight of their trunks and beddings, Param felt the onset of age. He had to stop every now and then and stretch to ease the pain in his back. 'Budhaapa, beta, budhaapa,' he said, but Pakwaan would have none of it. 'Leave it, Baba, old age is for someone else,' he cheerily proclaimed and Param smiled, wishing he could agree but aware that he was nearing his sixtieth year, this first-day-first-show conception.

It was past midday by the time they had settled in, a misty morning giving way to a blue, cloudless sky, the sun crisp and warm. Param decided that it was time to show his son the delights of the typical Delhi winter. They walked down the road to an open maidan and he found what he was looking for – a pushcart piled high with fresh radish and blood-red carrots, mounds of the green, white and blood-red, with dozens of nimbu, golden-yellow tinged with green, the vendor splashing water over the veggies, making them glisten in the afternoon sun.

'Aamaa, yaar,' his father said to the young boy manning the cart, wiggling his index and middle finger. 'Do gajar aur do mooli. Sprinkle the masala with love and squeeze the nimbu with care.'

The young boy smiled, pleased that this customer cared for taste. He held the vegetables grandly, snipping off their leafy crowns, scraping off roots and bits of mud, and Pakwaan watched, fascinated, as the radish transformed from whitish-brown to a pure white, the carrot from dull orange to a juicy blood-red. The boy slit them down the centre, squeezing the lime in the gashes, sprinkling them with rock salt and masala. The crisp pungency of radish tinged with the sourness of lemon, the piquancy of masala; the sweetness of the blood-red carrot balanced by the tartness of lime.

'Ah! Jannat,' his father said. And memories of Dilli spread deliciously in his head.

Dilli with its distinct seasons. Hot summers, when the vegetables were the boring lauki, tinda, tori, karela – gourds of all kinds; when appetites shrank but were sweetened by the availability of mango. The mango, as it marked the passage of summer, starting off with the safeda, the large, fleshy variety full of sweetness and only a hint of flavour, a teaser for what was to follow. The delicacy of the dussehri, the robust stringy flavour of the langda, the small choosnewalla mango that fit in a palm, its juices dribbling down one's chin as its sweetness was sucked out and, finally, the chausa, the thin-skinned greenish-yellow fruit, its flavour a combination of the safeda, the dussehri and the langda, the last mango of the season, an all-in-one memory of yet another mango season gone by. A brief and intense monsoon, when fresh ears of corn were roasted on a wire mesh over hot coals, sprinkled with salt and masala, rubbed in with the juice of a lemon, the soft sweetness of fresh corn tinged with spice – a tasty little snack picked off the street, taking the edge off a grumbling hunger – the pleasures of drinking hot chai and eating freshly fried pakora under dark skies pregnant with rain. With winter came the freshest, whitest cauliflower and the bright green peas that were impossibly, lusciously sweet. It was in winter and spring that the appetite returned, and kebabs and daals, khameeri and naans, kormas and ishtoos, gajar-ka-halwa and jalebi in hot milk were petty indulgences that were easily digested. Tasty memories tucked away for sustenance when summer announced her arrival.

'Beta,' said Param with a flourish, putting an arm around around his son's shoulder and pointing in the direction of the Old City. 'Tomorrow we shall go to Purani Dilli and the start will have to be early, for the day has to be long enough.' There was a ring of mystery, a lilt in his voice and Pakwaan's eyes shone with the excitement of delicious discoveries.

They left the next morning before the sun rose, just as the city was stirring awake. Morning walkers, their shoulders hunched, blowing air into cupped hands to keep the cold away, workers on their haunches warming their hands over fires while sipping hot tea. Old men walking in groups, invoking the Lord Ram's name in short, loud, intermittent bursts, muttering about their health in between. Some complained of constipation, wishing for squeaky-clean stomachs that guaranteed longevity, others complained of flatulence and sour belches, the experienced amongst them ready with their nuskaas that would guarantee immediate relief.

'A jhalak, a glimpse of early morning Dilli, my son, but wait and you shall surely witness a sight, a nazara that will thrill you, remind you of the bounty of dharti mata,' Param said grandly. His sentence was timed to perfection, it seemed, for as soon as he had finished, there, right in front of their bus, a tempo loaded with the freshest, whitest cauliflower stacked with such precision that they formed a pyramid of fresh cream nestled in brilliant green was making its way to the mandi. Pakwaan was dazzled by the sight.

They got off at the end of Daryaganj and turned left into Urdu Bazaar.

'This is the place my son,' Param said, bowing, and with a grand sweep of his hand ushered him into the walled city. 'Here is the Jama Masjid, Chandni Chowk, Matia Mahal, Gali Kebabian, Khari Baoli, Lal Quan, Fatehpuri, Chauri Bazaar, Nai Sadak,' he rattled off with the familiarity of an old waiter who knew the menu of his establishment like the back of his hand. 'This is the heart of Purani Dilli, where the food is robust, the chaats tasty, the masalas pure, the lassi thick and creamy, the pista ki lauj loaded with pistachio and desi ghee, and what we are about to eat in a few moments, the nihari, is uplifting in more ways than one.'

It was good to see his father excited and happy, reminiscing about memories that were very much his own. Pakwaan smiled at Param with affection, shaking his head at his theatrics.

They walked up Urdu Bazaar, the magnificent Jama Masjid on their right, an Emperor's monument to prayers and gatherings when he shifted the capital from Agra to Delhi and named the city Shahjahanabad. They turned left at Matia Mahal, now narrowed and encroached by commerce. 'Matia Mahal,' Param reminisced, 'once the street of hamaams and perfumes, where nobles of the court washed off the sweat and dirt of the day, scrubbed down by attendants with loofas, dabbing perfume on their wrists and behind their ears, the khushboo of the perfume lingering for hours as they enjoyed an evening of poetry that spoke of bitter-sweet love and of gracious times gone by. Matia Mahal was where gracious ladies of the Mughal court caught up on gossip and skilled mixers of attar sold their essences of sandalwood, rajnigandha, raat-ki-rani, musk, amber and even the glorious fragrance of the first rain on dry earth.' They were skilled, like good cooks, Pakwaan thought to himself, feeling the rumblings of hunger in his belly.

ZABARDAST NIHARI, the sign read, and below it, in a confident flourish, 'Asli Nihari ki Dukaan', the shop for true nihari. The early birds milled around, able to put their nihari and khameeri on tables as they ate standing up, the late lateefs sitting on the floor, eating with plates on their laps. Pakwaan hoped that they had not run out.

'Fikar not, Beta,' his father said, as if reading his mind.

'Oye, Zabardast Mian,' he bellowed, hands cupped around his mouth, his voice floating over the crowd.

'Abbe saale Kathua, Param,' the man behind the degchis and the pateelas doling out the nihari acknowledged, without so much as looking up. The crowd allowed them passage to the open kitchen, the delightful joys of reunion, their hugs and their handshakes, their being served out of turn, even making space for them on the tables so that they could eat in relative comfort in deference to an obviously long and warm friendship.

'Asli nihari is always made with thin cuts of meat from the muscles of calves and thighs, simmered overnight on the gentlest of coal fires with onion, turmeric, garlic, red chillies, sprinkled with a touch of the freshest garam masala and a generous dash of saunth, and is ready to eat after the first morning prayer, a bowlful of thanks to Allah for the bounty of dharti mata.' People around the table and those within earshot fell silent and Param realized that he had an audience.

'But my good friend Zabru Mian,' he said, pointing at Zabardast, 'gives his nihari a special twist and adds a rich black extract from the bark of a tree, which when cooked in meat arouses flagging desires. Many who have tried in vain to become fathers have fathered many sons after a few helpings of Zabru's concoction. Glue or gond in everyday parlance, shilajit in Sanskrit, meaning the invincible rock, if you know what I mean,' he winked, smiling mischievously. Pakwaan blushed and the men who had gathered around laughed. Zabru shook his head, breaking into a smile, and some, who had eaten, walked off with the swagger of confident Lotharios sure that the day held exciting promises.

The pateelas and degchis were empty, the last bits of gravy and nihari scraped off the bottoms and served to those who had arrived a little too late. Zabru's establishment opened every day for only two hours in the morning – six-thirty to eight-thirty, enough time for the nihari to be finished. Two generations, serving nihari for two hours every day of the week, allowing them to lead their life at the pace they chose. Pakwaan was amazed. He asked Zabru why he did not expand his business and Zabru's answer was that of a simple, contented man, happy with his life. 'Listen, beta, always keep supply a bit short of demand, otherwise how will there ever be longing?'

Philosophical, Pakwaan thought, though he was not sure he agreed.

Nihari was just the start of a staggeringly vast buffet, Param leading the way, reliving his memories of taste and smell. The streets filled up with rickshaws, tongas, scooters and carts loaded with goods. Pedestrians jostled for the right of way and the occasional 'behenchod' and 'behen ke laude' was aggressively spoken if somebody butted in or stopped too suddenly.

At the corner of Hauz Khasi, Param and Pakwaan shared an aloo-dahi ki chaat – bland boiled potatoes infused with the excitement of a little dash of yogurt, garam masala, amchur or dried mango powder, a splash of imli ki saunth and red chilli powder, crowned with a chutney of coriander leaves, green chillies and a hint of garlic. Next was bedvi aloo at Nai Sadak – wholewheat puris, plump and puffed, their insides lathered with dashes of the magical mixture of ground urad daal, aniseed, red chilli powder, fresh ginger and coriander – dipped into a curry of little pieces of boiled potatoes fried in mustard oil, spiced with ginger, red chillies, coriander, tomatoes, tempered with yogurt for balance and the delicate flavour of heeng – asafoetida – Pakwaan's grandfather's choice of weapon to expel hot, pompous airs.

Tongues and palates tingling with the pleasure of spices used with an instinctive feel for balance, it was time, Param decided, for a bit of sweetness. They walked towards Dariba Kalan where, at the entrance, stood a jewel in it's own right – 'Old and Famous Jalebiwalla'. No family names to describe it, no 'Mahal' as prefix or suffix, no name of a god to embellish it – just 'Old and Famous' in bold letters, sure of it's reputation, sure of it's quality.

Pakwaan watched, fascinated, as the rotund cook sat cross-legged, proprietorial, watching over huge kadhais sizzling with desi ghee, squeezing the batter through a muslin cloth, moving his hands in circles. The stream of batter sizzled as it hit the ghee, puffing up in neat little concentric circles that turned from milky-white to a deep golden-brown, and were then transferred to a kadhai of concentrated, viscous sugar syrup, which changed the colour of the jalebi to a crisp golden orange on the outside and filled it with syrupy sweetness. It was eaten with one hand under the chin to collect the syrup that invariably dribbled down. The shop deserved its name, Pakwaan thought, picking off with his tongue pieces of jalebi stuck between his teeth.

Father and son topped off the jalebis with lassi from a place across the Fatehpuri Mosque. Sweet lassi, stiff with malai, part eaten, part drunk – rich, sinful and delicious.

They took the bus back home from the Red Fort and as it passed under Tilak Bridge, Pakwaan was amazed by the contrast. New Delhi, with its wide, tree-lined avenues, water bodies around the lawns of India Gate where families enjoyed boat rides and spread their chaddars on the grass, picnicking with their families and friends. Purani Dilli, once Shahajahanabad, a garden city at its peak, chipped away by history and commerce. Its narrow gullies and its cheek-by-jowl existence had allowed a once gracious era to crumble away. Now the Walled City was sealed off, as if deliberately kept apart from the new. It had become a museum of sorts, which an outsider could visit to marvel at the expressions of life's energy in cramped and crowded spaces and quietly escape to better planned spaces.

The power of asli nihari, cooked in gond or shilajeet (*Asphaltum punjabianum* in Latin), kicked in after Pakwaan slept. He felt the beginnings of rock-hard invincibility as the same long-limbed, golden-haired firangi pari floated into his dream once again. She wore a blouse of the finest gauze, the sensuous slopes of her firm white breasts exposed by a plunging neckline, and a most generous ghagra, yards and yards of voile, printed with green parrots with the reddest of beaks, bright intricate paisleys, yellow-orange marigolds and pinched into the smallest of gathers around her slim-supple-young-narrow waist. Pakwaan saw himself standing at the rim of a giant cauldron, stirring the nihari mixture. He ladled her a portion and she sucked in the pieces of meat hungrily, marvelling at the taste and, with her blue eyes lidded with lust, she waggled her finger languorously at him, sure that he would join her. Pakwaan floated down, using his long ladle as support and his father's voice – a deep, mischievous baritone – could be heard from the skies, providing the soundtrack for his dream with Angrezi subtitles, like in a movie.

Pakao nihari, banao dihadi.
Hai shaa, hai shaa.
Aur woh,
Pehle bijli ka khamba, Phir dus gaz lamba
Ban jayegaa.
Hai shaa, hai shaaaa.
Cook nihari, make your daily wage,
And that thing between your legs will grow at every stage.
From electric pole to ten yards length,
For Nihari gives you solid strength.

She pushed Pakwaan down, lifting her ghagra agonizingly slowly, revealing ankles, calves, knees and gorgeous white thighs. She wore nothing underneath. She flicked at his erection, checking it for hardness – *thunnnn*, the sound of a bell resonated in his dream. She slid down gently on his erection, covering his body with her ghagra and, amongst the parrots, paisleys and the marigolds, he watched her ride him, hips straining. Ahh-oohing, he came, like the fountains in full flow outside the Town Hall in Chandni Chowk.

A while later, as he crept towards the bathroom to clean himself, his father woke. 'Dekhaa, nihari ka kamaal,' Param chuckled, reminiscing about his youth. Pakwaan blushed the deepest shade of red and hurried away.

While Pakwaan's pyjamas, clipped to the clothesline, flapped gently, drying in the early morning winter breeze, he lay on his bed, head on the pillow, looking up at the ceiling, sure now that cooking would take him places, thinking fondly of Vilayat, the land of his firangi pari.

Tikky's Progress

'YOU are a bloody disgrace,' Mahadev shouted, holding the final, school-leaving mark sheet in his hand. Tikky jumped, feeling a familiar bolt of fear and shame zip through his body.

'Low second division,' Mahadev muttered, almost to himself. 'Low bloody second division,' he repeated in a much louder voice and thrust Tikky's mark sheet inches from his face, two 'bloody's in three sentences more than enough proof that his temper still had a long way to go. 'I was an academic loin, always a first-class-first, and this bloody duffer gets a bloody low second division in such an important bloody exam,' he said, looking at Jhelum. 'Do you have any bloody idea what this bloody well means?' Without waiting for a reply he carried on, 'No good college will bloody admit you, unless I use my bloody influence and lick the bloody boots of college principals and their bloody ilk. I will have to bloody grovel in front of the same people who would bloody wait for hours outside my bloody office and be grateful if I bloody granted them an audience. And all bloody because of this useless bloody duffer,' he finished off, wagging his index figure at Tikky, looking at Jhelum, his face distorted in disgust. 'Sometimes I wonder if you are the bloody product of my loins,' he said sarcastically, pronouncing the word correctly this time.

'Bas darling, that's enough,' Jhelum interrupted, a bit more firmly than she had intended, upset at this slur on her fidelity.

Mahadev saw it as a gesture of defiance and hell broke loose. The direction of the tirade changed, from father to son to father to son via mother. The matter of a bad result became a contest between the status of his family and hers, his efforts to drill some discipline into Tikky versus hers to constantly contradict him. Then things just spiralled out of control. The gloves were off and Tikky watched his parents accusing each other and their respective families of all sorts of pettiness with a bitterness that left Tikky despondent, frightened and burdened with guilt. He slinked out of the room, shutting out their noisy, vicious allegations and flung himself on his bed. For some strange, random reason he thought of the Meekers, of Betty Crocker, McDonald's and kathi rolls.

It was the beginning of the year 1970. The baby-boomer sixties' angst with its strong Indian flavour had seeped into the country. Hashish, the poor man's high was now fashionable amongst the hip. Zealous admirers of yoga were growing, but were still in the fringes. Long hair and bell-bottoms were 'in' and Nam had vociferous desi protestors. The *Junior Statesman*, abbreviated to a spiffier *JS*, with its glossy covers and Peter Max artwork, flew off the printing presses and brought in little bits of baby-boomer angst to India. Indian teens discovered they were teenagers and the generation gap became a reality. It should have come earlier but communications were slow, validation from the West took its time – imitation's limitations in a way. And, fortunately for Tikky, *JS* now had a column for foreign pen pals. He bunged in his name and address and waited, expectantly, for contact from saat samundar paar.

KNOW YOUR WORLD, MAKE A PEN PAL!
CALL 212-PENPALS, TODAY!

The sandwich board with a man's head sticking out proclaimed in the middle of Times Square, and Svetlana was sure her kare-ma had come calling. She grabbed the pamphlet from the man and dialled the number as soon as she got home. The voice at the other end was sharp, efficient.

'How may I help you?'

'I am looking for a pen pal.'

'Any country prefer . . .?'

'India,' Svetalana said before the voice could even complete the question. She gave her address and telephone number, and a few days later the list arrived.

Andy, Bobby, Birdie, Bertie, Capsy, Charlie, Don, Derek, Doddie, Ellie, Jasper, Jazzy, Lucky, Larry her eyes went down the list in alphabetical order, surprised by western names followed by Guptas, Sandhus, Singhs, Malhotras, Nayyars, Iyers, Chawlas, Aroras. At T she was sure her search had ended, for the first name she saw was Tek Ram. She remembered how consumed she had been by the idea of India when she lent her voice to the 'Ram, Ram, Ram, Ram' chant at Woodstock and decided there and then that Tek Ram it would be. She would make Tek Ram her pen pal.

She wrote to him gushing about an India she imagined. A magical land of elephants, tigers, snake charmers, of yoga, spiritualism and holy men meditating in caves in the Himalayas and by the banks of the Ganges, who would show her the way, help her to discover her spiritual self buried by the curse of the meaningless materialism of America. *Please write back*, she wrote in the end, sure that she would meet him and they would become friends. Her first real Indian friend! She folded the letter and while slipping it into an envelope realized she had forgotten to include her photograph. She slid it in – there she was in a gauze off-shoulder blouse, a hint of her breasts outlined against the light, worn over a voluminous turmeric-coloured ghagra with bright green parakeets, paisleys and marigolds printed in vivid, vibrant colours.

She prayed it would reach him soon.

Cricket had saved Tikky, the sports quota at St. Stephen's College coming to his rescue. The future now looked more hopeful – he had moved, quite effortlessly in the end, from a desi Eton to a desi Cambridge, the logical progression to brighter prospects and better futures.

While Tikky and his mates had studied in Mayo, the hirsute and the hormonal had lusted after the smooth and the chiknaa, the tuck shop the starting point of a statement of horny intent. The buggerer would buy Coke and cream rolls, crisp, phallic-shaped pastries wrapped around thick sweet cream, and hopefully shake hands with the intended bugguree, tickling the palm with his index finger, praying for the tickle back, the seal of agreement for the expression of lust. This boy-boy lust wasn't for Tikky. He had always dreamt of voluptuous women, marvelling at the shape of their bodies and their breasts, enjoying vicariously the feeling of soft flesh in his hand when he bought small, water-filled balloons tied with a strip of rubber as they bunged back into the palm of his hand.

'Fantastic feeling,' he would mutter to himself and feel the beginnings of a firm erection, apna hath Jagannath, hand-practice, sufficing for release.

Delhi University teemed with the possibilities of hands-free sex, but mingling and mating had its rituals, the 'lookers' choosing from either/or options quite rigidly defined. Left of centre, just plain leftist, communist, the ability to spout Marx and dialectical materialism were admired, the admiration tempered, almost lukewarm. The Naxalites, way left of centre, were hotly admired, sometimes worshipped. Chairman Mao was their Chairman, the shining red star over China, the guiding light to their utopia. They demanded death to the running dogs of imperialism, a violent and bloody end to the reactionary capitalist state, painting their slogans the colour of blood on walls, spending hours in the café filled with the smoke of cigarettes without filters, plotting the downfall of the capitalists and the revisionist states with great-looking women by their side willing to join them in their struggle.

And at the other end was the hip crowd, and their hipness, like leftness, had its own bandwidths. Hair worn reasonably long, just over the collar, the occasional joint smoked, taste in music safe – Beatles, Creedence – sort of testing the waters of true hipness. A notch above were the hair-below-the-collar-wallas, drawn more to the edgy music of Led Zepp, air-guitaring with their hands on either side of their crotches, thrusting their heads, eyes squeezed shut. At the pinnacle of hipness, was the desi version of the phoren hippie, but cleaner. Shoulder-length hair glistening like in advertisements for shampoo and bouncing rhythmically against their backs as they loped about (for they never walked or ambled). They swayed, never vigorously gyrating to music, and plucked the chords in the air with such nonchalance that everyone believed they knew how to play. They fiddled with the fashions of the day, not feeling the need to tom-tom their use of drugs, flashing peace signs and 'be-cools' condescendingly to the rest, who struggled to arrive at the peak of coolness. They were the centres of female attraction at music fests (never festivals), where desi bands belted out imitations of 'Pinball Wizard', 'Tommy' and 'The Star-Spangled Banner', doing their bit to create the Woodstockian spirit.

Tikky fell somewhere in the middle, neither hip nor red enough, keeping his options open, hoping, impossibly for a hit. He mouthed his Marx and his Mao, paid lip sympathy for the proletariat so mercilessly exploited by the bourgeoisie. Lip sympathy had small advantages. At least his awareness was admired, in a condescending sort of way, allowing him to hold reasonably attractive women around their waists when songs like 'Nights in White Satin', which offered huge opportunities for a good letch, were being played. He went out with gangs, never on solitary dates, their dances on disco floors communal affairs. He gyrated and air-guitared vigorously, one hand plucking the imaginary strings near his crotch, the other 'jamming' an imaginary fretboard when Mick Jagger, aggressive with passion, sung 'I Can Get No Satisfaction'. Tikky hoped to transmit Mick's message to any one of the girls in their dancing group, but all he could do, like Mick in the number, was 'try, try and try'.

When *Woodstock, the Movie* came to town, he went enthusiastically to watch it, hoping his luck would change. They had cut and chopped, edited and finessed the festival of peace, love and music, shrinking it into three hours of concentrated baby-boomer angst, the *voice* of the sixties, for all to hear and see. It was a resounding success. The queues were long, the cash registers rung and the young came in droves wherever the movie played – America, Canada, England, France – it was a worldwide hit, a benchmark for all concert movies, one of the most entertaining documentaries ever made. It did its rounds and, having run its course in the West, made its way to an India primed to experience, vicariously, bits and pieces of the Age of Aquarius celebrated in Woodstock, America.

Shiela Theatre, Paharganj, got the honours. It was India's first 70mm screen built with state-of-the-art American technology and the latest six-track sound system. The devotees came, dressed for the occasion – American Army surplus picked up cheap in Azad Market and Sadar Bazaar. Grey or blue jackets ending just above the knees with brass buttons embossed with martial motifs on plackets and pocket flaps, epaulettes braided with silver and gold threads – eagles, stars and stripes – worn over faded jeans now flared into gloriously exaggerated bell-bottoms, outseams ripped apart till the knee, inserted with triangular pieces cut from the American Flag. 'Make Love not War', 'Draft Beer not Boys', 'Eighteen today, DEAD tomorrow' – popular anti-war slogans printed on large, round plastic buttons were pinned onto chests, sleeves, lapels and plackets in sympathy for their brethren across the seven seas. Extremely hip bikers had converted their Jawas to look like the souped-up Harley's Captain America bikes in *Easy Rider*. As they rode into Shiela, their sawed-off exhausts made rich, booming noises announcing their arrival. Hell's Angels in Paharganj. The left was also present – pyjama-and-kurta-clad, with jhola across the shoulder to enjoy a bourgeois protest against an imperialist war. The charsis, too, arrived, having emptied out their Charminars and mixed the strong tobacco with the finest charas and ganja. And, of course, the middle-of-the-roaders, like Tikky and his gang of girls and boys. They all sat, waiting for the movie to begin.

The hall was packed, thick with smoke and the sweet smell of hashish. Richie Havens began his gummy 'Freedom', the rabid air guitarists in the audience plucking their imaginary fretboards, shaking their heads and tapping their feet with passion, feeling heady swatantrata, and when Joe Cocker air-guitared and hip-thrusted his way through 'With a Little Help from My Friends', the groovy and the stoned danced in the aisles. When Country Joe and the Fish belted out their 'Gimme an F, a U, a C and a K' and Shiela reverberated with 'FUCK, FUCK, FUCK, FUCK', Tikky felt the stirrings. He let his hand wander and placed it on the thighs of one of the girls in his gang, hoping for a little action, considering the charged atmosphere. All he got was a sharp stinging whack on his wrist.

'What the hell do you think you're doing?' she spat out.

'Don't you want . . .' he said pointing to the screen, hoping she would see the logic.

'Definitely NOT!'

'But I do,' Tikky said, mustering up a false bravado as he removed his hand.

Ardhnangi, half-naked bodies were jumping into ponds, kissing and fondling on the screen. 'Oh! Uninhibited America,' he sighed. Steady couples were holding hands, hugging, and those sure of their feelings but not bold enough to articulate them found the right moment to declare their affections and start their feeling, fooling, kissing-shissing right there in front of India's first 70mm screen. Crestfallen, limp, Tikky left the hall before Sly and the Family Stone took the crowd higher and a stoned Jimi Hendrix played his version of 'The Star-Spangled Banner'.

When he reached home he found a letter had arrived in his name. It had the stamp with the Statue of Liberty on it, the first glimpse of the New World when the immigrants arrived, and he saw the glimmer of a silver lining. Svet's photograph fell out when he opened the letter. She looked lovely, he thought – dark-blond hair, white skin with just a hint of charming freckles, bright blue eyes, dressed like the bohemian women he had seen on screen. He imagined her as a wild child of the sixties, passionate believer in free love and flower power – till he read her letter. The India she imagined was not the India he knew. Holy men? Finding yourself? Snake charmers? Elephants? Spirituality?

Khade lund pe dhoka, what a letdown for an erect penis, he thought, for the first time in the vernacular, hitting his forehead with an open palm. But at least he had a female American pen pal, and who knew what kismet had in store?

He wrote back to her about the India he inhabited – about his family, school, college, and his visit to temples only when the family insisted, his vision of America as the land of opportunity and his desire to visit the country. And just in case she thought he was not his type, he admired her for her quest for the higher life at such a young age, inviting her to be her guest when she came to India. He slipped in his photograph, where he was dressed in white trousers and black bandhgala, with a flowing pink saafa tied on his head, and stood framed by an arch, in flawless white marble, at the entrance to the main building in Mayo. He felt it gave him an impressive aura of royalty.

And so it did. She must have replied as soon as she got his letter, for he received a reply within the month. Her first line after *How are you?* was *Are you a Maharajah?* He smiled when he read that line, feeling the wonder in her every word. He preened, thanking the Eton of India, and when he replied he skirted the issue of her quest for spirituality, providing her instead with basic Hindi words and forms of address that would make her passage to India more convenient. She found it charming. And as time passed she began her letters with *Namaste* and *Kya haal hai*, and signing off with *Bahut pyaar*. He felt happy with his contribution to her Hindification, the *Bahut pyaar* bit in the end filling him with hope. The lingua franca, it seemed, did have its advantages.

I trust this letter finds you in the best of health and spirit, his letters always began, another bit of pithy advice passed on by Mahadev on behalf of luminaries like Sir Maurice Gwyer at the National Academy of Administration. A simple *How are you?* was too clichéd, too perfunctory and signified nothing; asking after health *and* spirit addressed the whole human condition. This was followed by paragraphs, each para dedicated to an event. A para by para, point by point letter. Para 1: personal; Para 2: general; Para 3: activities sort of thing; and the signing off with *Yours sincerely* and a signature with a flourish.

Svetlana's letters were less structured, like conversations written down while talking to a friend. Only, she always addressed him as

Tek Ram, never Tikky, robbing him, he felt, of a little 'hipness'. Still, he looked forward to her letters, charmed by her curiosity and her notions about India. *Gee whiz!*, she wrote when he told her that people drove cars and did not move around on elephants, horses and camels, taking care to mention that cows, buffaloes and other assorted animals roamed the streets, in an effort to keep an Incredible India alive in her head. *Far out!*, was her reaction when he confirmed that most marriages were arranged; *Gimme a break!*, when he wrote saying that they had permanent help to cook, clean and drive; *Awesome!*, when he told her in Para 1 that they went to a discotheque on a weekend.

What a wonderful thing is the letter, capable of conveying across continents the warm hand-clasp of friendship, he wrote. It was a quote he had committed to memory. Sentiment welled up inside her when she read it, happy that she had found a true Indian long-distance friend. She asked for the Hindi translation for 'I like you very much'. There was nothing like conveying her affections in his mother tongue, she believed. He wrote back, thrilled, using the more formal 'aap' – *Aap mujhe achhey lagte ho* – aching for the 'like' to transform to 'love', dreaming of the day when she would ask him to translate 'I love you'. He would then use the more informal 'tum' or 'tu', sealing their relationship with intimacy.

The family was in Delhi when his first-year results were declared. 'A bloody third division!' Mahadev spat out angrily, as always holding Jhelum responsible for doling out protection and misplaced ma ka pyaar, always contradicting him, shielding their ne'er-do-well firstborn from the 'harsh realities of life'.

Mahadev's collection of clichés, 'Well begun is half done but badly begun is disastrous', 'Life is not a bed of roses', 'Cricket will get you nowhere', and the clincher, 'Duffers like you will be better off as puncture repairmen at cycle shops in Daryaganj', filled Tikky with a deep sense of dread. America now beckoned him with an irresistible sense of destiny and he lived in horny hope, sure that one day the sweet and loving Svetlana would hold his hand with feeling and show him the way to the American dream. Academic stagnation, wrist-slapped at first attempt when hopeful of fornication – there was now promise only in migration.

And kismet! It was time for a transfer once again, the home state wanting its senior gladiator back, and this time the shift would have to be immediate. It was decided that the family would be back in Bhubaneswar while Tikky would stay in Delhi, in the St. Stephen's College Residence, and return home only for vacations. Tikky packed up his bags quickly and left to enjoy an extended period of relief.

'Thank god for the silver lining,' Tikky sighed.

But if dark clouds have silver linings, silver linings surround dark clouds. There, in the suburbs of New Jersey, Svetlana sat putting the finishing touches to her letter, licking the edges of the flap with the tip of her moistened tongue, sealing it securely and mailing it to Tikky's mailing address, his home in Delhi.

Thanksgiving is around the corner, and I look forward to the gathering of cousins, uncles and aunts and helping my mother in the kitchen. The table will be laden with food. The stuffed turkey and the pumpkin pie mandatory, but dotted with piroshkis, pickled herring and beef stroganoff, small but important reminders of our Russian heritage. Stolichnaya will be chilling in the freezer for days and everyone will raise toasts to good health, fortune and to America's bounty for giving us a life so much better than what our elders had left behind. But all through this I am dying to come to India and meet you.

Bahut pyaar, lots of love,

Svet

The middle of December, the beginning of the winter vacation, was the time for Tikky to get back home. Three weeks, without the wait for the dreaded examination results. The finals were some months away. Heartfelt, sincere promises to do better next time at the dining table did not cut much ice with Mahadev. 'The proof of the pudding shall be in the eating,' he would laconically say, but it did allow meals to pass without incident. All good for Tikky, for the food in Residence was even worse than what was served in Mayo. The porridge had the consistency of cement, the chicken and mutton gravies were watery apologies for curry. Cold boiled eggs, congealed fried eggs, omelettes thin and unappetizing, and toasted bread so mouldy that one had to use both hands to tear a piece. He would miss home at times like these and a week before his departure he telegraphed Jhelum his favourites menus. Fried brain on toast, lachcha parantha and ande ki bhurji for breakfast, palak gosht, arhar ki daal with the tadka of desi ghee, fried chicken and mashed potatoes, gobi–aloo cooked with a simple garnish of cumin, ginger, turmeric, green chillies and, always, the Vindaloo with crisp fried okra.

Fortunately for Tikky, Mahadev was on 'toor' when he arrived. 'Tooring', never touring, was officialese for travel, the '-oor' extended when Mahadev's minions spoke, as if to signify long journeys. 'Sahib is tooring,' they would say, extending their hand in the general direction of faraway places. Mahadev's absence allowed Tikky relaxed expressions of a hearty appetite as he wolfed down his telegraphed delicacies, storing their taste and aromas somewhere in the back of his mind as a source of sustenance when served the culinary nightmares that lay ahead in residence.

He had finished a memorable breakfast – spiced brain on toast, sprinkled with rice flour and deep fried, the bite of crispy rice flour giving way to the softness of brain, followed by the crunchiness of a deep-fried toast, Pakwaan surprising him by adding on a thick spicy curry of thinly sliced masaledar liver sautéed in onions, golden and soft, with crispy lachchedaar paranthas. He was savouring the lingering taste, leaning back in his chair, sipping the thick, creamy cold coffee, when the letter arrived.

RE-DIRECTED, the stamp on the letter officiously announced, from their Delhi address to the new address in Bhubaneswar. It was from Svetlana, and he pounced on it and tucked it away to enjoy it at leisure. In his room he read the letter, thrilled once again with her *Bahut pyaar*, imagining the promise of a budding romance fulfilled. He should have informed her of the change of address and wondered if she would visit him when she came to India if he was in Bhubaneswar. Not likely, he thought as he sat down to write his reply.

Dear Svetlana,

I hope that his letter finds you in the best of health and spirit. Please accept my apologies for not letting you know my change of address. Thank God I managed to get your letter here in our new home, considering the Indian Postal Service can be quite erratic. My addresses for the next two years (unless one of those surprising transfers comes through), are my present address if you write to me between mid-December and mid-January and between April and mid-July. For the rest of the year my address is my room number c/o St. Stephen's College. I am sure you must have enjoyed Thanksgiving – it is always a joy to have family around and I know what fun it is when all my cousins get together in my mother's ancestral home in Amritsar, one of the larger cities in the Punjab and home to the Golden Temple, the holiest shrine of the Sikhs – like the Vatican to the Catholics.

My father's transfer to Orissa took me by surprise. I wonder if you will visit me and stay with my family in Orissa. It will be a pity if we cannot spend any time together. Imagine, coming all the way to India and not being able to spend time with your pen pal. Spiritual journeys can be tough you know. Life in ashrams can be spartan – you will have to sleep on thin mattresses spread on hard stone floors. Life will begin before sunrise and you will have to join the others and help with the cooking, cleaning and all sorts of chores. At times like these one may miss the comforts of home, and, like your American soldiers in Vietnam who are sent to Bangkok and Manila for much-needed rest and recuperation, for you, Spiritual Warrior, our home is always open. Puri is only an hour away from our home and has unspoilt sandy beaches that make possible glorious tans. The sunsets at Konark are stunning . . . and thought of describing the titillating erotic sculpture in its temples but decided against it.

I look forward, as usual, to hearing from you and hosting you in our home when you visit India.

He debated between *Lots and lots of love* and *Yours sincerely*, settling for the latter in the end. He reinforced the envelope with some cellotape, making sure that the letter would reach Svetlana securely sealed. He mailed it on his way to the club and prayed, as they say in bureaucratese, for a positive reply.

It was around the middle of February, when Tikky, just back from the cricket nets, found the letter slipped under his door. As always there was an Aum written in Devanagari, before the letter began. Tikky admired the care she took in crafting the Aum so beautifully.

My dear Tek Ram,

How could you imagine that I would not visit you when I come to India? This Spiritual Warrior (loved your turn of phrase, it did make me laugh) respects friendship and you are my only Indian friend. Guess I could do with a little bit of

R&R, like our soldiers in Nam, and a tan would be welcome. Brown is the colour of envy amongst us Whites! Get a tan, be with a friend and enjoy his family's hospitality. Gee, what more could a girl ask for?

Bahut, bahut pyaar.

It was the first time she had used the word 'bahut' twice. His spirit soared, his heart leapt, his hopes lifted. There was full chance of romance with its perks thrown in, full chance of migrating after academically stagnating and then failing at fornicating!

It called for celebration and he pulled out his porn magazines from under his pillow. He had the choice of *Mast Ram* in Hindi, with its descriptions of 'phad phadate hue laudey', stiff and shivering hard-ons, and 'phudakte hue phuddi' or jumping and restless pussy. Or Ted Mark with his Angrezi descriptions of sex-stiff rods, warm honey pots, soft and luscious breasts, licking, sucking, moaning, groaning. Today, he chose Ted Mark and sat on the edge of the bed with an old issue of the *Times of India* newspaper spread on the floor. Book in right hand, dick in left, he began apna haath Jagannath, the good old-fashioned wank. 'Here I come America, the land of Coke and McDonald's, the creator of Betty Crocker, the master of illusions, bhagwans of moh and maya, here I come . . .' he muttered and spurted all over the dated headlines, INDIA OR INDIRA GLORIOUS!

He wrote her the next day, unable to conceal his excitement, the opening line altered, a reflection of his joy – *I hope this letter finds you sailing in the same boat of health and happiness as I am* – and his last line – *So looking forward to having you with us* – before signing off with *Lots and lots of love* without the slightest hesitation.

Incredible India

EASTER was around the corner and Svet was fasting happily with the family during Lent. She enjoyed helping her mother clean and tidy up the house, helping her in the kitchen, kneading dough for the sweet kulichi, enjoying the sensation of the squishy dough escaping though her fingers. She peeled the skin of red onions, wiping off the tears with the back of her hand and not really bothered by the smell. She threw the red onion skins into a large pot of water, along with whole eggs, and watched, fascinated, as the white shells soaked up the red of the onion skins as the water boiled. Like large red rubies, she thought to herself.

The family sat together, painting the eggs, each one announcing in good-natured banter that his or her eggs were the prettiest, but they all agreed that Svetlana's peace egg with little peace signs painted in bright yellows and blues all over the egg was the most beautiful and apt for these troubled times. Svetlana enjoyed the compliment, happy that she was back in touch with family traditions.

And in the wings, history hastened her departure to India.

America was losing the war in Nam, but peace with honour was the new mantra of a nation not willing to admit defeat.

'Vietnamization' was the catch phrase – handing back the country to the locals after America had made sure they had done their bit to plant the roots of democracy and freedom on receptive foreign soil, but not before carrying out some intensive bombing of Vietnam to shake up the 'little people' and get them to negotiate. The television screens lit up, once again, with the horrors of war, B-52s dropping their bombs with immaculate frequency, followed by images of destruction – bloodied faces, mangled remains, the awful violence and gore of a war – and suddenly Svetlana thought of Rob. The memory of her love for him, their days of passion in the bunker, his wasted life, her lost love hit her with such tragic intensity that she wept, huge, wracking, uncontrollable sobs, an outpouring of grief that had been bottled up inside her for ages.

'I just have to go to India,' she repeated dramatically between sobs and the family looked at each other, baffled by her sudden desire. A curve ball straight out of left field, Vlad thought, shrugging his shoulders.

'So be it,' they said collectively and Svet hugged them, grateful for their permission.

She was surprised by her sudden, spontaneous catharsis but it had brought with it a sense of relief. The day of her departure was significant – 29 March 1973, when the last of the American soldiers were brought back home, the successful culmination of an operation christened Operation Homecoming. It was a nice name, warm, sentimental, a nation welcoming back its heroic sons to generous bosoms.

But the timing of her arrival could not have been worse for Tikky. He would be studying hard for his final undergraduate year – yet another chance to measure up to his father's academic pedigree. They had exchanged letters before she confirmed the date of her arrival. Her last letter had been brief.

Not to worry about the timing. Much as I would have liked to see you the moment I arrived, it will have to wait now as I will do the Agra–Jaipur route after spending a few days in Delhi. Then onwards to Haridwar and Rishikesh, perhaps Banaras as well. I will come to Orissa sometime in the beginning of June when you say you will be back home for your summer vacation, for the much needed R&R due to a Spiritual Warrior.

Tikky's letters had prepared her, somewhat, for an India that was different from what she had imagined. The hands folded in a namaste as greeting, the 'Aap ka kya haal hain?', 'Bahut achha' and 'Dhanyavaad' – 'How are you?', 'Very well' and 'Thank you' – spoken with an American twang, thrilling the listener. All those within earshot would be amazed and grateful that a foreigner had taken the trouble to familiarize herself with their language. They smiled when she spoke this way, always generous with their help, confirming her impression of India as the land of warm hospitality.

But then, she was from the land of suburbia where crew-cut lawns ended an inch above concrete walkways, where dust hardly ever flew around even when the breeze was strong. Neat and orderly – sterile, you could say, with the intention of being derogatory if you enjoyed chaos and dirt. The furthest she had been from the 'burbs had been Woodstock, and now she was in India. She spent a week doing Delhi, seeing the Walled City, the Jama Masjid, Red Fort, walking the gullies of Chandni Chowk and Paharganj amazed by the crowds of people.

Cows, cowdung, scooters, cyclists, tongas, trucks, cars, pedestrians, piddlers, shitters, beggars, hijras, street urchins selling newspapers, pens, torches, books – all on the streets, a giant, colourful circus packed with life, the rites of a clichéd tourist passage assured. She had a severish case of the Delhi belly, had her money stolen, was whistled at by the roadside romeos who, mouths and lips tinted a deadly blood-red with paan, asked her if they could hold her hand and make her body 'tingal'. Taj Mahal took her breath away and for a brief, sentimental, romantic moment she wondered when she would meet her knight in shining armour, her Shah Jahan. India was so far more colourful, more chaotic, hotter, dustier, dirtier and, in the end, more fascinating than she had ever imagined. A must-visit, she would announce to her family and friends when she got back home. A once-in-a-lifetime experience.

She whizzed through Jaipur in a day, seeing the Amber Fort on elephant-back and sitting behind the jharokas of Hawa Mahal, feeling the cool breeze on her face, watching, as the ladies of the court must have more than a hundred and fifty years ago, life go by on the streets below.

Tikky waited eagerly for the day he would meet Svetlana. Shaved and shampooed, cologne splashed generously on his face, hair blow-dried to look bouncy, he sat on the lawns of St. Stephen's waiting for her. She wore tight white churidars and a long loose Lucknawi kurta over a slip. She had pulled her back into a ponytail and there was a large, round red bindi on her forehead. India had rubbed off on her rather quickly, he thought, smiling.

'You look beautiful,' he said as she came up to the bench, meaning every word. She hugged him, replying, 'You're not too bad yourself.' Arm in arm, they walked to the café, Tikky's heart singing with hope.

The air was thick with smoke and intellectualism and as Tikky walked to his table with Svetlana holding his arm, he took in, with pleasure that bordered on a sense of victory, the envious looks he got from the men discussing their Maos, Marxes and dialectical materialisms. Svetlana stared, fascinated by the crowd. Attractive women, some wearing simple khadi sarees, some in white pyjamas and colourful kurtas, eyes lined with kajal, foreheads dotted with bindis of all sorts of colours and shapes, some smoking beedis, others their cigarettes without filters; the men in either jeans or kurta-pyjamas with jholas strung across their shoulders, long-haired and short-haired, their faces serious with intellectual angst. She heard words like 'imperialism', 'Marxism', 'Leninism', 'Maoist' bandied about in pitch-perfect English, the mood way off left and definitely anti-American. We deserve it, she thought.

'What an exquisite monument to love the Taj Mahal is! You must be so proud of your culture and heritage, an elephant ride and a camel ride one moment, a cab ride or a scooter ride the next,' she gushed. She absolutely luhhuved India, its warm people always smiling despite their poverty, the standard, clichéd gush of the foreigner visiting India for the first time. But Tikky listened without interruption, fascinated by her excitement, dreaming only about the possibility of a hot, intense romance.

When they said their farewells, she kissed him on the cheek, Tikky sure that in the fullness of time, their love would blossom and they would make a great future for themselves in the land of the free and the home of the brave.

Nirvana Ahoy!

RISHI or sage, kesh or hair. Rishikesh, hair of the sage, the city where souls, hungover after the mindless pursuit of materialism came for a whiff of freshness and solace from their confusions.

'Here your soul will bathe in the sacred energies emanating from nature and the forces that have lingered timelessly from the healing power of saints and holy men,' the plaque at the entrance to Swarg Ashram read.

Baba Bhola Bachcha was the ashram's spiritual head. A large black-and-white photograph, with the Baba looking straight at the camera, his face and eyes glowing with concern, hung on a wall.

'Welcome to swaarrg,' Ma Radha gurgled, her eyes half closed, lovingly stretching the word 'swarg'. She introduced herself as having been at the ashram for two glorious years, a shining example of the before and after. An American, like Svet, hers was a dukhbhari kahani that had blossomed into one of hope and happiness. She came to the ashram as Rolanda Smith, one of Timothy Leary's confused and drug-crazed children, but had battled her demons with the simple life at the ashram with Baba Bhola Bachcha showing her the way, christening her Radha, the playful Lord Krishna's favourite gopi.

'Impish, innocent, mischievous like a child, my Baba is,' she said stressing on 'my' possessively, placing her hand on an ample bosom, 'but so full of wisdom, always radiating love, peace and happiness around him.' The Baba was away on a spiritual world tour, Ma Radha informed Svet, her voice thick with admiration and awe. 'I miss him only in the physical sense but I can feel his good vibrations at all times,' she gushed happily. Firangi Das Ramka's and Ma Radha's experiences of finding a goo-rooh were so similar, almost exact, in fact, Svetlana thought, marvelling at the coincidence, convinced that Swarg Ashram and the Baba would show her the way.

The next morning onwards Svet woke before sunrise and walked to the banks of the river, where she watched the rising sun, its gentle rays bathing her soul with warmth and peace. She sat by the banks of the Ganga in the lotus pose, her familiarity with yoga evident, the heels of her feet resting effortlessly on her thighs. Her breathing started from her stomach, moving upwards, filling her chest, gradually extending her shoulders. Her surya namaskars were rhythmic, her body moving smoothly through the entire asana. She was thrilled by the authenticity of it all – right here in the lap of the Himalayas, by the banks of the holy Mother Ganges in the land where yoga started. This was as real as it could get.

The Indians in Swarg, and there were many, were an older lot – 'fifty plus', most would say when asked their age. They had religiously followed the advice of the ancient Hindu sages. From the time they were born till they turned twenty-five, they observed brahmacharya, the life of the celibate student, controlling pulsating libidos, sharpening their life-skills to successfully enter grihasta, or family life, which allowed them to express their pent-up libidinal urges while fulfilling their responsibilities as householders. Sons settled, daughters married, they were now in Swarg Ashram living out the third stage, the vanaprastha or the hermit in retreat, during which they would think of God and prepare themselves for the final frontier – the wandering recluse, or the sanyasi, who would see Narayan or God in every man.

They spoke heavily accented English, swallowing their vowels, mixing up their As and Es. They 'sported' good ideas, loved to eat 'epples' and 'bnanas' because they were good for health, and reminisced about 'alephant' rides with their family when they were in householder mode. Wallets were purses or moneybags, toilets were latreens or sundaases. Have you done your latreen/sundaas today, was a standard plaintive whisper from those obsessed by but deprived of a good bowel movement the first thing in the morning.

Latreen/sundaas, the one place Svet felt India could have made a minor concession to authenticity. Sun-daas resonated dangerously in her mind with 'stunned arse' as she walked towards the toilets set at a distance from the main ashram. They were large key-hole shaped porcelain pots embedded in the floor, with foot-shaped blocks on either side. One squatted instead of sitting, and washed instead of wiping. Arse-wiping was discouraged. There was always the danger of soft paper fluff being stuck to your bum if one wiped vigorously, besides feeling an uncomfortable dryness between the cheeks throughout the day.

Thus spoke Kailash Chand, or Kaycee, as he called himself because that's the way he liked his name. He was Svet's age, in the brahmachari stage, too young to be in Swarg, if one believed in tradition, an oddity amongst the rest of the locals. Public-school educated, independently wealthy enough to keep away from the awful rat race that celebrated those who had 'arrived'. 'Arriving', with its attendant accoutrements – the high-status job with fat salary and chauffeur-driven car – was just too commonplace, like a matrimonial advertisement in the *Hindustan Times*. Like Svet, he had done his 'thing', indulging vicariously in the protests of the sixties, hitting the Kathmandu trail, smoking dope, dropping acid, sucking on chillums stuffed with the freshest hash picked from cannabis plants that grew wild in Manali. But there came a time when he realized he had overdone 'living life by instinct' and wandered into Swarg, where he found solace in yoga.

The fifty-plusses treated him with disdain. 'Bluddy rich-man's buoy, just wasting father's money, eediot,' they would mutter amongst themselves and send up silent prayers thanking Bhagwaan that their children had not turned out like him.

Kaycee was aware of the vicious bitching but he understood their disgust – they had struggled through their lives, the lot of the middle classes – and he thanked god that he had never belonged there. He kept his distance from the self-righteous, enjoying the snobbery of it all. 'Remember, Gautam was a prince before he became the Buddha,' he would say to them, sure that it would wind them up.

Sewa or service was Swarg's leitmotif, right up there in the heavens, so to speak, in the spiritual scheme of things. 'It is sewa that accelerates the dedication of a seeker and lights the path to God' – the Baba's quote was stencilled neatly in Sanskrit, Hindi and English in the common prayer hall, above doors and entrances, and on walls for all to see. Svet was most enthusiastic, squatting on her haunches, made easier with practice at the sandaas, wiping the floors with pochhas dipped in soap solutions, making sure they shone. She polished the woodwork with vigour, cleaned the brass bells with brasso, so that they gleamed golden in the light.

With her smattering of Hindi learnt from Tikky she was the darling of the fifty-plusses, who spoke in awe of her capacity for sewa. 'Bahut paseena bahaya hai bitiya ne,' they would say affectionately, the pouring of sweat a metaphor for hard work. She was touched that they called her 'bitiya', daughter, and was delighted yet again by the warmth of India. And they were equally taken by her fair skin. Fairness was beauty, and Svet was fair and therefore a beauty, or haseena. 'Ma Paseena Haseena,' they would say with genuine admiration as she walked past them, truly the sweating beauty, with a bucketful of water, pochha and broom in hand. She would blush happily at the compliment.

Kaycee enjoyed the solitude and calm of Swarg, doing his bit of sewa without the passion that Svet displayed. He was dedicated to yoga and mastering the asanas, treating it as a form of physical exercise and *not* a means to achieve moksha or approaching a divine force. All this moksha-voksha, dissolving into the divine, was too esoteric for him. Yoga had eased his restlessness, but not enough to welcome set routines. Yoga was 'happening' in the West and it was just a matter of time before it would 'happen' in India. Some day, he was sure, he would be teaching it in his motherland or, if he was lucky, abroad. 'And who can say, for strange are the ways of the world. I could find my pretty little yogini along the way and experience the bliss of grihasta,' Kaycee laughingly told Svetlana.

Kaycee gave Svet what he felt was good advice. He was grateful to Swarg for all it had done for him, he said, but found the paraphernalia of spirituality a bit overdone, almost melodramatic. The constant competitive, cloying attitude of the Ma Radhas, Laxmis, Pujas, the Sant Bhagwan Dases, the Sant Rams, mainly the foreign crowd – she clenched her teeth when she heard this, he sounded so facetious – was like a spiritual circus, with everyone clamouring to be the star disciple. And the spiritual leader, Baba Bhola Bachcha was nowhere close to being blessed with the innocence of a child. See the way Ma Radha gushes on about him, Kaycee said conspiratorially. During the day they are guru and disciple, an elder brother caring and guiding the young sister, but at night God only knows. 'Din ko behen–bhai aur raat ko charpai,' he muttered, smiling wickedly at Svet's uncomprehending frown. It was impossible to get the lilt in English, but 'Brother and sister during the day, and in the night they roll in the hay,' was a good enough translation he thought.

As fond as she was of Kaycee, Svet refused to hear anything against the Baba. She had mastered her mantras, devoutly served and cleaned, learnt with precision the art of yogic breathing and could do twenty sets of surya namaskars without breaking into a sweat. She was sure that news of her devotion would reach the Baba's holy ears and she waited eagerly for the Baba to appear in flesh and blood and light up her path to God.

Swarg looked fresher, more heavenly, when they heard the news of Baba's arrival. Floors sparkled, bells gleamed, Ma Radha was more ecstatic than usual. 'You wait and see,' she said to Svet and anybody else willing to listen, 'the ashram will hum with good spiritual vibrations, better energies, and a collective enlightenment around every corner.'

The weather turned for the worse a few days before the Baba's arrival. Rain fell constantly, Rishikesh became slushy, the blue waters of Mother Ganga turned brown and muddy. The days were dark and a heavy grey, depressing to say the least for the welcome of a spiritual leader returning from international spiritual sojourns. The Ashram prayed for better weather and a day before his arrival the heavens heard Swarg's collective request. The skies cleared, the sun shone brightly, the waters of the Ganga transformed from a muddy brown to the original sparkling blue, nature making way for the devout and the faithful, rolling out its welcome for the Baba's return.

The Baba arrived the next day, arms raised in triumph, his face aglow with victory, new foreign devotees in tow as proof.

'Your new friends,' he said, and began the introductions to his flock assembled for his welcome.

'Ma Akash, for her heart is as large as the skies,' he said pointing to the lady with ample breasts to his left. She blushed, bowing her head and doing her namaste.

'Ma Sitara, for her soul twinkles as brightly as the stars in the sky,' he said, indicating the one closest to him, who smiled at the Baba with warmth and familiarity. Svetlana glanced at Ma Radha looking jealously at the newcomer.

'Sant and Ma Shanti,' the Baba announced, showing the couple to his right, 'husband and wife who have finally found peace with themselves.' The whispers that went from ear to desi ear praising the Baba's ability to so easily convert White people became louder and louder. The hall hummed with admiring whispers at the Baba's amazing powers, the Baba finally raising his hands, requesting silence, his flock now ready to welcome him.

The welcome was hierarchical. The inner coterie came forward first – Ma Radha, Ma Laxmi and Ma Puja went up to him, touching his feet, the Baba placing his hands on their heads and blessing them, after which they stood by Ma Akash and Ma Sitara. The men followed, Sant Bhagwan Das, Sant Ram, doing the same and then standing by Sant and Ma Shanti to the Baba's right. The elders came next, some actually touching his feet and others, either because of bad backs or squeamish at the thought of touching the feet of someone so much younger, just going through the motions. Right shoulder dropping, the right hand reaching a little below the Baba's knee, the Baba's hand at a height, making adjustments for the feet toucher, always in the air, never touching their heads but his blessing understood. Thus aerially blessed, they went to their earlier positions, distance between the laity and the devout accepted. The newcomers in the ashram, like Svet, were the last to welcome the Baba, giving Svet time to observe the correctness of procedure. The touching-the-feet bit was strange, but she saw it as an exercise in taming the ego, a step in the right direction to light up her path to God.

Finally, it was her turn. She walked up, her eyes lowered, bent down and touched his feet, straightening up to look at him. Ma Radha walked past Ma Sitara and whispered in the Baba's ear, 'We call her Ma Paseena Haseena.' The Baba threw back his long black curly hair and laughed – full-throated, spontaneous, uninhibited. 'What a lovely name,' he said, looking at Svet with delight and placing his hand on her head, blessing her. 'May you live long,' he said piously, his hand moving from her head, resting on her cheek for a moment then sliding down her neck and along her arm. He held her arm, squeezing it ever so lightly. Echoes of Kaycee's 'behen–bhai–charpai' flashed through Svet's mind as Ma Radha shot her a jealous, dangerous look.

The word of Baba's arrival spread quickly through Rishikesh. Swarg's Sadhana Kutir, or the house of spiritual practices, was packed with foreigners, tourists and even acolytes from other ashrams, eager and expectant to receive Baba's gyan. Rows of men on one side, rows of women on the other, a broad enough passage in the middle to allow four people to walk abreast on to an elevated stage set up with microphones, a harmonium and a tanpura. The Baba arrived, his inner coterie on either side, their palms joined in greeting, heads and joined palms graciously moving left and right, acknowledging the presence of the assembled audience.

The Baba sat in the centre of the stage, flanked by Ma Radha on the harmonium on his left, Ma Puja with tanpura on his right. The rest of them sat behind the three in no particular order.

'We will begin with chanting and meditation, and please remember that for meditation what you need is not dollars, not eggs, or sweets, or chocolates, or cakes. What you need is strength, this solid' – and he clenched both his fists – 'seminal vigour.

Therefore I insist on total celibacy as long as you are staying at the ashram.'

Kaycee was so wrong about the Baba, thought Svetlana, rebuking herself for her doubts at the welcome. He was a truly pious being.

'We will begin the day with a chant to the great and powerful Lord Shiva, so full of glorious energy. Lord Shiva, the destroyer *and* the transformer of the world, from whose locks of hair the holy Mother Ganga flows, and by her banks our Swarg flourishes. Close your eyes,' he drawled into the mike in a slow, thick, loaded voice. 'Let the mantra seep into your mind. *Hear* the words, rid your mind of all thoughts, focus on *nothingness* and imagine a peaceful void. *Feel* the spiritual vibrations of AUM NAMA SHIVAYA.'

The Baba nodded at Ma Radha, the signal for the chanting to begin. Ma Radha pumped the bellows of the harmonium with one hand, the other flitting across the keys, Ma Puja plucking at the tanpura to set up the structure for the chant. Pitch set, structure outlined, the two Mas filled their lungs with air, opened their mouths and, from the bottom of their throats began with the first sound of Aum, stretching it from a silent whisper to an audible hum, moving on to 'Nama' and 'Shivaya' in the same style – AAUUMM, NAMAA, SHIVAAYAA'. This was repeated by the Mas for what seemed like a long time, with the Baba joining in once in a while to lend the chant more spiritual weight. Swarg's Sadhana Kutir buzzed with heavenly energy, most people closing their eyes, Svet included, soaking in the atmosphere of spiritual devotion. Finally, the chant wound down, the last SHIVAAAYAAA elongated more than usual, the sound from the harmonium and the tanpura became softer, tapering into silence. The Baba looked at his assembled flock, now primed to receive spiritual gyan.

'The greatest gift from the Almighty,' he began, 'is the gift of life. Unfortunately, in most humans it lies there placid, indifferent to its true potential. There are some who stamp their greatness on the pages of history, but as time flies and ages pass they fall off its pages, forgotten. But the truly enlightened defy time and continue to shine through eternity. These are the men who have dedicated their lives to the search of divine truth and have found it by awakening the power of their kundalini.' He paused, repeating the word, breaking it into two syllables, stretching each for effect. 'Kundaah-leeni. Remember this word, *burn* it into your mind, *work* towards its full activation and experience its divine joy.

'Just as the week has seven days, the human body has seven chakras or spinal centres, each chakra possessing amazing powers waiting to be released on the activation of your kundalini. At the base of the spinal column is the muladhar chakra, the resting place of kundalini shakti, which lies coiled like a snake with three-and-a-half coils. In meditation, this is visualized as a four-petalled blood-red lotus. Activation of the kundalini at the muladhar results in true happiness, beauty, perfect health, physical strength and a magnetic persona. This chakra lies right in the mid-spot between the anus and the penis or vagina, depending on your gender.' He looked at the female section of the crowd as he said this, smiling fondly. Some bowed their heads, avoiding his gaze and hiding their blushes. Svet looked straight at him, rapt. As his gaze flitted across the gathering of women he made sure that his eyes held Svet's for a moment. He nodded his head to acknowledge such focused dedication.

But Svet's thoughts were elsewhere. Instinctively, her head for numbers had worked out the logic of it all. The three-and-a-half coiled snake, precisely half of seven, a half-a-coil release per chakra starting at her blood-red petalled first chakra or the moolah-dar, she thought to herself. Simple when you broke it up into small half-a-coil by half-a-coil stage releases of the kundalini.

'Ordinary mortals,' the Baba carried on, 'would be happy with the release of their muladhars – after all, happiness, beauty and life without tensions are achievements not to be scoffed at. But the true seeker will strive to uncoil his kundalini, half-coil by half-coil.'

Svetlana was thrilled at the possibility that they may be spiritually connected, for the Baba thought just as she did.

'From the muladhar to the swadisthan, to the manipur, to the anahat, to the visuddha to the ajna,' the Baba continued grandly, indicating the spots with graceful movements of his hands. 'The ajna,' he repeated, pausing, his eyes looking over the heads of the devotees past the banks of the Ganga and beyond, 'is located opposite the mid-spot between the two eyebrows, the teesri aankh, or the third eye. And when kundalini unites with ajna, the third eye will open and give the seeker wondrous powers. The seeker will become clairvoyant, gain telepathic powers, have the power to curse or bless, allowing the seeker to even interfere with nature.'

He sipped water from a glass, looking at his gathering. He was sure he had had the desired effect. A hushed admiring silence had descended upon his flock as they waited for him to explain the miraculous effects of the uncoiling of the last half-coil.

His voice was now low, thick with the promise of the fabulous, as he said, placing his finger between his eyes, 'From the ajna, the kundalini shakti will unite with and rest at the sahastrar located in the subtle centre in the middle of the brain.'

'Ah! The sahastrar!' he loudly proclaimed. 'That thousand-petalled lotus, the abode of the most powerful and important Lord Shiva, will open and welcome the Kundalini to its final resting place. With the activation of sahastrar, in keeping with the Shiva lingam tradition,' he said smiling mischievously, 'a fine elixir-like secretion will flow forth, permeating the entire body, making it free of all ailments, and the seeker will experience permanent and infinite bliss, be finally emancipated from the painful cycle of life and death, achieving the final beatitude.'

An appreciative murmur waffled through Sadhana Kutir, some getting up to leave thinking it was the end of the lecture. But the Baba had not finished. He raised his arms, motioning to the restless to sit down.

'Full activation of the kundalini,' he continued, 'is a joyous journey never to be undertaken alone but always under the guidance of a competent guru. Understand that when the process of activation starts, there is a gush of negative and positive energy that can attack the seeker's weaknesses, like anger, jealousy and ego. Sometimes this churning can be so intense that the person can lose his mental balance. I have had to attend to aspirants who began to vomit blood and only through right guidance were they saved from terrible fates. Blessed are those who find their divine guru, the one who can lead them lovingly down the correct path, protecting them from evil, and I am there for all who seek this.'

Finished with his sermon, he rose to leave. The crowd, too, were on their feet and parted reverentially, allowing him and his entourage generous passage. Svetlana stood there transfixed, happy and grateful that she had chosen to come to Swarg. She felt the beginnings of divinity twitching expectantly between her legs, at her moolah-dar, waiting for divine guru, Baba Bhola Bachcha's spiritual titillation, that would open the doors, show her the way to nirvana.

Sadhana Kutir was the Diwan-e-Aam, where the masses gathered to receive gyan from the guru. Atma Nidhi, the House of the Treasure of the Self, was the Diwan-e-Khaas, for the khaas, or the special. It was attached to the Baba's quarters, a step up in the spiritual hierarchy, where the Baba was available for a spiritual one-on-one to guide the devout, pointing them in the right direction. No appointments were necessary, meetings were strictly on a first-come-first-served basis from sunrise till ten in the morning and again from sunset till dinner. Svetlana, obsessed with getting her kundalini released from her moolah-dar, was eager to be the first to knock on the doors.

She slept fitfully that night, her dreams full of snakes with three-and-a-half coils uncoiling, making their way till the moolah-dar and upto the ajna, but slithering down to visuddha, anahat, manipur, all the way down to the original resting place – like a disappointing game of snakes and ladders. But she managed to rise early and rush to the banks of the river and, as the sun rose, perform her salutations – twenty sets of rhythmic surya namaskars. She felt her body open up, its stiffness slowly seeping away. Her arms glistened with the hint of perspiration, her face flushed with the rush of blood. Ma Paseena Haseena was now ready to be the first for a spiritual one-on-one.

The Baba, too, had woken early, readying himself for the desperately devout, his preparations studied, ceremonial, a celebration of his devotion to the great Lord Shiva, the most important, according to him, of the triumvirate.

'Jai Bhole Nath,' he intoned three times, thankful for the new day and, after his ablutions, applied the paste of multani mitti and keora on his forehead, face and neck, enjoying the taut stretching of his skin as the face-mask hardened when it dried. He bathed, scrubbing himself energetically, washing off the last bits of the grit of the multani mitti and looked into the mirror. He was happy with what he saw – his eyes shone, his face glowed gloriously, reinforcing his aura. Dressed in a crisp white dhoti, torso clothed in nothing but his janayu and a three-stringed mala of the largest rudraksha beads about his neck, a bottle of the purest sandalwood oil in his hand, he entered Atma Nidhi.

There, in the centre of the room, lay the Shiva ling, comfortably embedded in the yoni. Ling and yoni, yin and yang, male female coupling – symbol of the most divine creative energy, waiting for his devout and daily attention. He lit a bunch of incense sticks, waited for the fire to catch and then in one powerful exhalation blew out the flames. The lit ends glowed a dull orange-red, smoke curling out from the tips.

'Aum Nama Shivaya, Aum Nama Shivaya,' he chanted as he walked around the ling once, placing the lit incense at the yoni. In between his chanting, he poured cold Ganga-jal on to the ling from a brass jug whose spout was the shape of a bull's head, Nandi the bull to be precise, the mount of Lord Shiva. 'Aum Nama Shivaya, Aum Nama Shivaya,' he hummed, pouring the oil on the ling, watching it slide down the sides. Thus bathed, the ling glistened magnificently and Baba finished off his devotion by showering rose petals on the Shiva ling – a caress after a bath. From the time he lit the incense sticks till the showering of the petals, he chanted 'Aum Nama Shivaya', his ritual perfectly timed so that he chanted the mantra exactly one hundred and eight times – nine times for the planets that moved through the twelve astrological houses, nine times for each astrological sign to diminish bad vibrations and enhance the good ones, a cosmic prayer to improve the condition of the universe.

The clichéd fingers of a rosy dawn crept up in the sky, but before sunrise would announce the opening of the doors of Atma Nidhi, Baba Bhola Bachcha had time to reminisce. He thought, amazed, about his success, especially in foreign lands. His lectures on sewa, detachment and the general search for spiritualism went down well, but the response to his kundalini lectures were always spectacular, especially amongst the women. Flower power, free love, the general indulgence in the pleasures of the flesh because India was the spiritual flavour of the season, made kundalini fit right in. The muladhar chakra, the base of all kundalini activation, was suggestively placed. The chanting of 'Aum Nama Shivaya' was the start of the uncoiling of the kundalini snake, but foreign devotees seemed to be in a rush. Chanting was too slow and they sought direct intervention from the guru, the spiritual fuck, for quicker results, and he happily obliged. He smiled at the memories of his muladhar kindlings.

It was his mentor, the great guru Falaudi Fauji Baba or the strong-as-iron armyman baba, a worshipper of Lord Shiva, who had shown him the way. He smiled when he thought of Falaudi Fauji Baba and recalled with much affection the memories of his guru telling him the story of the Shiva ling drawn from ancient texts, the guru's version sung in a lilting rhyme full of fun and mischief, the words fresh in his mind. Falaudi Fauji Baba would rub his hands gleefully, chortle wickedly and begin,

'O all you Shiv bhakts, let me sing you a gaana,
A legend from the very old Shiv Purana.
It has a lilt, it has a rhyme,
This story from the most ancient of time.
In the dense and virgin forests of Daruk, pristine for many ages,
There were some women who were single and some married to holy sages.
They prayed to the great Lord Shiva, with devotion without dearth,
So our Lord came to test them and descended on Mother Earth.
He had ash smeared on his body and wore not a thing,
And stood there in the centre wickedly holding his ling.
Some women swooned in fright, but others with him they played,
And when the sages saw this their tempers were terribly frayed.
"Chhee chhee chhee chhee," they said, "this is such a paap,"
So they all got together and gave him a deadly shraap.

They cursed him with so much venom that his ling just fell to
the ground,
And after did this happen there was mayhem all around.
The ling bounced all over the Universe in one mighty rage,
Burning everything it touched, confounding the holiest sage.
"Forgive us! Forgive us!" The sages cried, "Hum ko karo
kshama,"
As they sought the august audience of the one and only Bramha.
Bramha heard them patiently and this is the advice he gave –
Advice they would remember till they all went to their grave.
"You maybe the holiest of the holy but what you have done is
very odd,
He came as a guest to your ashram and a guest must be treated
like God.
You're lucky I know his wife well enough to call her Paro,
So listen to me carefully and you won't have to worry, yaaron.
Pray to the goddess Parvati with devotion and great grace,
And the troubled ling will very surely find its resting place."
When this was done, all was well, no doubt with some loss of face,
The troubled ling finally found its rightful resting place.
Wisely Brahma told them to never curse in careless haste,
And to drench the ling with water, flowers and pure chandan
paste.
Remember this, remember this – it's a fixed and steady rule,
For this is the only way the ling will forever be cool.'

Faulada Fauji Baba would laugh when he finished reciting, his chelas joining in, enjoying the lilting legend, marvelling at the power of the ling and the placement of the starting chakra, so suggestive, so libidinal, so sexual. Baba Bhola Bachcha chuckled at the memory. He had announced celibacy as a virtue in the ashram but his living quarters and Atma Nidhi were the exception.

The sun was up, its rays filtering through the windows, lighting up one side of the already glistening Shiva ling. He was sure Ma Paseena Haseena would be the first to arrive. He had seen the look of complete rapture on her face and knew that the kundalini obsession had taken hold. Ma Radha was becoming tiresome, cloying, too sweet and syrupy, and too devoted. Paseena Haseena would be a refreshing change.

'Come in my Paseena Haseena,' he said laughingly when he heard the knock on the door.

Svetlana stepped in, amazed that he had known it would be her.

'My third eye sees all,' he said with authority, placing his thumb between his eyebrows, and Svetlana felt the half-coil at her moolah-dar fluttering, all ready for kundalini ignition. The soft light of the sunrise filtered through her gauzy slip dress worn over a sporty boob tube and leotards, outlining a young firm body – long legs with just the right hint of muscle, hips that gently flared from a slender waist. It was the first time that he really looked at her, a bottom-up gaze, his eyes resting briefly on round, fleshy breasts. Garmagaram maal, is what he would have called her in his Lotharian and horny pre-spiritual days, 'hotshot goods' not quite encapsulating the lecherous flavour of the expression in the vernacular. His muladhaar, too, felt the libidinal pull, desparately desiring direct divine intervention, but he reminded himself that meditation and chanting was phase one of the journey.

He sat in padmasana, the lotus pose, motioning her to sit opposite him. She took off her slip and sat, her boob tube and her leotard like a sensuous, shining second skin, slashed by a firm white stomach and a white slender waist, much younger and fresher than his old faithful, Ma Radha's. He was impressed with the ease with which she placed her feet on her thighs, her back erect, breasts thrust out as she sat in padmasana without the slightest hint of strain. And more flexible, too, the Baba thought, salivating at the possibilities.

'We shall begin by chanting "Aum Namo Shivaya", a prayer to Lord Shiva, who resides in the sahastrar. Focus on the Lord as you chant, your thoughts still, not restless like a monkey.'

Svetlana closed her eyes and they began chanting. The Baba watched the rise and fall of her stomach and the heaving of her breasts as she inhaled fully and exhaled completely in perfect rhythm with her chanting, his ling, like Shiva's in the legend, hotting up imagining the coupling, he shoving between his Shivayas, she moaning between her Aums. No longer able to resist, he grabbed her by her shoulders and tried to force her down pulling at her leotard.

Scared, frightened, she screamed, kicking him in the genitals, right there in the front of the mid-spot between the anus and the penis, where his muladhar lay. 'Lecherous fucking con artist,' she spat out, kicking him once again, thoughfully this time, on his fleshy arse, and put on her slip, all set to leave.

'I am only human, Paseena Haseena,' he bleated pathetically, as he massaged his balls to ease the pain, wondering how easily he was allowed his direct intervention on his foreign tours. What was it about Bharat, he wondered moaning in pain, that even the phoren maal, bilkul garmagaram, became so virtuous when they visited here?

'Yeah, right, only human,' Svetlana shouted as she marched out, slamming the door behind her.

Ma Radha was at the entrance, expectant and hopeful, awaiting her turn.

'Forget about your bloody moolah-dar, dear, all you are getting is fucked,' Svetlana said firmly and stormed off to her quarters, leaving behind a baffled Ma Radha.

Like Woodstock, her search for nirvana had been a bummer.

Banaras, Varanasi, Kashi, that most ancient of ancient cities, older than history itself, sinking below the earth when measured on the scale of holiness with Swarg on the other side, would be a given a miss. She left Swarg quietly, taking the first bus out of Rishikesh, an old and rickety trundler packed with people, groaning its tired way to Delhi, seemingly hitting every pothole on the road. Travel-sick people puked noisily with their heads stuck out of the windows splattering the sides of the bus with freshly digested rice, daal, veggies and rotis, the smell of sweat and grime getting worse as the bus hit the plains burning in the heat of June. People stared at Svetlana, and when she met their gaze they smiled. It irritated her now, this constant display of happiness and warmth.

BOOK III

Vindaloo Dreams

DELHI–Howrah, Howrah–Bhubaneswar. Two days and two nights of travelling time for a little over 1000 miles. New York to Chicago was a much longer distance and Amtrak would have taken half the time. The journey seemed to take forever – time for Svet to reminisce and compare.

Her grand, romantic, spiritual view of India lay shattered. The crowds, colour and chaos that were once an affirmation of a 'real' sort of life, was now chaos and nothing else. The crowded compartments of the train were filthy. Grit stuck to her body like a thick, scaly second skin. The stinking toilets, people sleeping in the corridors indifferent to the dirt and filth, the odours from bodies a strange, disgusting mix of mustard oil and the smell of burnt, gritty coal, mothers hurriedly carrying their children when the trains stopped at stations and sang their 'soo-soo's, happily watching them piss on the platforms – all of it got to her now.

She missed the orderliness, the cleanliness of America, her space not hemmed in with so many people. She realized she envied her parents' life – solid, predictable, her father the provider, her mother the homemaker, unmoved by passions, content with carrying on with the business of life. Her life of a seeker had come to nought. One big zero, she thought, consumed by self-pity and loathing. Yet she could not help but count her blessings. She had not succumbed to the Baba's lecherous intentions and had quite enjoyed the kick to his balls – the bastard deserved it. Whatever happens happens for the best, she convinced herself, and by the time she reached Bhubaneswar she had put her demons to bed. Her spirits were high, her attitude positive, the timing of her arrival auspicious.

With Mahadev on tour, his household was relaxed. Jhelum, the gracious hostess who believed that a house was as blessed as the number of guests that visited it, looked forward to making Svetlana's stay in her home memorable in every way. All signs, as the soothsayers would say, for kismet to bestow its bounties.

Tikky was at the station to receive her, the memory of the peck on his cheek allowing him the comfort of the grand gesture. 'Welcome, great Spiritual Warrior, welcome to humble Bhubaneswar,' he bowed grandly as she stepped off the train and hugged her. She smelt of the Indian Railways, coal mixed with dirt, topped with the lingering smell of aloo-puri, paranthas and achaar.

'The first thing this warrior needs is a shower,' she said, reading his mind.

'And so it shall be,' he said.

Jhelum was out on the veranda drinking her morning cup of tea when they arrived and, after Tikky was done with the introductions, insisted that Svetlana join her for a cup before moving to her room to freshen up for breakfast. The tea rejuvenated Svet, its flavour surprising her – two parts Lipton Green Label leaf tea, one part Brooke Bond Red tea dust for colour, laced with cardamom for that welcome hint of spice.

When she stood under the shower enjoying the waters flow, thick and generous, she realized how much she missed the simple pleasures she had always taken for granted. It was the first time she had taken a shower since her arrival. Swarg had no showers and the showers in the seedy hotels she had stayed in had been ridiculous apologies – stringy little streams that could take forever to wet your body. The bucket bath had been the only option – bending low, filling the mug, standing up, pouring from head to toe. Squatting was an option, popular amongst the locals to avoid this workout of sorts but by the end of it she had had enough of sitting on her haunches on the sundaas. Ah! The pleasure of sitting on the washing closet! 'Going to latreen', as the fifty-pluses in Swarg used to say, always sounded to her purposeful, focused, like going to war, apt for the sundaas; 'visiting' was so much more relaxed, perfect for the WC, she thought. There was toilet paper as well, but she had proudly switched from wiping to washing, something that would serve her well as time passed. The towel was soft and fluffy, not rough and threadbare; the soap creamy and aromatic, not carbolic like in the rest of the places. First, tea served in bone china, and now this – the simple pleasures, the comforts of civilization!

And if the bathroom welcomed her back to civilization, the dining table at breakfast was a salute to America. Warm pancakes, like the ones at home, topped with honey, with thin, caramelized slices of kadauli, that little Oriya banana, one-tenth the size of the chiquita but so many times more flavourful, followed by scrambled eggs, the egg, milk and butter cooked to perfection, firm yet soft. Jhelum coaxed her to eat more of everything till Svet covered her plate with her hands to convince Jhelum that she was truly sated. Nevertheless, she could hardly resist the mangoes that were served to finish off the breakfast – bainganphali from Puri, known for its sweetness and flavour. She covered her mouth with her hands to stifle a burp, leaned across the table and gratefully squeezed Jhelum's arm.

'So nice of you to have me,' she warmly said, looking first at Jhelum and then around the table.

'You must come more often, we are having pancakes for breakfast after ages,' Gauri wickedly acknowledged.

'Always complaining, these children,' Jhelum said in playful banter. The table laughed.

Lunch was even closer to America than breakfast, Jhelum on a mission to bring her home to Svetlana. Fried chicken that would have done the Colonel proud, shaked and baked, evenly coated with flour, salt and pepper, with a hint of chilli flakes appearing as dashes of red for the right touch of colour and piquancy. The potatoes had been mashed and whisked with care, no lumps to surprise you when you chewed, rich with the flavour of milk and butter, all proof of lessons from Jo Meeker well learnt. Dessert was Mango Fool, 'a speciality of our house,' Jhelum proudly proclaimed: mango pulp whisked with cream and crushed ice, topped with a scoop of vanilla ice cream, served in stylish, large martini glasses.

Nourished and relaxed, Svet slept through the afternoon, her soft, clean body enjoying the pleasures of moving on soft cotton sheets that were spotlessly clean. Tikky waited eagerly for her to wake so he could take her to the Bhubaneswar Club and show her off to his friends. Gauri and Govinda teased him, looking at each other, rolling their eyes dramatically and ribbing him about kissing and hugging, pyaar and mohabbat.

'It's not *that*, okay?' he weakly retorted and they laughed, not believing a word.

His life till now had been sterile, almost boring, when compared to Svet's. His sympathies were with the exploited proletariat, the people of Vietnam in their struggle against imperialism, but he would not even think of painting the Lal Salaam or joining protest rallies. He was nothing but a gutless a fence-sitter. And here was his pen pal who had lost her love to a war, marched with protestors on the streets of her homeland, been at Woodstock for that mother-of-all concerts, smoked her pot, dropped her acid, passionately expressed her varied angsts, and was finally in a strange land searching for herself, living in the present, her future to be taken as it came. His life had been hemmed in by a future conjured by his father, and even that seemed wobbly. With Svet came the possibility of adventure, maybe romance, and the chance of going to America.

When Svet finally emerged, hair combed and face washed to rub off the effects of sleep, looking fresh and pretty, it seemed to Tikky that she had walked out of the first photograph she had sent him with the very first letter she had written! She wore the same ghagra, eleven yards of ghera, pinched and gathered skillfully at the waist, the base the colour of turmeric, printed with bright green parrots with blood-red beaks, paisleys and marigolds in vivid colours, topped off with a gauzy off shoulder blouse. And when Pakwaan got them their nimbu paanis and saw her, he almost dropped the glasses, sure that she was the pari of his after-nihari wet dream when he had gushed like the fountains outside the Town Hall in Chandni Chowk! Two young men, one American woman, ek phool do maali, two gardeners one flower, the eternal triangle at the core of so many novels and films.

While Tikky and Svet were at the Bhubaneswar Club, Noddy, Randy, Chuk and Rocky drooling over Svet, envious of Tikky's good fortune, Pakwaan in his kitchen prepared another of Tikky's telegraphed-from-college requests. The meat had been marinated overnight, each spice roasted separately to assure full release of their aromas, then ground with vinegar, Pakwaan using jaggery instead of sugar this time to round off the tartness of synthetic vinegar after checking with his father that it was a good idea.

His grandfather had masked the Vindaloo to expel hot, pompous, pretentious airs. His would be the perfect balance of spice and chilli, of tartness and sweetness, a perfect blend of flavours guaranteed to deliver jolts of excitement to a jaded palate used to the blandness of boiling and sautéing, to food to which spices were added by misers. Breakfast and lunch had been a tribute to mehmaan-nawazi, to connect a guest in their home to the familiarity of hers; dinner would be his grandfather's signature dish at Veeraswamy in Vilayat. It was the way Pakwaan went about his task that at once puzzled his father and made him proud. There were no grand flourishes, no exaggerated displays of confidence. His son seemed intent, studied and focused, leaving nothing to chance.

Param helped Jhelum to set the table, five thali settings of bell-metal, the metal famous for its quality and finesse, the outside oxidized a rich rough black, the inside a shining beaten brass. An indigo runner was laid across the length of the table, with rows of saffron flowers woven at either end. The centre of the table had a brass urli filled with water, sprinkled generously with the flower of the raar-ki-raani, the queen of the night. The sweet fragrance of raat-ki-raani lingering over the aroma of spices ground in vinegar and accented with indigo, saffron and polished artisan brass created an ambience pregnant with possibilities. And while Pakwaan watched the Vindaloo simmering sexily in the kitchen, kismet played its slow and langorous hand.

Pakwaan served the rice first. Basmati on a shiny silver salver, steaming hot, each grain blossoming separately, slightly swollen in the centre and tapering off at the edges, like the fingers of the very artistic. The Vindaloo and okra came next. The okra thinly sliced, dipped in besan and fried crisp. The table had helped itself to rice, and Pakwaan served the Vindaloo and the okra – enough curry to pleasantly moisten the rice, then pieces of mutton, boneless and on the bone, with a small serving of okra on the side for that bit of crunch while marvelling at the softness of rice and curry.

Svetlana salivated between bites, her palate, mouth, tongue, lips, all receptors of the sensual, luxuriated in the taste of the sting of chillies and cinnamon, the tartness of vinegar so deliciously rounded with the sweetness of gur, the tang of mustard with the sweetness of onions, the sound of the gorgeous crunch of okra in her mouth.

'I have never tasted anything like this before,' she panted, barely audible, her senses completely aroused. She had just felt the flutter of the half-coil in her moolah-dar region when Pakwaan walked in enquiring if anyone wanted seconds.

'My friend, Pakwaan, the man behind this fantastic meal. He proudly carries the baton of family tradition for the third generation,' Tikky grandly announced. Jhelum looked at her son, puzzled, Govinda and Gauri tittered and gave each other knowing looks, aware that he was just trying to impress his foreign friend.

While Pakwaan served Svetlana, bending over to pour the Vindaloo gravy, their hands touched for a brief moment, soft, white, feminine against firm, manly brown, the hands that had cooked this meal leaving her smouldering with passion.

'I am bhooki for you Pak-vaan,' she whispered sexily looking up at him. Pakwaan felt the heat and passion in her voice. Embarrased, he left the dining room, though chuffed at the thought that his food had stirred her so.

She feigned tiredness after dinner and went off early to her room. She lay in bed and, raising her hips, slowly slipped off her underwear, feeling the softness of the voile between her legs, her hands feeling the warm flesh of her thighs. Her hands moved under the gauze blouse to fondle her breasts, pinching her nipples, feeling them harden against her palm. The moon was bright, the summer breeze typically coastal – cool but heavy with moisture, the stars bright and clear in a near cloudless sky. Svetlana tip-toed across to the servants' quarters and entered Pakwaan's room.

Pakwaan lay on his stomach on the mattress on the floor. She stood at his feet and took off her blouse. Then lifting her skirt till her hips, she stood astride him and squatted just above his buttocks, spreading eleven yards of ghera printed with parrots and paisleys over his face and body, her haunches strong after all that sundaas practice. She squeezed his firm, young buttocks, running her hands down to fondle his balls. Pakwaan groaned, turned over to free his full-blooded erection, the timing and positioning perfect for Svet to impale herself on him. She rode him, Pakwaan holding her arse firmly, thrusting his hips to match her rhythms, the ghagra slipping off his face. He could see her now, her hands languorously holding her hair, her breasts firm, bouncy and inviting. He let go of her buttocks and roughly grabbed her breasts.

'Vindaloo, Vindaloo, Vindaloo!' she moaned.

'Chudai zindabaad, zindabad,' he groaned.

As their passions reached frothy crescendos, Pakwaan was amazed at how closely her seduction of him matched his nihari-inspired wet dream.

Afterwards, she lay beside him, deliciously spent, and turned her head, glancing at his face. His mouth was agape, his eyes open wide, surprised, shocked at this sudden, fortunate, intense fuck. She smiled as the path to her nirvana lit up in a flash, astonishing in its clarity.

Till now her quest for spirituality had not allowed her to think of her talent for business as a virtue – her head for figures, her love for playing around with them and quantifying ideas to spot trends. All that was now a thing of the past. While working at the store she had been sure that America's love affair with heat and spice had just begun, and now she was convinced of it. India remained the flavour of the season, the market for Indian food was growing, and with Vindaloo as a starter, with Tikky and Pakwaan to help in its production, she was sure she could make enough money for the rules of the world to not apply to her. Yes, this was a nirvana of sorts, she convinced herself. She patted Pakwaan perfunctorily on his cheek and chest, flashed him a thumbs-up sign, quickly put on her clothes and left as suddenly as she had arrived, robbing a grateful Pakwaan of post-coital tenderness. Strange, these firangis, was the last thought that came to his mind before he slept, his sleep deep and dreamless.

While Svetlana and Pakwaan fucked lustfully, Tikky slept, too, dreaming of Americana, his large house in suburbia, his Cadillac and Mustang parked in the garage, a porch surrounded by a white picket fence and a loving Svetlana by his side.

Svet woke the next morning breathless with optimism – imagine the hand-wringing excitement, the desperate need to speak with Tikky, to describe her redefined nirvana with Tikky and Pakwaan as the major props. Breakfast hastened her restlessness, Svetlana somehow controlling herself to appear calm, saving herself the embarrassment of blurting out the plans she had for the three of them.

Pakwaan was a genius, the breakfast that was served made her more sure of that. Her appetite edged by the previous night's seduction, she helped herself to the simple fare of ande ki bhurji, lachchedaar parantha and home-made mango pickle – the Indian-style scrambled eggs spooned onto bite-sized pieces of crisp, layered parantha, dipped into the tangy pickle, the hotness of chilli layered with the relief of the sweet-sourness of mango. A simple breakfast magically transformed. Oh, the mouth! What a gorgeous little organism, she thought. Lips and tongue to kiss and talk, to suck, to eat, the source of all pleasurable titillation.

As soon as they left the table, she gripped Tikky firmly by the elbow, took him to her room and sat him down on the bed.

'This spiritual warrior has finally seen the light,' she began, then paused, closing her eyes. 'I've had it up to here,' she said, stretching a hand over her head, 'with all this fuzzy spiritual bullshit, its promises of self-realization and happiness. Maybe good for the Boodah but then he was a prince who could afford his aversion to wealth and lead the life of an ascetic, find enlightenment and found a religion that has so many followers. Would you rather be rich and unhappy, or poor and happy, is a question often asked by the goo-roohs. I say now I would rather be rich, period. So, let us be princes first, then think of that higher' – she mimicked the inverted comma with the middle and index finger of her hands – 'life later. Being rich and spiritual is far better than being spiritual and poor. America is *the* land of opportunity that rewards hard work and talent more than anywhere else in the world, where wealth and profit are celebrated as achievements worthy of emulation.' Her tone was spirited, her eyes bright with hope, her words soaked with infectious optimism.

'America is ready for exotica and there is nothing more exotic than India,' she gushed, carrying on without missing a beat. 'America will continue to get its instalments of goo-roohs, swamis, Aum Shantys and such.' Tikky heard her quietly, not missing her dismissive tone. 'But we must take advantage of the beginnings of America's love affair with heat and spice. America is ripe and ready, eager for more flavour from India, and there is nothing more physical, more tantalizingly sensuous than a spicy Indian curry that you can touch, feel, taste and smell. And Pak-vaan is a genius who has taste in his hands and magic in his fingers,' finished Svetlana, looking nostalgically at her breasts, squeezed the night before, as confirmation.

'We will bring product to the table. We will start small and finish BIG,' she said, shaping her hand into a victorious fist, already sounding like the entrepreneur who is written about after they become successful. She fleshed out for Tikky her version of the American dream – an apartment in Manhattan overlooking Central Park, a place in the Hamptons where they would go for their well-deserved rest and recuperation and hobnob with the generally rich and sometimes famous, vacations in Europe, and other accoutrements of unimaginable wealth. Tikky's version of the American dream was minuscule by comparison and he looked at her, amazed, seduced by America, the expression on his face much like Pakwaan's after she had fucked him.

Svet's transformation from gentle spiritual warrior to hardnosed, driven businesswoman was sudden and dramatic. There was no point in letting the grass grow under her feet – she cut short her trip and left for home, telling Tikky and Pakwaan to be ready for an adventure that held rich and glorious promise.

Fresh off the Boat

HER letter arrived three weeks after she left, a week before Tikky's final-year results were to arrive. This letter had no Aum sign, none of the charming little references in the lingua franca. It was brief, focused, to the point, but the excitement and optimism were clearly evident.

Dear T.R.,

I have spent a few days with my friends where I worked at the supermarket before I came to India to find myself (hah!).

If the sell-throughs on the shelves are any indication, I believe we are sitting on an incredible opportunity. The sales of spices, chutneys, chillies, pickles are increasing, and I will not be exaggerating if I say ASTRONOMICALLY so in New Jersey, a suburb not exactly cosmopolitan. 'Very conservative' would be the right description – like Bhubaneswar, if you want to place it in an Indian context. I have also managed to meet folks who work in large-format supermarket chains in Manhattan and here the increase in sales is even more dramatic.

Ready-to-eat food sales are on the rise, the gap between sales in this segment is wide when compared to Manhattan and the 'burbs. Funnily, there is nothing remotely Indian in the ready-

to-eat area and I think this should be the area of our focus in the future. But I am getting ahead of myself. Like I said, we must start small, test the waters, then make our leap of faith.

Let us start by selling Vindaloo, crisp-fried okra and rice (how can I forget it?) at weekend fairs in Manhattan, see the reaction and take it from there.

Exotica is the *flavour. It would be a great idea to 'dress up' Pakwaan at these fairs – in those long coats buttoned till the neck (sherwanis?), tight white churidars and those curled at the end genie-like shoes. And please don't forget the headgear – what you were wearing in the first photograph you sent me. Pakwaan, like you, must look royal enough to attract the crowds and with his magic finger-lickin'-good cooking, to borrow the Colonel's line, we are sure to become the pioneers (hopefully very rich ones) of Indian food in America.*

Lots of love,

Svet

Tikky could not help getting caught up in the excitement. Ah! America, my lucky charm, he thought, imagining the rosiest future in a world across the oceans, more than just a distance away from that dreaded cycle shop in Daryaganj! Letter in hand, hope in his heart, he loped out of his room and went straight to the kitchen to share the news with Pakwaan.

'Yeh sab Bhagwaan ki dua hai,' Param said, looking skywards, thanking the heavens. He hugged his son warmly and then, placing his hands on Pakwaan's shoulders, held him at arm's-length, shaking his head in wonder, amazed at how quickly the boy had become a man. Palmer Sahib's letter had allowed his father to showcase his skills at Veeraswamy and now the same good fortune had crossed Pakwaan's path. Kismet had been kind to them. 'You must be grateful to God for the skill he has blessed you with, but NEVER take it for granted,' said Param. Good, solid advice that somehow sounded like a warning.

In Tikky's case permission for better futures in far-off lands was not so easily granted. Mahadev, at first, loathed the idea. 'First you protect him under your petticoats and then my firstborn hangs on to the coat-tails of our cook's son,' Mahadev sneered when Jhelum informed him of Tikky's plans.

Jhelum, sick of his barbs and weary of the constant taking-up-of-cudgels on her son's behalf, tired also of praying for the spectacular academic result that never came, decided to calmly say her piece. 'But mai kya, darling, it is bleak for him here and maybe I am to blame. But don't you think things can only get better in America?' In the end it was a clinching argument, and for the first time since she could remember she had had the last word.

Tikky wrote to Svet immediately, all excited and rushed, skipping the Mahadevian flourishes of health and spirit, cutting to the chase.

Dear Svetlana,

Finally, permission from Father granted, passports and visas applied for, so look forward to seeing you.

The tone of the letter was that of a telegram with URGENT scrawled on top, but he remembered in the end to add *Lots and lots of love, Yours truly, Tikky*.

The bureaucracy was cranked into motion, prodded by seniority, their passports got done in a rush. Their visas were done in 'due course' and by the middle of September Tikky and Pakwaan were all set to travel to the promised land. Pakwaan's outfitting took more time. They would fly out to America from Delhi and the sherwanis, Param insisted, had to be cut, sewn and stitched by

Mohammad Umar and Sons near Majestic Cinema at Kashmere Gate, trusted tailor to families settled in Purani Dilli for generations. Well made, the garmeat draped the body comfortably, lent an air of understated elegance; badly done, it looked obscene, buttons at the chest threatening to pop out of their buttonholes, seams puckering dangerously as if about to come apart, the sherwani riding so obviously in front that it could be mistaken for a hand-me-down.

The young men were in a rush, but Mohammad Afzal Umar, fourth-generation darzi, khandani kalakaar, would have none of it.

'Sahibzade,' he addressed father and son after a particularly long, whining, insistent plea to 'jaldi karo' and give them an express delivery, 'this is a sherwani, not some petticoat that can be cobbled together by any mochi. If a sherwani *has* to be made, please remember it has to be done' – his hand moved slowly, rhythmically, mimicking the movement of a needle through cloth – 'it-mi-naan se,' his voice soft and gentle, stretching the word lovingly, 'with leisure and love, at peace with yourself and the rest of the world.'

'Spoken like a true kalakaar,' Param said as an apology, remembering the pride in his father's voice when he talked of his skills as a Kathua. The measurements were taken, the fabric and lining cut, spread on the table to allow it to relax and while Mohammad Afzal Umar supervised the making of Pakwaan's sherwanis, Pakwaan learnt the art of tying his saafa in the Jodhpur style. Six yards of tie-dyed fabric in bright pinks, mustards, greens and indigos tied around his head, stretched broad and flat on one side and, on the other, sensuous coils of colour that covered most of his right ear. The sherwanis fit perfectly, Param insisting on getting a photograph taken of his son in full regalia – sherwani, saafa, churidar and jootis. Their journey was delayed but Pakwaan was happy that Mohammad Afzal Umar had stood his ground. It was worth the wait. Pakwaan felt like royalty, astonished at how vividly he remembered his dream.

They left for America on 6 October 1973, amidst tearful farewells, hugs and handshakes. It was the first day of ramzan. Strange, uncanny, when Param thought about it. When his father left Banaras it was Muharram and now, when his son was leaving home for foreign lands, it was the day the Muslims began their month of penance and fasting. What was it with Muslim festivals and Kathuapan? He smiled at the irony and put it down to coincidence.

As the two young men flew to America 30,000 feet above sea level at just a little less than the speed of sound, the captain of their ship rather proudly announced that down below on Mother Earth history, once again, was being made.

Sixth of October 1973, was a rare day – one of the few times (perhaps in all of history) when the Jewish and the Muslim, both kat-huaed, began their fasting and their penances at the same time. Ramzan on one side of the Suez, Yom Kippur on the other. On this day Egypt *and* Syria had attacked Israel, taking it by surprise. History would call it the Yom Kippur War, America once again tilting the balance by sending arms and ammunition, planes and tanks to Israel just in time, like the Japanese when they managed their inventories in the automobile industry to give them the competitive edge. It was a short war, peace was brokered by Russia and America, icy adversaries in the Cold War, but there were some amongst the learned who predicted that this was a war that could have 'far-reaching consequences'.

It was chilly when they arrived in New York and war was headline news, the prophets of doom predicting possibilities of a World War III that ran 'imminent risks' of going nuclear. But Svetlana, familiar with ducking and covering, knew there was no need to panic. All manufactured fears, she told the two young men, nothing to worry about. A nuclear war would have proved the doomsayers right – far-reaching consequences indeed – but Svet was right. No bombs were dropped anywhere and the world carried on more or less as before. But all wars leave their legacies, and the Yom Kippur War was no exception.

The automobile was an American icon, an important example of the might of American manufacturing muscle. Mustangs, Chevys, Ford Impalas, Buicks, Cadillacs had been immortalized by Hollywood and used-car salesmen, the American suburb with neat lawns and trimmed hedges made possible by the motor car. So when the vanquished struck back by banning the export of gasoline to America, there was chaos across the country.

SORRY, NO GAS! EMPTY! CLOSED! FUEL SHORTAGE IS GOING TO GET THE WORLD BACK ON ITS FEET, the signages outside gas stations and on billboards announced.

Gas was rationed, speed limits imposed to ensure optimum consumption, life in general slowed down, gas prices quadrupled, the long queues for gas with people praying that gas would not run out till their turn came caused patience to wear thin, and those with shorter fuses shot at others if they thought the queue had been broken. Petrol pumps across the country wound up, unable to deal with losses, and the born-again Christians saw this as an opportunity to spread the message of their Lord Jesus. 'Fill up with the Holy Ghost! Fill up with old-fashioned salvation!' they painted in bold black letters across gas dispensing contraptions, hoping that the errant would realize the folly of their ways and return to the welcoming bosoms of Jesus and Mary. It was *toe-tull kay-oss*, Pakwaan imagined his father waving his hands while telling this story.

A depressing time, when sentiment, that strong emotion which drives markets to bubble furiously, was tepid, the desire to consume watered down. But Svet, Tikky and Pakwaan's collective kismets were bulund and their fortunes held up, their rise not meteoric but fast enough to embellish the tales of entrepreneurship with romantic masala.

The war added to the woes of New York City, already struggling with crime, drugs, bankruptcy, the backlash of the Vietnam War and a general hangover of excessive angst. Rents were low and spaces could be leased for a pittance – good signs for the optimistic, enthusiastic entrepreneur convinced of profitable futures despite depressing times. And Svetlana, having grooved through the sixties had finally discovered her own groove, hitting the ground with confident stride. She rented a loft off the Bowery, inhabited by the drunk and the decrepit but spacious and well-lit, where they would have enough space for themselves, the kitchen big enough to experiment with food, and fix recipes and yields, before they moved on to bigger things. 'An example of the humble beginnings of great businesses' – Svetlana imagined the headline after they had 'arrived' on the business scene.

Tikky, meanwhile, was simply grateful to be in America, sure that he would realize the top end of the American dream, allowing him to cock his snook at his father. The possibility of a blossoming romance with Svetlana filled him with warm thoughts of snooking his cock as well. And Pakwaan was grateful to kismet. The memory of Svetlana's spontaneous expression of lust post her Vindaloo and fried okra dinner was delicious, passionate, always creating that warm flutter between his legs. It was astonishing how close his life had run, until now, to his dream. The pot of gold beckoned – he was sure of it – and, if he was lucky enough, fucking as a perk after a well-cooked meal!

But Svet, pari of both Tikky's and Pakwaan's dreams, had changed. She talked in staccato bursts, bullet-point language, ticking off each point on her finger tips. Her language was peppered with business jargon – daily sell-throughs, percentage point growths and market penetration. Her vision for the company was grand – she wanted it to become the most well-known Indian food brand, loved for it's ability to deliver delight to it's customers *every time*. 'We will call the company Aum Foods Inc.,' she told the boys. 'Aum' was easy to pronounce, even for Americans, and it resonated with the spiritualism of India, which was sure to remain in flavour for some time to come. Just listening to her, Pakwaan felt the chances of the 'fuck as perk' slip away, but Tikky girded up his loins, determined to contribute to her vision in significant ways, gain her respect, affection, love, rise in her esteem and, finally, park his girded loins in hers.

The oil crisis was a little blip on a culinary landscape that bubbled with potential. Fast food restaurants, where sanitized, standardized, homogenized snacky foods were consistently served in a jiffy to hungry customers, were growing. Svetlana's plan was simple. Money was in short supply and necessity was the mother of invention. They would start small and see if they could finish big. They would begin with Vindaloo – chicken, lamb, pork, beef – served with rice and crisp-fried okra at neighbourhood fairs. With Pakwaan's flair and genius, the word of mouth would spread. Catering orders would follow from small gatherings to large affairs and profits would be stashed away till, in the fullness of time, there would be enough to put money down for their own restaurant. They imagined great futures, leaving their mark on the history of quick-service restaurants in America. They thought of an ADAR's – Aum's Dosa and Rolls – where kathi rolls would fly off the griddle, dosas would sizzle on tawas glistening with oil, and idlis would steam in giant gleaming steamers, fluffy and delicate to the bite. It would be *the* one-stop shop for the vegetarian and the non-vegetarian. Or maybe ARACC's – Aum's Rice and Curry Corner, where rice could be served with Vindaloo, chicken curry, lamb curry, dal and vegetables, where customers walked in, helped themselves to a bowl of steaming basmati, topping it with curries of their choice that simmered in hot bain-maries, and paid at the till at the end of the counter. Quick, easy and very scaleable. The possibilities were endless, and their spirits were made even more buoyant by an issue of the *Time* magazine that Svetlana always kept at hand to spur them on to greater heights.

On 17 September 1973, McDonald's had featured on the cover of *Time* magazine. A bun drawn to resemble a mouth with two corners of cheese shaped like incisors hanging over a rich brown burger dressed with lettuce leaves. The top part of the bun was a caricature of a face – large dreamy eyes and bulbous Idaho-russet-number-one-potato-shaped nose dotted with sesame seeds. The burger floated in the sky, over the American flag, with a drawing of the drive-in with the golden arches in the background. 'THE HAMBURGER EMPIRE' was printed in bright golden letters on a red background, the headline in red and gold, the colours of the McDonald's brand.

'But if we have to make our mark, add our very own dots to a landscape being furiously dotted upon, we have to, like McDonald's,' said Svet jabbing the cover with firm intent, 'be *consistent* – recipes have to be fixed, quantities of spices and masalas measured, weights and measures of chillies, onions, garlic, ginger mentioned, yields determined, portions costed. Even times have to be set to determine the doneness of a dish.'

Sub kuchh likhat mein, everything in writing, Pakwaan imagined drearily, but Tikky saw the merit in laid-down procedure. De-skilling, idiot-proofing, assembly-lining the production of food would ensure that whatever they served tasted the same, time after time after time.

'Like a bloody kaarigar the cook will be, following instructions, no scope for feel or flair,' burst out Pakwaan, expressing his displeasure.

Svet and Tikky immediately jumped to consistency's defence and soothed Pakwaan's ego, telling him that to get so many cooks as skilled as him for the number of restaurants they had planned would be impossible.

'Look at it this way,' Tikky would say whenever Pakwaan objected to their overzealousness for standardization, 'the cooks will follow *your* recipes, allowing you to take credit for an army of people that carry out their little part in taking forward the lessons of three generations of cooking.'

The 'fixing' of the recipe for Vindaloo, rice and crisp-fried okra posed a challenge and a welcome relief for Pakwaan from the dullness of the constant weighing. Chicken cooked faster than beef, beef cooked a little faster than pork, lamb took the longest time. With his sense of timing, the setting of cooking times was easy. But the taste of the rounded sweet-sourness was elusive. Cane sugar was hard to come by and rarely available in the few shops that carried Oriental and hardly any Asian spices, the synthetic vinegar, as usual too tart for the tongue. The combination of rice vinegar and sugar was not robust enough, vinegar and sugar was too raw, the aftertaste like a pickle not allowed enough time in the sun. But like all great cooks Pakwaan had a memory for taste. He remembered the sweet-sourness of a salad that Svet had made and discovered the delights of balsamic vinegar. A generous splash (later measured and specified) of the sweet grape balsamic in synthetic vinegar, the spices ground into this magical mix, and the result, he thought, was better than the palm sugar substitute, maybe as good as the original. It was his moment, his individual stamp on the Vindaloo, made in America! There was much backslapping and congratulations, Svet sure that it was more delicious than the Vindaloo she had tasted in Bhubaneswar.

They slept well that night, Svetlana even feeling the beginnings of horniness, smiling wickedly at the thought of surprising

Pakwaan. But they were in business now and having the company pen dipped in the company inkpot could be risky. She sucked her fingers sensuously, first one and then two, and once they were delectably moistened proceeded to pleasure herself.

With the recipes for the various kinds of Vindaloos finally fixed, serving portions were costed and the selling price set at four times the cost of each portion. There were handsome profits to be made. They would launch their range of Vindaloos – chicken, beef, pork and lamb – served with rice and crisp-fried okra from a stall in Astor Place on the first weekend of November.

The weather was tricky – brief spells of snow or rain, with patches of the clearest skies and crisp warm sunshine in between. Typically New England weather, Svetlana told them, the use of England a concession to the mother country. Ulta-pulta, upside down Vilayat No. 2, Tikky and Pakwaan had christened America when they observed the differences between America and England. As in India, the English drove on the right side of the road, these Vilayatis on the left. Like us, they lit up their homes with 220 Volts of electricity, here they managed with 110 Volts. A switch flicked down in England, and the lights and fans came on; up, and they were off. It was exactly the reverse in Vilayat No. 2. Cricket was played over five days with everyone dressed in white and it was possible that in the end nobody won. America's baseball was like cricket, but aerial. The balls were thrown on the fly, there were no stumps, the batter struck out if he swung and missed thrice if the ball passed in the hitting area, and one team would always win. The game finished in hours, each team wearing colourful uniforms, different for every team. American football was played mainly with hands and bodies, English football with feet. They looked at time differently, England mentioning first the day, then the month and finally the year, America first the month, followed by the day and then the year. Here it was never 'quarter to' or 'quarter past' the hour but 'quarter off' and 'quarter after' – as if they realized the dangers of blind imitation, making a statement, as if, of a new and original arrival. But they loved the English accent – charming, posh and classy when compared to their own nasal drawl.

The weather during the last week of October had been horrendous – wind howling through tunneled streets and a damp, bitter cold that seeped into their bones. The week was well spent by Tikky and Svet, recipes manualized, copies of menus printed for their catering business – Astor Place a good spot to hand them out as Pakwaan dished out his magic.

'Bund-phaad thand, or arse-tearing cold,' Pakwaan thought, blowing hot air into cupped hands when he went out to buy groceries, stepping gingerly to avoid slipping on the icy sleet, the gush of warm air as the doors to the supermarket parted a welcome relief. Pakwaan was always amazed at the size of the vegetables and fruits in this country. Tomatoes the size of apples, cauliflowers the size of a bouquet, the okra long, fat and thick, curling at the end, as if protesting at being longer than nature permitted, the sizes of fruits and vegetables so similar that it seemed they had been extruded from a mould. And most fruits and veggies – okra, cauliflower, strawberries, peas, carrots and even mangoes – seemed to be available throughout the year, without as much as a thought for the seasons, the pleasures of longing for those times of the year associated with one's favourite fruits and vegetables denied. The lines for gas may have been long and the people frustrated by shortage but in the supermarkets America was the land of plenty, the aisles were well-stocked with all sorts of food, the range of choice often confusing.

Pakwaan's first stab at shopping had been a spectacular,

hilarious failure. Sent to buy chicken and Coca-Cola, almost tumbling into the supermarket when he tried to push the door open and the doors automatically parted, he stood there wide-eyed and gaping at the shelves overflowing with produce.

'May I help you?' an energetic voice enquired.

'Chicken?' he asked.

'Breasts, breasts and legs, legs and thighs, legs, thighs, giblets, whole?' the voice rattled off at high speed. For the first time Pakwaan wondered how buying chicken could become such a project. He changed tack, thinking Coca-Cola would be simpler.

'Coke,' he said more confidently.

'Regular? Diet? Classic? Cherry?' The voice rattled off again.

'Maderchod, all I wanted was a simple Coke and bloody chicken,' he muttered to himself and bolted out of the door.

He smiled at the memory as he picked the okra-on-steroids for the fair the next day.

Pakwaan woke early, grateful for a clear blue sky and a bright, sunny day. He had washed the okra the night before and left them on a cloth to dry – they had dried well, not a trace of moistness to be seen. Moistness was disastrous for deep-frying okra and resulted in stringy, moist bites chewed to a gummy pulp swallowed ultimately with reluctance. He prepared the batter, thankful for the convenience of the sifter – a mound of golden-yellow gram-flour sifted onto a platter, sprinkled with the blood-red of chilli powder, a dash of turmeric, the muddy green-brown of amchur, dried mango ground to a fine powder, for that hint of sweetness in the batter, with a generous handful of roasted and powdered coriander and cumin seeds for that touch of spice. Okra cut, batter ready, Pakwaan showered, slipped into his churidar and tied the six-yard leheria saafa on his head. He looked at himself in the mirror, flicking off imaginary pieces of dirt from his sherwani, running his palms down his chest and stomach to iron out the little creases, remembering his nymphet-on-highways-of-fluffy-clouds dream. The day throbbed with the promise of his Vindaloo exciting the firangi palate lathered with blandness.

Svet and Tikky crunched the numbers, determining the number of portions to be sold, each portion fixed and measured, break-evens calculated – if they sold only a fourth of what they had made, they would recover their investment, a thought that filled them with the pleasure of riches. So off they went, their responsibilities clearly defined. Tikky would ladle the portions according to the quantities budgeted, Svet would handle the cash and hand out the fliers for their delivery and catering business, while Pakwaan dished out his magic.

FOR DELICIOUS INDIAN FOOD SERVED AT YOUR DOORSTEP CALL 212-AUM-FOOD, the board read. '212-Aum-Food' sounded mystical, nifty *and* efficient. Below this headline was printed the menu of the Punj Pyaara at Veeraswamy bordered by a frame of red roses, with 'Enjoy three generations of perfection!' under it in Svet's stylish, slanting calligraphic hand, the exclamation mark tall and plump, filled in black, the dot a bright red, guaranteed to attract attention.

They reviewed the competition – a Gyro Stall serving the Greek sandwich roll stuffed with meat, greens and choice of sauce, a Salad Bar that advertised organic produce (maybe a bit ahead of its time, Svet surmised), and Gloria's Gorgeous Quiches and Apple Pies, 'as American as you can get' stencilled below the heading. The rest of the stalls were mainly clothing and knick-knack shops – bits and pieces of old embroidery and crochet work, old grandfather clocks, old porcelain pieces, tiny little cups to dress mantlepieces and such and, of course, the worry beads, Aum signs, patchwork cushions, tie-dyed scarves and kaftans, bits of colourful, exotic India randomly splashed across Astor Place.

But Pakwaan was the star attraction, sherwani–saafa attired, faux three-stringed pearl necklace around his neck, every bit the maharaja as imagined by the West. He tossed the okra-with-batter into the hot oil with a flourish, fascinating spectators with the hissing noise. He stirred the Vindaloo gravy with style and passion, ladling the gravy, then pouring it back into the big degchi from a height, the stream of curry lit golden by the sun, taking a bow graciously when customers complimented the chef, and blushing when a pretty girl wickedly propositioned him wondering if he was as good a fuck as he was a cook. The Vindaloo was a hit, customers lapping it up so quickly that the last of the Vindaloo, bits and pieces of chicken, beef and pork that stuck to the edges of the degchis had to be scraped off to feed the few customers who insisted on having just a sample, a little taste of this new and delicious flavour. Svet and Tikky were sure they had a winner. Svetlana did not even need to hand out her fliers announcing their menu for delivery at doorsteps. The enthusiasts grabbed them from her, assuring her that they would call, chanting '212-Aum-Food, 212-Aum-Food' as they salivated and went their merry way.

'212-Aum-Food, how may I help you?' either Tikky or Svet would answer the phone and take down the details, efficiently asking if they wanted their food spicy, regular or mildly spiced.

Pakwaan was irritated at these concessions to the firangi palate. Mildly spiced versions seemed more popular, always a challenge for Pakwaan who was used to spicier tastes, finding the end result just about rescued from blandness – an insular palate may be, but willing to flirt with change, Pakwaan thought, consoling himself.

Business was brisk enough. They averaged around five caterings a week, Pakwaan often having to rush off to cook for catering orders, barely being able to take the bow for his Vindaloo at Astor Place in the weekend. The menu of the Punj Pyaara was the most popular and the most profitable – they had priced it at a premium, and rightly so. The wazwaan meant Pakwaan had to hunt for the right cuts of lamb, the three of them pounding away at the meat till it reached the right consistency to be rolled into gushtabas and ristaas. The meat for the kakori, too, required effort, Pakwaan grinding it himself till it reached that silken smoothness, and the mixing of the spices required precision. The sheermal was problematic – the tandoor, always on hire, could only be used in homes with patches of lawn or some sort of outdoor space, and for the homes without such spaces the sheermal had to be substituted with the ulte-tawa-ka-parantha, parantha cooked on an upside down tawa, the dough a mix of flour, egg, milk, sugar and ghee, like the dough for sheermal, but a little less rich and not left to ferment overnight.

There were other combinations that were popular – 'Combos', Svet had christened them for that abbreviated energetic feel. The butter chicken, paneer makhni, daal makhni with saag, raita and lachchedaar parantha found its takers, as did the 'Budget Combo' – home-made basic chicken curry, with jeera-aloo, a choice of greens between spinach and cauliflower, tawa rotis, plain wheat rotis cooked on the griddle and biwi-ki-dal-tadkedaar, the yellow dal with the 'wife's special' tadka, Vidhaata's contribution to the family's vast repertoire.

Profits were being stashed away, the margin money for downpayment for their first restaurant no longer such a distant dream. Life was hectic, but good. But what can you do about kismet? So benevolent when the going is good, dangerous when the tide turns.

Like all years, this year, too, wound down. Thanksgiving had been celebrated, families had come together around tables laden with food and downed their eggnogs, eaten their turkeys with cranberry sauce and stuffing, each family agreeing that their stuffing and sauce was unique. Christmas was only a week away, the organized already loaded up with their gifts for their near and dear ones, happy to know that they would avoid the mad rush of last-minute Christmas shopping. The streets were brightly lit, the Christmas tree at the Rockefeller Center glittered with lights and shiny Christmas decorations and families enjoyed the pleasures of togetherness as they skated on ice in the skating rink in the sunken plaza. Stores announced their sales with gusto, announcing tempting discounts, hoping to suck in footfalls titillated by the pleasure of consumption and a good deal, the oil shortage being pushed back into some insignificant corner of collective memory. In short, all was well with America, more or less, till everyone tuned in to the late-night television show on the fateful day, six days before Christmas, beamed all the way from Burbank, California, at a chosen time when night had descended on all parts of the United States despite its three time zones.

'Heere's Johniee,' the compere said with great flair and style over the typical music in the background that announced grand arrivals with Johnny Carson sitting behind his desk, America readying itself for witty one-liners, jokes, funnies and humorous insights. And while his one-liners drew some laughs, he announced that America would run out of toilet paper. It was meant as a joke, but the rationing of oil had created a culture of shortage. Toilet paper vanished from the shelves with alarming rapidity and there was talk of rationing as the whole of America (or so it seemed) rushed to the supermarkets to buy all the tee-pee they could lay their hands on. Johnny was back a few days later telling America it was a joke but the damage had been done, and it took some time, three weeks, give or take a few days, for America to feel secure about having enough toilet paper to wipe their bums whenever the need arose. Tikky and Pakwaan wondered what the fuss was all about, shortages were a way of life in India, and in this entire fiasco even Svet believed America had overreacted. Thank God for sundaas and her conversion to washing – she was grateful that she had been saved the jostling, the elbowing, as masses of people tried to ensure soft, fluffy wipes for their behinds after they did their jobs.

But business suffered. Catering orders were cancelled and people ate less at the fairs, past experience confirming the ease of great bowel movement after they consumed food rich in fibres and spice.

'Oh, for a nation of arse-washers,' Svet, Tikky and Pakwaan fervently sighed in unison.

Profits shrunk, the stash for their margin dwindled, the restaurant suddenly seemed so much further away. Svetlana was the pillar of strength, sure of their future, handling every catering order, every foray in the fair with zeal and passion, reminding her team that they had a great product that was consistently delivered, which was half the battle won, waving the hamburger on the cover of the *Time* magazine at Tikky and Pakwaan to strengthen belief.

Time passed, winter giving way to warmer weather, and soon spring was in the air, as they say, the planets so aligned that the malevolent effects of Saturn or Shani, the planet of misfortune, were lifted and kismet, once again, flashed its benevolent smile on the young strugglers. Aum Foods got their largest catering order – dinner for fifty in the Upper West Side in 'an apartment with four large bedrooms and a terrace with a panoramic view of Central Park', a real-estate blurb would have read.

Faith and Ben Dylan welcomed Svet, Tikky and Pakwaan to their home, gushing about their love for India.

Completely and hopelessly in love with the country, they admitted, eyes shut, face crinkled to emphasize the depth of their love. 'Absolute Indopheels,' they said with feeling. 'We love everything about India but hope you have been careful with the chillies and spices as we've both had our Delhi bellies,' Faith said with a titter. 'Better safe than sorry, and so what if the tee-pee crisis is over.' Everyone laughed, Tikky assuring them that care had been taken, Pakwaan smiling at them reassuringly.

Faith and Ben Dylan were older than the three. They had flirted with the sixties but always from a distance, protesting the war, showing concern for world peace and happiness and the rest, but always from within the confines of their comforts. They had done the fashionable thing, taken time out – their sabbatical from the daily dust and grind of everyday life made possible by rich parents – and backpacked. England, Europe, Afghanistan, Pakistan and, finally, India. India stuck to them, allowing them their lifestyle, their efforts of bringing India to America, with a healthy profit margin tagged on, successful so far. Besides, their affair with India had other advantages – a 'unique positioning' the marketing pundits would say. Their familiarity with India gave them the status of the refined cosmopolite, more than a touch grander than just cosmopolitan.

'Today is our Indian soiree with Indian food and seetar music by a young American being trained by Pandit Rah-vee Shanker,' Ben told them.

Their home was an ode to India. At the entrance stood a statue of the Lord Balaji, framed by golden arches, his body draped in an exquisite red-gold-black temple saree. Incense sticks with the aroma of sandalwood burnt at Balaji's feet. Jamavar shawls casually draped the white silk sofas, the window blinds were creatively cut from colourful sarees. Phulkaris in their mustards, vermillions, oranges and fuschias were framed stylishily and hung on the walls, a giant Gujarati dowry chest with gold inlay work had been cunningly carpentered to function as a bar. An Eames chair and Ottoman at the end of an Afghan kilm with a Pichwai as the backdrop completed the idea of eclectic, ethnic-chic, like the rest of the evening.

A low diwan upholstered in a creamy gold handwoven fabric served as the stage for the musicians, with white bolsters in mirror-work embroidery providing back rests for the sitar and the tabla player, and brass urlis filled with water, generously sprinkled with rose petals and floating candles, little pools of exotica, lay scattered across the terrace.

The guests were a collection of struggling artists, slightly left-of-centre intellectuals, not quite completely reformed hippies, who mixed and sold their own organic muesli breakfast cereal down on 125th Street and Columbus bordering Harlem, a sprinkling of businessmen who were tasting their successes selling shiny ebony masks and other bric-a-brac all the way from Africa. And, finally, Moh and Maya Urban, the Heads of Creative of Sutchee and Sutchee in New York.

The Pandit's disciple started with Raag Yaman, the first raag taught to learners, the evening setting allowing it a contextual aptness. As the tempo increased, the tabla and the sitar player shook their heads in rhythm, closing their eyes, as if soaking in the beauty of the music. The fading strains of the end of the performance were followed by a gentle clapping from the audience impressed by this display of virtuosity. A little like Woodstock, Svet had to remind herself, but without the rain and frenzy. Tikky found it too precious, Pakwaan likewise—too much dikhawaa, unnecessary show-shaa.

And then it was time for dinner, the menu the same as the one served by the Punj Pyaara at Veeraswamy in London.

Mulligatawny Soup, the hotness of pepper tempered for the firangi palate with a generous squeeze of fresh lemon; rice, chicken and arhar ki daal, Pakwaan refusing the convenience of the banal curry powder, making the garam masala just the way Ramaswamy had taught his grandfather, with just enough spice to clean the palate and prepare it for the subtle taste of Abdul Ahad's gushtaba, pounded meat balls cooked in yogurt and dried ginger. The spicier rista in a rich red curry and the saag cooked with the sprinkling of Kashmiri masala followed, preparing the guests for a rush of the stinging mustard of Santoo-moshai's machher jhol, fish curry, toned down by the subtle flavours of chaurchori, the flavour of the korma and the kakori, the sweetness of the sheermal allowing the palate enough relief to welcome the sweet-sour spiciness of his grandfather's Vindaloo.

The guests loved the food and asked the hosts to present the chef.

'PAAK-VAAN,' Faith and Ben Dylan said in chorus, pleased that their India soiree had been a success, and Pakwaan took his bow to enthusiastic applause – just like at Veeraswamy when the Punj Pyaara were presented, Pakwaan thought, sure that his father would have been proud.

The Vindaloo TV Dinner

THE guests left as Svet, Tikky and Pakwaan wound up. Moh and Maya Urban, Faith and Ben Dylan were on the terrace, huddled together. Moh and Maya were convinced that they were staring at an opportunity not to be missed – it was exciting, new and, thank god, off the beaten path. If handled right, it promised much more than just the proverbial pot of gold at the end of the rainbow.

'Where do the three of you want to go with this?' Moh asked them, and Svet spoke about the plan with purpose and intent – sell at food fairs, cater at parties, build up good word-of-mouth and profit, and set up the first of many restaurants . . .

'All good but not good enough, even risky,' Moh rattled off without waiting for her to finish. 'One,' he said making his index finger erect, 'it can take too much time. Two –' now the middle finger went the same way – 'the restaurant business is the riskiest, seventy per cent mortality rate, for your information. Three' – the ring finger joined the other two – 'the restaurant as a business has possibly the lowest entry barriers. I wonder if you are aware that in Manhattan alone there are so many restaurants that if one ate three meals in a different restaurant each day, it would take him more than five years to eat in every one of them, provided, of course, that all them do not shut down in that time,' he said, sniggering.

'And, therefore, four,' he concluded, straightening his pinky, 'the best option is to adapt this wonderful product you have, starting with the Vindaloo, to the ready-to-eat business. The process will carry with it intellectual properties. It will, in all probability, be patentable and create entry barriers. It will be a far easier project to scale up than a restaurant. The RONA – return on net assets – and the ROCE – return on capital employed will be more attractive. In the end, the business will be easier to exit, if we so desire, with a valuation so attractive that we can put up our feet and live comfortably ever after.'

'So, five,' he said, his thumb joining the circus of erect fingers, but remaining horizontal because of the dictates of anatomy, 'let us toast to the future successes of Vindaloo ready-to-eat with Sutchee and Sutchee advertising, Faith and Ben Dylan financing, and you guys doing the product, being paid a decent wage, with some generous sweat equity attached.'

Pakwaan was diddled by the jargon, but Svet and Tikky were convinced by Moh's confidence, sure that he was pointing them in the right direction, and began to feel the realization of their American dream.

'Cheers to the success of ready-to-eat Vindaloo,' Faith and Ben Dylan said as if on cue, uncorking a bottle of champagne, pouring the frothy bubbly into fluted glasses.

'Chin, chin,' they all trilled, clinking their glasses as Moh and Maya fished out their visiting cards, handed them to Svet, Tikky and Pakwaan.

Things moved quickly. Recipes in hand, cost of goods described in detail, Tikky and Svet arrived at the offices of Sutchee and Sutchee to meet with Moh and Maya the very next day.

I CONSUME THEREFORE I EXIST, the sign on top of the entrance read. Existentialism simplified, Tikky thought and remembered the debates that followed drinking sessions at St. Stephen's. Soren versus Jean Paul: 'Did you think therefore you were, or were you because you thought?' The chickening or egging and hours of intellectual masturbating that led to no concrete conclusion. Moh and Maya had got it right. For them you existed because you consumed, take it or leave it, buy it or sell it, no argument – the ultimate marketing mantra.

From here on end, it was business. Brainstorming and ideating, segmenting and positioning, size of market and projections of year-on-year (abbreviated to YOY to save time), growth Svet and Tikky insisting on 'product, product, product', Moh and Maya more ambitious about the BRAND, the product just a concept to be placed in a mystic exotic niche. A product it was, but accessorized with the compelling concept of mysticism and the right touch of exotica, Vindaloo could become an ideology for a counterculture that had offered nobler and more humane alternatives.

To and fro their discussions went, Moh and Maya allowing Svet, Tikky and Pakwaan (when he accompanied them) a glimpse into their creative arsenal of managing words and images inserted into efficient time slots to convince the masses to consume with passion.

'Simple, but our pride and joy – our first award,' Moh said as he set up the projector and Maya went about drawing the blinds. The projector whirred, a beam of light illuminating the screen, no sound, no image, but a still blackness and a sentence on the screen in bold caps.

EVER WONDER HOW LONG YOU
CAN SPEAK ON AT&T FOR 50 CENTS?

The sentence faded away in a moment, leaving the screen black. Seconds later, squiggles, stars and such appeared on the screen to keep the viewers' attention, accompanied by a voice-over: 'Getting bored? Need something to do?' Then black blankness again. A minute later the screen lit up with the words,

ISN'T A MINUTE A LONG TIME?

The audience was amazed. A minute had been stretched to feel like it was so much longer, and AT&T, Moh and Maya proudly proclaimed, had a fresh batch of enthusiastic subscribers.

'The power of advertising, my friends,' Moh took a bow and Maya switched on the lights.

Now Maya took the stage. 'Of course, we need air, water, food and shelter to survive but there is another absolute necessity and that is novelty, continuous titillation for our eyes, ears, senses of smell and touch. Vindaloo will be positioned as novel, as *the* exciting alternative to an American taste that has lived with monotony for far too long. We are exploring various options and will come up with a campaign that will blow your socks off.'

Faith and Ben Dylan clapped, excited financiers to the project, privileged to be part of such esoterica – their business – buying cheap from India, selling dear in America, was, well, so profitable, but mundane in comparison.

Pakwaan scratched his head with one hand, his balls with the other, bemused but impressed by all this tamasha. Moh and Maya were like new-age Arth Purabiyas with a great feel for the word and the image. Once again Pakwaan thought of his dream and for a brief, flashing moment thought of the grief Arth had caused his grandfather but quickly shrugged it aside.

Money from the Dylans, concepts by Moh and Maya, produced by Svet, Tikky and Pakwaan, like the roll of credits at the end of major motion pictures, the role of each player in the team clearly defined – a sure-shot recipe for success.

Moh and Maya and their team of researchers prised out priceless details and insights from the marketplace. One, heat-and-eat foods was the fastest-growing segment in the already fast-growing food market. Two, the hot and spicy segment was the fastest-growing category in the fastest-growing segment. Three, there were hardly any players in the heat-and-eat segment in the hot and spicy category. And four, twenty-five per cent of all food eaten is eaten between meals. (*Can Vindaloo be given a snacky character?* was underlined vigorously on their concept sheet.) Five, shoppers seemed to be buying stuff quicker in a round package than in a square one. (*Should Vindaloo packaging be round?* Again vigorously underlined.) Six, play with *How long can you live with monotony?* This has to be the core message. Seven, Pakwaan in his saafa and sherwani adds to the flavour of exotica and can be the face of a television series that showcases Indian food for a growing cosmopolitan segment willing to experiment. A great synergy for the brand!

The concept was now getting clearer in their heads. Money was pumped in whenever needed, Faith and Ben Dylan thrilled by the novelty of it all. But the product lagged. 'Heat-and-eat' may have a bouncy rhythmic ring suitable for an advertising byline, but the cooking of food on a large scale was so industrial that it was alien to Pakwaan.

The first instalment of advertised exotica, it had been decided in one of the brainstorming sessions, would be the TV Vindaloo Dinner (with fried okra and rice) in three versions – mild, normal and spicy. Sensible gradations to cater to the levels of spiciness that jaded palates were willing to experiment with. But the manufacturing of it puzzled Pakwaan. It seemed simple at the start – make the three components, ladle fixed portions of each in a moulded aluminum tray, cover with a lid and freeze; taste it some days later to check if there were any variations in taste; and if all was well it was good to go to the market. But Pakwaan soon found himself a bit out of his depth, even intimidated by the strange newness of it all.

He made food, but had never manufactured it. He was familiar with kitchens but this was a karkhana, a large factory, where people wore white coats, like doctors. Heated grills more than three feet long sizzled with sautéed vegetables. The pieces of meat were of the same shape and size, as if cut from a mould, cooked on fired-up grills. Tilting pans oscillating on hinges, where voluminous quantities of sauces and gravies simmered before they were poured onto the meats and vegetables, then blast-chilled in chillers, and frozen in 'walk-ins' as big as Mahadev Sahib's pantry!

Pakwaan made the first batch (mildly spiced), enough to serve fifty, each portion measured and ladled into containers, a few set aside for themselves, the food technologist and flavourist. It was the first time he had heard of such terms, the flavourists especially unique, qualified chemists with a 'nose' and a 'taste' for the fine things in life, who played around with chemicals, emulsifiers, stabilizers, salts and other substances, imparting unique flavours to foods that allowed them their distinctive aromas. They sat around a table, Svetlana, Tikky, Pakwaan, the food technologist and the flavourist. Just like the Punj Pyaara, Pakwaan thought as he placed a tray in front of each. The technologist looked at the Vindaloo, examining it for colour, texture and general appeal, the flavourist brought his nose close to the tray and inhaled, closing his eyes, trying, it seemed, to 'locate' a familiarity of flavour but not quite succeeding. And then they ate and did not even spend time mulling over the taste to place it before they commented. The applause was spontaneous, they were generous in praise.

'Bravo! Bravo!' the two of them said as they clapped and Pakwaan gratefully took his bow.

But post the blast-chill and quick freezing, after the same team heated and ate from the same batch of dishes, nothing seemed to be right.

'Textural variation massive, colour degradation. Unacceptable,' the technologist said gravely, like a doctor giving bad news.

'Aroma and flavour completely absent,' was the verdict of the flavourist after he inhaled the smells from the tray.

And they were right – the meat had become leathery and difficult to swallow, the gravy looked like it had a watery top layer, the flavour of the balsamic and vinegar was barely traceable, the okra was mouldy and rancid. The basmati, at least, was fine.

'Hey Ram, I am hopeless,' Pakwaan said, slapping his forehead with an open palm.

This time it was Tikky, loins permanently girded, who came to the rescue. Shopping for the groceries, checking of service at caterings, helping and observing Pakwaan in the kitchen, generally working with his hands, so to speak, had given him the confidence to make a suggestion.

'Can we,' he started hesitatingly, 'marinate the meat, fire it on the grills, make the gravy separately, a little thinner than the original recipe, pour it over the meat before we blast-chill and freeze it? That should prevent textural issues and allow the meat to cook and absorb the flavour of the gravy when heated before being eaten. It would thicken the gravy . . .' he said, gaining confidence, 'and, as for the okra, maybe we need to drop the idea of crisp-frying and do a bhindi do pyaaza as an accompaniment,' he finished off with a flourish.

'It could work,' muttered the technologist, thoughtfully shaking his head.

'He may have a point,' the flavourist said, nodding in agreement, 'and just in case there is a loss of flavour, I am here to top note it. Come,' he smiled, throwing his arm across Pakwaan's shoulder, 'let me show you the Alladin's cave of flavours.'

Shiny test tubes, arranged in a row filled with liquids of different hues, neat little stacks of fragrance filters like the kind handed out in the cosmetic sections of Bloomingdale's and Macy's. 'Dip,' he said grandly, 'and smell.' Pakwaan dipped and smelled, amazed at how close these were to the aromas in a kitchen. A whiff of manufactured pungent mustard that brought tears to his eyes, the aroma of cinnamon from the filter instantly bringing back Tuesday baking days at Jhelum Memsahib's when the house smelt of fresh dalchini as he took the cinnamon rolls out of the oven, the smell of meat and coal so real that he could have sworn it was bottled in Jama Masjid. A true kalakaar this man is, Pakwaan thought.

A bit of a hit, a bit of a miss, a little trial and a little error – and, finally, the heat-and-eat met the specifications for mass production. Tikky's instinct about the meat had been right, and Pakwaan was easily able to solve the lack of crispiness in the okra. He undercooked the okra before freezing, then sprayed the okra with vegetable oil, sprinkling the dish with a mixture of finely ground rice flour, amchur, chilli powder and salt. While the Vindaloo heated through, the okra cooked, the rice-flour mixture turning a rich crispy brown. The flavourist's contribution was significant – he laced the dish with the aromas of food cooked on coal and wood fires, the air in the dining room lingering with smells of age-old tradition.

Svet felt a burst of admiration and the usual horniness when she tasted the Vindaloo. 'I am proud of you, Tikky love,' Svet moaned through pouted lips and heavy-lidded eyes, Tikky's heart all aflutter, months of loin-girding finally getting their just rewards.

Hot for each other, bodies burning with passion, they rushed off to the nearest chiller room, kissing, fondling, feeling, gasping, thrusting, exploring each other amongst the batches of vinegary Vindaloo waiting to be blast-chilled.

They had finally 'fixed' the product, but Pakwaan was not convinced. To him the product seemed touched up; he could never quite be sure that it tasted like the original. It bothered him, but just for the moment.

The Vindaloo was ready to roll out amongst much congratulatory shaking of excited hands, joyous back-thumping, the atmosphere charged with a brilliant shining optimism. It called for celebration, and Faith and Ben did the honours, inviting the 'V Team' (Svet's title for the players involved in the Vindaloo project) for dinner at La Caravelle, 'unfaltering and the top French dining place for high society,' a leading food critic had gushed.

La Caravelle in Vilayat No. 2 was to French food what Veeraswamy must have been to Indian in the original Vilayat, Pakwaan imagined when he entered. Veeraswamy had its tiger skins, portraits of maharajas and other sepia-tinted memories of the Raj, he remembered his father telling him, and La Caravelle had murals painted by French artists that showed French aristocracy celebrating life. And life on the floor imitated the art on the walls. La Caravelle's tables, like at Veeraswamy, were graced by the powerful and the rich, the well-known and the interesting, their kitchen filled with such talent that it changed its menu every day, never allowing its many customers to be jaded by monotony.

Pakwaan loved the place, its elegant tables, the grateful looks on the patrons' faces after they tasted their food and sipped their wine, and the murmur of contented conversation. The restaurant was popular and a table had to be booked days in advance. Tables for twos, fours and sixes were the norm, but a table for seven was an odd request, the number ideal for the round tables placed in the centre of the restaurant, vantage points from where regular and rich patrons could have an all-round view and preen at other rich and regular patrons not lucky enough to be placed in the centre. But the Dylans had done the maître d' a favour, allowing him first choice from a batch of the most exquisite kilms from Afghanistan, charging him a price only a fraction over the cost. He was gracious enough to remember the favour and it had served the Dylans well. This celebration was impulsive, but a table for seven was managed in the end.

The maître d' met them at the entrance, arms open in welcome, shaking Faith's hand, two warm pecks on either cheek, telling her how beautiful their kilm looked at the entrance to his home, and led them to their table. The restaurant was full, the importance of their favour underlined, the regulars looking at them, foreheads creased in doubt, wondering if they could recognize anyone. The maître d' pulled out a chair for Faith, settling her in, swishing the starched damask napkin to air it and placing it gently on her lap. A waiter appeared, crisp white shirt tucked into black trousers, their knife-edged pleats immaculately ironed, a black tuxedo, the lapels pinched together with brass buttons held together by a delicate brass chain, his hair gelled and brushed back smartly. He carried a large silver tray with seven fluted glasses filled with bubbly. 'The house champagne, compliments of the house,' he said brightly and got his look of approval from the maître d'.

'To champagne,' Ben Dylan said, 'that elixir that washes the tongue, refreshing the palate to taste good food.'

'To the success of Vindaloo,' the V Team chorused, and everyone clinked their glasses.

The meal was an orchestrated ceremony, each course accompanied by a suitable wine suggested by a sommelier and approved by Ben enthusiastically from a gigantic wine list.

Pakwaan and Tikky were fascinated by the effort of matching drink with food.

'Pamplemousse rafraîchi au Marasquin, Vivaneau farci aux Aromates, Supreme de Poularde en Chaud-froid, Asperges Vinaigrette,' Pakwaan read off the menu, intimidated by dishes he had never heard of. The appetizers and the first course were decided by the rest of them, with Pakwaan just going along. For the main course he went with whatever Tikky ordered – Poularde Maison Blanc – the easiest to pronounce, at least.

'Great choice, Monsieur, a favourite of President Kennedy, the vichyssoise and chicken in champagne sauce renamed in his honour, Poularde Maison Blanc or the White House Chicken,' the waiter said in a sweet French accent, the 'r's gargled out from the throat, 'vishyswaaz' said with such elongated delight that Pakwaan was sure he had made the right choice. He asked for directions to the men's room.

'Follow me,' the waiter said, bowing graciously. The men's room was on the way to the kitchen. Pakwaan was washing his hands after taking a leak when he heard the waiter's voice. 'Hey Joe,' he yelled in a typical American drawl, 'two of Shafty's favourites at the table for seven.' He heard laughter in the kitchen and wondered what the joke was.

The meal took its time, the conversation all about an exciting future, Moh and Maya hinting at a campaign that would be wildly successful. Pakwaan found French food too subtle for his palate, enjoying the crisp flakiness of the buttery croissants dipped in the vichyssoise, the soufflé at the end of the meal delightfully lemony and light. At the end of the meal, the bill was presented to Ben. 'That will be thirty per head,' Ben announced matter-of-factly, passing the bill around for verification. Each person paid for themselves.

Pakwaan was appalled. What was it about this Vilayat No. 2?

Invite people for a celebration and ask them to pay their share? Behen-di-lund, he thought, gaand mein goo nahin aur sooar ko dawat de rahein hain. Not enough shit in your arse and you call a herd of pigs for a feast. That seemed to sum it up brilliantly. He was surprised that Tikky thought it normal. 'Nice way to settle things,' he said casually, 'the obligation is squared off immediately.' Tikky had changed, Pakwaan thought. Gracious hosting was always for the pleasure of the guest, no question of obligation whatsoever.

But Pakwaan loved the idea of La Caravelle and thought wistfully of the day when he would have his own establishment that served the best Indian food in the city, his ode to the Punj Pyaara. The variety in Indian food was astounding – he could cook a different menu everyday without repeating a menu for months. But, for now, there was a product to be launched, huge impact to be made, virgin markets to be penetrated.

Brand Vindaloo

THE branding was superb, Moh and Maya's choice of the core message, *How long can you live with monotony?* was apt, the execution for print and media advertisements brilliant, the choice of the tongue as the medium for their message so obvious that it was a masterstroke. The tongue with its taste buds that filtered taste, the organ that spread word of mouth, salivating instantly at long-lost flavours of food suddenly remembered.

For the sides of buses and the top of bus shelters, two photographs of a tongue in close-up – the first coated yellow, dull, slouching, as if tired, with a *How long can you live with monotony?* scrawled angrily below, the second a pink-red, healthy tongue, its 'taste buds' dancing in celebration, *The Vindaloo Dinner – Taste the Difference!* written bouncily alongside.

The ad film was spectacular. The main prop was that of a fashion show, the ramp rolling out from a giant, stylized, Warholesque mouth like a tongue, upon which stale burgers, BLTs with wilted lettuce leaves, limp French fries and limper hot dogs moved along slowly, mechanically, the boredom getting heavier for the viewer till a sudden fading out of light with the image sucked off the screen. Blank darkness for a moment, then a voice-over, tired, exasperated in tone, with the message, 'How long can you live with monotony?', followed by the beginnings of a buoyant tune that reached its crescendo as the screen lit up and waiters dressed in tuxedos poured out from the mouth holding TV trays of steaming Vindaloo dinners, pirouetting and prancing around on a tongue that bounced delightedly, saliva dripping off its edges. 'The Vindaloo TV Dinner,' the voice-over said, enthusiastically now. Pause. 'Taste the difference.'

The sales took everyone by surprise. Vindaloo dinner trays flew off the shelves in supermarkets, 7-Elevens, mom-and-pop grocery stores, as if the national palate, if there was such a thing, sleepy and jaded for decades by burgers and BLTs and such, had woken up, desperate to consume a new, delicious, spicy flavour cooked on a traditional hearth. The sell-through in stores was dramatic, especially in Black and Hispanic areas, thirty per cent sell-through being achieved week on week. It was unprecedented, record-breaking. Demand was at a gallop, supply just at a trot, and 212-Aum-Food was ringing off its hooks. The press raised their written toasts to the spirit of America where ideas well-executed, irrespective of their origin, were rewarded. Faith and Ben Dylan were lauded as visionaries who had realized the potential of Indian food, and when Moh and Maya gave a bite saying, 'This is just the teaser, the tip of the iceberg,' the media went into a tizzy.

MOVE OVER MCDONALD'S, THE VINDALOO IS HERE!
HOW LONG WILL THE BLT SURVIVE?
VINDALOO, THE NATIONAL FLAVOUR?

Other variations on similar themes made headlines. Tikky was a bit of a surprise package for the journalists, not their idea of India because he was like them in so many ways. But his accent was so English that they were charmed. Pakwaan was the closest fit to their idea of India. The magical Maharaja, with his sherwani and saafa, peacock brooch and pearl strings, his smattering of English thickly accented; this third-generation cook, who cooked with recipes handed down from father to son, was so traditional, so timeless. They were fascinated by the way he shook his head, bobbing or shaking it from side to side, never letting on whether he meant a 'yes' or a 'no'.

First there was spirituality, then yoga, and now Indian food. And Pakwaan was the man of the moment. CBS, the channel partners with Moh and Maya were eager to sprinkle their channel with a bit of ethnicity and throw in an Indian cookery show and see how far it went. And so Aum Sutchee Sutchee Productions presented *Pakwaan's Pot of Indian Treasures*.

Montage shots of the Taj Mahal, camels silhouetted against an orange Pushkar sunset, kebabchis at Jama Masjid vigorously fanning sigris, seekh kebabs glistening a rich brown-black in the light, the sizzle of jalebis twirled around in hot oil, sitar and tabla in the background mixed with the chanting of Aum in soothing baritones. Cut to a studio kitchen with Pakwaan, dressed in sherwani, saafa, necklace, standing behind the cooking range with hands folded, saying, 'Namaste,' to the camera. Incense sticks burnt on the cooking counter and the soulful sound of plucked tanpura strings create an almost mystical mood.

'Remember,' Pakwaan said slowly, 'from earth sprang herbs, from herbs food, from food seed, from seed man. Man thus consists of the essence of food. From food are all creatures produced, by food do they grow.' Moh and Maya, thinking it would be appropriate, had loaded the episode with a bit of depth and heaviness at the start. Pakwaan's transformation after the opening gambit was dramatic, obviously rehearsed. He grandly took off his faux pearl necklace, unbuttoned his sherwani lined with paisley motifs on a bright maroon silk background, his young muscular body visible beneath a see-through Lucknawi chikan kurta. With his saafa still on, he rolled up his sleeves. 'And now,' he said, spreading his hands expansively, 'on to the Vindaloo.'

Schlick, schlick, schlick, the onious were accordioned in a flash, the ginger julienned delicately with effortless ease. And when he poured the marinade over the meat and rubbed it in with vigour, 'Rub it in with luuhv,' he said in a plaintive sing-song voice. He sprinkled the spices and salt from a height, streams of spice and salt lit up by clever camera-work as they floated downwards to the pot. He stirred the ladle and remembered his father's description of the handle-ghumanewallas and smiled, moving his hands to the edge of the pot and back to his face as if scooping up the flavours. Aah, he said. The Vindaloo had been made before the show and dressed by food stylists to appear delicious before the camera. 'Mmm, fun-taastic,' he gushed as he tasted. Everything was performance.

'Fantastic synergy for the brand,' Moh and Maya excitedly agreed. All a result of good collective karmic energy, Svet felt, briefly remembering her quest for spirituality. Karmic energy, successful strategy, advanced technology, great synergy – what more could one ask for?

Moh and Maya's 'tip of the iceberg' spiel had not been an idle boast. The Mild version was just a teaser, the carrot metaphorically dangled to gauge the reaction of a niche market that held the promise of phenomenal growth. In the wings and waiting to be launched was Medium, one red curled chilli by its side, and Spicy, two curled red chillies by the moniker. Medium and Spicy, pitched to those with adventurous palates, Aum Sutchee Sutchee Productions once again proving that they had their sensitive fingers placed firmly on the market's pulse.

This episode of *Pakwaan's Pot of Indian Treasures* began with montage shots of red chillies drying in a Rajasthani courtyard under a blazing desert sun, the spices being ground by women in voluminous ghagras and skimpy cholis, the camera cutting to Pakwaan sprinkling masalas from a height. 'I prefer Spicy,' he said, smiling at the camera as he took off his sherwani, 'but then I am more adventurous,' he signed off, his voice the right mix of inviting and mischievous. Curiosity, eagerness, suspense were at fever pitch. The market could not wait! Medium and Spicy, along with Mild, flew off the shelves. When they reviewed sales six months later, the trends were encouraging. The sale of Mild Vindaloo TV Dinners was up overall but showed a dip in Black and Hispanic areas, though here the sales of Spicy were much higher than before.

Moh and Maya reminded the market that they had cut down the time from concept to plate – six months for Mild to arrive on the shelves from concept, less than half the time for Medium and Spicy. 'Our strategy of launching new variants has resulted in a spurt in overall sales and opened a whole new franchise for the Mild variant,' they told the press. The markets applauded and the pundits predicted the brightest of futures.

'Behen-di-lund,' Pakwaan said, not understanding a word but impressed by all the ballyhoo.

'Onward, ye soldiers of commerce,' Moh and Maya joked, though they meant every word, 'we do not have a moment to lose.' No one was allowed to rest on the laurels. There still remained Point Five on their concept sheet – one quarter of the entire food business comprised in-between-meals eaters. 'Twenty-five per cent of such a huge market,' Moh and Maya said to each other with round eyes and awestruck voices. 'At twenty-five per cent, this segment is a treasure chest for profitable growth. Mouth-watering and definitely worth a shot.' They had already decided on the byline – *The V Snack will hit the spot, you betcha!* Free love still had top of mind (or thereabouts) recall, the 'G' spot the most longed for yet elusive destination. 'V' rhymed with 'G' and 'hitting the spot' so Moh and Maya felt, hinted at the possibility of post-snack sex.

'We need a share of that twenty-five per cent,' they told the rest. 'A whole bloody quarter! Imagine the traction, the brand extension and market share if we get a piece of the action.'

'Action, traction, extension may be fine,' Tikky said, irritated that they had not been allowed enough time to savour their success, 'but what about perception?'

'How do you mean?' Maya asked, pert and businesslike.

'A snack is a bite-sized, dry, finger-food eat, and the packaging is throwaway. Vindaloo is a curry eaten with rice, a meal not a snack,' he said, condescension creeping into his voice.

'What you see as a problem, we,' Moh said grandiosely pointing at Maya and himself, 'see as an opportunity. I am sure it is possible to do small pieces of boneless meat that are barbequed and have the flavour of the gravy, and develop an attractive, round package for product differentiation.'

'Like tikka?' Tikky asked.

'Exactly,' Moh said, 'Like teeka.'

'If the pieces are cut smaller, a little bigger than bite-sized,' Tikky said, thumb and forefinger apart, 'the marinade for the Vindaloo made thicker, and the batch is marinated for longer, then fired on the grill with a shortened freezing time, we may have a Vindaloo tikka!' Tikky looked at Pakwaan for approval.

'Wah, Tikky-baba, wah, you are a quick learner – this will definitely work,' Pakwaan said, looking at Tikky, amazed that the Sahib's son had observed so much about cooking.

'You *are* a genius,' Svet whispered in his ear, squeezing the insides of his thighs, Tikky closing his eyes, sighing at the thought of the intense pleasure when her creamy white body would thrash with his own dark brown. Unable to wait till the meeting got over, they excused themselves immediately and rushed home. They kissed and fondled while wriggling out of their clothes and like desperate lovers united from past lives fucked like there was no tomorrow.

'Will you marry me?' Tikky asked her, spent and happy.

'We are married already,' Svet lovingly fluttered back, ducking the question.

The V Snack was historic, a once-in-a-lifetime spark that set the business firmament alight. The time taken from concept to plate had been reduced from three months to two. 'Thirty-three per cent!' Moh emphasized to the market, leaving it to the analysts to figure out the math. 'Aum Foods has demonstrated capability to now launch six new products a year instead of four,' the media gushed, and when the Aum Sutchee Sutchee Productions' cameras rolled for *Pakwaan's Pot of Indian Treasures* just before the V Snack launch, they made changes that ensured fantastic success (with the benefit of hindsight, of course).

The episode opened with the dance of the whirling dervishes, cutting to Pakwaan with his hand folded in the traditional namaste. But instead of the saafa he now wore a fez, his face framed by an ornate Turkish grill in hand-beaten brass and copper embellished in a profusion of delicately carved flowers and skewers. Pakwaan whisked the marinade, the camera showing the change of colour as the red chillies, pepper, cumin, mustard seeds, cloves and turmeric melded with the ginger, garlic, vinegar and balsamic. He reduced the mixture in a pan to thicken it slightly and poured the marinade on the pieces of meat, rubbing it in with 'luhvvv.' He put the pieces on a skewer, its handle moulded to look like the grip of a sword and laid it on the grill. The camera panned to a batch of styled tikkas, moist pieces of delicious brown with the rich brown serrations of the grill showing on their surface.

'The V Snack, will hit the spot, you bay-chaa,' Pakwaan grandly announced, his pronounciation of 'betchaa' so exotically quaint that Moh and Maya winked at each other greatly amused. It was auspicious in a way, for in Pakwaan's own language 'baycha' also meant SOLD!

And sell it did in a never-before-in-history sort of way. Eight pieces of boneless meat in the Mild, Medium and Spicy variants top-noted by the flavour of wood fire with a sweet, sour and chilli follow-through, packed in a box that looked like the round old biscuit tins so typical of mother country England. It was a phenomenon! More than fifty per cent sell through, these lovely round packages barely having time to rest their frozen bottoms on the air-conditioned shelves. Aum Foods were now major players in the snack-food segment and the TV-dinner space, and a juicy target for larger food companies who would pay good monies to acquire them and expand their 'product portfolios inorganically'.

They bought the loft they had rented – cash-down, Tikky would love to say. The company's cashflow was healthy enough to afford full payment for the loft by cheque. They spiffed up the place with hardwood teak floors, screens handcrafted by Japanese craftsmen, the work of up-and-coming avant garde American artists adorning the walls, rare silk carpets casually thrown across the floor. Tikky bought himself a Mercedes, the ultimate status symbol back home to announce your arrival. He wrote to Jhelum with photographs of himself in the Merc with Pakwaan, a photograph of Svet and him, his arm around her shoulder with the Merc in the background, smiling as he imagined his mother's reaction when she saw it. Merc was his choice of car, but his mother's fear had always been BMW – Tikky getting hitched to a girl who was either Black or Muslim or White. Tikky had never been quite sure if she meant it as a joke. Of course, she would show the photograph to Mahadev as proof that she had always been right about her son, enjoying the 'See I told you so' bit, leaving Mahadev with no choice but to agree.

- Launch of Mild Vindaloo variant: March 1975
- Launch of Medium and Spicy: October 1975
- Launch of V Snack: January 1976
- RONAs and ROCEs much healthier than industry averages
- Profits doubling every year

So a roster in bullet-point format would have read when the media plotted the growth of Aum Foods Inc. And Aum Foods Inc. was showing no signs of letting up. Chicken or lamb curry and rice, chicken tikka masala, steamed rice, lentils and spiced potatoes were now on their concept-to-plate list. The meteoric rise of Aum Foods Inc. in the larger historical context was another feather in the cap of America as the land of opportunity, a haven that rewarded the spirit of entrepreneurship.

Vindaloo Hijacked

BUT the observers from objective heights would have noted a flagging national self-esteem in need of a bit of topping up.

America's entry into the pages of history had been dramatic till World War II – a hundred per cent track record, if you will, with their doughboys, GIs, Fat Men and Little Boys, great tonic for the self-fulfilling prophecies of manifest destinies, their status as saviours of democracy and other essential freedoms well deserved. Post 1945, however, their track record had become iffy. Their Korean foray had been nothing to thump the chest about. Vietnam was a disaster and Watergate justified the epithet 'Tricky Dick' for the leader of the nation. It was the first time in the history of the New World that a President faced the possibility of being impeached and was forced to resign to avoid the shame. That, too, on 9 August, the same day America had dropped the Fat Man on Nagasaki twenty-nine years ago!

But America still had global appeal. It was the land of brands loved the world over – McDonald's, Coca-Cola, Wrangler, Levi's – popular TV serials, blockbuster Hollywood films. It was the land where the have-nots were never envious of the haves, because they believed they had a fair shot of getting there themselves. And, of course, there were the American cars, Dodges, Buicks, Lincolns, Cadillacs, Plymouths, their manufacture the incontestable symbol of American machismo, as American as apple pie. In short, the national morale was evenly balanced, but stretched a bit taut.

But somewhere in the horizons of kismet, Shani, the planet of misfortune, had made its unobtrusive entrance yet again. The predictors of the 'far-reaching consequences' of the Yom Kippur War had been wrong so far but, tucked away, a consequence had gently bubbled with the potential of being far-reaching. The long lines at gas stations were a distant memory, but the prices of gasoline had risen astronomically, by close to sixty per cent – enough for car owners to reminisce about the 'good old days', like the 'refugees' who moaned about prices after Partition when they remembered how reasonable the cost of everything was in their beloved Lahore. Suddenly, American cars, which were big, roomy, luxurious, but gas guzzlers became less popular. And from the Land of the Rising Sun, the very land that America had bombed into submission less than three decades ago all the way across the Pacific, there came the Hondas and the Toyotas, cheaper, compact, more reliable, using far less gasoline and cheaper to run. The sales of the Hondas and Toyotas climbed steadily upwards while those of the American icons went in the opposite direction.

It started in pockets, the lament of how America had declined and, with it, as generally happens in history, came nostalgia for those good old days when Americans consumed stuff proudly made in America. Foreign imports were the cause for national weakness, to be avoided at all costs, it was concluded. 'Be American, buy American, export to the rest of the world,' became a rallying cry of sorts. Nothing like a healthy dose of the feeling of those good old days layered with a healthy dose of xenophobia! Naturally, Vindaloo, as a brand, as a business, as a source of profitable revenue streams, was threatened.

Moh and Maya's skills were stretched to find a way to take Vindaloo from its Goan origins and place it as believably as possible as American or, second-best, to position it as originating from a 'Whiter', more 'cultured' place. Moh and Maya knew the power of the printed word, the fascination for the beautiful image, and were masters at moulding both. The challenge of taking a product from its original context, placing it in a different one and yet guaranteeing success excited them no end. If they could pull it off, what a feather in the cap it would be for Sutchee and Sutchee! The entire market would come knocking at their doors, and ah the power they would have! They sent off their missive to Ben and Faith, copied to Svet and Tikky, asking them to meet 'sans Pakwaan'. It was the first time they had used the word 'sans' instead of 'without' – a hint of things to come.

'This sudden discovery for the love of an America imagined in the past and the fear of the foreign as a result,' Moh began sarcastically, 'can be disastrous for our brand. Vindaloo is not even *close* to being American. The way I see it,' he carried on, picking up a marker, moving towards the white board, 'we can . . .' ONE, he wrote, *Wait.* 'We assume that this is temporary and wait for some sort of normalcy to return but the timelines on emotional horizons are impossible to predict. If this lasts longer than we expected, we will lose top-of-the-mind recall in the heads of our customers.' He looked at Maya, as if passing on the strategic baton.

TWO, Maya wrote. *We need to REPOSITION the Vindaloo.* 'We play around with the origins of Vindaloo, positioning it as close to America as possible in . . .'

'Play around with its origins?' Tikky asked Maya, not waiting for her to finish.

'Strictly business, nothing personal,' Moh cut in brusquely, allowing Maya her say.

'India is still a strong flavour but with all this made-in-America codswallop, one never knows how long it will last. We played with the idea of positioning it as American, keeping the colour of the gravy as the core idea – a rich red-brown like the skin colour of the native American. "Red Indian Vindaloo" has an authentic son-of-the-soil feel about it but we felt it would be too far-fetched.'

The Dylans, Svet and Tikky nodded their agreement.

'It was Vasco da Gama, a Portuguese who brought with him the art of cooking in vinegar to Goa. The original version was called Vin d'alho – from vinho, wine, and alho, garlic. More like a pickle, less like a curry with the Portuguese but transformed to fiery Vindaloo with the Goan fondness for chilli and spice. Vindaloo with a Portuguese positioning might increase market share in our fast-growing Hispanic segment but will not cut it in an overall sense. Portugal, pardon my political incorrectness, is too tanned and Portuguese positioning will have limited appeal in White America.' Maya finished off, passing the parcel to Moh.

'So we have decided we will rechristen Vindaloo and call it Vinthelieux, the V Snack will be called the "Oui" snack and the byline for both will be "So delectably French",' Moh finished off, playing the pitch-in-tandem to perfection. 'Like India, France is also considered exotic but in a more sophisticated sense. It is the centre of fashion, art, style, design, wine, food. *Culture,* really in an all-embracing sense. In my opinion, there is something about France, a . . .' he paused for effect in search of the phrase, 'a *je ne sais quoi*, that will make the Vinthelieux positioning fly. Pakwaan would most definitely object, what with three generations of cooking he carries in his DNA, but times like these call for drastic measures. We have built a brand and now the time has come to protect it and, in the end, business, as they say is . . .' He stopped, waiting for the rest to complete the sentence.

'BUSINESS!' the rest of them said, thumping the table in unison.

They would have to be allowed their freedom to Frenchify the product – leach out the original robustness, replace it with little hints and soft notes of garlic and ginger, spices and chillies tailored for sophisticated palates that salivated at the mere suggestion of a little excitement. Three variants would be unnecessary, one bland version good enough.

'We will save on production cost, good for margins,' Moh and Maya enthusiastically proclaimed.

'Okra will be replaced with a version of a potato gratin baked in cream and cheese. It will give our effort at Frenchification more authenticity.'

For Pakwaan, who they all agreed would be the stumbling block to this fascinating project, there would be a long vacation as a reward for all the effort he had put in. It would sound sincere enough. But Tikky, party to this subterfuge, refused to be the messenger.

On the face of it, Pakwaan had nothing to complain about. He was a minor celebrity, people sometimes stopped him on the streets and asked, 'Aren't you Paak-vaan, the Vin-duh-loo man?' He would smile and nod his head. 'Love your show!' they would say, and congratulate him, shaking his hand, and he would be thrilled at the recognition. The country had been kind to him, he always admitted. He could never have imagined a life of such comfort. The loft was heated, running hot and cold water taken for granted, he bought whatever he needed and sent money home to his father, and still had enough saved for more than just a rainy day. 'It can happen only in America,' Tikky and Pakwaan agreed with Svetlana when they took stock of their individual successes. Pakwaan had adapted well to Vilayat No. 2, wearing his tan chinos, slipping on his brown moccs with fringes and without socks and throwing on his blue Oxford chambray shirt, 'dressing down' like the others to announce the beginning of the weekend. He loved the pace of his life, short periods of intense effort setting recipes and such followed by what felt like pushing a button – standardized product cooked, packed and frozen, barely touched by human hands. He enjoyed performing for his TV programme, cutting with skill, ladling with rhythm, the food styled to photograph well in the end. He had perfected the gesture of closing his eyes and saying 'Delicious' with a certain believable sincerity.

Yet, the little things bothered him. His accent had improved, he had become more American and was easily understood, but he could feel the aura of exotica around him diminish. Svetlana and Tikky Baba's disappointment was palpable. And at times Pakwaan missed his kitchen, missed being surrounded by spices, chillies, vegetables and meat, missed cooking for people and enjoying their applause. Somewhere deep down inside there grew a nagging fear that when he entered a kitchen to cook a meal for friends, something would go wrong. It never had, so far – people always applauded – but he believed that he had been lucky. The kitchen was no longer a place where he felt the joy of being completely at home. It had become a place somehow tinged with fear. He could feel that he had moved away from food, but could not guage how far. He had been feeling for a while that he needed time to think, to be by himself. And so Svet's suggestion for a vacation came as welcome relief.

He did not suspect a thing. He went to Disneyland and photographed himself with Mickey and Minnie, Donald and Goofy against the backdrop of the Magic Kingdom, got on every ride and loved each one. It amazed him, where his skills had brought him, unimaginable till a few years ago, and now he felt as though he had lived his dream. He left Disneyland for Vegas, taking in the experience of gambling and hearing famous singers strut their stuff on slick, well-designed stages. He admired how a strip of desert glowed with such intensity and throbbed with so much life. Moh and maya, desire and illusion, made so real that few could tell the difference! Only in America, Pakwaan thought, filled with wonder.

But the more he stayed away from the V Team and their activities, the more that nagging feeling of fear of cooking grew. The organized processes, the sameness of it all and the convenience of fast food, its empty taste, began to bother him. He oscillated between the pleasures of his prosperous present and swells of nostalgia as he reminisced about the times spent with his father in his kitchen, inhaling the aromas, watching the spices sputter delightedly in hot oil and the genuine applause of appreciation for meals well made. He had not felt such joy in a long time and regretted that it did not bother him too much.

He left the tables at the casino, cashing in his chips and felt the brief thrill of victory when he realized he was ahead of the house. He wandered aimlessly, squinting at the exaggerated brightness of the streets, till he came to a restaurant. The Dining Room, the signage simply read over a door of the brightest, most vibrant red. Pakwaan looked curiously through the glass frontage. Immaculately crisp white tablecloths, white bone china settings edged with the same red to match the colour of the door, an arrangement of fresh flowers on every table, elegant candelabras with delicate, tapered candles waiting to be lit. Like Jhelum Memsahib's table when she had their parties, he thought. The space had a warm familial air about it, a promise of graciousness, where the art of hosting or mehmaan-nawazi was not learnt by training and instruction, but naturally understood.

He walked in a little hesitantly and was shown to a table. He had judged correctly. The candles were lit as soon as he sat at the table. The waiter returned with the menu and a glass of Kir Royal.

'Compliments of the house,' he said, smiling, and moved away, allowing him to go through the menu at leisure. The waiter was the youngest in the family of five that ran the restaurant. Pakwaan saw the daughter helping the parents in the kitchen and could sense a joyful energy about the place. He placed his order quickly.

The Kir Royal had been delightfully mixed, the tartness of champagne and the thick sweetness of Crème de Cassis perfectly balanced, cleansing his palate. His order of shrimp arrived, grilled to the right shade of pink with the rich flavour of rock salt served on a warm plate with melted butter. The young waiter sprinkled pepper on the serving from a long wooden pepper mill till Pakwaan motioned him to stop. Black flakes on delicate pink, golden butter on a white plate edged by the boldest red – a feast for the eyes and the taste buds. 'Wah,' he said aloud, throwing his hands in the air, and the family took a bow, graciously accepting the compliment. The aubergine soup was excellent – charcoal-grilled aubergine melded in a rich natural chicken broth with the sweetness of onions, a red pepper garnish mixed in cream, a touch of genius. They talked. Pakwaan was amazed at the effortlessness of conversation and felt an indescribable sense of pride when they expressed their sense of wonder at him being the third generation of a cooking tradition.

Fresh ingredients, food prepared with love and care – the results were naturally stupendous. From the décor to the aperitif, the starter to the soup and the mains, the meal was a delight to the senses, and after ages Pakwaan felt his deeply natural connection with food return to him. It filled him with a wholesome joy. Bilkul khushi se bharpoor, he thought in his mother tongue, and felt guilty at how easily he had acquiesced to idiot-proofing a skill that had given him so much happiness, ashamed at having sacrificed real pleasure for mere convenience.

'Thank God for the skills he has blessed you with but *never* take them for granted.' His father's parting words resonated with astonishing clarity. It was his moment of realization. A small restaurant, his ode to heredity, a set menu for every day of the week, made with the passion he had when he learnt the art in his father's kitchen. He recalled the story of the standing ovations at Veeraswamy, sure that his establishment would be worthy of the same.

He left for New York bubbling with energy, filled with hope and the promise of happiness, sure that he had found the way to his personal nirvana.

Yet, when he discussed his plans with Tikky and Svet, his enthusiasm evident as he waved his hands excitedly, admitting to his foolishness at being carried away by the grandeur of scale, he was surprised by their indifference. They hardly heard him as he chattered on, and expressed interest by peppering the conversation with 'How interesting!' and 'How quaint!' and 'About time someone thought small and intimate instead of big and impersonal.' This throwing about of condescending clichés irritated him and he felt the beginnings of a dangerous, bubbling rage.

Tikky had contributed easily to the Vindaloo's Frenchification. Like a good technician, he had added and subtracted hotness and spiciness, sourness and sweetness, till the taste satisfied the lowest common denominator. This was what the market wanted, and Moh and Maya desired for the brand they had created. Xenophobia had thrown up a new, interesting set of statistics – mildly spiced Vindaloo had shown the largest dip in sales, the spicy variant more or less holding on to its pre-xenophobia volumes, as if patriotism was coloured. The new flavour had been enthusiastically accepted amongst middle-class White populations, the largest market segment by far. So said their dipstick analysis, and Moh and Maya were sure that they had positioned Vinthelieux correctly for a society marked by xenophobia soothed by an aspiration for sophisticated culture. The packaging, too, was artistically French – Toulouse-Lautrec's Moulin Rouge poster variants, with women in ruffled skirts kicking up their legs in celebration after tasting the Vinthelieux.

Pakwaan accompanied Tikky and Svet for the soft launch of Vinthelieux to Faith and Ben Dylan's place. They had bought the apartment upstairs. Cash down, Tikky smugly informed Pakwaan. A staircase connected the two apartments, so now they had two commanding views. The occasion was an exercise in studied, rehearsed elegance – another soiree, so evidently French. Pakwaan was reminded of the evening in La Caravelle, but here there was neither character nor charm. The waiters, dressed in black culottes with short black frock-coats and white stockings up to their knees, their shiny black patent leather shoes with bows shining in the evening light, seemed like out-of-work actors, their accents pitched perfectly in French. 'Oui, Monsieur,' they acknowledged when guests asked them for wine, trotting off elegantly towards the bar. 'Merci,' the guest would say in turn when they were served, taking care to pronounce the 'r' as 'gh'. A smattering of conversations in French floated around and the not-so-cunning linguists took care to speak English in French accents. The pretension was appalling.

Then the food was served. The original mild variant had bordered on the bland, but the Vinthelieux was an insult. They had sucked out the flavour from the gravy. The potato gratin was the worst choice as accompaniment – a tasteless mish-mash of nothingness without any hint of texture. Pakwaan felt an intense rage at such tremendous betrayal wash over him. He looked at Tikky accusingly.

'You call this . . . this . . .' Pakwaan struggled angrily in search of a word, 'this bloody chutiapa, this tasteless bloody concoction – *food*?' he sneered at the plate, his eyes moving from Faith to Ben, Moh to Maya, from Svet and, finally, boring into Tikky.

'Don't take this personally, it's just business,' Svetlana said in her clipped, businesslike tone without a trace of guilt.

Pakwaan was gripped by a maddening rage. 'Don't take it personally, don't take it personally,' he repeated, shaking clenched fists. 'So bloody easy for you to say – a family recipe handed down through generations, hijacked and repackaged to become a tasteless concoction.' He wrenched off the white damask napkin tucked into his collar and flung it across the terrace. 'Behen-di-lund,' he shouted, banging his fists on the table, the fancy stemmed glasses rattling dangerously with the force of the thump. Ben Dylan looked up, thinking Pakwaan was addressing him.

'Merde,' the out-of-work actors playing waiters said in fine polished French accents.

'I will show you how it is done,' Pakwaan said angrily and moved towards the kitchen. He looked around for a pan and, finding it, put it on the fire. He threw in a bit of cumin, mustard seeds and dried red chillies, roasting the spices separately as he remembered from his father's instructions. He watched the mustard and cumin seeds pop, and smelled the aromas, the memories of his father's kitchen spreading deliciously in his head. He chopped the garlic and delicately julienned the ginger, but all the while he felt a sense of fear, as if something had got to give. When he began to slice the onions, his right hand moved in a speedy blur, but he did not move the fingers of his left hand fast enough, a mistake even a beginner would rarely make – and the knife sliced off bits of his fingertips. Blood spurted, tainting the chopped onions a sickening shade of red. Pakwaan grabbed a napkin, tore it into a thin strip, tied the makeshift bandage as tightly as he could to control the bleeding and rushed out of the kitchen. The swing doors parted as he shoved his way through and he came face to face with Svetlana, her fists clenched, her face rigid with anger.

'I have forgotten how to cook,' he said, humiliated by the pathetic, bleating tone of his own voice.

Her fists opened slowly and those slim, long fingers, those

graceful hands that had stroked and fondled his body with such sensual generosity now roughly held the back of his head, bringing his face close to hers as if to kiss him. She knew he expected sympathy, but she had none to give.

'Frankly, my dear, I don't give a damn,' she said viciously, enjoying the moment, her lips twisted into a sneer.

Pakwaan looked at her, shocked by her cruelty. Tikky moved to console him, but Svet held Tikky back and he stayed, his girded loins having found their parking place after all.

An Ending of Sorts

PAKWAAN lay in bed, propped up on huge pillows filled with eiderdown, his head enveloped by their sensuous, comfortable softness, the silence broken every now and then by a wail of sirens – fire tenders or ambulances, he could not tell. He held up his left hand to take a look – a misshapen, grotesque lump of gauze and bandage. The flow of blood had stopped somewhat, thank God, and for that he was grateful. But the pain he carried was unbearable.

Tikky had visited once in the past week, with a ticket to Delhi as Pakwaan had requested, and had gestured grandly at the symbols of material progress that lay around Pakwaan's apartment – as though offering him bait, like the goat in Galeecha's story, to convince him to stay back. Pakwaan felt the beginnings of an intense self-loathing when he thought about how easily he had allowed himself to be seduced by the grand yarns that the new-age Arth Purabiyas – Moh and Maya, desire and illusion, heads of Sutchee and Sutchee, truth and truth – had spun. It brought back to his mind the joy and pride on his father's face when Tikky had announced the news that they were going to America, and he could not forgive himself for ignoring his father's warning never to take his God-given skills for granted.

He left for home a few days later, and on his way to the airport was amazed by the advertisement campaign that had been rolled out for Vinthelieux and the Oui snack. Humongous Lautrec-type graphics were pasted all over town – on the sides of buses, on bus shelters, billboards, on the roofs of yellow cabs. The photography was superb. The food glistened richly, he had to admit, grimacing when he recalled the memory of the awful, empty, artificial taste of the dishes at that pretentious launch. But he knew in his bones that the products were going to be a huge success, and it filled him with sadness and an impotent rage.

He rolled down the window of his cab and felt the cool air caress his face, blow through his hair, and, like a balm, magical memories of his father's kitchen rushed into his head. Salivating smells surrounded him and the sight of curries on a simmer, gently bubbling, enthralled. His father cutting onions, holding one end firmly with the tips of his fingers, exposing just enough so that very thin slices would be cut. *Schlick, schlick, schlick,* the knife moving in a blur, and in an instant the onions were finely sliced. Spices being roasted, cumin seeds popping on hot tawas, paneer and mushroom being diced, fresh meats being marinated in yogurt and spices, the marination being worked in with the hands. Ah! For him it was an indescribably sensuous feeling. And the transformation, the food changing colour and texture over heat – the gobi just the right golden-yellow, the chicken and mutton the desired rich dark brown. All this achieved without written recipes, without a reminder from wound-up clocks that time was up. Just smell, feel and texture to determine the doneness of a particular dish.

He felt a warm surge of glorious hope and, with it, a much-needed top-up of self-esteem. He was, after all, the grandson of a Kathua-turned-cook-extraordinaire, son of a first-day-first-show conception and proof of the passion of the palangtod paan, inheritor of skills of two generations steeped in the fine art of cooking. In his heart, he knew that his wounds would heal and his fears would vanish.

And tomorrow would be another day.

Acknowledgements

TO my wife, Shefali, whom I nudged, bothered, pushed, cajoled, to read whatever I wrote, whenever I wrote it. A lady of substance and patience, she generally complied and more often than not liked most of what I had done.

To Mini Bahadur, with whom I did all of the above (except nudge) and am thankful for her suggestions.

To the delightful Mukul Kesavan for his wicked, funny take on *Gone with the Vindaloo*.

To Azhar Waziri, maker of the finest kakoris and galoutis, for the secret of well-made niharis and Wajid Ali Shah's murgh musallam.

To Amit Judge, for telling me the story of Lord Mayo's statue, which I could use as a revenge of the Hindi-speaking story at the Eton of India.

To Arvind Wable, for his knowledge of the traditions of Mayo, which I tapped into often.

To Krishan Dhawan, family polymath, for checking if my knowledge of 'events' served me correctly.

To Aruna Ghosh for some brilliant suggestions inspired by sun-soaked sessions at the India International Centre and an evening at home inspired by more ardent spirits.

And, finally, to Aditya Bahadur, now a PhD, who pushed me so hard to finish the book and gave the incomplete manuscript to

Diya Kohli at Hachette India, who convinced Poulomi Chatterjee to run with it. To the two editors, despite our run-ins, thank you for making the book, we all hope, a much better read.

Gone with the Vindaloo is a first-time effort written between trying to run an export business and a restaurant business. It took more than ten years to finish. Taking time out to write would not have been possible but for the excellent team at Matrix Clothing and Sahsha Foods that allowed me a degree of redundancy to indulge in my diversions.